TRAC

ASENA BLESSED

BOOK TWO IN THE CHRONICLES OF ALTAICA

ODYSSEY

Published by Odyssey Books in 2016

Copyright © Tracy M Joyce 2016

All rights reserved. No part of this book may be reproduced or transmitted by any person or entity, including internet search engines or retailers, in any form or by any means, electronic or mechanical, including photocopying (except under the statutory exceptions provisions of the *Australian Copyright Act* 1968), recording, scanning or by any information storage and retrieval system without the prior written permission of the publisher.

www.odysseybooks.com.au

A Cataloguing-in-Publication entry is available from the National Library of Australia

ISBN: 978-1-922200-48-8 (pbk)
ISBN: 978-1-922200-49-5 (ebook)

Cover design by Karri Klawiter (www.artbykarri.com)
Map of Altaica by Magic Owl Design (www.magicowldesign.com)
(Based on colour original by Marilyn Jurlina)

Dedication

You can't write books without a support team, and I have the best team helping me.

The following people have my thanks!

Michelle Lovi of Odyssey Books—you really are a 'wonder woman'. Thanks for having faith in me.

My outstanding, overworked and definitely underpaid beta-readers—Bronny, Maz, Elleni, Jenna and Clive.

To my husband Robert, who has to put up with my constant state of vagueness because I'm pretty much always writing in my head.

To Matt Easton from Schola Gladitoria, who provided me with wonderful military information. Any errors of interpretation are mine alone.

To my fellow authors, Belinda Crawford, Jenny Ealey and Carl Sundstrom, Thank you for your unfailing encouragement, support, understanding, and at times forgiveness.

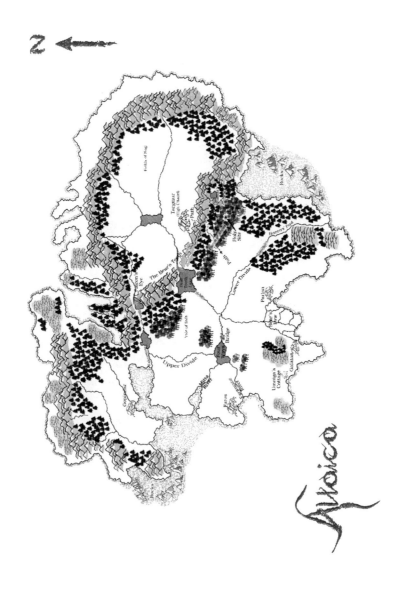

For more detailed maps please visit
www.tracymjoyce.com

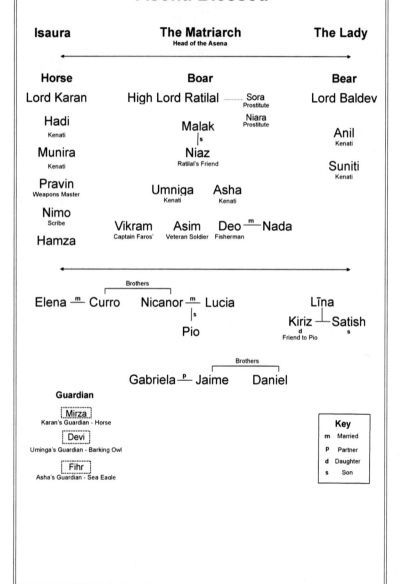

Chapter One

ISAURA SHOOK UNCONTROLLABLY; goose bumps prickled her skin, her teeth chattered loudly. Memories flashed back to her. The Lady, the wolves … no, the Asena … and the old woman, Pio and his music. The fragments became whole. They had pulled her from her home, from oblivion. *I suppose I should be grateful. Gods, where am I?* The noise—everything was so loud. She curled on her side. *Enough! Make it all stop!*

A quiet voice spoke to her. Strong arms held her. After being unable to touch anything for so long, of thinking she would never be able to feel or hear anyone else, she was overwhelmed with emotion, with gratitude. His voice was so calm, so soothing. Safe.

Karan held a water skin to Isaura's lips. She tried to hold it but fumbled. He tipped it slowly and she sipped at the water, too weak to do little else.

'That's it, but not too much now,' he said softly as he withdrew the flask.

What's he saying? I can't understand. She tried to open her eyes, blinking furiously in the dull morning light. He pulled the hood of the cloak forward to shelter her face.

'Thank you,' Isaura murmured. Her throat burned. Gradually she opened her eyes and smiled gratefully at the man who held her.

Karan drew a sharp intake of breath. Her eyes were a deep green, but flecked with a glowing vibrant blue that also rimmed her iris. The same blue as eyes of the Asena.

Isaura instantly liked this face before her. Deep set, dark brown eyes scrutinised her from under prominent eyebrows. His face was framed by wavy dark hair; two curls strayed across his forehead. He had a close-cropped beard and a hawkish nose. *Don't let me go.* He frowned; his face appeared tough and ruthless. Inexplicably, she felt hurt—as if somehow she had failed to measure up. He must have noticed her confusion, because he quickly smiled, transforming his face. Laughter lines crinkled around the edge of his eyes and she envisioned a man who could be strong, kind and ... *Gods girl, get hold of yourself!*

Cowering against him she tried to take in her surroundings. A circle of people? Weapons? A forest clearing? Autumn leaves—red and yellow against the fog. Asena. *My friends—they're meant to be here. The Lady said they were here.* Frantically she craned her neck searching for them. *There! Gabi, Jaime, Curro ... Elena. Ugh, some things don't change.*

A cry of anguish reached her. *Lucia?* Moving bodies blurred past her—one of them mountainous. *Nic?* Isaura struggled against the arms holding her, but soon gave up. She could barely speak, let alone break free.

Lucia and Nicanor scudded to a halt beside Pio. He lay curled on the ground, with his arm over the neck of the Asena and his face partially buried in its ruff.

'Pio?' Lucia asked worriedly as she shook him gently.

'He merely sleeps,' Asha said in a soft voice.

Lucia scowled, unable to understand her and angry that her son seemed to have been put at risk by the strange ritual. She looked with distaste at his flute lying on the ground. *Magic. Pio had used magic.* Nausea rolled through her.

'Ma ...' Pio grumbled. 'It's too early to get up. Let me sleep.'

Lucia caressed his brow. 'All right, sweeting, you sleep.' The Asena's fur brushed her arm. Lucia stiffened, her breath caught in her throat, yet the creature lay placidly beside Pio.

Isaura stirred in Karan's arms. In a hoarse whisper she asked, 'Pio? What's wrong? Is he all right?'

Karan sensed her consternation and weakness. He guarded her as if she was precious and fragile. 'Ssh, Bright One, ssh. All is well.'

'Lucia?' Isaura called out plaintively.

'Isaura, Pio is well. Rest.' Lucia darted a fearful look at Karan and the two Asena who surrounded Isaura. Isaura nodded and relaxed again into Karan's embrace.

'Umniga, are you with us?' Karan asked softly. She did not reply. 'Umniga?' She had collapsed after the Ritual of Samara. Still in the position she had held in the circle of Kenati, she lay spread-eagled on her back. He nudged her with his foot.

'Must you do that? I'm bone weary. How is the girl?' she asked.

'Overwhelmed, weak.'

'The Asena?'

'Only three remain. These two and the one with the boy.'

Asha and the other Kenati converged on Umniga and Karan. They helped Umniga sit up and began talking at once.

'You're all right!'

'Thank the gods.'

'It worked.'

'Of course it worked!' Umniga snapped.

Karan quirked his brow at this. 'Without the Asena you would have been lost.'

Isaura moaned and held her hands over her ears. She tried to burrow deeper into Karan's arms to escape the onslaught of the sudden babble.

'Quiet, all of you!' he commanded in a harsh whisper. They fell silent, chastened at the sight of Isaura's cringing form.

'Karan,' Umniga said softly. 'We should examine her.'

'No. Leave her be. She's been through enough. You will have time with her later, when she is stronger.' He rose and strode back to the camp with Isaura in his arms.

Baldev's eyes watered in the smoke that lingered low from the burning of the bridge and the fort. Sweat and grime covered his face while blood covered his armour. The smutty tang of the air coated his nose and when he wiped his face he tasted the bloody taint on his hands. Cries and groans of wounded men carried through the polluted air; injured horses squealed nearby. The roadway that led to the former bridge was barricaded. Their own partially built palisade could now be finished and improved upon without threat.

He summoned his captain. 'Send a rider to Gopindar for reinforcements. Get word to Captain Javal at the northern-most watchtower on the Falcontine that the northern patrols will need to be stepped up. We need to get a move on finishing those last watchtowers and beacon fires.' He jerked his head to indicate the palisade. 'Eventually I want this transformed from a palisade to a fort; one day to a citadel.'

The captain nodded hurriedly.

'Start construction on bridge towers and a bloody great gate behind those barricades. They'll provide a good vantage point over the bridge foundations and lookout. Keep the enemy from rebuilding the bridge. Get the walls closest to the river rendered quickly to reduce fire risk. One day we'll replace that bridge and I want something more permanent than these barricades barring the way. Go, see to it.'

Baldev wandered over to the picketed horses to check on their injuries. 'How goes it?' he asked an old warrior who was stitching a long cut that ran directly along the underside of a horse's belly.

'Not as bad as I'd expect. This one's lucky, stitch it up and salve it; it'll heal in no time. There's a few with 'em bastards' arras stickin' out of 'em that won't be much good for anythin' for a while. But most will recover. Bloody lucky really.'

'Can you care for them here?'

A thoughtful look crossed the wizened face. 'Yep, if our medical kits get resupplied. Between the 'orses and the men, there'll be bugger all left.'

Baldev nodded. 'You will.' A squeal caught his attention and he spied a horse with an arrow protruding from its rump.

One man stood at its head, another at its rear, calming the animal. A woman picked up its hoof, bent its foreleg tightly, and pressed her fingers into its chest. The horse lowered itself to the ground and they rapidly restrained it.

Baldev slowed as he approached them. 'Well done,' he said softly. 'I thought you'd have trouble.'

One of the warriors knelt beside the horse, talking to him quietly while he covered its eyes with his cloak; others held the leg ropes tautly. The youngest, a teenager, sat at the horse's rump with his med kit beside him. He stared anxiously at the arrow.

Baldev put his hand on his shoulder. 'He's yours?'

The boy nodded, pale and sweating.

'Just do as I say, yes?'

He looked gratefully at Baldev.

'You can't pull it straight out. You will have to make a wider cut next to it and then you will be able to work it out.' Baldev smiled encouragingly. 'That's it, well done … a bit more, it's deep …'

The horse squirmed under the blade; the young warrior's shaking hand paused.

'Don't look so pale, boy.' Baldev passed him a needle and silk. 'Stitch it up. You've done it.' Baldev sprinkled a brown powder on the outside of the cut and the horse's leg restraints were removed.

The young man wiped the sweat from his forehead, getting out of the way as his trembling horse quickly stood. Not taking his eyes from his horse, he said, 'Thank you, my lord.'

'Just let him rest.' Baldev patted him sympathetically on the back. 'He'll recover and lead you to victory another day.'

The boy smiled and nodded before fainting.

'Ah, shit!' Baldev cursed. He pulled him clear of the horse and lay him down on the grass. His armour showed no sign of damage. Wadded up in the band of his pants, at the base of his cuirass, was a bloody length of cloth. 'Young fool.' Baldev scooped him up and made for the field hospital inside the palisade walls. He left him there, saying simply, 'See what you can do.'

Every clan member learnt basic healing skills, from the time they were children. As warriors they each carried a simple medical kit of supplies. They had to know how to tend to their own injuries and those of others in the field—the sooner they were treated, the sooner they could fight. Warriors who were less able-bodied or too old often became more specialised in healing, thanks to experience and extra training from the Kenati. Yadav was one such warrior.

Baldev spied his grizzly old face amidst a cluster of warriors. A roar tore through the air and Yadav staggered back. More warriors around him leapt forward to bear down upon something. Baldev strode over to help, finding them restraining a large young man whose lower leg had been shattered. A flat blade sat heating in the nearby fire. 'Yadav?'

Yadav looked up with a scowl. 'What?' Seeing Baldev, he grimaced then shrugged. 'What, my lord?' Yadav growled in consternation as the young man struggled again. 'For the love of the gods! Just let me pour the bloody poppy juice down your throat!'

Baldev pushed past the warriors, put both his hands on the patient's shoulders and pinned him in place. 'Be still!'

'They'll take my leg. Don't let them take my leg!'

'BE STILL! It's your leg now, or your life later. You either let them give you the juice, or we'll take your damn leg without it. Make up your mind, boy!'

The young man opened his mouth to speak. Baldev grabbed his jaw, pressing his thumb and index finger into his cheeks, preventing him from closing his mouth. Yadav poured the poppy juice down his throat; Baldev held his mouth closed until he swallowed. The youth glared at him.

Baldev was blunt. 'Don't look at me like that. We're going to save your life. It's the lower part of your leg, below the knee; once you're healed you'll still be able to ride, shoot, fight and bed a woman!'

'You'll be back in the saddle in no time,' a gruff voice said. Wry grins broke out among those around him.

'Understand?' Baldev asked.

The youth nodded reluctantly.

'Good, because I have work for you when you are well.' Baldev gestured to two men near him to replace him in pinning down the young man's shoulders. A piece of thick leather was placed between his teeth. Joining Yadav at the lower end of the table, Baldev put all his strength into holding the boy's legs still. 'Gods, what a mess.'

Yadav removed his tools from boiling water. 'Blade went right through the muscle and got stuck in the bone. Bugger it! It'd have been easier for us if it had gone all the way through.'

'Just cut it off,' Baldev said bleakly. At the first cut the young man passed out.

Yadav worked quickly, sawing through bone, tying off the large blood vessels.

'Stop,' Baldev said quietly.

'Pass me the cauterising blade,' the old warrior said without looking up.

'Stop, Yadav. He's gone.'

Heads bowed, the warriors stepped solemnly back from the table. With a flick of his head Baldev dismissed them.

Yadav's tired face twisted in bitterness. 'I hope those strangers are worth it.'

'Ratilal would have made his move eventually,' Baldev grunted. 'It's better that we deal with him now, before he gains more strength.'

Yadav didn't answer.

Baldev thought of the battle, of the men—of this young one, of the horses, and he prayed to the gods that it wasn't all for nothing.

One of Vikram's eyes was black and swollen and the white of the other was bloody. He struggled to see clearly as he sat beside Deo in the wagon while they made their way back to Ratilal. Every bump and rut of the dirt roads jolted through the unsprung old wooden cart and sent pain lancing through his ribs. They had stopped at numerous farms where Deo had spoken to the locals. He had no idea what Deo had said and he didn't care, but they now had a ramshackle convoy carrying the wounded from Parlan.

Nada had taken charge of caring for the wounded; she sat in the rear of Deo's wagon keeping a sharp eye on them. She had enlisted the newcomers to help and they had proved themselves useful. Vikram hoped it would pacify Ratilal. The villagers from Parlan had the flimsiest of excuses for not aiding his men during the short battle—if they didn't appear to help now in every way, they would face his wrath. His thoughts strayed to Asha—nobody deserved that.

Well into the morning, their convoy encountered Ratilal's battered band camped off the roadside near the valley in which they had been ambushed. All those in the convoy stared in silent shock at the number of wounded and dead men and horses. Ratilal sat on a throne of salvaged tack. He stood at the sound of wagons and, with Niaz beside him, limped towards them.

Vikram had witnessed Ratilal's anger before, yet he had never seen his face like this; it unnerved him. He appeared calm, though his eyes were glassy, cold and hard.

Ratilal's words were clipped as he took in Vikram's battered appearance. 'What. Happened. To. You?'

'Karan returned with a band of his men, ambushed us, we battled, and lost. They beat me halfway to Karak, tied us up, locked us in the lodge, took a few of the strangers, and left with Umniga and Asha.'

'Umniga! Asha!' His face coloured and his hard, cold eyes took on a manic gleam. 'Did they seem aware that he was coming?'

'They gave no sign of it earlier, yet they must have known something for they aided the ambush.' The words left a sour taste in his mouth, though he knew no alternative to utter.

'Bitches!' Ratilal spat. 'Damn those bitches to Karak! They have betrayed their clan. I will flay them alive if I catch them. I …'

Niaz put a hand on Ratilal's arm and whispered. Ratilal shrugged off his hand, but subsided sullenly.

He appeared thoughtful for a moment, before looking cunningly at Deo and the others. 'Did no one help you? Did no one hear the fighting and come to your aid?'

Deo's fists clenched the driving reins. Before Deo could speak, Vikram replied, 'Many had gone home to their outlying farms, so had no knowledge of the battle.'

'The others?' Ratilal demanded.

'The others were too drunk to hear …'

'Too drunk! Ah! They were not drunk when we began our chase …'

Vikram shifted in his seat, deliberately wincing, drawing Ratilal's attention away from Deo. 'They were difficult to rouse and reeked of ale.' Deo did not reek of ale when Vikram 'woke' him, but he did now. *Clever old bastard.*

Deo cleared his throat. 'Aye, we was well on the way when you gave chase to those bastards.' He spat on the ground in disgust. 'But at the news of the murder of your father, we drank some more in misery, then some to bless his journey. We slept like logs.'

Well done, old man, Vikram thought.

Ratilal pursed his lips, muttered to Niaz and flicked his head in their direction. Niaz approached and within three feet of Deo he wrinkled his nose as he took in his dishevelled appearance. Looking back at Ratilal, he nodded. A look of disappointment crossed Ratilal's face, but the mask of control slipped back onto his visage.

'Vikram, get down from that wagon and report fully. Niaz, find room for the wounded on this convoy. They need to get to Faros, where we can better care for them. Leave those with minor wounds to see to the injured horses. Find a farm nearby where we can take them. We'll probably lose most of the horses, but send supplies and help anyway. The injured are in the care of these good people.' He gestured to the locals driving the wagons. 'Consider it payment for your laxity in aiding Vikram and my men. Take very good care of them, make sure they all survive or you will incur my wrath. The levies will be called and your village shall lead by example, providing all its able-bodied men.'

'The dead, my lord?' Niaz asked.

Ratilal looked at the corpses in disgust. He drew Niaz aside. 'We need to burn them. They'll be ripe by the time wagons get back.'

Niaz moved closer to him, whispering, 'You can't leave them here.'

'Of course not,' Ratilal said quietly. 'We've no oil and in our state we can't gather wood to burn them.' His nose wrinkled with distaste. 'And we need to show Faros and those who supported my father that the old ways will not be forgotten. In the face of our dedication to the dead, how can they not follow me?' Loudly, he finished, 'If you have room, take them. If not, send wagons back. It is only fitting that they have a proper farewell before their families.'

Niaz bowed deeply. As he rose his eyes locked with Vikram's and a flash of sympathy danced across them before he spun on his heels and left.

Ratilal swept his gaze over Vikram's battered face. 'Well, what happened?'

Vikram related the night's events in detail.

'Had you seen any of these men earlier? Were they part of his original force?'

'No, High Lord, I do not think so.'

'*Think*?' Ratilal asked icily.

'They were not, High Lord.'

Ratilal debated scenarios to himself. 'Karan must have had a force of men hidden somewhere. Could they have split off from the main force during our ambush?'

If he keeps going, he'll figure it out; they need more time. 'Either way, High Lord, they killed your father and took what they wanted. And they must have wanted those strangers very badly,' Vikram said bitterly.

Ratilal glanced up quickly, distracted from his musing. 'Yes, you say they took some of the strangers.'

'In fact, High Lord, I believe that was their only purpose. They said that Clan Lord Shahjahan had promised the strangers to them. They were only interested in the unconscious girl and the young boy and his family—no others.'

'Why? He risked much by this. What could be worth it? Did you notice anything special about them?'

'If they were sent by the gods, High Lord ...'

A horse, lathered and exhausted, rounded the road's bend. Vikram leapt protectively before Ratilal, drawing his kilij. Warriors drew beside him shielding their lord. The horse skidded to a halt.

The rider slid from its back shouting, 'High Lord! I must see the High Lord!' Jabr, the young warrior Ratilal had sent out scouting with Mas'ūd, floundered his way towards him.

Ratilal cocked his brow imperiously at the breathless young warrior and ordered, 'Report!'

'High Lord! Mas'ūd found them. They passed, via a hidden trail, down to the river and were resting their horses.' Jabr wheezed and gulped air.

'For the love of the gods, someone give him some water so he can finish.'

Jabr gratefully took a water skin.

'Drink, boy! Finish your report!'

Jabr's voice shook as he continued, 'High Lord, Lord Karan was not with them ...'

'I know that.'

'The one we thought was Lord Karan was in disguise ...'

'I know that!' Ratilal bellowed, spittle flying from his mouth, as he barely resisted beating the dolt.

Jabr, ashen, replied haltingly, 'High Lord ... I ...'

'How many men were in the group you saw? Did it look to be the full force? Did Mas'ūd notice if any had turned off anywhere?'

Jabr quailed under Ratilal's intense scrutiny.

'High Lord, forgive him his tardiness—he is green and nervous. Report, lad. Slow down. Breathe. The high lord is fair; he'll not punish you for the truth.' Vikram smiled at him. *C'mon lad, pull yourself together.*

Ratilal coolly appraised Vikram before he replied in an even tone, 'I need the truth—speak.'

Jabr licked his lips nervously, then drew himself up. 'High Lord,' Jabr continued, his voice gaining confidence as he did so. 'Mas'ūd saw no sign of the enemy splitting the main force. Other than the absence of Lord Karan, the entire force seemed to be there. We killed one of their sentries. When we left they were still resting their horses. Mas'ūd has gone to warn the crossing guard, hoping to stop them at the bridge.'

'Dismissed, join the others,' Ratilal absently ordered.

Jabr bolted.

'Don't assume that you know the extent of my benevolence, Captain Vikram,' Ratilal said harshly.

Vikram bowed, contrite. 'High Lord, what would you have us do?'

Ratilal shook his head and sneered. 'We can do nothing and you know it as well as I. We are too depleted. Better they had not killed the sentry—doubtless they've discovered him and moved on. Too much time has passed, Vikram; we wouldn't catch up and if we did,' his hand encompassed the wounded around him, 'we could do little. We must trust that Mas'ūd made it to the crossing.'

Anger and hate welled within Ratilal, begging to be unleashed. It roared like a living flame inside him. He constantly struggled to control it, yet it bubbled to the surface all too often; it felt so good to unleash his anger and let it burn. He loathed that his father had been right about him needing patience and control.

Ratilal breathed deeply. 'Right now, we look after the men. After that, we plan.' Pre-occupied, he resumed pacing while slapping his gauntlet impatiently against his thigh. 'How did they get extra troops in undetected? Have you any ideas?' Ratilal demanded.

Vikram scrambled for an answer. 'High Lord, I do not.'

'Nothing? Surely a man of your experience has some ideas.'

Deo and Nada had been discretely listening while they worked with the wounded.

'Deo, get me the spare bag from the wagon,' Nada said. He looked at her as if she were mad. She glared back at him. 'Just do it, you lazy old bugger.'

He shrugged and went to the wagon to look. In consternation she said to the warrior she was treating, 'Oh, for the love of the gods. He won't find it, daft old sod that he is.' She moved hastily to the side of the wagon.

'Well?' Deo hissed.

'Help him,' Nada said, shifting her eyes to Vikram. Deo glowered at her, but her scowl silenced him. 'Just do it. There's more going on here than you think.'

'You better be right,' he mumbled as they both turned and wandered back. 'High Lord,' Deo said deferentially, 'I … we couldn't help overhearing your conversation.'

'Well?' Ratilal demanded.

'There is a way they could enter Boar Clan lands, High Lord,' Deo replied. Ratilal stiffened, his gaze predatory. 'It's an old way and not well known anymore. They could have come by Hunters' Ford.'

Ratilal spun to Vikram. 'How is it you did not think of this?'

'A lad like Captain Vikram wouldn't know of it,' Deo said hastily.

Vikram apologised. 'High Lord, it is an ancient track. In truth, I am ashamed to say I had forgotten its existence.'

'You'd have to be a local to know it, High Lord.' Deo shook his head and casually hawked up a gob of phlegm before continuing. 'Entrance is totally overgrown. Be bloody stupid to use it this time of year anyway—river usually floods. Treacherous bloody crossing at the best of times.'

Ratilal fisted his hands; his head pounded. 'Idiots, all around me—idiots!' His hand strayed to the flask hidden in his pocket; quickly he stopped himself.

He summoned Niaz. 'Old man, tell us how to find the entrance.'

'Entrance?' Niaz asked.

'To the track to Hunters' Ford,' Vikram said.

'Oh that.'

Ratilal's face turned puce and a vein throbbed in his temple. 'You knew!'

'I did not think ...' Niaz paled. 'By the gods! Karan, that's how ...'

Ratilal's face contorted in rage. The urge to punch his friend in the face nearly overwhelmed him. 'Niaz, find us some horses. I need to see this track.'

'Will you not take some men with you, High Lord?' Vikram asked.

Ratilal hesitated. 'Yes, only a few. Karan will be long gone and you'll need all the help you can get. Sort things out here and head back to Faros; be careful. I don't want these men put at more risk. I need them tended and back to fighting strength. We'll catch up with you before the Four Ways. Gods only know what we'll find there, but we'll tackle it together.'

—ᴍ—

Karan carried Isaura from the sacred site where the Ritual of Samara had been held into the main camp and sat on the ground near the campfire with his legs stretched out. The early morning fog was slipping away through the trees and the glow of the sun was shifting from grey to golden.

Isaura sat nestled between Karan's legs, leaning against his chest. The Asena had followed and lay stretched alongside them. Isaura shuddered and she held her arms tightly against herself trying to warm them. More cloaks were thrown around her. Her arms and legs were grabbed and rubbed vigorously.

She knew they were trying to get the blood flowing through her limbs, but with each touch it felt as if a thousand pins speared her. Isaura moaned, trying to raise her leaden hands and move away. Karan held her fast with one arm around her middle. Her head rested against his chest while he caressed her brow. He tipped his head forward and, as she fought the pain in her legs, Isaura heard him murmuring in a soothing tone.

Isaura concentrated on his soft voice. Karan's lips were right next to her ear; his breath warm against her skin. 'Ssh, bright one. All will be well, hush now. I've got you. You are home, ssh.' Karan repeated this mantra until Isaura began to settle.

Asha summoned Āsim. 'We need her to try to move her legs some more.'

Āsim placed a hand around Isaura's foot and under her knee, bending each of her legs repeatedly, while Asha continued to rub them. Isaura groaned as the pain increased, crested, then eased as more of the feeling returned.

'Stop.' Isaura's words were foreign, but her intent was clear.

Āsim looked up and tightened his grip on her leg.

'Stop!' Isaura's voice growled a low, bass tone, which rumbled through those nearest her. The Matriarch watched her closely.

Āsim stopped, the hairs on the back of his neck rose, and he shivered visibly.

The Matriarch pushed him out of the way and sat on her haunches directly between him and Isaura, baring her teeth.

Karan's hand tightened around Isaura's waist. 'Āsim, I think you've been told.'

'Aye. Asha, I'm sorry. You're on your own.'

'Karan?' Asha asked.

'Leave her be. Just bring me some food.'

Karan tipped Isaura's face to his, scrutinising it carefully under the protection of the cloak's hood. He said softly, soothingly, 'You must learn control—relax.'

The hood of the cloak slipped back as Asha returned and Isaura's eyes met hers. Asha gaped. Karan quickly shook his head at Asha to remain silent. He pulled the hood back up, sheltering Isaura's face.

Asha knelt before them with a bowl of watered-down stew. She stirred it slowly, thoughtfully. 'Karan, what just happened with Āsim?'

Karan turned a stony gaze upon her. 'I believe we'll find out in due course, but for now, not a word.' Asha nodded reluctantly.

The motion of Asha's hand as it stirred the stew mesmerised Isaura. *I hope I'm not drooling.* Asha moved the bowl up to Isaura's lips. Karan laughed as she licked her lips and she wriggled impatiently. Isaura frowned at him. *Laugh, will he? It's not him who's bloody well starving.* He caught her annoyed look and schooled his features. *Yes, that's right, but your damn eyes are twinkling. You still think this is funny.* Isaura pursed her lips, glaring at Karan, daring him to laugh again, but she could not resist returning his smile. Her stomach grumbled loudly. She chuckled hoarsely, wincing at the dry irritation of her throat. A water skin was pressed against her lips.

'Slowly,' Karan said softly. 'Sl-ow-ly.'

Nodding, Isaura raised her eyes to him again, scowling. 'I'm not an idiot.' She attempted to sit up properly. The effort exhausted her and made her dizzy. Isaura leaned back against Karan's chest with an exasperated huff. His hand rubbed her shoulder sympathetically.

'Here,' Karan said to Asha. 'Give me the bowl. Go see to Umniga. I'll take care of her.' He held Asha's hand firmly when she handed him the bowl and in a voice that brooked no disobedience said, 'Not a word to her, Asha, not yet.'

Chapter Two

KARAN HELD THE steaming bowl before Isaura. It took all her concentration to grip the wooden spoon. She managed two mouthfuls with a shaking hand and the spoon slipped from her fingers. *I'm like a damn baby.*

Though physically exhausted, Isaura's mind raced. The language she was hearing fascinated her; its complex rhythm and cadences were lyrical and it resonated deep within her. Isaura leaned back, closing her eyes to listen.

Karan's arm draped loosely around her waist. He had much to plan and they needed to reach Bear Tooth Lake and rendezvous with Baldev, yet it felt wonderful to rest after their flight. Karan was surprised at his reluctance when he lay Isaura on the ground. 'Rest, bright one,' he murmured as he left her. The Asena, ever her sentinels, promptly spooned alongside Isaura, one facing her feet while the other faced her head.

Karan found the Kenati away from the main camp, deep in discussion. He strode into their midst. 'Effective immediately— Hadi, you will return to the High Citadel in Targmur and work with Chancellor Khayrat. I want him to send word across the High Plateau and mobilise all my forces. Hadi, Khayrat is in charge while I am absent. You'll assist him in any way he deems fit and I need you there to ensure communications. Munira, I need to send you and your guardian to reconnoitre the Four Ways. I need to know how Lord Baldev fared. Then you will go to the squad at Hunters' Ford. Keep me informed of any developments through Asha or Umniga. Anil, Suniti, go to the Bear Tooth Lake. You'll make better time on your own. Find Baldev, I'm sure he'll have need of you. Spread the word of what has happened to any homesteads on the way. Tell them we'll do our utmost to protect them, but we offer the protection of the High Citadel for any young children. Their parents must bring them to the lake in two weeks' time. From there they'll be taken to Targmur.'

Shocked looks passed amongst the Kenati. No low-lander had ever visited Targmur.

Seeing their astonishment, Karan laughed harshly. 'These people are under my protection, mine and Lord Baldev's; they are ours.' *How better to cement their loyalty than by protecting and educating their children.* 'I will endeavour to protect them, but this is a large territory ... I'll not suffer their children to be victims if I can help it. Asha, Umniga, you remain with this lot and teach them—quickly. The sooner they learn and are useful the better.' His glance encompassed them all. 'Now go. Not you, Umniga.'

Karan watched them leave then addressed her. 'What do you know about the Ritual of Samara?'

She frowned. 'Not a great deal. It was the time of the last Bard Kenati. Samara was dying; he loved her and wanted to save her. He conceived the ritual in desperation, and she lived.'

'How did it change her?'

Puzzled, Umniga said, 'There are no accounts of any change. She lived to an uncommonly old age, though. Why?'

'The girl—Isaura.' It felt odd saying her name aloud. 'Her eyes are flecked with the blue of the Asena. I've already seen a glimpse of Undavi in her.'

Umniga's jaw dropped and her eyes widened.

Good, she's off guard, maybe I'll get the truth. 'Tell me exactly what happened in this ritual.'

Baldev was confronted with the horrified face of Mirza's rider. 'He's gone, my lord ... Mirza is gone,' he said.

'Was he among the dead?'

'No, my lord. I checked twice. What will I tell Lord Karan?'

'What? That you've lost his horse … no, not just his horse, but his guardian too.' Baldev's lips twitched.

Another warrior looked up from tending an injured horse and took pity on the man. 'Bloody horse has always been trouble, ever since he was a young 'un.' Mirza's rider looked between the two of them in confusion. 'Don't worry about it, man. Damned horse hightailed it out across the bridge at the end of the battle.'

Baldev laughed at his look of relief. 'He's gone back to Karan, that's all. Find another horse to ride to the lake—you'll be safer anyway. Go on.' He turned to the warrior. 'What do you think has made him happier: that he won't have to tell Karan, or he won't have to ride him again?'

'Not getting on that bloody horse, I reckon.'

Yadav approached Baldev. His arms were no longer gloved in red, yet his clothing was stiff and darkened from crusting blood.

'How goes it?' Baldev asked.

'Not as bad as it could've been, but bad enough.'

'The young one who saved his horse—the one I carried to the hospital?'

'Dead.'

Baldev gripped the side of a wagon and hung his head. Yadav put his hand on his shoulder, squeezing it in sympathy. They had both seen this before—too often—but it never got easier. Baldev breathed deeply and raised his head, looking squarely at Yadav.

'He was going to die anyway. You couldn't have changed it,' Yadav said. Baldev nodded in thanks.

'We're lucky there's only a handful of severely injured men and women.'

'How many of them will survive the journey to Bear Tooth Lake?'

'Gods alone know,' Yadav said tiredly.

Isaura snuggled into the fur of the Matriarch. She needed the reassurance of touch to know she was back and would not slip away.

The Matriarch huffed gently through her snout. *You will not slip away, not now.*

Isaura's eyes snapped open. *You can talk to me! Like her? Here? I'm safe?*

Yes, Isa-cub. You will not slip away. At least not unwillingly.

Thank you. An idea occurred to Isaura; she could not shake it. The Asena's voice was intrinsically familiar and comforting, yet it was not the voice of the woman who had spoken to her in the spirit realm. Isaura tried to curb this thought, remembering that the woman had wanted her involvement to remain secret. A wave of amusement radiated from the Matriarch.

Too late, Isaura thought with misgiving. *You can see into my mind just as the Lady could.*

Don't chastise yourself, Isa-cub. She cannot keep secrets from me. Derision for the Lady exuded from her.

You don't like her? Nothing. *Why? Who is she?* Nothing. Isaura's mind rapidly turned over the events of her rescue. They worked together to save her and bring her here—why? Her instincts demanded her to be cautious. *You knew the Lady had spoken to me, yet she was unaware that you knew. Aren't you worried that she'll read my mind here and find out? In fact, can she hear us, even now?*

The Matriarch snorted. *In this realm she can do little other than watch—not enter your mind. And now ...*

Yet you can do so in both realms ... Isaura interrupted.

Very good, Isa-cub. The Matriarch's scrutiny intensified.

So, am I the fly caught in a web of two spiders?

Spiders kill that which is caught in their web. Clearly you have been saved.

Clearly you want something from me, both of you.

Nothing.

Do I even have a choice?

The Matriarch appeared to be waiting for something.

I don't like games. I'm grateful to be saved, but I—don't—like—games. Isaura's ire rose; her eyes flared blue. *I won't be used.*

You are ... interesting, Isa-cub. Satisfaction and wry amusement rolled from the Matriarch. *There is always choice, Isa-cub—always. Sometimes we walk the trails before us, sometimes we make our own. I give you a gift. It might help you decide which trail to walk.*

Immediately those blue eyes narrowed and bore into her. At once Isaura's vision altered, becoming sharper and showing her colours outlining and surrounding the Asena and herself. She looked at the people scattered around the camp. Shades of brown and green surrounded them; occasionally she saw a flicker of red ripple across them. *Auras.* Isaura had no idea where that word had come from, but she knew it to be correct.

Her own aura appeared markedly different. It flashed blue, violet and red over subdued browns and greens. The same blue haloed the Asena. Worry took root within her. *This is the spirit realm again,* she thought. Her skin prickled. The hairs on her arms stood up. *This is different. I couldn't feel it before.* The familiar lure of The Wild tugged at her to join it. *No. I know you now. No. Never again. Never.* Isaura remained resolute, speaking to The Wild as if it were a living entity. She felt recognition from it.

Good, Isa-cub, very good.

Gradually the tug at her spirit disappeared, to be replaced by another sensation. Goosebumps formed on her skin as a sensation akin to water flowed across it.

What? Isaura saw nothing to account for this. There was no breeze, yet the sensation persisted. The current slowed and eddied around her limbs. *What's happening? It's attracted to me.* Suspicious, Isaura asked, *Why?*

Your essence is different now. It cannot lure you away, though the same attraction to your power still exists. Since it cannot steal, it must come to you.

Isaura grinned widely as she began to feel more alert, stronger.

There is more, Isa-cub. Here is your gift. Pressure built up around her. Isaura's head began to pound. It was as if something was trying to drill its way through her skull. She held her head in her hands as agonising power seared her mind.

A burst of energy flared around them, buffeting Isaura's form before ceasing abruptly. The Lady appeared, angry. *Stop! You'll ruin …*

Too late. To stop would kill her. The Matriarch, un-cowed and smug, said, *You don't want her dead, do you?*

Irate, the Lady's face distorted. The air crackled with energy as her image became a more intense shade of blue. Her lip curled with disgust. In agony, Isaura moved away and watched them warily. Immediately the Lady moulded her features into a visage filled only with concern. The pent up power surrounding them dissipated. Her voice radiated compassion and kindness as she said to Isaura, 'Don't fight it, child. If you want to survive, don't fight it.'

Isaura looked at the Matriarch for help, reaching out with her mind, only to hit a wall. The pain was becoming unbearable. She had to make a choice—fight or surrender? *Choose the path. Bastards.* She couldn't resist much longer. *Damn it!* Isaura gave up. The pressure in her head intensified. It exploded in one magnificent wave of energy that formed a torrid confluence within her.

'Isaura?' the Lady asked.

Isaura raised her head and shot both the Matriarch and the Lady a venomous look. *I HATE BLOODY GAMES!* Her words boomed through the figure of the Lady, causing her image to fracture, then reform. The Matriarch, however, remained impassive and unaffected.

'What have you done?' the Lady accused the Matriarch, shooting her a look filled with malice.

I levelled the playing field.

Chapter Three

'YOU KNOW SO little about the ritual,' Karan said.

Umniga shrugged. 'It was a hunch. We had little option and I could think of nothing else. It worked anyway.'

Karan scowled at her. 'There was more at work in that ritual than you ever considered.'

She remained silent.

'When this is done ... when ...' Karan's skin began to prickle, distracting him. 'No. I was going to wait until the strangers are trained and taught our ways, but anything could happen. I'll send for Nimo ...'

'I'm not talking to that bloody scribe! She's just a chit of girl; she shouldn't be privy to all our knowledge.'

'Yes you will,' he replied too quietly.

'The Kenati have never written down their teachings. They are only for the chosen.'

Karan leaned down, so close to Umniga's face that their noses almost touched. 'You have no choice. If the Kenati had kept written records, you would have had better knowledge of the ritual. We are at war; your numbers are few. We cannot afford to lose our lore.'

Umniga glowered, yet said nothing, knowing he was correct.

'Hadi and Munira have already spent time with Nimo.'

Indignant, Umniga said, 'They had no right!'

Karan silenced her with a glare; his finger pointing inches from her face. 'I want all the Kenati to work with her, so we can compare your stories and compile accurate records.'

'She will tell.'

'She will not,' Karan replied. Scorn etched itself upon Umniga's face. 'She will keep it a secret or she will die. The records will be locked in the vault. I'm not asking you, old woman, I'm ordering you.'

Umniga scowled, but nodded.

Karan rubbed his arms, as if chilled. Looking about warily, he straightened and turned from her. *No wind.* The hair on his arms stood up. *What is … ? Isaura?*

—⚡—

Curro and the others were clustered at the outskirts of the camp's perimeter. They avoided the gaze of the Altaicans and murmured amongst themselves.

He saw Karan race across the campsite, making directly for Isaura. Umniga trailed in his wake. Curro leapt to his feet. 'What's going on? Isa? C'mon, Nic.' He moved to leave Elena's side, but she anchored his wrist firmly.

'No, Curro. Leave her be.'

He could see the anger and hurt in her eyes, but remained torn.

'They'll take good care of her. Right now I need my husband,' she said.

Nicanor shook his head in disbelief at Elena.

Lucia took his hand, saying, 'Pio is fine—he's just sleeping. I'll stay with him. Go, see if you can help Isa.'

'I'll come too,' Gabriela added quickly.

Curro looked at Elena apologetically. 'I'm sorry, Leni. I'll be quick—I promise.'

'Someone needs to stay to protect Lucia, Pio and me.' Elena reached out to Jaime, snagging his arm.

He shrugged her off. 'Protection from what?' he muttered as he followed the others.

—⚡—

Isaura clutched her head and began writhing on the ground. Foam came from her mouth and blood streamed from her nose.

'Isaura!' Karan skidded to a halt beside her, grabbing her flailing arms. He struggled to hold her still. Āsim leapt up to help, placing a stick across her mouth to stop her biting her tongue. The Asena lay nearby, calmly watching. Karan narrowed his eyes at them in suspicion.

Isaura's friends hovered around him, jostling his arms. He shot them a warning look.

Her thrashing subsided. Soon she lay still. Āsim removed the stick, flicked the foam out of her mouth with his fingers and rolled her on her side.

Asha passed Karan a water flask. As he bathed her face, Isaura's eyes fluttered open. She sat up, coughing violently. Isaura grabbed the flask and gulped the water. Resting on her hands and knees she heaved in air. Her shuddering breaths quietened and a string of expletives erupted from her lips.

Nicanor laughed in relief. 'Welcome back, Isa! Thank the gods Pio is asleep. He doesn't need to learn that language.'

Gabriela laughed, though she eyed Isaura anxiously. 'You don't even know what she said! None of us know what she said. She always curses in Matyrani.'

'Because it sounds so damn good!' Isaura ground out. 'Blast them. I hate games,' she grumbled as she sat. Isaura drew her knees up and rested her head on her arms, before taking another swig from the flask.

Āsim quirked a brow at Karan, shaking his head. 'She seems remarkably recovered.'

Isaura cast him a brief withering glance. 'Apart from a bloody headache that is,' she retorted. 'Ugh! It's like worms in my head.' She stiffened and rubbed her temple. 'Wriggling bloody worms!' Reaching out, she took Karan's hand, holding it tightly.

'By the gods!' Āsim exclaimed.

Isaura looked up, startled at the complete silence that

surrounded her. Her mind raced. *Oh shit! I understood everything he said. Did he understand me?* Someone else spoke from across the fire. Isaura turned her head quickly in their direction; the sudden movement sending a sharp stabbing pain through her skull. Although the language was foreign, she understood what they were talking about. The words were like living things, writhing within her brain, then settling. Isaura held her hand over her mouth, trying to quell her rising nausea. She looked at the sleeping Asena. *What did you do?*

'Greetings, Isaura. I am Karan,' he said, inclining his head and holding his free hand to his heart.

'Greetings, Karan.' Confused, still holding his hand, she whispered, 'What's happening?'

'Umniga, do you know?' Karan asked. There was no reply. Karan turned to see the old woman staring in open-mouthed shock at Isaura. With a wry smile he said, 'I think you've been given a gift.'

'Nic? Curro? Are you here?' she asked plaintively.

Karan remained by her side, her hand still locked around his.

'We're here, Isa.' Nicanor seated himself beside her and placed his arm around her. Her eyes met his. His arm dropped from her shoulders; he looked momentarily stricken.

'Curro, you can still understand me?'

Curro cleared his throat. 'Yes. How're you feeling?' The others joined him, clustering around Isaura.

Gabriela embraced her. 'Isa! I'm so glad you're back. We feared the worst. How are you?' She released her and Isaura smiled warmly. 'Your eyes! Oh no!' Gabriela withdrew, horrified.

Elena, who had been unable to let Curro out of her sight, joined them. Curro put his hands on either side of Isaura's face while he examined her.

Karan fingered the hilt of his kilij and quashed an urge to chop off Curro's hands. Curro stepped back, shaking his head in dismay. Hastily, he wiped his hands upon his trousers. Elena grabbed his arm and hauled him away from Isaura.

'What about my eyes?'

Nicanor would not meet her gaze.

'What. About. My. Eyes?' Her tone was steely, unfamiliar. The others put more distance between them.

'They're blue. How?' Gabriela whispered from the safety of Jaime's arms. Isaura arched her brow in disbelief.

'Her eyes? You're wondering about her eyes? How is she even up and about? Let alone speaking in two different languages!' Elena spat. 'None of it is natural. It's magic.'

'You don't know that,' Nicanor said.

'What else could it be? It hasn't happened to any of us.' She looked with revulsion at Isaura and said accusingly, 'It's you. It's in your blood.'

'I didn't ask for this,' Isaura retaliated.

'You didn't have to. Your blood is tainted. Like all your kind.'

Elena's shrill voice had drawn Lucia part of the way to them. She kept one eye on Pio as she barked, 'Elena! What are you going on about?'

'It's true,' Elena continued. 'You're all thinking it. She's Hill Clan and always will be.'

Curro looked askance at her, before averting his eyes. The others looked anywhere but at Isaura. No one contradicted Elena.

Lucia hovered and glanced anxiously at Pio sleeping soundly. 'Blasted woman,' she muttered, before pushing her way to the fore. 'Let me look. Have you all lost your senses?' She paused before Isaura, gaped, but rapidly composed herself. 'Actually … the green is still there. They … are green … They've just got flecks of blue about them.' She spun around and shooed the others way. 'I'm sure they'll return to normal soon.' Hastily, she returned to Pio and bent over his face in concern. Her hand hovered near his eyes.

'She's worried he's the same,' Isaura said with dismay. The pain of rejection creased Isaura's face as she tracked the departing backs of her friends. Only Nicanor remained, but was poised to leave. 'I'm not contagious, Nic.' Tears welled in her eyes.

'Give us time, Isaura. We don't understand ... when you are better ...'

'I *am* better,' came her toneless reply. Nicanor retreated.

Karan moved to her side. 'My eyes are blue?' she asked him softly.

'Green, with bits of blue—and beautiful,' he told her.

Isaura smiled half-heartedly. 'Blue, like the Asena, yes?' He nodded. Isaura, her face blank, turned from watching her friends. *Time to be strong.* 'Time to get up. I've had enough sitting on my arse for a lifetime.'

'Isaura ...' Umniga began.

'Later, Umniga.' Karan's tone brooked no argument. He hauled Isaura to her feet. She stepped confidently forward, only to stumble. Karan caught her as a tirade of cursing, worthy of his most coarse warrior, erupted from her—half in a foreign, yet oddly familiar, language; half in Altaican.

'Damn it!' she yelled at the Asena. 'You cunning bloody fur balls. Couldn't you have fixed my bloody leg as well?' The Asena slept on.

The surrounding warriors looked nervously between the Asena and Isaura. Karan tried not to laugh. 'We revere the Asena. They have never heard anyone speak directly to them let alone abuse them. You might want to remember that. Do you want my help?'

Stiffly, she shook her head. Head high, jaw set, determined to show no weakness, Isaura walked forward doing her best not to limp. Beads of sweat broke out upon her brow and she tried not to grimace.

A warrior stood up and handed her a quarterstaff. 'Use this for the time being,' she said, scowling at Isaura's friends.

Isaura smiled in gratitude as she took the staff and experimented walking with it. The more she practised with the staff, the wider her grin became. 'Thank you.'

'C'mon lass, come over here with us. Perch yourself on that log there.' Āsim shepherded her along until she sat near them. The strange sensation within her head was lessening; overwhelming it was a ravenous hunger. Isaura found herself fixated by the camp oven.

'Ya daft old bugger,' Umniga said. 'Give the girl some food.'

Someone put a bowl of stew in her hands. Her benefactor did not let go of the bowl until Isaura looked up; his eyes widened in shock at her gaze.

'Enough. You've seen. Now go and tell the others,' Karan said. 'Isaura has been blessed by the Asena—she bears their mark upon her.'

Isaura ploughed through the food and held out the bowl for more.

Conversation around the campfire resumed. Karan looked at her. 'Do you know what happened to you?'

She shook her head. 'The Asena … the Matriarch.' She shrugged. 'It was as if my skull was being stabbed. Like my mind was sliced, tossed up and rearranged. Now it's like some *thing's* in my head … Like the words are in my head—alive. They move and settle. Each time I hear your language, I feel a bit more of a change.' She sighed. 'It's lessening … I'm alive.'

'What you describe would test the mettle of the best of us,' Karan said.

'It's a gift,' Umniga said reverently.

'Some gift,' Isaura snorted.

Umniga looked surprised at her dismissive attitude. 'The gods have …'

'Gods … ?' Isaura seethed. Karan squeezed her thigh in warning; she said no more. She would not be the easy convert and tool that Umniga would undoubtedly want.

The warriors talked of war. War with the Boar Clan. War with Ratilal. 'You are at war because of us?' Isaura asked. *They should hate us.*

Karan spoke quietly, yet his voice carried clearly. 'It was bound to happen sooner or later. Ratilal just needed an opportunity.'

'Aye, I've lived with them and the things I could tell you about that bastard.' Āsim shook his head. 'I wish more of their clan knew it, but he's too good at hiding his tracks. Asha was the first slip up he's made in while. I'm glad we got you and your friends out. I wouldn't leave a dog in his care.'

We ran from one war, now we're in another. Isaura looked at the warriors around the fire, noting with satisfaction that there were women amongst them. Her choices were getting easier. *No more running.*

—⚒—

The Kenati regrouped away from the main camp. In a grave voice, Hadi said, 'I've never heard of, or seen anything like this.' No one replied. 'This is beyond the Ritual of Samara. Umniga, what have we … ?'

Umniga scowled at him. 'Stop being such an old worry wart! No, it's not in any history of the damned ritual. It's new. I told you she was important … I knew she was important. Just look at the boy if you need confirmation that we should've helped them. By Rana and Jalal, we have not seen a Bard Kenati in generations. Think about what he did!'

'A Bard Kenati is one thing, but this …'

Umniga narrowed her eyes. 'Isaura is different, that is all.'

'We have never …'

'Check her aura.' Asha's voice was firm. Hadi and Umniga stared at her. 'Instead of butting heads like two old goats—check her aura.'

Merging with Devi, Umniga examined Isaura's aura. Her face paled as she broke contact with him. 'Somebody get me a drink. No, not water—kefir.' Astonished, they passed her a flask— Umniga never drank alcohol, but she swilled the kefir like it was water. She appraised Asha. 'You knew.'

'No, only suspected.'

'What?' Hadi barked. 'Will I have to summon my guardian to see?'

Karan's younger Kenati, Munira, rolled her eyes at him. 'Tell us, Umniga, before I strangle him.'

'Her aura ... not only is it at full strength, which shouldn't have happened for days, maybe weeks, but ...' She took another swig of kefir. 'It's totally different from when I found her ... It's totally different from when we returned.' She took another drink before passing it to Hadi. 'Here, you'll need that.' He looked at her suspiciously.

'It's the same as the Asena, isn't it?' Asha said.

'Virtually.' Umniga nodded absently. 'It's almost entirely blue.' She scowled at the bottle of kefir in Hadi's hand and snatched it back, taking another long gulp before thrusting it at him again. 'There's your answer, Hadi, not that it's any bloody answer at all. The Asena have always been a mystery, but if they've helped her then by the gods we will too.'

Hadi took the flask from her, saying resignedly, 'We'll have to. I've a feeling we don't want her as an enemy.'

chapter four

RATILAL STARED FROM atop his mount at the flooded river. Old Deo's directions had proved sound—though unnecessary. As they had drawn near the hidden entrance, a loose horse had happily whinnied at them and emerged from between the low hanging branches of some sheoaks to greet them. As they'd ridden the winding forest trail to Hunters' Ford, his men had gathered a string of horses that Karan had stolen then abandoned. For that alone the journey was worth it—even if it was thanks to Karan.

The rising river had submerged the pebbled beach; the crossing was a muddy torrent.

'It may not rise further, unless there's more rain in the hills.'

'It matters not,' Ratilal said bitterly. 'We can't get the horses across that! We've no boats handy to ferry men across and, even if we did, we are in no fit state to fight him and he knows it … but we will be.'

Niaz stared across the water. 'He'll have troops—waiting.'

'Of course,' Ratilal bit out as he spun his horse and headed back along the trail. 'How many spots are there like this on the river, Niaz?'

'This is the only ford—if you can call it that.'

'No, just places where we can get a handful of men across undetected.'

'In the north there are more, up near the Falcontine.'

Ratilal scowled. 'They'll be expecting that—like last time. I'm not thinking of an invasion force to begin with. Small squads might be able to sneak past his patrols and, if we're lucky, become an itch he can't scratch.'

'Hit and run.'

Ratilal cocked his head. 'Mmm, or an assassination squad. If they don't cause havoc they could get even closer. Kill Karan and you remove the brains of the operation.'

'Multiple teams could do both. Have them looking one way while we move deeper into their territory. Though such a blow … Karan is well loved—it may enrage the clans to a full invasion before we are ready.'

'True.' Ratilal paused, thoughtful. 'Though we could hit another target—one that he obviously values. He's probably got them somewhere safe.' Ratilal grinned as he mused. 'Imagine his shock if something were to happen them. It'd be a chink in his armour and tarnish him before his people.' Niaz looked at him questioningly. Ratilal laughed, explaining, 'The newcomers. He went to so much trouble to get them, it would be a shame if something happened to them.'

The air had been still all day and smoke hung low in the cold, shadowed valleys through which Ratilal's convoy travelled, filling them with misgiving. As they rounded the bend in the road and stared up the straight, the sight of the burnt out fort confirmed their fears. A dead horse lay across the track halfway to the fort and the ground on either side had been trampled by the charge of Baldev's warriors.

A new encampment had been set up, further back from the remains of the burnt fort, along the road to Faros. Groups of soldiers were finishing digging a trench around the camp. The debris had been thrown backwards and others were building a wall out of it, topped with wooden stakes, to finish the temporary defences. Those at rest were shaking their heads and gesticulating wildly.

Ratilal drew a deep breath, frowning at the sight before him.

'There's nothing to defend against,' Niaz said.

'Not yet, but I daresay that their commander knows they need a job to do. We'll rebuild the fort. Morale will be low, anger high. Give them a job and they won't do something stupid.'

They stopped outside the camp. 'Report!' Ratilal demanded of the officer before him.

'High Lord, I was not here during the battle. I was amongst the reinforcements from Faros. Allow me to summon one who was.'

Ratilal nodded.

A young soldier raced over to stand nervously before him. 'Don't just stand there, you dolt—report to the high lord!' the officer ordered.

With a nervous gulp he began, 'We barricaded the road as best we could, but they split their force, attacking from two sides at once. Our men fought bravely, but the archers on the walls had to divide their attention. They targeted our archers first, thinning their ranks, then those across the river began to shoot too and attempt to cross. We faced enemies from three sides. With the archers thinning, they assaulted fully and engaged with our shield walls at the road barricade and at the end of the fort where the wall was not finished. Once they broke through there, the archers had no choice but to redirect their fire within the fort. Those of us on the ground fought tooth and nail. The commander …' Here he paused, drawing a steadying breath. 'They chopped off his head as they broke through the shield wall on the road. They set fire to everything …'

Ratilal remained silent, staring at charred remains of the fort. Finally he said, 'I have no doubt that you all fought bravely—no doubt at all. Dismissed.' He waved the young soldier away. To the commander, he asked, 'The wounded, have they been seen to?'

'Yes, High Lord. They left us the wagons. The worst have already been taken to Faros. The others we could treat here.'

'Very good.' Ratilal left, signalling for them to stay where they were. He stalked toward the burnt out ruins.

Vikram leapt from the wagon, calling out, 'High Lord, wait.' Ratilal spun toward him. Vikram approached, saying quietly,

'You may be vulnerable to their arrows, now the fort is gone.'

Ratilal's lips twisted in a parody of a smile. 'It would be a lucky shot, but you are correct.' Ratilal stood there, arms folded, scowling at the faint wisps of smoke that still wafted from the blackened stumps of two remaining uprights. 'What would you suggest at this point, Captain Vikram?'

'Rebuild the fort, High Lord. It will be needed again one day and while they continue to build their fort across the Divide we need a presence here. In the meantime it will keep the men busy and harden them up.'

Ratilal quirked his brow at Vikram. 'My thoughts exactly.' He paused. 'Captain, I'll not lie to you. I distrust your sudden change of heart toward me. We have never been "friends" or even of similar dispositions, yet now you support me.'

'May I speak frankly, High Lord?'

'I don't see why not, since that's what we're about.'

'You're correct. I don't share or approve of your ...' Vikram paused, struggling for a word that wouldn't enrage him, '... peccadilloes, but I'm loyal to my clan above all else and you are now clan lord. I did not swear my oath lightly.'

Ratilal laughed. 'Peccadilloes? Vikram, really?' Vikram's lips thinned and he looked away. 'Ah, you're angry.'

Vikram cursed inwardly; in all the years of working for Karan this was the only time he'd let his emotions rule him. *Damn it! I could jeopardise everything.* 'You take what you do ... what you have done very lightly, High Lord.'

Ratilal appraised Vikram carefully. 'My peccadilloes as you so quaintly call them are limited to women who specialise in such things and are happy to be paid for their time. I learnt my lesson when I was younger ...'

Vikram met Ratilal's gaze fiercely. 'Asha.'

'Asha? You've a thing for her, do you?' Ratilal scowled, kicked a rock into oblivion and began to pace. His eyes darted to the remnants of the fort, the convoy of wounded and the fresh troops at the encampment. Clearly distracted he murmured, 'I meant to scare her and have a bit of fun, but she said ... she reminded me ...' He rubbed his stomach and let out a frustrated breath. 'She angered me.' *She and my sister ... I thought I'd buried that a long time ago.* Ratilal shrugged, returning to the present. 'We've all got tempers. Even you, Captain. How's the strength of your oath right about now?' he goaded him.

'Unwavering, High Lord. You are an able commander, you need only ...'

'Oh, there's more? Do go on, Captain. Since we're having this frank discussion you should get this out of your system. Tell me.'

'You need only control your temper.'

Ratilal's hand clenched into a fist. He forced it open one finger at a time. 'Are you done? Anything else you'd like to enlighten me on?'

Niaz had watched them warily from his horse; he now stood beside his friend. 'High Lord?'

'All's well, Niaz. Go on, Vikram, finish.'

Vikram cursed inwardly. *I should have kept quiet. If I stop now, I'll seem weak to him and that's guaranteed to work against me.* 'High Lord, be discreet. The people will want to follow you. Civilians and soldiers alike want the reassurance of a strong leader now more than ever. They'll want to trust you, but you must not provide fodder for the rumour mongers.' *What in Karak am I doing? Making my own job harder!*

'Is that all, Captain?' Ratilal's tone was blasè, yet his eyes bored into Vikram. 'Return to your wagon.'

'High Lord?' Niaz asked, shocked.

Ratilal smirked and clapped him on the back. 'Niaz, I asked him for the truth and I got it. I'm satisfied. If he'd said he was my friend and loved everything about me, then I'd be worried.'

'You trust him?'

'Niaz, he couldn't hide anything, even if he tried.' Ratilal took one last look at the ruins of the fort. 'Now to work. Time to put on my statesman's hat and make an inspiring speech.'

Niaz groaned inwardly. The men followed Ratilal because he was their best warrior and a cunning and able commander; the speeches were another matter. Every time Ratilal put on his 'stateman's hat' to make a grand speech Niaz thought he sounded like a pretentious git.

Ratilal spun around, remounted his horse and rode into the campsite. 'Men, we have work to do and a war to win! This has been a dark day. My father, your clan lord …' Here he paused, appearing grief stricken. 'Murdered! Murdered on the very day he signed a peace treaty! Before he was murdered, he told me that he wanted to see our clan return to its former glory. And by the gods we will see that happen! We will see Horse and Bear, relegated back to the far North and the Plateau, back to the wastelands they deserve! We will reclaim our ancient land across the Divide! We will restore our clan to its former glory. We will rise, like never before and we will cut a swathe through our enemies' ranks and retake what was ours!'

Chapter Five

KARAN'S FACE BECAME stern as Isaura finished telling them about the enemy they had fled from.

'Where were you sailing to? Certainly not here, by your state.'

Isaura grimaced and flushed in embarrassment. 'Er … no. We were hoping to sail down the river and up the coast to Matryan. Nice, simple, tidy plan.'

'What went wrong?'

She laughed harshly. 'Everything! Utterly unseasonal winds, ocean currents we didn't know about, storms … The list is long. The upshot is we were not, are not, sailors—only luck saved us.'

'Not luck,' Umniga added. 'The gods—you were sent here.'

Isaura's expression grew dark. 'You don't believe in the gods?' Umniga chuckled. 'Well, child, it looks like they believe in you.'

'Gods?' Isaura's jaw clenched as she restrained herself. The old priestess didn't deserve her scorn. 'I'm not sure. I've never needed them. My mother never talked about religion—*ever*. Based on the stories people tell, even if they are real, I don't think I could trust them.'

Umniga's eyebrows shot up, disappearing into her hairline.

Karan held up his hand, forestalling Umniga. 'In order to stay here you and your friends must learn about our culture. You must follow our gods and learn our rituals. The others must learn our language. You all must learn to fight. There will be no exceptions.'

'If they refuse?'

He shrugged. 'We have no need of those who refuse, and having been in our clan lands, you will not be allowed to leave.'

She nodded. 'For me, I agree. I want to fight.' Umniga narrowed her eyes at her; Isaura smiled back sweetly. 'And it can't hurt to learn about your gods.' Looking at her friends, Isaura said, 'The men will be fine, but the women ... It was forbidden for women to learn skill at arms in Arunabejar.'

'Why?'

Isaura shrugged. 'It's got something to do with the Great War generations ago. They developed a fear of magic and women who could fight well. Some clever woman probably kicked their superstitious arses.'

'They must learn. You must convince them,' Karan said.

Isaura sighed. 'Given the choices I'm sure I can think of something; then they'll be *your* problem.'

Interesting, Karan thought, *she speaks as if she is not one of them.*

Ratilal and his retinue rode through the outskirts of Faros along the main thoroughfare. Timber boardwalks had been laid before the shop frontages in preparation for winter; already the dirt road had become churned up and the damp soil stuck to the horses' hooves as they moved, deadening the sound of their passage. The street was crowded with merchants hawking their wares, and people haggling over prices as they shopped.

At the sight of Ratilal's convoy, the crowd became silent and the eerie quiet spread like a disease.

'Not quite what I had envisaged,' Ratilal murmured to Niaz as solemn faces stared at him. Yet, once one man bowed formally, slowly the rest followed. A ripple of submission preceded them as they passed along the street. 'Better,' he quietly commented, 'but they could look a little happier.'

'High Lord,' Niaz said. 'They've just lost their clan lord and we are at war. Should they smile at you on the occasion of your father's death?' Ratilal jerked his head around to glare at Niaz. 'Forgive me, High Lord, I meant no rebuke upon yourself. I merely believe that they've had so much news ... They've already seen the injured from the fort, the bodies. It's too much for them. Give them victories, then they'll shout your name from the rooftops.'

Ratilal stared at him for a moment longer before grunting, 'Doubtless,' and turning away.

In the courtyard of the citadel, Ratilal and Niaz dismounted beside Vikram's wagon, thrusting the reins of their horses at one of the men.

It was customary for the Chatelaine and the Chancellor to greet their lord. Other than the soldiers in barracks, no one greeted him. No one had been set to watch for his arrival. The usual guards at the doors were absent.

'Vikram!' Ratilal barked. 'See to the wounded.' Scowling, he strode up the citadel steps with Niaz racing to catch up.

'You're not limping, at least not much.'

'Can't feel it.'

Niaz snagged his friend's arm, halting him. 'It's that damn tea,' Niaz hissed. 'You must stop taking it. You know what will happen.'

Ratilal grabbed Niaz's hand and forced him to let go of his arm. 'Don't do that again,' he bit out with a glare. 'I'm fine. Come, let's find out what in Karak's going on.'

Ready to vent his frustration, Ratilal continued down the main hall of the citadel. He threw open the doors to the Great Hall. Rows of camp beds lined the walls; a scream issued from the room at the rear of the dais. Around the hall, women worked with the wounded, cleansing, stitching and bandaging wounds. He lost count of the buckets full of bloodied bandages being carted out. His countenance moved fluidly from anger, to dismay, remorse, then to bitter determination. *Damn it!* Here was evidence of his failure. *Damn Karan.*

'Chatelaine Gita,' his voice carried across the vast room.

The old woman straightened stiffly, summoning another to take her place tending the wounded, and headed over to Ratilal. Her lined face looked grey, large dark circles hung under her eyes; her apron was stained with dried blood.

'High Lord.' She bowed and rose ponderously with a hiss of pain. 'I am sorry for your loss, but bid you welcome as new clan lord and high lord. I pray the gods bless your rule.'

Ratilal scrutinised her. He could detect no trace of rancour in her tone, despite the fact that she disliked him.

'The wounded—was there no better place to house them?'

The Chatelaine sighed. 'No, High Lord. The sick bay in the barracks is small. I assumed you would call the levies and they would fill all the barracks.' She stood, her hands clasped before her, eyes lowered slightly. Tiredly, she continued, 'Traditionally, when there are this many wounded, the Great Hall is opened up for their care. Forgive me if I have displeased you, High Lord.' She bowed again, remaining bent before him.

He surveyed the hall. *Tread gently.* He noticed Niaz's mother, Malak, and several other women of noted families working among the wounded. *There are too many eyes here.*

'You have not displeased me, Chatelaine.' He gripped her arms, raising her to stand before him. 'You're doing well. I hope that you'll continue on in your role now that I am high lord. I've need of your experience now more than ever.'

'Of course, High Lord. If you wish it.'

Ratilal nodded brusquely. *It was not a request, old woman.* 'Good, come with me.'

The Chancellor, breathless, met them in the hallway. Ratilal's lips drew into a thin line before he spoke. 'A little tardy, old man. Follow.'

In the courtyard, the Chatelaine gasped and her hand went to her mouth in shock as she saw the fresh wounded. Her grief at the sight was so plain that Ratilal felt his anger soften. He put his hand on her shoulder. 'Chatelaine, you know your duty. Your priority is the injured. Put all your staff to the task,' he directed the two household heads. 'Requisition whatever you need from the town.'

'Vikram, get fixed up and get me a report on the state of Faros's defences; I want it by eventide tomorrow. Niaz, see to the opening of all the barrack wings. Call the levies. Sort out how many silahtars of real experience we have left, no matter how old—we'll need them to get the levies in shape.'

News of his arrival had spread and the courtyard had begun to fill with servants who were hastily helping unload the wounded. Chancellor Sudhir and the others in the courtyard stared at the refugees.

'These are the newcomers,' Ratilal said loudly, drawing more attention to them.

Sudhir and Gita cast their eyes disparagingly over the group. Uncertain and awkward, the strangers tried to avoid the bustle, but were jostled constantly and abused for their idleness.

'For these our clan lord was murdered?' Chancellor Sudhir asked.

'No!' Ratilal's voice boomed across the crowd, his gaze withering. The silence in the courtyard was absolute. 'Shahjahan was not killed because of these poor souls. They were merely in the wrong place at the wrong time. He chose to help them. Let us honour his choice. Don't forget that they have helped care for our wounded. We will take our hostility out on the battle field with honour, not on these poor wretches.'

Chancellor Sudhir asked, 'What is to be done with them?'

'Make use of them here. Put them to work. Surely you can use the help? They know nothing of our language, pair them with staff, ensure that they teach them. They can earn their keep.'

'Perhaps if they're seen to be helping here, then they may be accepted more quickly,' Vikram added.

'Perhaps,' Gita said with a sniff. 'First, High Lord, I would tend to your injuries.'

'Really, not so long ago you were far more reluctant to do so, though I was even more in need of your aid.'

Gita swallowed nervously. 'High Lord, then you had your friends who could ably assist you. Now …' Her gaze slid to procession of wounded. Gita's eyes widened and her speech trailed off.

Ratilal's words were clipped. 'As you rightly see, many of my friends are in these wagons.'

'High Lord, forgive me.' Gita bowed quickly and deeply.

Ratilal seethed. His jaw clenched, as did his fist. *Breathe, patience, breathe. Damn Karan and his dog, Baldev. No ... if I'd been more careful ... No, those damned Kenati. If they'd not betrayed me, Karan's plan may have failed.* He raked his eyes along the procession of wounded until they came to rest upon Niaz's mother, Malak, and other high born women as they stood at the citadel door watching the wounded being carried in. Malak's gaze met his, trapping him with their severity. With a clap of her hands, she spun and began ordering the other women to work. Released, Ratilal remembered the Chatelaine bowed before him.

'They have more need of your aid than I, old woman.'

—⚘—

'Come, the boy—Pio, is awake,' Karan said.

'I know,' Isaura replied softly. 'I heard him complaining. They won't want him near me.'

Karan laughed. 'From what Āsim tells me, what they want won't matter.' His lips thinned in disapproval as he held her hand and drew her to him. 'What they want does not matter to me either—come. You can inform them what is required if your friends wish to remain.'

They walked to the others; several guards fell in with them.

Facing her friends, Isaura gripped the quarterstaff so tightly that her knuckles shone white. She dreaded Pio's reaction to her. Drawing near, she could hear him.

His back was to her and he was whining at his mother as she restrained him. 'I don't see why I can't—it's Isa!'

'Not yet! Isaura is not the ...' Lucia looked up hastily, realising Isaura and Karan stood before them. She turned to Nicanor for reassurance; Pio slipped from her grip, spun and ran into Isaura.

'Isa!' He wrapped his arms around her waist. She fell to her knees and embraced him. 'I knew it! I knew they'd save you.'

'You saved me, Pio. You and the Asena.'

'Me?' He clung to her, his face buried in her neck. Pio shook his head, unwilling to look at her. 'But Isa, they say you're not the same. They say your eyes are different—not natural.'

Isaura stiffened, pushing him gently from her. 'Look, Pio, tell me what you think.'

He took her face in his hands and peered into her eyes. 'Well, they are different,' he said, his voice worldly wise. 'But they're kind of pretty.'

Elena snorted in disbelief. Curro put his hand on her shoulder urging restraint; she shook him off in irritation. Lucia and Nicanor glared at her, but were torn in defending their son—to do so would support Isaura and neither was certain of her anymore.

Pio ignored her. 'But how, Isa?'

'The ritual. The Asena.' Hesitant, Pio's face twisted in confusion. Isaura placed her hand on his chest. 'It's all right, just ask. I don't care if others hear.'

He drew a deep breath, looking over his shoulder in concern at his parents. 'They say … is it …' Afraid to voice the words, he whispered, 'Is it *magic*? They say it's *magic*.'

Isaura looked straight into his eyes, shrugging. 'I don't know, Pio. But I didn't do it. I didn't ask for it.'

Elena stepped forward, her hands clenched into fists. Isaura eyeballed her and her eyes flared blue.

Pio's eyes widened at the sight. 'Wow! Aunty Leni said you can speak their language too?'

'Yep. The Asena did that one, for sure.'

He nodded sagely, as if he expected no less. 'Will you teach me?'

Isaura laughed in relief. 'Of course, we've all a lot to learn now.'

Lucia and Nicanor had faint, sad smiles on their faces as they observed the two. 'Pio,' Nicanor said softly, but firmly. 'Return to your mother.'

Pio was ready to protest, but Isaura stopped him. 'All's well, Pio. I am back. I am still your Isaura. Go to your parents.' She stood up, face hard, and swept her gaze over them. 'There are conditions upon you … us remaining here.' They looked with unease between her and Karan. 'We must all learn their language, their religion and their laws.'

'What of our own religion?' Lucia asked. Isaura turned to Karan, speaking briefly with him.

'In the privacy of your own home, you may pray to your own gods. But you'll also learn and participate in all our …' Elena laughed bitterly at Isaura's slip. '*Their* religious celebrations and services. You'll find many are not unlike yours.' She paused. 'There is one more thing. We must all learn to fight—women included.'

Lucia gasped in shock. 'Surely not!'

Elena's face twisted in anger. 'Never!'

Oddly, Gabriela did not appear perturbed.

Nicanor and Curro were angry. 'The language, the law, even the religion we can do, but our women are not fighters. I will not risk my wife,' Nicanor stated.

'It is not negotiable,' Karan said calmly. Isaura repeated his words, matching his tone.

Outraged, they moved to argue en masse. Isaura thumped the quarterstaff into the earth as a bass, rumbling, growling, 'NO!' emerged from her mouth. Her eyes glowed with blue fire and those around her felt the vibration of her voice through their bones.

Karan briefly considered calming her, but was curious to see the extent of her power and content to let her teach them a lesson.

Isaura continued, 'These people saved us! We would all be bloated corpses on that stinking boat if not for them.' Her voice rumbled through them again. '*Do not forget it!* They're now at war, because of us. Every man, woman and child in this land learns to fight. They're not asking you to do something extraordinary. They're asking you to fit in—to do your best! There is nowhere left to run. You want to protect yourselves and your families? You want to live, then learn! Decide!'

Karan had not witnessed such raw force before, though he kept his surprise hidden behind an impassive facade. He noted Asha and Umniga watching intently from where they sat around the campfire; protectiveness toward Isaura flared within him.

Pio gaped in shock and he backed away from her. Eyes wide, he pressed against Lucia's legs. She held him to her, automatically looking to Nicanor for safety. Nicanor stared at Isaura, wary, defensive.

I'll never hurt you—fools. Her own bitterness and rage surprised her as she struggled to quell it.

Nicanor embraced his wife and child—his instinct was to protect them, but he never thought it would be from Isaura. 'Isa, no. What's happened?' His heart was breaking. His hand trembled as it rested upon Lucia's shoulder. They had been saved; Isaura had been instrumental in their saving, yet they had lost her. There was a hardness in her that he had never noticed. The certainty that it had always been there settled like a weight upon him; he had never seen the danger.

Finally Curro spoke. 'We agree. We've no choice.'

Isaura's words whipped him. 'There's always a choice, Curro.'

Chapter Six

BALDEV HAD PASSED several deserted farmsteads on their journey. Many of the farms that had been around the Four Ways Lake and bridge area had been abandoned, or the inhabitants killed during Ratilal's incursions. The derelict buildings and broken fences were a bitter sight to Baldev. *We failed to protect them.*

This farm though, was clearly not deserted. The animals were well tended and fat; the outbuildings were well maintained. Baldev approached the main house, a sturdy mud brick building. Uncut beams, worn smooth with age, surrounded the door. He knocked loudly. No answer. A small child rounded the corner of the house, froze and stood staring in dismay at him. Baldev followed her gaze to his small convoy and the wagon of wounded. Her eyes met his; she darted away towards the barn.

Damn. He followed in her wake. Striding into the barn he saw her disappear into an end stall. Muffled voices reached his ears. He spun as he sensed a movement from a dark stall behind him. A pitchfork lashed out at his belly.

'Satish, stop!' a woman's voice cried out.

Instinctively Baldev sidestepped, grabbed the haft of the fork and pulled on it. A teenage boy tumbled from the shadows into the dirt at Baldev's feet. 'What in Karak do you think you're doing, boy?' Baldev grabbed him by his shirt front, hauled him up and thrust him against a large round post.

'You should teach your son better manners!' Baldev barked at the woman now standing beside him.

'I'm sorry, Lord Baldev.'

'Lord Baldev?' squeaked the boy.

'Correct,' Baldev ground out as he shook him.

'I ... I ...' the boy stammered.

'You thought I was the enemy.'

The boy gulped nervously and managed a small nod despite the fact that Baldev's fists were under his chin.

'Dolt.' Baldev shook his head in disgust as he let him go. Still looking at the boy, Baldev continued. 'Mistress, I wish we had got off to a better start, but I would ask your help and the use of your barn for the night for my men and I.'

'Mama!' The little girl's voice cried out in panic from the rear of the barn.

'Of course, you can have the hospitality of our house and hearth,' the woman said in a rush, turning her back on him and hurrying to the last stall.

'Tell my captain to bring the wounded in here,' Baldev ordered the boy. 'Help them with whatever they need for the horses.' The boy made to leave. Baldev halted him, saying tiredly, 'And try not to attack any of them, or we'll have to pick up your bits and put them in a bucket when they're finished with you.'

A bellow bounced off the walls of the end stall. Frowning, Baldev made his way forward to see the little girl, holding a rope, watching her mother intently. The woman knelt before the rear end of cow, her arm buried inside it. 'Can you get it, Mama?'

'Nearly, Kiriz. Its head's in the wrong place and ... the feet are ... It's big ... Every contraction is squeezing the life out of my arm. Just a bit more ... Got it.' She was red faced and sweating. 'Slippery thing!'

Baldev winced; she laughed at him. 'What's wrong, Lord Baldev?' she panted as she worked. 'Big strong lad like you. Put off by a birth? I hope not, I'll need your help.' She pulled two hooves into the open. 'Kiriz, pass me the ropes.' She looped the ropes around both feet. 'Right.' She nodded at Baldev. Quickly, Baldev knelt beside her. 'I'm not going to get this one out on my own.' She passed the ropes to Baldev. 'Pull when she has contractions.'

'I've done this before.'

'Not with that face you haven't,' she replied acerbically. Kiriz giggled and strategically moved back.

Baldev waited, then pulled. 'Wait … Again … Wait.' Baldev's men were filtering into the barn. 'Again.'

'I know!' Sniggers erupted behind him. He looked around to see his guards in a semicircle watching in delight. *Marvellous.*

'Come on, man, stop glaring at them. I can't afford to lose the cow and calf. Help her.'

Baldev, on one knee with the other leg bent before him, braced his boot and waited.

'Get ready … not too hard yet …'

'Damn it, woman. Do you want me to pull or not?' Baldev complained as he pulled again, then waited as the contraction eased. The nose of the calf appeared.

She cast him a disparaging look. 'Pull, now. Pull!'

Baldev hauled on the ropes. His boot slipped in the rush of fluid and muck and he landed flat on his back. He was nose to nose with the slimy calf draped along him. Laughter erupted around him.

'Looks like he's a Dada, boys!'

Baldev scowled and pushed the calf aside as the woman cleared muck out of its throat. He looked in disgust at his zirh gomlek— his chain and plate armour—as he stood up.

'Is it alive?'

'He. Yes, he's alive. Help me drag him to the mother's head. Gods, he's a big one.'

'Just like his pa.'

Baldev shook his head and glared at the man who spoke. 'You'll keep.' Baldev, the woman and child backed away as the cow began to lick her calf. Baldev had a small smile on his face. 'All good?'

'As long as she gets up and keeps going.' She shrugged. 'Just like the rest of us.'

Baldev's warriors began to disperse. 'Get back here,' he barked at the wise-cracking warrior as he winked at the small girl. 'Your job …' He smiled wickedly. 'Your job is to clean my armour. Get this,' he gestured to the blood and muck, 'off it. I want it spotless.'

The warrior nodded resignedly. 'What are you going to call your calf?' he asked Kiriz.

Kiriz grinned and winked. 'Little Baldev!'

—☫—

Daniel entered the Great Hall, half carrying an injured soldier. The feeling of eyes upon him stopped him in his tracks. The wounded man he was helping gave his shoulder a squeeze. Whether in support or as a reminder to get on with it, he didn't know. Daniel glanced about looking for instruction. A young woman approached him. Her lip curled; she eyed him with distaste and distrust. Her brusque voice battered him.

When he didn't respond, she rolled her eyes and spoke slowly in a scathing tone. The wounded man barked a rebuke at her. Raising her chin defiantly, she pointed imperiously to the far end of the room. Daniel nodded deferentially; she smiled smugly. With satisfied condescension she led him to the end of the room.

Together they assisted the soldier to sit upon a solid table at the end of the hall. Daniel noted the raised dais and throne-like chair upon it. The chair had been covered with a heavy black cloth and no wounded were upon this dais. An ante-room was set up as a surgery. The girl unbound the man's wound, inspecting it carefully. Another set of bandages crusted with dry blood were wrapped around his chest. She peeled away the sticking bandage. The wound started bleeding profusely.

Daniel had his back to her as he made a move to fetch more wounded. Her hand shot out, snagging his arm.

'Wait!' She tugged him back and placed his hand on the pile of old bandages on the wound. 'Hold it. Press firmly.' She darted off, returning quickly with two older women, one looking decidedly harassed and the other with a regal air.

'Chatelaine, it just started bleeding again.'

'You should've waited until they were ready for him.'

The regal woman added, 'Looking at the state of the bandages you should have known this could happen.'

'Mist ... Lady Malak. I didn't think.'

'Be more careful in future. I'll deal with this. Go,' Chatelaine Gita said. She lifted Daniel's hand from the bandages and examined the wound. Both the older women grimaced. Gita replaced Daniel's hand upon it. She disappeared into the back room returning with an armful of supplies, depositing them with a huff as someone called her name.

Malak had known Chatelaine Gita for years; they were from different social strata within the clan, but at times like these Malak knew she should put that aside. 'I'll do this, Chatelaine.'

Gita looked at her with wary gratitude. 'Lady Malak. It's not necessary for you to do this.'

'It is. It's our duty. And Mistress Malak will do, Chatelaine Gita. Let the young have their new pretensions—I'll have none of it.'

Gita could not keep the look of surprise from her face. The title of 'Lady' rankled Malak, not because of the implications of status—she needed no reassurance on that scale—but because of the source of the change. Ratilal. There was a plethora of 'Lords' and 'Ladies' when there should only be two: the rightful clan lord and his wife.

'Mistress Malak has suited me all these years; it will suit my remaining ones. You, Chatelaine, appear worn out. I am perfectly capable of handling this, though it has been a while since I've had to. Tomorrow I'll make sure more of the younger elite help out. Even if I have to drag them here. Leave me the young man. He can help, I'm sure, even if it's just to hold this man down. Go, they are calling you again!' She dismissed the Chatelaine from her presence.

'Name?' Malak barked at Daniel. Daniel looked blankly at her.

The wounded soldier whispered, 'Dan-i-el, his name's Dan-i-el.'

'Brace yourself, man,' Malak directed the soldier. 'You're going to have more stitches than a quilt. Poppy?'

He shook his head adamantly.

The soldier groaned as Malak commenced cleaning the wound. 'With any luck you'll pass out.'

'Do I look lucky?'

Chapter Seven

UMNIGA AND ASHA commenced their instruction of the others. Isaura translated for them; each time she did so, the fluidity of her speech drove a deeper wedge between her and her friends. She was not going to point out that Pio was rapidly assimilating the language.

'Enough,' Umniga declared with a smile. 'More tomorrow, tonight it is enough. Well done!'

Everyone, except Pio, looked relieved.

'What's wrong, Pio?' Isaura asked with a smile.

Pio looked cheekily at her, briefly forgetting his fear. Though quickly a small disappointed frown creased his brow. Uncertain, he looked at his mother who said nothing, lowered her gaze and looked away. Isaura waited. A torrent of words flowed from Pio. 'I'm not tired. I've been asleep most of the day. Do I have to go to bed again?' He spun his head looking at his parents. 'I want to explore. Can I go and sit by the fire with the warriors? I want to look at their weapons. I …'

'Pio, enough.' Nicanor was stern.

Umniga observed this exchange with mischievous delight. She held out her hand to Pio, who grinned at her, jumped to his feet and grabbed her hand. Smiling at Nicanor and Lucia, Umniga said, 'He'll be fine. They already like him.' She extended a hand to Lucia, beckoning her, smiling wider, coaxing her to come. Lucia got to her feet with a reluctant smile.

'Lucia, you're going over there? Are you mad?' Elena said.

Lucia sighed, resigned. 'They've helped us and really their demands are simple. We said that we'd learn and for better … or worse,' her eyes flitted uncertainly to Isaura, 'this is home now.'

She let Umniga lead her and Pio into the group around the fireside. Nicanor followed her, but the others remained seated. Asha and Isaura walked back together, leaving the others in isolation.

Karan was pleased to see the boy's parents join them, but something would have to be done about the others. *Tomorrow. Tonight let them see this family being welcomed. Tomorrow they will have no choice.* Karan was disgruntled that Isaura sat with Āsim and was participating eagerly in conversation around her. He should have been pleased his warriors were taking to her so readily, and not peeved that she was not talking to him. He curbed his emotions, offering no interference in the mingling of his people and these newcomers.

Pio sat with Umniga, yet he could not take his eyes off the sword hanging by the side of the warrior nearest him. The woman, Sarala, while talking, was aware of his scrutiny. She deliberately changed her posture so that the sword swung before him. Pio's eyes remained glued to it; he kept craning his neck to better inspect it as she moved. He was so intent on the sword that he did not notice Sarala turn her head to him.

'Pio?' she asked, merriment dancing in her eyes.

'Pio, don't stare!' Lucia warned. He looked up hurriedly, embarrassed, but Sarala's face creased into knowing grin.

'It is no matter. Boy—Pio, do you want to hold this?'

Pio looked at his mother, who smiled half-heartedly.

Umniga said, 'Pio, ask. Practise.' He began well then halted, looking to Umniga for help. She whispered, 'Kilij,' in his ear; he finished triumphantly, grinning. Wide-eyed, he held his breath as Sarala drew the sword excruciatingly slowly from its scabbard.

'Hurry up, stop torturing the lad. He's about to burst!' Āsim laughed.

Facing Pio, Sarala laid the sword across her knees. It was inornate, yet beautiful in its simplicity. A plain metal crosspiece met the blade and the horn grip. Rather than end in a straight pommel, as Pio was used to seeing on the swords his uncle made, the grip ended in a graceful swirl. 'Uncle Curro, come look! It's so different to the ones you make!'

Curro grinned at him then looked at Elena. 'We should join them.' She wrung her hands nervously. 'We have to begin somewhere. You have to overcome your fear.' He could understand her worry. Magic was something they'd all been raised to fear, yet he had always thought of it as a myth—tales told simply to frighten children. He'd also been raised to treat people as he would like to be treated. Yet here was Isaura—with magic. Was she some kind of throwback? Was her blood bad? He shook his head, trying to clear his thoughts.

Seeing the play of emotion across his features, Elena said, 'You're right, it's fear, but it's not just the magic.' Guilt writ itself clearly across his face, then slid away. She wished he'd tell her the truth. 'It's fear of losing you.'

'Nothing happened. I told you nothing happened. Not that night, not ever.'

'Look me in the eyes and tell me that,' Elena said. Maybe tonight she'd get the truth.

He stared at her. 'Nothing happened. Not then, not ever.' Curro took her hand and kissed it. 'I swear.'

Elena watched him kiss her hand, wariness and longing in her gaze. She knew what she had seen. Each time he lied, a piece of her spirit withered inside her. She tried to keep it hidden, but she knew it was altering her behaviour and she felt helpless to stop the blackness consuming her. Part of her wondered if she really did want him to speak the truth, or if hearing the words would seal her fate. Her eyes strayed to Isaura.

'You don't have to talk to her, or … even look at her, but we have to get to know these people,' Curro said, smiling encouragingly. They moved to Pio's side.

Curro was fascinated by the style of the sword. 'Indeed, Pio, I have never seen its like.' Not only was the grip different, but the blade had a slight curve and the last section flared out. Curro bent close to it, trying to examine it in the firelight.

Isaura noticed Āsim discretely withdraw a dagger from his boot as Curro got closer to the blade. She said nothing, even though she noted more than one hand resting upon their weapons. *I'd be cautious too.* She admired the aplomb of the woman as she allowed Curro near the sword. *He wouldn't stand a chance.*

'Maybe they'll let you hold it so you can see better.'

'Ah, I don't think so, Pio. A soldier does not readily give his weapon away, least of all to a stranger.'

'I'll bet they'll want you to make one.'

Curro laughed. 'One day, Pio, but I think I'll have much to learn if I am to make a blade as fine as this.'

Pio frowned. 'It's different—the shape is lovely, but it doesn't look special in any way. What would you have to learn?'

Curro knelt next to him. Pointing at the steel, he said, 'Even in this light I can tell that this steel is far superior to anything I've worked with before. This sword is plain, but its beauty lies in the quality of its steel and the mastery needed to create it. I will need to learn much before I can do this.' Pio looked disappointed. 'Ah, Pio, it's not something to be sad about. It's something to wonder at and want to discover,' he said as he ruffled Pio's hair. He nodded his thanks to the warrior and sat near Elena.

Pio still gazed at the sword. He gave the woman the most disarming smile he could.

Wait for it, Isaura thought. Pio asked and gestured if he might hold it. *And there you have it—little imp.*

Sarala stood close behind him. She moved him so they faced the fire. Leaning down she placed the sword in his small hands. Her calloused hands encompassed both sword grip and Pio's hands. Pio was agog. She released her hands from around his. Pio gritted his teeth, determined not to let the blade drop, but its tip quickly lowered to the ground. She took it from him; he mournfully watched her slide it back into its scabbard.

To Pio's surprise, a short straight stick was placed in his hands and another warrior stood before him with a similar stick, beckoning him to fight. Pio enthusiastically lunged and swung the stick at his opponent, to a chorus of cheers. The warrior corrected Pio's stance and adjusted his grip before they recommenced. Nicanor watched his son fiercely wield his 'sword'—the determination and concentration on Pio's face astonished and disconcerted him with a vision of his gentle son as a killer.

Lucia, observing his pensive gaze, took Nicanor's hand. 'This will save him. It will save all of us.'

Karan beckoned Isaura to him. *Better,* he thought when she moved to his side. Suspicion gnawed at him. *Why do I feel this contentment near a woman I don't even know? What has Umniga done?*

'Translate,' he told Isaura. 'Tomorrow will be a long day. We leave for Bear Tooth Lake. It will take many days to ride there. Each of you will be assigned to a warrior. You will ride beside them for the entire journey. They will continue to teach you Altaican, and how to properly ride and care for your horse. In the evenings you will receive further instruction from Umniga and Asha in our history and lore.'

'And their military training, my lord?' Sarala asked.

'Āsim and Pravin will commence that at the lake. Pio will be paired with you for the journey. If he has energy for training then work with him, but I doubt after riding all day if any of them will even be able to lift a finger let alone a sword. These next days will toughen them up; then the real training will start.' He laughed with the others.

Isaura's lips curled in amusement. Though tempted to translate the entirety, she did not.

Karan quirked his brow at her silence. 'Just tell them that military training starts at the lake.' That signalled an end to the evening and the newcomers drifted away. Those not on sentry duty bedded down for the night.

I'm certainly not going with them, Isaura thought, watching her friends settle to sleep. *But I don't belong with these warriors either … I will though.* She stared into the fire trying to suppress her welling bitterness. *Superstitious idiots.*

'I need to walk. Am I allowed to walk away from camp for a bit?' she asked Karan.

He rose, holding out his hand to her and hauled her to her feet. 'Come then, we'll walk.'

'Alone.' She ground the end of the quarterstaff into the dirt; her eyes glowed.

'No,' Karan replied. She glared at him. He leaned forward and whispered in her ear. 'You feel alone, but you don't want to be alone.'

She put her hand on his chest, rested it there and bowed her head. They stood like this, close—but not touching save for her hand for several minutes. When, finally, she looked up at him, the blue fire in her eyes had lessened. She nodded with a half smile.

He held out his hand to her in invitation. 'Come, walk with me, Isaura.'

It felt good to be moving. Although her leg was stiff, as she walked the muscle began to hurt less. Karan had been right, she didn't want to be alone. Yet, unsure of his motives, she didn't speak to him. Instead Isaura ploughed ahead, finding a trail and following it mindlessly. *Why do I trust him? I don't know him. He has only been kind, yet …*

Abruptly she stopped, turning toward him. 'What do you want?' she said without rancour. 'What do you expect from me?'

'Only what I expect from the others, no more.'

'Umniga seems to believe I've been sent by your gods. She seems to think that I'm special in some way.'

Karan heard her scepticism, but felt her distrust. 'Umniga may think a lot of things, but you must …' He grinned wryly before continuing. 'No, you will make your own path.'

Path! Isaura scowled.

'Isaura?'

'It's just …' *Damn it, go with your instincts.* 'It's not the first time today I've been told to make my own path.'

He waited, doubting that Umniga would suggest such a thing.

'The Matriarch told me,' Isaura said quietly.

'The Matriarch?' Isaura nodded. 'The Matriarch spoke to you?' Karan said, stunned.

'Damn it! Now you're going think I'm a freak too.' Isaura turned and began to walk away.

Karan grabbed her hand. 'No, I don't. Yes, you've got special gifts, but here, they are gifts, not a curse. Come.' He led her further away from the camp and kept her tucked into his side, so that he could whisper to her. 'Don't tell anyone, particularly not any of the Kenati, that the Matriarch spoke to you.' He grinned. 'Or Umniga will never give you any peace.' Isaura rolled her eyes. 'Tell me how she spoke to you.'

'In my mind. She can hear my thoughts.'

'And you can hear hers?'

'Only if she lets me.' Isaura's gaze became momentarily distant as she thought about the Lady. Though aware of Karan still holding her hand and staring intensely at her, she said nothing.

There's more, Karan thought. Rather than ask, he squeezed her hand. 'It's enough, Isaura.' They kept walking, until the horses were before them. 'Do you know your eyes flare blue when you're angry?'

'Really? Another reason they're terrified.'

His face remained serious. 'I want to teach you how to control your anger. It's not always to our advantage to have people read our emotions so easily. Your anger shows your power. Keep it hidden. Keep it as a surprise. It may give you a tactical advantage.'

Isaura nodded and shrugged. 'That makes sense.'

'It's not just that. Your voice. You can channel your power through your voice, when you desire it. We call it Undavi. You used it without meaning to when you woke and Āsim and Asha were trying to help you. Again you used it when you told your friends my terms and reprimanded them.'

'I'm not sure …'

'Isaura, it can be used for many purposes, subtly. Yours, in anger, is not subtle and it reverberates through the world around you.'

She dreaded what he alluded to. 'You're worried I could hurt someone?'

He nodded. 'Few of us can use Undavi. I can, but not as you do. My power is like a light snowfall. You are like an avalanche.'

Isaura gulped. 'Don't mistake me. It's a gift. I …'

'You just want me to avalanche in the right direction.'

Karan smiled. 'Yes. Power without control consumes. Control makes heroes or villains of us all.'

They reached the picket lines. 'Ah.' Isaura stopped several feet from the nearest horse and pulled her hand from Karan's. 'Um … I should tell you … I can't ride. I've never been around horses much.'

'Never?'

'Once as a child. It was … not pleasant.'

'Since then?'

'I've only been near them when they were at the forge.'

'How did you travel?'

'I walked. We were too poor to have a horse. Most of us were.'

'You'll learn.'

'Uh huh.' Isaura moved no closer.

'But not if you stay over there.' Isaura pursed her lips. Karan laughed. 'You're really afraid of the horse!'

Isaura glowered, crossed her arms and her lips drew into a thin line. 'Nervous, not afraid.'

'No, afraid.' Incredulous, Karan said, 'You, who have sailed an ocean, walked the spirit realm alone, and not only spoken with the Asena but had the temerity to yell at them … You're afraid of a horse!' He grinned broadly, looking, Isaura thought, absurdly pleased with himself.

'Stop being such a smug bastard!' She stepped closer and tried to ram the staff into his foot. He kept laughing as he stepped easily away. She scowled at him before continuing wryly, 'Well, I suppose when you put it like that, it's a bit stupid.'

The chestnut horse in front of them stretched its neck out toward her midriff, sniffing at her, while his lips mouthed her clothing. He grabbed her tunic and pulled it vigorously.

'Hey!' Isaura jumped back.

'He's cheeky.' Karan patted his neck. 'He belongs to Sarala, the warrior who showed Pio her sword. She always has a treat for him. Now he expects everyone to have a treat. Just growl at him if he tries it again. Tone of voice is important. Like a child, if he gets away with it he will try it again.'

'A child? It's not a child. It's a horse. It has a mind of its own and a lot of weight to throw around. If it wants to throw me off, then I'm off. If it wants me dead, then I'm dead.'

Karan laughed and shook his head. 'You're in the Horse Clan. You've got to learn. Lessons start now.'

'Lessons? You're my instructor then?' Isaura smiled.

'Pleased by that, are you?' Isaura looked away. 'Move to his side,' Karan said.

Her fear of the horse briefly overwhelmed her embarrassment. Karan took her hand and laid it on the horse's neck. His hand remained covering hers; she swallowed nervously. *What's going on? My head doesn't get turned by men.* She hid her confusion by concentrating on the feel of the horse's neck. The hair under its mane was warm and surprisingly soft. Karan moved her hand with his, encouraging her; tentatively she began to relax. The horse roughly pushed his neck into her hand. She jumped back.

'He's itchy. If you haven't got a treat for him, the least you can do is give him a scratch.' Isaura found herself vigorously scratching the horse's neck; the more she scratched the more he leaned into her hand. She moved her hand toward his ears, causing him to cant his head. Isaura, delighted, forgot her fear. She turned to smile at Karan. Disgruntled because she'd stopped scratching, the horse's head butted her in the middle of her back.

'Ow, you've got a bony head.' She braced herself with the staff and let him scratch himself. Finally, she stepped out of reach. 'Enough!' she growled, pushing his head away.

'Do you want to go back?'

She gave him a pensive look. 'Not yet, do you mind? Teach me some more about the horses.'

'Tomorrow. We can walk some more if you like. If your leg can take it.'

'I have to get it strong, this'll help.'

Karan chose a circuitous route through the forest. They stopped to rest on a fallen moss-covered log. The fog had crept in and thickened the night.

Karan had so much he wanted to ask her, yet he felt it wise to keep his questions for another day. There was a connection between them that he didn't understand and he was certain Isaura didn't either. He needed time to think it through; she needed time to adjust to all the changes she had faced.

'When can I start my training?'

'Your leg will hinder you …'

'Not from archery. I'm already …'

Karan interrupted her. 'I was going to say that it will hinder your sword training, but you can start with other weapons tomorrow.' She grinned. 'You have used a bow before?'

'Yes, a great deal.'

'But your women do not fight.'

'I've never been fond of their rules.' She shrugged. 'Besides, if I wanted to eat, I had to hunt. Trapping and shooting provided plenty of meat.'

'Have you killed in battle?'

'Yes.' She refused to look at him. 'I shot several of the enemy when we were leaving.'

'Did you hesitate?'

'Never.'

'Did you find it easy?'

'I suppose I should say no. That's what everyone wants to hear, right?' When he said nothing, she slid her gaze in his direction. 'It's the lives taken out of battle that are hard.' She needed to confide in him. 'The Zaragarians are ruthless ... I left poison with the elderly who remained in our village in case they chose to end their lives ... on the boat I gave some to a young girl to end her suffering.'

'Would you do it again?'

'Honestly ... I don't know. The act was easy—appallingly so. It's the consequences ... the guilt ... that troubles me. But I know I should feel it, to not feel it would be worse and I'll carry the weight of those lives forever. Yet in one way my guilt is a small price to pay ...'

Karan didn't press her to elaborate. 'Can you use a sword?'

Isaura laughed. 'My archery is fine, but any time I pick up a sword and don't chop off my own leg I think I've done well.'

Karan smiled. 'You've plenty of work ahead of you then.'

'So do your instructors.' Shivering, Isaura wrapped the cloak about her tightly.

'It will be colder by dawn and your clothes are old and thin. Umniga should ...'

She waved her hand dismissively. 'It doesn't matter. I don't blame them ... why would they give their good clothes to a stranger who looked liked she'd die. I wouldn't. At least they kept my boots, although they're almost worn out.' She shrugged. 'I can't wait for training. Do you know how long I've been stuck as healer, and frowned at for having the temerity to want to learn such things, to be doing anything other than what was expected?'

Karan gazed at her with a queer look that seemed to penetrate her.

Feeling unusually coy Isaura blurted out, 'Shall we go back to the fire?'

Rising, Karan made a flourishing bow. 'Lead the way—*if* you remember it.'

'Of course I do!'

He leaned close to her face, smug. 'Prove it.'

Despite the thick fog, Isaura stood, saying with utter self-assurance, 'We came that way, but the quickest way should be this way. I could hear a creek near the camp and the sound of that creek has wavered in and out of my hearing. Now it's over there.'

Karan raised his eyebrows. 'Really? It could be a different creek. Are you sure?'

'It feels right. The lay of land, the contours … I can't explain it. It's like asking how I know how to breathe.' She put her hand on her hip, tapping her foot impatiently. 'Are *you* lost, Karan? Well, follow me—I've never been lost in my life.'

Unerringly, Isaura led him back to camp. With a conceited grin she sat before the fire. Everyone else, except the sentries, was asleep. *Where do I sleep?* Isaura lay curled on her side with the cloak tucked tightly about her, trying not to shiver. *Damn it, if I get any closer to the fire I'll be in the bloody thing.* She pulled the cloak's hood over her head.

—ɯ—

Karan threw more wood onto the flames and mulled over the events of the last twenty-four hours. The coming of the foreigners had already wrought change. His eyes flicked to Isaura. *Not bad change.* He analysed his reaction to Curro touching her. *It was merely the embrace of a friend, yet I loathed it. Why? I don't even know her. What is it about her?*

Lost in his thoughts, he had no idea how long he sat there, but the fire had again burned low. He placed a large log on the glowing coals, knowing it would burn until morning. Karan lay on the ground, but could neither settle nor get warm. Remembering where his cloak was, he all but groaned when he looked toward

Isaura. Quietly rising he went to her. Lying behind her, he felt her stiffen.

'What are you doing?' she whispered.

Karan moved closer so he could whisper in her ear. Isaura remained silent—rigid. Her stomach began to knot.

'Don't be afraid, Isaura. It's cold … You've got my cloak. I'm just cold, that's all.' *It's not all.*

'I'm not afraid.'

'Just nervous?' She heard the teasing in his voice.

I am so afraid. 'Just nervous.'

'Let me tell you a secret.' His lips brushed her ear and his words sent a shiver down her spine. 'You make me a bit nervous too.'

The knot in Isaura's gut blossomed into a spark of warmth. She smiled and turned her head. 'Only a bit?'

'Only a very tiny bit.' In the glow from the fire, his face appeared serious—except for his eyes.

She rolled towards him, grinning. *What am I doing?* Isaura's hand reached toward his face. *Stop thinking.* Her fingers tentatively caressed his lips. He closed his eyes. 'Only a bit?' she whispered. Her hand moved to cradle his cheek. Karan's eyes were still closed as he nodded and tilted his head into her palm. 'Liar,' she whispered as she left a lingering kiss upon his lips.

Heart pounding, she rolled over, putting her back to him again. 'It is very cold. You'd better stay with me.'

Chapter Eight

KARAN LAY ALONGSIDE Isaura with his arm draped around her. She was curled snugly against him. His first thought on waking had been to run his hand along her belly and thigh. They were surrounded by others. He drew his hand back. *What in Karak was I thinking?* Isaura stirred, wriggling in her sleep against him. *Gods, I know exactly what I was thinking.* Karan rose up on one elbow and looked down at her. His hand moved involuntarily to smooth strands of her dark hair from her face. Isaura rolled over and smiled sleepily up at him. Instinctively he smiled back as his hand tucked a stray strand of hair behind her ear and lingered, gently brushing her cheek.

'How did you sleep?'

'Well, really well, considering.' Chuckling, Isaura stretched then placed her hand over his, which he realised with shock had lain to rest upon her belly.

I can't do this. A bit of sport with someone who knows the rules is one thing, but not this. She's not even one of us … yet. Hastily Karan removed his hand from under hers and rose. Isaura's eyes darkened and a slight frown creased her brow, yet she took his proffered hand and let him haul her to her feet.

'Your training begins,' he said bluntly.

—⚔—

Curro woke early with Elena, snug within his embrace. *Things will work out.* Hearing a stirring across the camp, he noticed Karan waking. He watched him partially rise onto his elbow. Karan leaned down, murmuring to someone. Curro looked away, feeling intrusive, then snapped his head back at the sound of soft familiar laughter. *Isaura*. Karan slid his arm out from under her head, disentangling himself and rose, pulling her to her feet. Curro's fist clenched involuntarily as he stared from where he lay. *What's she thinking?* Elena stirred in his arms. Quickly, he looked upon her, smiling, traces of guilt erased.

—⚊—

Baldev leaned against the yard railing, deep in thought, watching Kiriz and Satish carrying water from a well to the house and the vegetable garden in the twilight. *Will Asha and I have this? This peace, how long will they have it?*

'The wounded are settled, my lord,' his captain said. Baldev didn't answer. 'My lord?'

He nodded distractedly. 'Set up a perimeter guard, but I doubt we'll need it—not yet anyway. Rest, we've a long day tomorrow.'

Baldev still stood in the same spot when darkness came. In the yard behind him he could faintly discern the silhouette of the cow and her calf. As it greedily suckled, its head butted her udder, demanding more. *Little Baldev, indeed!* Sparks flickered from the farmhouse chimney and vanished into the night sky.

He bowed his head, kicked the timber fence and drummed his fingers along the top rail. Coming to a decision, he left the yard and headed toward the house. A dim glow came from one of the windows, but as he drew near the timber shutter closed and Baldev heard it barred from the inside.

He knocked on the door and raised his hand to knock again. The woman opened it to see his fist aimed at her face. Startled, she stepped back. Hurriedly Baldev lowered his hand. 'Mistress ...' Embarrassed he said, 'I didn't even ask your name.'

'Lords don't need to know the names of the likes of us.'

Baldev scowled. 'This lord does.' In a milder tone he continued, 'You know Lord Karan and I are not of the same stamp as Ratilal;

nor are our men. If we were ...' His eyes shot to her children.

'I know. Līna, my name is Līna.' She remained blocking the doorway.

Kiriz wandered up to stand beside her mother. She looked between them curiously.

Baldev smiled at her and cleared his throat. 'Mistress Līna ...'

'Mama, it's just Big Baldev. Can't we let him in?'

Baldev groaned and bent down to look her in the eye. 'Kiriz, please don't call me that in front of my men again, will you?'

'You are big,' Kiriz countered.

Līna laughed at Baldev's embarrassment. 'Promise him, Kiriz.'

'Promise,' Kiriz swore. Baldev sagged with relief.

Līna relented. 'Come in, Lord Baldev. Stop standing outside in the cold.'

Kiriz led Baldev to the fire, while Satish stood up from a stool with a look of awe on his face.

'You haven't got another pitchfork hidden somewhere, have you?'

Satish reddened and shook his head quickly.

'No fire poker either?'

'No, Lord Baldev, I swear.'

Baldev laughed. 'Good. I'm glad that you've not been trained properly. If you had, you might've struck me with the damn thing before I heard you.' Satish hung his head. 'Oh, boy, don't be down. You thought you were protecting your family. No harm done.'

Līna passed Baldev a mug of tea and put her hand comfortingly on Satish's shoulder. 'What is it you need, Lord Baldev?'

'You're here on your own with the children? No husband?'

She stiffened. 'My husband was killed in one of Ratilal's raids. He was visiting another farm, closer to the Divide, to trade ... You're the first man to set foot in this house.'

'Ah ... I'm sorry ... You've been managing here on your own since then?'

'I help!' Satish exclaimed.

Līna squeezed his shoulder; he subsided. 'Satish is a good worker. He's nearly fifteen … nearly a man.' She smiled at her son. 'Together we manage.'

'Hey, me too! I help!' Kiriz piped up.

Baldev grinned at her. 'Of that I'm certain.' His smile faltered before he addressed Līna. 'You understand what could be coming? We'll do our best to protect you, but …'

'You can't be everywhere.'

'No. In the morning I'll be sending out riders to outlying farms. We'll need information from you about those nearest. They'll be spreading the news about Ratilal's treachery … about the start of war. Real war this time.'

'It seemed *real* enough last time,' she said bitterly.

He stared at her, saying solemnly, 'They'll also be letting them know that their children can be taken to Bear Tooth Lake. From there we will take them to a safe location.'

'*Safe?*'

He nodded. His eyes slid from her to Kiriz and Satish, before resting sombrely upon her again. 'Safe,' he repeated before turning and leaving.

As he walked back to the barn he heard Satish's adamant voice. 'I don't care. I'm not going!'

—⚞—

Isaura looked at the metal object she held in her hands. It was flat, square with a strip of leather on one side, under which she placed her hand.

'It's a curry-comb. Each of us has one, and a hoof pick.' Karan stood beside Isaura. Gone was the quiet warmth she had felt from him last night. 'Brush him. No, not there. There, where the saddle will go, and the girth. We don't have time to groom them all over. Get him smooth and clean. No sticky sweaty hair left, no lumps. If you leave any there, it rubs and pulls the hair out and they'll get sore. Get a move on, the others are nearly done.'

'Pick up his feet,' Karan commanded when she'd groomed the horse. Isaura stepped away, shaking her head warily. 'Watch. Run your hand down his leg. Put a little pressure here … he should just lift it up like this.' She took the hoof from him. 'Look under his foot. You're looking for stones, but you've got to clean out the muck to find them. Use this.' He handed her a slightly hooked small, blunt metal tool. 'Don't worry, Toshi's a gentle fellow.'

Patronising ass! Isaura snatched the hoof pick from him. She dug the tool into the muck compacted upon the sole of the hoof, flicking it in Karan's direction. Growing in confidence, she dug harder. 'There's something here.'

'Caref …'

'I know what I'm doing. I've seen Curro do this a million times.' The horse leaned away and tried to pull its leg from her grasp. 'Damn horse. Stand still,' she muttered. 'Nearly … ow, ow, OW!' The pebble flew out. Isaura dropped the hoof. 'Bloody thing bit me!' She shot sideways as Toshi tore a hole in her pants. She scowled at Karan. 'Gentle!'

'I tried to tell you.' He soothed the horse, who was eye-balling Isaura. 'They don't feel much on the sole except right where you were digging like you were mining for gold. If you'd gone a little more carefully, you wouldn't be rubbing your behind as if you'd been stabbed. Toshi won't put up with poor handling.'

Isaura chafed at this public rebuke. Others were readying their horses, and while no one said anything, she saw their grins.

'Now do the rest,' Karan ordered.

She eyed Toshi warily. He canted his head and glared right back at her. *I swear he just bared his teeth at me.*

'Now you've just got the hind legs to do.'

'Marvellous.'

'He can't bite you there,' Karan said.

'No, but since he's such a *gentle soul*, I suspect he's more accurate with that end than his teeth.'

Karan shooed her dismissively toward the horse's rear end. Isaura kept peering over her shoulder to find Toshi staring at her. Beads of sweat formed on her brow as she hastily cleaned out the final hoof.

'Grab the saddle. No, not there. Put it there. Reach under, do up the girth and surcingle.'

Isaura looked dubiously at the saddle she had placed on Toshi's back. *It's so light.* It had a high pommel and cantle over which sat a thick cover that formed a soft padded seat and skirt. This transformed the pommel and cantle into firm cushioned barriers. Below this hung wide supple saddle flaps and deep barred stirrups. It looked impossible to fall out of. *I'll be trapped on the damn horse.*

'Mount up,' Karan ordered.

Isaura stepped back, pale and sweating.

'Get on.'

Her anger rose with her fear. 'Nothing could be easier.'

'He's the best teacher you'll get,' Karan snapped back at her. 'He's also the lowest to the ground in case you land on your behind.'

'Perhaps someone else should teach me,' Isaura muttered.

'No,' he said forcefully. 'You'll have no other teacher until you reach the lake.'

Though she held the reins, they drooped. She lifted her foot a few inches off the ground and Toshi's head swung at her. 'Hey!' He stopped and swung his head away. With dread, she lifted her foot, keeping one eye on him. As she put her weight in the stirrup he began to walk off. Isaura hopped on her bad leg, unable to get on, and grimaced in pain.

Karan stopped smiling and grabbed the reins, halting Toshi.

Embarrassed, Isaura mumbled, 'Sorry.'

Karan steadied her, while his thumb rubbed comforting circles on the small of her back.

Isaura began to relax, but stopped herself. *Why can't you just make up your mind? One moment you're ordering me about, the next you're nice.* Irritated, she shrugged him off.

Karan stiffened, his tone perfunctory. 'Try again. Shorten the reins a bit and keep this one, your inside one, much shorter—force him to turn his head. That way if he moves he'll move in a circle. You won't have to chase him. Stand here, side on, your back to his head. Try again and be quick.'

Isaura placed her foot in the stirrup, pushed off and swung her leg over the saddle. She thrust her other foot quickly into the stirrup. Uncomfortable and nervous, she held the reins tightly. Toshi walked backwards; Isaura squealed.

'You're making him walk backwards. Just relax the reins a bit,' Karan said.

'Are you mad? This animal hates me!'

Karan ground out, 'He doesn't hate you.' Toshi was backing himself into the bushes. Soon he'd have nowhere to go, except perhaps upwards. 'He just doesn't respect you. But …'

'And you want me to let go of the bloody reins?'

'Not let go, loosen. *You* are making him go backwards!' Isaura frowned, finally comprehending the sense in this. Karan raised his voice. 'Do it now! If you don't he'll run out of room and either lose you in the bushes or he'll rear and dump your stubborn arse on the ground!'

'Rear!' Isaura dropped the reins. Toshi backed himself under a low bush. 'I hate horses!' she said as she lay clinging to Toshi's neck.

Annoyed, Karan strode forward and led the horse out of the bushes. 'Next time do what I say, when I say it.' Before Isaura could retort, Karan spun on his heal with the parting comment, 'You've got enough twigs in your hair for a nest.'

Isaura gritted her teeth, barely restraining her temper. Keeping the reins loose, she glowered at Toshi. Slowly a wicked smile crept over her face. She emitted a low menacing growl. 'Move a muscle and I'll turn you into a thousand meat pies, understand?' Toshi's ears flicked. 'Stand.' He stiffened, terrified. 'Good.'

She removed one hand from the reins and felt her hair. *Damn it!* Cautiously she raised the other hand, leaving the reins draped over the horse's neck. Tense, waiting for Toshi to exact revenge upon her, she tugged the twigs free from her hair. Finished, she hastily grabbed the reins. Isaura carefully observed the little horse. It was as if he were frozen. Triumphant, she grinned, giving him a perfunctory pat in reward. 'Good lad. Now, remember who's the boss.'

Isaura was still grinning when Karan returned upon a horse. She said sardonically, 'One twig doesn't make a nest.'

'Gave you something else to think about though, didn't it?'

Her eyes narrowed; her lips twisted in irritation.

Karan indicated the loose reins. 'You're very brave all of a sudden.' He looked at Toshi closely, pushing his horse forward into him, yet Toshi remained immobile. Karan's wry grin vanished. 'What have you done?'

Isaura gave him a smug smile. 'We had a little chat.'

Karan opened his mouth to rebuke her, but Āsim rode up before he could comment.

'Everyone is ready. The newcomers are each partnered with a warrior,' Āsim said.

'Problems?'

Āsim chuckled. 'None that a day's riding won't iron out. I'll take the rear.'

'Come on, Isaura, we're up front. We can have a *little chat*,' Karan said coldly.

Annoyed, Isaura kicked Toshi, harder than she intended. He shot off at a rough trot after Karan. Bouncing awkwardly, one hand on the pommel of the saddle and one on the reins, Isaura cursed. 'It's going to be long day.'

Chapter Nine

VIKRAM GRINNED AS he eyed the small column of his troops as they turned down the street that led to Pramod's brothel. He had sent a messenger to summon Paksis, the head of the Masons' Guild, to attend him in the watch house at the citadel. Paksis had declared that he was unable to attend at the watch house at the requested time and would call by later. *Damn Paksis. I know that bloody man has a lot to answer for. I want him there when I inspect the city walls.*

Vikram rode through the winding streets of Faros to the section of the city that housed all the masons. Located as they were on the very outskirts of the lower city, they had ease of supply of raw materials. He drew to a halt before a long low stone building with a slate roof. The sound of chisels clanging against stone filled through the air.

Vikram entered the workshop of Master Māhir, who ran the second largest masonry workshop in Faros.

'Master Māhir, I would have the benefit of your expertise this morning,' Vikram said.

Māhir looked up briefly from the drawings he was perusing. His desk was the only surface not covered with a film of stone dust. 'It'll take longer than that.' Vikram frowned and quirked a brow at him questioningly. Māhir sighed. 'You want to go over the fortifications, yes? Well, it'll take longer than a morning to cover it.'

'I see. I should have come to you first.'

'Keep your flattery, Captain Vikram. I assume I'll be paid for this?'

Vikram's lips twitched. 'The rewards will be great.'

'I want more reward than the inner glow of knowing I'm helping my clan and this city—though someone should have a long time ago.'

'You'll be in better standing with the high lord than Paksis. Who knows what will happen from that? It may benefit us both.'

'Paksis is an idiot to refuse you.'

Vikram gave a wry smile. 'News travels fast.'

'We both know that. Paksis can't see which way the wind is blowing. Though I note you haven't talked about payment.'

Vikram grimaced. 'I'd be surprised if you weren't paid. However, I wouldn't presume to negotiate away the treasury's funds.'

Māhir snorted. 'Well at least you're honest and it's better to be seen to be willing.'

Vikram smiled softly and inclined his head in acquiescence. Māhir looked back at his plans for one last time, rolled the scroll up and tucked it away. He disappeared into the workshop, bellowed instructions to his foreman and reappeared with a grin.

'That ought to keep them busy.' Standing beside Vikram he fumbled as he put on his hat and coat, using the time to murmur, 'Did you see Sarala?' Vikram shook his head. Māhir looked grim. 'Do you think she is well? Alive?'

'I would've had word if she were not.'

Māhir nodded sadly. 'I know she made the right choice. The Horse and Bear didn't kill the old lord, did they?'

Vikram's mouth turned down and his gaze grew hard. He couldn't keep the disgust from his tone as he whispered. 'No. It wouldn't have served their purpose, but it did serve Ratilal's.' Māhir looked at him quizzically. 'Our lord was going to make many changes,' Vikram added. His eyes darted to the door to the workshop, before he laughed loudly. 'Do you always take this long to get ready? It's a wonder you make it to your workshop before noon. Come.'

On their way to the citadel they joined the troops who, surrounding Paksis, were escorting him to the watch house. Vikram ignored him, but Māhir smiled in greeting as he passed, moving to head to the small column beside Vikram.

Vikram heard Paksis spluttering in indignation and muttering imprecations upon them both. He wheeled his horse around, stopping the column and faced Paksis.

'Paksis, enough! You brought this on yourself. Now, you've a choice: shut up or, rather than allowing you the dignity of a private conversation, we will have one here on the street for all to see.'

'I resent this treatment. I've done nothing wrong!'

'You refused to attend me this morning in the watch house. You dolt! We're at war! The masons must start on repairs to our defences. In refusing, you defy the high lord, you fail your clan, you bring shame upon yourself. Gods help you when the high lord hears of this.'

Paksis's eyes darted at the crowd and he licked his lips nervously. 'I …'

'Quiet! Save your breath until we reach the citadel.'

'Y …'

Vikram cast him a scathing look, silencing him. Paksis subsided, but cast a poisonous glance at Māhir.

Māhir shrugged at him, falling in beside him as they rode. 'Don't blame me,' he said quietly. 'You should've got out of bed … one of Pramod's girls, was it?' Māhir laughed as Paksis grumbled in affirmation. 'He does have the best, doesn't he?'

Paksis remained mute until they were in Vikram's office, where the head of the Master Carpenters' Guild waited patiently. He raised his brows in disbelief as Paksis vented his anger.

'I say again, I resent this! If I had known the reasons then I …'

'I command the City Watch. I am not accustomed to giving my reasons for a summons to appear; nor may I add is the high lord. You refused us both, so you could dip your wick.' Paksis opened his mouth. 'Stow, it Paksis, just stow it. You dig yourself a deeper hole with every word.' *If I'm lucky when Ratilal gets back you will no longer be Guild Head, but Māhir will be.*

The young soldier, Jabr, stood waiting in the corridor. 'Good lad, on time. Come gentlemen, the day is gaining on us.'

They walked the outer battlements. Vikram peered at the sprawling web of the outer limits of Faros. *They should never have been allowed to build right up to the wall.*

'The hoardings will all need your attention, Master Carpenter, and that of your guild,' Vikram said. Together they inspected the nearest one.

'It's not too bad. There are always timbers needing replacement in these things, but considering ...' the master carpenter paused, looking sheepish.

'I know, you don't need to say it. Despite everything we tried, we only got the basics done. There were never enough resources allocated to do the work properly.'

The carpenter nodded sympathetically.

Māhir peered over the wall, inspecting the masonry and paying attention to the stonework around the hoarding. Frowning, he walked to over to a guard. 'Lad, lend me your spear.' Leaning back over the wall, Māhir used the spear to gently probe at the mortar lower down. The mortar drifted away like dust.

He spun toward Vikram. 'When were the last masonry repairs done to this section of the wall?'

'Last summer, why?' Vikram's narrowed his eyes and cast a glance at Paksis.

Māhir followed his gaze. 'He did them, yes?' Vikram nodded and Māhir launched himself at Paksis, knocking him to the ground. Vikram and Jabr hauled them apart as Māhir vehemently cursed Paksis. 'You greedy, lazy, son of a bitch!'

Paksis climbed unsteadily to his feet. 'How dare you!'

'What have you found?' Vikram demanded.

'The mortar there ...' He pointed, showing Vikram the crumbling state of it. 'It's disintegrating into powder!'

Vikram nodded to Jabr and the guard; they seized Paksis. 'Bring him.'

Paksis rallied. He stared at the section Māhir indicated. "'Tis nothing, Captain Vikram, merely the dregs of old mortar left at the edge—that is all.'

Māhir growled. 'Really? How can you tell?'

'I cannot, but nor can you.' Paksis shot back.

'Do you care so little for your work?'

Paksis's lips thinned to a tense line. 'Of course not!' he spat.

'Liar!' Māhir roared.

'Peace, Māhir. How, Paksis, do you explain this?' Vikram interrupted.

'It must have been an apprentice.'

'So, you do not supervise your apprentices? Even when they're working for the clan lord, on the clan's main defences?'

Paksis began to sweat; he said no more.

'We'll investigate this further and if necessary you'll answer to the high lord.'

They continued their inspections, finally coming to the southern gate which exited to the harbour. This wall withstood not only battering by gales and storms, but at times high seas. Vikram watched Māhir and Paksis inspect the stonework. It was obvious, even to him, that serious repairs needed to be undertaken here. Māhir looked up at Vikram, shaking his head in disgust.

'Paksis,' Vikram said. 'This was the main purpose of your work last summer—explain.'

'I wasn't aware …'

'You were the one who was responsible for this; you should have been aware. Māhir, what caused this?'

'The mortar mix ratios were probably all wrong. Lime, sand and ash—the right ones, mind you, must be used. They must also be in the right quantities. Whatever they did was probably cheap, knowing this one,' he said scathingly.

'It would've worn quickly here anyway,' Paksis retorted.

'Not this quickly.'

'And the wall? The same problem, you think?' Vikram asked.

'Most likely, Captain,' Māhir said.

'Paksis, you leave me no choice but to report this to the high lord.' *The gods smile upon me, this will be easier than I thought.*

—⚘—

Līna stood amongst Baldev and his men. She had drawn a rough map in the dirt. 'The nearest farmsteads are here and here. There's a creek below a rocky hill—Bald Bluff, we call it. It has a thin covering of sheoaks along the base and in a section across the middle. The children think it looks like a fat man's bald head, with a beard.' She smiled. 'You can't mistake it. The country's all undulating here abouts, but that sticks out and it's really one of the few rocky outcrops around here.'

Baldev nodded. 'The other side?'

'There are only a few farms towards the north.' Līna hesitated. 'Until recently our clan … er … we've been reluctant to settle too near to … the Falcontine.'

'You mean too near to the Bear Clan.'

'Yes, my lord.'

'You're under our protection now. To all intents we consider you part of our clan, though you're free to keep your Boar traditions and ways.'

'I understand. There are a few families who've moved up there, but old habits …'

'Die hard—I know. Do you know where they are up there?'

'I heard rumour that a couple of families, burnt out from closer to the Divide, moved north of the Vale of Safa, because they hoped the Forest of the Asena,' she shuddered, 'would protect them.'

Baldev laughed sardonically. 'Another old habit, yet one they seem to be overcoming. The Asena haven't been seen here in years. They stick to the Plateau.'

'Our tales remain strong, Lord Baldev. The tales of the Asena are still told as a warning to children.'

'So they hoped that the fear of the forest would keep Ratilal's men away. I doubt that will work. The old ways and tales may be strong here, yet they are all but forgot in Faros. My thanks, Līna.'

She bowed and turned to leave, but Baldev's words halted her.

'We'll be using your farm as a base of sorts. You'll regularly see mine and Lord Karan's warriors.'

Līna turned to face him fully, her voice flat, yet her eyes reproachful. 'You'll make us a target.'

'You were already a target. You don't even have the fear of the Asena to keep you safe here. This way you'll have some protection.'

Baldev looked at the map, now ignoring her. 'Send a pair of riders there.'

Shaking her head, Līna stalked to her house.

'Foolish,' the captain said as he watched her leave.

Baldev grunted. 'She knows her options, her choices are on her own head. Come, we've more to discuss.'

Isaura had lost count of the ways she'd devised for killing, skinning and cooking Toshi. *Damn horse would probably be tough as old leather.*

The ride had commenced with Karan's edict, 'You are not to use the Undavi on that horse again. You have to learn the same way as the others. Only a poor horseman or commander rules by fear.'

The only other words from his mouth were orders.

Isaura had hoped today would give her a chance to talk to Karan, yet looking at him she wondered, *What happened to the man I kissed last night?*

Karan drew the column to a halt near a creek on the edge of the forest. 'Time for a break. Kick your feet out of the stirrups and swing off, like this.'

'Please stand still, little monster,' Isaura said as she swung from the horse. Her legs touched the ground, nearly buckling underneath her. *Oh, damn! Just stand still,* she silently pleaded as she leaned heavily on the little horse.

'Legs?' Karan was brusque, yet he stood right behind her with his hand at her waist.

'Wobbly. As if they don't belong to me.'

'That's normal,' he said dismissively.

Do you actually care? She walked around, barely limping, but with a type of rolling gait. Karan kept pace with her and grinned.

'What?' Isaura asked him curtly.

'Nothing,' he replied with feigned innocence. Karan took the reins from her and tied the horses to a tree branch. Annoyed, she arched her brow at him. He laughed. 'You're walking like you've got a barrel between your legs.'

One minute you're detached and the next you're laughing. Damn you! Isaura resisted the urge to hit him. *Why did I ever kiss you?*

Isaura watched Pio kick his feet out of the stirrups and slide down the side of the horse. Hanging by arm's length, his feet wiggled in the air several inches off the ground before he let go and dropped to earth. Pio stood on tiptoes, trying in vain to flick the reins over the horse's ears. Isaura watched, amazed, as the horse lowered its head for him, and then gently nuzzled his tunic. Pio ran to his parents, grinning. Lucia and Nicanor seemed as stiff and sore as she was.

'The blonde and her man are over there. Both looking a little sorry for themselves. However, the thing that will really interest you is down the end,' Karan said.

Isaura shifted discretely to see what he indicated. Curro and Elena walked towards the others. Curro appeared fine, but Elena limped. She batted Curro's arm aside irritably when he moved to help her. Elena chanced to look in Isaura's direction and a scowl disfigured her face. She attempted to stand tall and walk without limping, yet only managed a waddle. Isaura's laugh carried clearly to her.

Umniga rode before Karan and Isaura, blocking her view. She slid from Nasir's back with astonishing grace. *She's not even got a saddle! Just the blanket!*

'How are you managing, child?' Umniga asked Isaura.

Upon her arrival, Karan's manner became perfunctory. The teasing smile vanished and a facade of bland politeness replaced it.

'Isaura is doing well, considering,' he said.

Considering what? Isaura thought. *Don't damn me with faint praise.*

Karan continued, 'And you, Umniga? You were complaining you were too old for this, yet look at you now.'

'I think my limbs are remembering the joy of riding.'

Isaura's mouth turned down at the corners. *Joy!* 'I need to stretch my legs,' she said sourly before stalking off along an animal trail through the trees. *By the gods the damn woman must be at least sixty and she makes me feel useless!*

Her pulse pounded in her head with each step. She flexed and fisted her fingers. Concealed by the trees, she picked up a rock and hurled it as hard as she could at a trunk, pushing her welling anger into the throw. It hit the tree but did not bounce off. *What in the world?* Isaura marched to the trunk. Her anger dissipated as she stared in disbelief. The rock was embedded within the timber.

Gods, did anyone see? She looked about furtively, spying Asha following her trail. She moved from the tree and waited for Asha to reach her. Isaura stood with her arms crossed, kicking at the dirt. Asha gave no sign that she had seen her throw the stone.

'I won't get lost, you know.'

Asha shrugged. 'Lord Karan wants you accompanied.' Isaura grunted. Asha continued, 'You're unarmed and not trained. You've no way to defend yourself and …'

'What do I need to defend against? The enemy is across the river, yes?'

'For now.' Asha continued lamely, 'You may see a bear. The bears are unpredictable …'

Isaura, sceptical, stared at her. 'A bear?'

Asha smiled wryly. 'It's unlikely, they're mainly in the northern forests around Gopindar. Still, these are strange days.' Isaura waited, staring at her. Asha sighed. 'You must remember you're not yet a member of our clan. You can't wander freely.'

Isaura nodded. 'Training. I have to pass the training.'

'Yes. You must pass all the training. I don't think even the Asena can change that.'

Isaura looked at Asha's bow. 'Let's get started then.'

Asha canted her head at her. 'Have you used a bow before?'

'Yes. But not like this. Yours are more curved and shorter, but a bow is a bow,' Isaura finished nonchalantly.

Asha drew her bow and shot at a stump. Isaura gaped at the speed with which the arrow hit its target.

'Fast! How? It's so much shorter than our bows, but the power!'

Asha grinned proudly. 'Your turn. Try to hit the stump. The wood is soft and I want my arrows back.'

Isaura reverently took the bow. She turned it over in her hands admiring the workmanship. 'Asha, this is a thing of beauty. It's so light.'

'It was a gift.' Asha coloured, before continuing abruptly, 'Just shoot it, Isaura. We'll have to head back soon.'

Isaura drew the bow; her eyes widened in amazement. 'So easy to draw.' Cocky, she aimed the bow at the stump and released her arrow. It sailed far too high and missed the stump. She groaned. 'I don't believe it.'

Asha watched her smugly, arms folded over her chest. 'Again?' she mocked.

Isaura lips quirked. *I'd probably act the same in her shoes, with some cocky newcomer.* She considered how much she'd missed by, and drew again.

Asha watched her concentrating and altering her aim. Clearly Isaura was worried she'd miss.

Isaura held the bow too tightly; she knew it, but couldn't help herself. Concentrating, she released the arrow. It embedded itself in the dirt. 'Shit!'

Impatiently she held out her hand for another arrow. Asha passed it to her saying, 'Do you always take so long and think so hard about it?'

'No. I never really think about it,' Isaura replied.

'Relax. It's just us.'

Rapidly, she drew again, not really aiming—merely looking at a different spot on the stump. She loosed the arrow into the wood. 'Yes!' Isaura said.

'Better,' Asha agreed.

'Oh, come on!'

'All right, much better!' Asha laughed. Isaura held out her hand again with an expectant look. 'Fine, one more, then we have to collect them and go. You're like a child.'

'Yep! Give me the arrow!' Isaura said as she bounced on the spot. She grabbed it, drew, and released in a heartbeat. The arrow landed right next to Asha's. 'Yes! I've got it now!'

Isaura went to retrieve the arrows, not noticing Asha silently agape at her.

Beside her again, Isaura asked cheekily, 'So, Asha, who gave you the bow?'

chapter ten

VIKRAM ENTERED THE council room, carrying a scroll, to see Ratilal standing before the great hearth. He nearly baulked at the sight. Ratilal had removed one of the great sinan, which rested in ornate brackets on either side of the fireplace, and was inspecting its soundness.

He bowed low before Ratilal; exposed, he struggled to keep his hand from his kilij. Ratilal let him wait. The sound of hoof beats, wagon wheels on stone, and voices carried from the courtyard through the window into the quiet of the council room. Yet the soft slide of the spear through Ratilal's hands as he hefted it dominated his hearing.

His mind raced as he remained bowed. *What does he know? Does he suspect me? Has something else irked him?*

'Rise,' Ratilal said as he returned the sinan to its bracket.

Vikram rose slowly, quashing the urge to rush.

'You've been busy,' Ratilal said.

'Yes, High Lord. I did as you instructed. I'm here to report on the state of the city's defences.'

Ratilal narrowed his eyes. 'Why are the walls covered in workmen?'

'The fortifications were in dire need of repair. I thought if you knew their state that you'd be angry at any delay in the work.'

'My father had Paksis see to the walls only last summer.'

'Yes, High Lord. But Clan Lord Shahjahan … that is, the work would have passed a cursory inspection, but he did not care to check the work thoroughly.'

'Why did you not check the work thoroughly?'

'High Lord, your father … he checked it. I did not think I

would need to as well. I mean no insult to your father, High Lord.'

Satisfied with Vikram's discomfiture, Ratilal waved his hands dismissively. 'I take no insult at that, Vikram. My father's better days were behind him and I know you were loyal to him.' His lips formed a thin line of displeasure. 'However, I take it you mean that Paksis deliberately did poor repairs.'

'Yes, High Lord. I believe he did so to save costs.'

'Yet charged the full amount?'

'Yes, High Lord. The current repairs are being undertaken by Māhir. He has supervision of all work to the walls. This scroll indicates all the areas needing attention. The workmen have started on the outer walls, but the inner bailey walls also need attention.'

Ratilal took the scroll and rolled it out upon the table. 'Gods! This is the last thing we need. The last thing I need to be bothered with. *All* these areas need repair?'

'Yes. Particularly the southern gate. The northern gate is sound.'

'Thank the gods for small mercies!' Ratilal said bitterly. 'At least the likelihood of them attacking from the south is remote, but that's not the point. Where's Paksis?'

'Paksis is in a holding cell, awaiting your judgement.'

'Good. What have you promised Māhir on my behalf?'

'Nothing, High Lord. That is for you alone to decide. Māhir is a loyal clan member. He realised the importance of the work.' Vikram smiled conspiratorially. 'It helped that he dislikes Paksis intensely.'

Ratilal smiled in return. 'Very good. Paksis is head of the guild, yes?'

Vikram nodded. 'There is no telling how deep his corruption runs.'

'Come show me the walls and I'll speak with Māhir. Then I'll decide Paksis's fate.'

Baldev mounted and the small column began to move out.

'Wait!' Lina called.

Baldev reined his horse in, spinning it toward the red-faced woman. She held a small sack and dragged Kiriz along with her. Baldev eyed her warily.

'Take Kiriz with you.' Baldev stared at her. 'Please, Lord Baldev … please,' Lina begged. 'I can't get her to the lake. I can't leave—we've other cows calving. I must stay here.'

Kiriz kicked her mother and tugged free. 'No! I want to stay. I'm not going!' She ran toward the house.

'Bugger!' Baldev kicked his horse into a canter; its strides rapidly caught up with Kiriz.

The pounding of hooves grew louder. *No, no!* Kiriz thought. Frantically she pumped her little legs harder. Kiriz looked over her shoulder and a massive hand loomed toward her. Baldev leaned down from the saddle, reached out and grabbed the girl, hauling her up before him. Kiriz wriggled and kicked. Her small heels pummelled the horse's neck and shoulder as she tried to escape Baldev's grip. 'Be still,' he said, giving her a shake and riding back to her mother.

'I don't want to go! I want to stay here, with my Mama. Satish can stay—why not me?'

'I want you safe,' Lina said. 'We're at war. The same men who killed your father may come here.'

'What about you?' Kiriz asked as she ceased struggling. 'Who'll look after you? Who'll run and tell you when strangers come? Who'll keep the fire going and watch so the stew doesn't burn? Who'll make you tea?'

Lina smiled and laughed. 'Oh, my precious little one. We'll miss you and no one will do such a good job as you, but Satish and I will manage. If the enemy comes we can't fight and worry about you.'

'I can fight too.'

'Not yet you can't,' Baldev told her softly.

'But I'm good with my slingshot.'

'It will not be enough, little one. You go with Lord Baldev, he'll keep you safe.'

'Who'll keep you safe?' Kiriz said plaintively.

Baldev had one hand on the reins and the other around her waist. She tried to prise his fingers away.

'My warriors will be stopping by on their patrols. They'll check on your mother and when they're here they'll train Satish.'

'So I could stay?' Kiriz asked.

Lina shook her head. 'No, little one, no. You must still go.'

Baldev bent his head next to Kiriz's ear. 'You're going to Bear Tooth Lake. You'll see Umniga and Asha.'

Kiriz quickly looked up at him. 'Really?'

'You like them, don't you? You like Asha's stories?' Kiriz nodded through her tears. 'And while you're there you can start training. There's someone there who greatly needs a friend like you who knows about our ways and stories. You can help him and teach him. I think you'd be the best person for that mission.'

'Why doesn't he know any stories?'

'Er ... he's new here.'

'New? What? I can't teach a baby, you know.'

'Baby?' Baldev shook his head, laughing. 'He's not a baby. He's just arrived here, that's all.'

'Arrived? From where?'

Baldev groaned. *This'll be a long trip.* 'Kiriz, this is an important mission. Do you want it or not?'

She sat up straight and half turned within Baldev's arms. 'Yes, Clan Lord. I can do it.'

Lina smiled at her daughter, though barely restrained her tears.

'Say goodbye to your mother then,' Baldev said. 'You'll be back with her soon.'

—∞—

Elena groaned, slouching despondently, as the old woman approached them.

Umniga scowled at her, poking her with her staff. 'Sit up, girl! Time to listen!'

Isaura was unable to keep the grin from her face. Elena's fist curled. Curro put his hand upon hers, restraining her.

Isaura dutifully translated as Umniga taught them Altaican, but she was losing patience. Pio was rapidly picking up the language, but the others were not really trying. *They're counting on me to always translate. Me! They don't even damn well like me anymore.* She glanced over to Karan sitting by the fire. *He barely spoke to me all day, other than to instruct me. Damn it! I kissed him.*

Isaura listened as they stumbled over words as if they were mountains. She ground her teeth in frustration as Umniga began explaining the Altaican religion. *Enough with the gods!* Her thoughts drifted to Karan again. *Bugger!*

With talk of religion, Lucia and Nicanor were now interested in what Umniga had to say. Pio attempted to translate when Isaura lapsed.

Her voice laced with derision, Elena said, 'Rana? Jalal? What kinds of gods are these?'

'It's not difficult, Elena,' Isaura said. 'In fact it's not so different from the old gods you worship, Araceli and Majula.'

'We're not all *possessed* of magic as you are, Isaura. It's not so easy for us.'

'Wake up, Elena. They're a mother and father god and goddess. The stories are nearly the same as your people's.'

Elena smiled at Lucia's shock.

'Your people? Isaura, you are …' Lucia said.

'No, Lucia. I was never one of you. The moment I couldn't help on the boat … I watched … I saw the looks cast my way. The same looks I got when I was a child.'

'We never looked at you that way. We protected you when you were ill.'

'No, you never looked at me that way … until I came back—until now.'

Pio sat watching this exchange with his head hung low.

'Pio is the only one of you worth a damn.' She cast a disparaging look at them, before rising and leaving the group.

Karan met her before she'd gone three paces and tossed a staff at her. 'Training time.'

—⚘—

Malak had seen her son, Niaz, enter on the heels of Ratilal. *High Lord Ratilal! The inflated notions the young have! If only I could have kept them apart when they were children.* The sight of Daniel hurrying about on the orders of a bossy young maid distracted her. Gita had placed each of the newcomers under the supervision of another staff member who were supposed to guide and teach them the language. Though an admirable idea, Malak thought the progress too slow, the staff too busy and their motivation lax, while some obviously enjoyed the power they held over them. Ratilal was unlikely to change this. *How are they to survive here?*

Chatelaine Gita is not getting any younger. Malak smiled at her folly. *She's the same age as me. She doesn't notice the attitude of her staff to the strangers—she doesn't care to.* The fact that this concerned her surprised Malak. Something about the young man who had been helping her had touched upon her conscience. Seeing him being harangued by the young harpy of a maid annoyed her.

Malak strode up to Daniel as he turned to leave on yet another errand. She placed a restraining hand on his arm, while glaring at the girl. 'Find someone else. Daniel is no longer your charge. He'll be helping me from now on.' Malak's haughty gaze cowed the girl, whose eyes widened in fear. She smiled as the girl scurried away.

Daniel relaxed visibly. Malak thought wryly, *Rarely do people relax around me.* 'Dan-i-el,' she said. 'Dan.'

He enjoyed the familiar ring of his shortened name. The lady before him returned his smile. Daniel had not seen her smile since she had been in the halls; he doubted that she did it very often. Her hair was greying, yet her skin was smooth; he could not guess at her age. Her hands were unblemished by work. 'Mistress Malak,' he said, bowing his head deferentially.

'Dan, food.' He shook his head, looking around the hall, knowing there was still work to do. She placed her arm upon his, tugging him along. 'Come, *come!*'

Daniel allowed this formidable woman to drag him along like a small child. They entered the kitchens where she stalked the room as if she owned it. Taking whatever food she wanted and placing it on a tray, she directed Daniel to pick up two mugs and a jug of water, before beckoning him through a side door.

They entered a large sunny, walled garden. One section grew herbs for the kitchen. The rest of the garden was given over for various plantings of vegetables. Fruit trees were espaliered against the wall.

He knew Gabriela would love the garden and strove to thrust the thought from his mind.

Malak sat on a stone bench nearby. She noticed Daniel gaze mournfully at the fruit trees. She'd seen such an expression of deep sadness cross his face before. *Fruit trees! Why on earth would they make a lad miserable?* The only time she knew young men to be made miserable by the sight of inanimate objects was when they were pining; even then it didn't happen very often. *Over a woman then—foolishness.* Yet, she felt sorry for him. Clearly, a sensitive young man; he was not what she would call sturdy. He'd obviously lost weight thanks to whatever trials had brought them here, but he would never have been built like an ox—he had none of the qualities her clan prized.

Malak tugged his hand and, trying to keep the impatience from her tone, said, 'Daniel, sit down.'

Frightened, Daniel backed away, shaking his head and holding up his hands.

Malak rose and dragged him to the bench. 'Sit, Dan,' she said, tugging him down. Impatiently she grabbed a slab of bread, dumped a hunk of cheese upon it and thrust it into his hands. 'Eat!' she said in full frown. Daniel looked around cautiously to see if they were being observed. 'Eat!'

Daniel tore into the food. Malak's suspicions regarding the strangers' treatment within the citadel deepened. She shook her head in self-disgust. *What are you thinking, Malak? Why do you care about the fate of this one? You've never looked beyond your family before ... Yes, and look how they turned out.* Lips pursed, she was roused from her darkening thoughts by Daniel rising. Ruefully she snagged his hand and urged him to sit once more.

Niaz remained hidden, studying his mother from the shadowed doorway. He could just hear them. She looked as if she were trying on a new garment that fit too tight for comfort. His smile faltered and his jaw dropped as she reined in her usual impatience, schooled her features and began to teach the newcomer Altaican.

—w—

Baldev was impatient. It had been two slow days since they set out for Bear Tooth Lake. Asha was never far from his thoughts. He trusted that Karan would do everything in his power to get them to safety, but knew that might not have been enough.

Kiriz had taken to riding with Baldev during the day and attending the sick in her own inimitable way. She lay curled in a blanket beside him as he sat gazing into the fire.

'Big B?'

Baldev groaned, replying sternly, 'Kiriz.'

'Baldev,' she mimicked, frowning back at him. 'I want them to get better,' she finished plaintively.

'I know, little one. We're doing all we can. For now go to sleep.'

Baldev occupied the long nights watching over the sick. Often he thought of the young man who'd died when they took his leg. Kiriz snuggled into her bedroll at his feet. *How many others like her? I hope their parents send them to safety.*

He needed distraction. As a warrior, he could kill skilfully, brutally and efficiently, but beyond that he was an accomplished craftsman. Like many of his clan he loved working with wood; immersing himself in the craft could clear his mind or distract him. He allayed his frustrations for the time being by carving a small bear. He had roughly shaped the wood and could now commence more detailed carving.

The boy, Pio, should like it. The boy ... Asha was right. Ah damn it. He needed to see Asha again. Baldev nearly pitched the carving away in frustration. *Gods, I don't even know if they made it to safety. I just want to get to the lake.*

He sighed, placed his cloak over Kiriz's sleeping form and returned to his work. *I'll make two to wear as a token and talisman. So all will know to whom Pio and Kiriz belong and who will protect them.*

Chapter Eleven

KARAN AND ISAURA stopped a short way from camp. He marked a tree trunk with his knife. Isaura could just see it in the waning light. 'Knife first.' He passed her a dagger. 'Hit that spot.'

She hefted the dagger and hurled it at the tree. The dagger spun end over end and embedded itself in the tree trunk right on the mark.

'You've done that before.'

Isaura shrugged. 'Whenever I was angry.' She glared at him with eyes still brilliant blue from her encounter with Elena.

'Throw the knife again. Like this.' The knife lay concealed along the inside of his arm. Karan's arm shot forward and the knife stuck in the target.

'Why like that?'

'Surprise. Try it.'

Isaura threw the knife and it bounced off the trunk.

Karan sat on a stump with his arms crossed. 'Again. Until you get it right.'

Eventually she hit the mark.

'Enough. Here, take this.' He handed her a stick. 'Let's see your swordsmanship.'

Isaura gripped the stick and waited for his attack. Karan sighed. The longer Karan stood eyeing her like some dud recruit, the angrier she became.

'On second thoughts, we'll start with some basics. Relax a bit—you're too tense.'

'Of course I'm tense. You were supposed to attack me.'

'Too tense. You hang on too tightly to the sword. This will quickly tire your wrist and arm and make it easy to knock the sword from your hand. You stand too rigidly. All this will tire and slow you. Relax—bend your knees a little.'

Shrugging and rolling her shoulders, Isaura adjusted her stance.

'Good, you don't want your legs too far apart. Weight a bit more on the balls of your feet, but feel balanced.'

Isaura rolled her eyes. 'Anything else?'

'No. We won't fight. Mimic my moves. This originated from our training. It evolved into what we call the dance of swords—each move is based on guard and attack positions. Think of it as a dance.'

'Dance?'

'Yes, dance. You've danced before, yes?'

'No.'

'No? Never? Really?'

'The opportunity never presented itself.' Her lips drew into a thin line. 'Let's get on with this. I'm sure I'll figure it out.'

'See if you can get this right,' Karan quipped.

Concentrating on copying Karan's movements, Isaura forgot her anger. He moved slowly at first—making sure she was following. Gradually his movements sped up and became increasingly fluid.

'Now, we add some footwork in. Watch. You must be able to move rapidly, smoothly. Never step too wide. It will unbalance you. Both feet move. Be balanced.'

'I am bloody well balanced!'

'We'll see.' Karan stepped forward, attacking her using the stick like a sword. Isaura barely blocked his first swing. His second swing swiped the side of her good leg. She moved backward, stumbling, landing on her backside. Curses spilled forth from her lips and her eyes flared blue.

'Balanced? Isaura, stop ranting. This is training. You were wrong, accept it.'

She scowled at him, smacking the ground with her fist before nodding tersely.

Dropping down beside her, he asked, 'Were you always this quick to anger?'

'Yes … no … maybe not this quick.'

'You looked like you wanted to kill me.'

Isaura reluctantly replied, 'Briefly. My anger is worse than it used to be. I wanted to rip Elena's throat out and I was livid at the rest break with everyone and everything.'

'I'll teach you something that will help. It'll take some practice, but you'll eventually be able to use this skill anytime to maintain your equilibrium. Close your eyes. Concentrate on your breathing. In and out through the nose. Equal breaths in and out, so that it makes a hollow sound in the back of your throat.' Karan spoke quietly, guiding her through a series of relaxation techniques. 'Now, listen to your surroundings. Feel it.'

Isaura heard the brittle rustle of the drying leaves in the breeze and the distant scuttle of a small creature through fallen bark. She caught the scent of rabbit and deer wafting on the air. Isaura let the smells and noises around her saturate her senses. *I felt like this on the boat. I wonder …* Relaxed, she slipped into the spirit world.

Karan's stomach dropped as if he was falling. He felt a shift in the atmosphere around him and a dim tug. 'Isaura?' he asked urgently. He caught her as she slumped.

So it's that easy. She felt the energy around her merge into her aura, invigorating her. Her form appeared more solid and stable in this world than it had in the past. Isaura heard Karan speaking to her and static danced across her cheek when he slapped her face. *Curious.* The thread from her spirit to her body was strong, not the tenuous thing she'd had on the boat. Her gaze travelled its length. *I'm firmly anchored to my body and … to Karan?* A thread of blue ran from her to Karan, winding into his chest, and a bright blue spark rested there. *How romantic,* Isaura thought bitterly. *The one man I've been interested in and he likes me because of magic.*

Isaura. The Lady's voice was like silk sliding through air as she coalesced beside her.

I wondered how long you'd take. Isaura did not take her eyes from Karan.

I've been watching, waiting. You're far more robust than I'd hoped. You survived the reckless interference of those animals. I'm pleased. You progress well.

Annoyed, Isaura replied, *I'm not sure that pleasing you should be one of my priorities.*

You're still angry?

I feel like a bone you and the Asena are ready to fight over. I don't trust you because, while what they did was agonising, it also helped me immensely and you didn't want that. Why? Why would you want me kept in ignorance? Isaura's stare challenged her.

The Lady's eyes narrowed slightly; irritation flicked across her face.

Isaura ignored her and returned her watch to Karan.

The Lady followed her gaze. *Interesting,* she said, frowning when she noticed the bond between Karan and Isaura.

So now there's another in your game?

Affronted, the Lady replied, *They are mine. They have always been in my game, as you call it.*

Isaura turned a baleful glare upon her. *They're people, not possessions!* Isaura's form began to fade.

Isaura, we should talk. I want …

We'll talk when I choose. Isaura gave a curt wave as she returned to her body.

Anxiously, Karan raised his hand again to slap Isaura. 'I don't want to do this,' he muttered.

'Then don't,' Isaura said, catching his hand mid swing.

Karan let out an explosive breath, then held her face between his hands. Resting his forehead against Isaura's, he said with relief, 'Don't do that without warning me. I thought you were lost again.'

'No danger of that,' she replied flatly. She sat up, pushing his hands away.

'You've no guardian to anchor you,' Karan said.

Her eyes snapped to his briefly before she looked away. *Do I tell him?* 'I … I think the ritual made me strong enough not to need one. I don't feel The Wild calling me when I'm in the spirit realm.'

'The Wild?'

'That's what I call the power that lives there.'

'Lives?'

Isaura nodded. 'It's what the Kenati worry about. It tricks you and tries to take you further from your body.'

'This I understand,' Karan said. 'But they don't talk of it as if it were alive.' Isaura shrugged. 'And you don't feel the pull at all?'

'Not anymore. I don't think it needs to call me.' Despondent, eyes downcast, she added, 'I think it's in me—me and the Asena.'

Karan sat back, momentarily stunned. 'Your eyes … I suppose that makes sense.'

Isaura sighed. 'There's more.' She hesitated. *What will he do? What will he think? Magic is no hindrance here …* 'We're connected.'

Karan stiffened. 'How? What do you mean? What did you see?' His eyes narrowed; his jaw clenched.

'My aura is linked to you—here.' She placed her hand over his heart. His gaze darkened.

'So that's it.' Karan's voice was clipped. Isaura's hand fell from his chest as if scalded. He stood up, moving further away, and paced. 'This was too quick. This thing … this attraction between us.' Karan spat the words like a foul taste from his mouth. Isaura sat rigidly, her face like stone. 'It's merely the product of the ritual—Umniga's doing. Now it makes sense.'

'What makes sense?' *Breathe, Isaura, breathe—relax.*

'Umniga likes to play matchmaker. She thinks you're special, so she wants you with me. I warned her not to dictate who I would marry.'

Isaura's jaw dropped. Her hurt at his rejection transformed into astonishment. *Marry!* 'What? Why? Because you're so special?'

'I am clan lord,' Karan said, affronted. 'I am the only clan lord with a guardian. Yes, I am special.' Isaura barely restrained curling her lips in amusement. 'It was too soon. I've never ... that quick.' He stopped abruptly, embarrassed, as her eyebrows rose in surprise.

'I don't think Umniga had anything to do with it. She wasn't in control.'

'The Asena?'

'Maybe. I'll ask if I see them again. They might tell me.'

'Good.'

'What difference will it make? The bond is there.'

'There might be a way to break it. I'll not have my future dictated by the whims of others.'

'You're clan lord and a *special* clan lord at that. Some aspects of your life have always been dictated by others.'

Karan pointed his finger at her like a dagger. 'Don't ...' He began pacing anew.

'Look, you're worrying over nothing. I mean, I think you're handsome and probably worth a quick tumble, but I'm not going to pledge myself to you.'

Karan stopped pacing and stared at her, stunned. He clenched his jaw tightly and a vein bulged on his neck.

'I think you should do those breathing exercises,' Isaura said casually. Karan spun on his heel and stalked off into the woods. 'Wait, you'll need this. I wouldn't want you to get cold!' Isaura tossed his cloak at him.

'That went well.' She kicked a fallen pinecone into the forest. Karan's reaction hurt her. After years of being the freak, being singled out as a latent danger to all around her, she should have been used to it. His words came back to her with painful clarity: *'beautiful eyes'*. She'd never been someone with beautiful eyes, let alone someone anyone could find attractive. Isaura shook her head at the irony of it all. The problem wasn't that he didn't find her attractive, but that he thought magic had caused it. Magic had always seen her feared, yet had never materialised until now.

'Great timing! Stupid man. Could be that we just find each other attractive—pure and simple. Not because of some sort of *bond magic*,' she said, waving her hands theatrically as if casting a spell. '*Marry!* I've really got to talk to those dogs.'

—⚹—

Baldev approached the camp in the twilight. To his left Bear Tooth Lake lay still and dull, tendrils of fog creeping from it to wend their way around the camp. The tips of the snow-capped Bear Tooth Mountains were blazing in the last gasp of sunlight. The sparkles of many campfires slowly grew and smoke hung heavy in the air.

Kiriz slept against his chest. She had become their little mascot. Baldev could have given Kiriz to any of the others or put her in the wagon with the wounded, but he had grown used to her chatter and the feel of her small form in his arms. It made him think of his future with Asha and whether they would have children. 'Gods, man,' he murmured. 'You haven't even asked her to marry you.' He grinned, remembering Asha's face at Parlan. From the look in her eyes, she was interested in him. *She will, you fool, she will.* He reined his horse in before the sentry.

'My Lord Baldev, it's good to see you returned,' the sentry said.

'Have Lord Karan and his party returned yet?'

'Not as yet, my lord.'

Baldev's mouth drew into a thin line. The sentry's gaze strayed to the wounded in the wagon following Baldev.

'Your brother is safe. He fought well and is still at the Four Ways. I pray you'll see him soon,' Baldev said.

The sentry smiled with relief.

Turning in his saddle, Baldev addressed his captain. 'See to the wounded. Get them settled, tended and fed. I'll be in my tent.'

Kiriz sat up, rubbing her eyes as Baldev rode along. 'How long did I asleep? What'd I miss? Big B, you should've woken me up.'

Baldev laughed. 'You didn't miss anything, don't worry.'

'Where are they going?' she asked as the wagon of wounded veered away from them. 'Will they be all right? Who'll look after them?'

Baldev stopped beside a large yurt. A thick felted wool banner emblazoned with a standing bear covered the entrance and a brown pennant featuring the same motif stood near the door. He dismounted, lifted Kiriz down and placed her on the ground. Warriors ran from several directions to meet him. His horse was led away and he was rapidly surrounded, separating him from Kiriz.

Baldev began moving into the yurt; his aide joined him. 'Lord Baldev, I'm relieved you've returned.'

'As am I. How have things progressed in my absence? There are more tents and fires than I expected.'

'Many of the Boar remained after the festival. They knew what was at stake with your meeting. They feared the worst and have stayed to hear the outcome.'

'When they see the wounded they'll know it.' Baldev rubbed his face tiredly. 'Gather everyone. I'll address them all and tell them the truth of what happened. Then we'll see how many will fight alongside us. We'll need their numbers.' The aide turned to leave. 'Wait. Your rotation is due to finish soon, but I think I'll need to keep you with me a while longer.'

His aide nodded, smiling broadly. Young warriors who distinguished themselves were given the privilege of working closely with the clan lord, who in turn personally oversaw their training.

'Don't let it go to your head. War is no time to train a new aide.'

Baldev abruptly halted at the door of his yurt and spied Kiriz standing wide-eyed, subdued and alone. Gone was the precocious young girl of the last few days.

He strode over to her, the men and women around him parting like scythed grass. 'I haven't forgotten you, little one.' Baldev scooped Kiriz up and entered the yurt. 'Get us some food and drink.' As his aide left, Baldev called out, 'Something suitable for my young adviser here too.'

Paksis stood before Ratilal in Vikram's office. Vikram and Niaz stood to either side of him.

'Paksis, not only have you shamed yourself, you have betrayed my father, betrayed your clan and you have betrayed me!' Ratilal said.

Sweat ran down Paksis's jowly face. His eyes darted, pleading to Vikram. Vikram remained impassive.

'In the morning you will be flogged and your hand branded so all will know of your dishonour.'

Ratilal's skin itched and his stomach roiled. He gripped the edge of the table that he sat behind to prevent his hand reaching for the flask in his breast pocket. Though there was no point—it was empty.

'Paksis, you are henceforth stripped of all your assets.'

Paksis fell to his knees. 'High Lord …'

'Do not look at me! You stole from me! Your assets are now my property. Your workshop is mine. It will be used exclusively for the repair of Faros and this citadel. Your house is mine. It will be sold and the funds used to aid the war effort.'

Vikram spoke quietly. 'He has a family, High Lord.'

'Really?'

'Yes, High Lord. A wife and a daughter,' Vikram said.

'Good,' Ratilal barked, inordinately pleased. 'Your disgrace tarnishes your whole family. Your wife and daughter will live here in the servants' quarters. They will work here with the wounded until such time as you have redeemed your family name and honour.'

Paksis raised his head and hands imploringly. 'High Lord, they did not know!'

Niaz thrust him forward onto the flagstones.

'Stay down,' Ratilal barked. 'I'm not finished. Send in Māhir.'

Māhir entered and bowed deeply before Ratilal. While bowed, his eyes locked in sympathy with Paksis's. He rose cautiously.

'Māhir, Paksis's workshop has been sequestered. You will now manage it on my behalf. You are to continue to oversee all repairs to the citadel and Faros.'

'Yes, High Lord.'

'Vikram and some of the watch are to ride to the workshop and then on to Paksis's home. You may as well ride into town with them to the workshop and take charge. Inform the workers fully as to Paksis's fate. Make sure they understand they'll be fairly treated if they work well. You are dismissed ... Wait.' He barely refrained from smirking. 'Inform your guild they need to decide on a new head—Paksis has just volunteered to serve at the front.'

chapter twelve

RATILAL AND NIAZ surveyed the training field below them. Orderly rows of tents lined the west of the field. Archery butts resting against earthen mounds dotted the northernmost end, and training fields extended through the east. In one field, riders combated with practice swords atop their horses; the winner was the last man still on his horse. On foot in another section men trained with a variety of polearms—bills, glaives and spears.

'I want longer spears made like the sinan in the council room,' Ratilal directed Niaz. 'You and I are going to get down there and train them hard for a while yet.'

'The city defences?'

'Vikram.' Ratilal laughed at Niaz's stunned expression. 'Vikram can handle it. He's been doing a good job, so far. Gods know I don't want to liaise with the merchant class and hold the dispute settlements every week.'

'It's monthly.'

Ratilal rolled his eyes. 'Whenever it is. We've got more important things to do. We need to keep an eye out for some special talents, not just brute strength. We need several teams of excellent all-round soldiers, each with some specialised skills whose combined talents make them ideal for working together behind enemy lines for months at a time.'

'We'll need to select the teams soon, before the rains restrict where they can cross the river.'

'I've been thinking about that. They're not taking mounts. A small force may be able to cross in canoes at night undetected. Come.'

They entered the command tent and examined a map of

Altaica rolled out upon a table. Ratilal reached for the flask he always carried.

'High Lord, you need to stop drinking the shadebell tea.'

'It's dulling the pain.'

'And slowing the healing. How strong is it?' Niaz asked.

'I'm reducing the strength, don't worry. It's been giving me the runs and a rash.'

Niaz looked at his friend. 'That's because it's too strong. Ratil ...' Ratilal arched his brow at him. 'High Lord, you need to stop.'

Ratilal stood rigid. 'Niaz, watch your tone.'

Niaz persisted. 'How long since you had it last?'

'A few hours.'

'You want it again, don't you?'

'Enough! We've work to do. I've allowed you to speak thus, because I know you're concerned, but enough! Either help me plan or leave.'

―⁂―

Isaura glared at Karan's departing back. She continued staring long after she lost sight of him, hoping for his return—to no avail. A current of air curled around her face and ruffled her hair. There was no breeze. *Great, an audience!* Isaura found a mossy patch at the base of a tree and lowered herself to the ground. The current continued to circle her.

'I'm not in the mood to deal with you, woman,' Isaura ground out. Abruptly it ceased. 'That was easy.'

Isaura's skin prickled. *More company.* She searched the forest. 'You may as well come out,' she said softly. Seeing nothing, she twisted, peering around the tree. A wet nose delicately prodded her neck while she looked the other way. Isaura yelped in surprise. 'Blast, don't do that!' Turning hastily back she met the blue eyes of a younger Asena and a warm raspy tongue licked her cheek.

Isaura grinned as the Asena sat upright next to her. She tried to put her arm around it, but its head and shoulders were higher than her and its breadth made it impossible. Instead, Isaura leaned her body sideways into its fur, ran her hand down its chest and scratched its chin. It stretched its neck out in enjoyment. *'Just like a dog.'* More Asena came out of the forest.

Dog, Isa-cub? The Matriarch asked as she lay alongside her.

You don't know what dogs are? Aren't there dogs here? Isaura thought about the dogs she'd seen in Arunabejar—farm dogs and pets. She focused on the play and crazy antics she could remember.

The Matriarch's eyes narrowed as she viewed Isaura's memories. *I don't like this comparison, Isa-cub.*

Isaura's loud laugh faded. Pensive, she rested her hand in the Matriarch's pelt. *I thought you'd gone.*

No. For a while yet we will watch over you, though you may not see us.

Isaura's hand tightened in the Matriarch's fur. Her face twisted in grief. She drew a deep breath and forced her features into a mask of calm. *You heard? You saw?*

Yes. The bond was there the moment you returned.

Did you bind us?

No.

Did the Lady? Isaura asked. *She seemed surprised when she noticed it—genuinely surprised.*

If you noticed that then the chances are she didn't do it. She does not like to reveal her emotions.

Isaura snorted. *Well, I seem to be able to make her do that relatively easily.*

You do seem to have a gift for it, came the distinctly amused reply.

If neither of you did it, then how did it happen?

Random or planned ... it is the by-product of your return. You are changed ... Many things are now unknown ... which can only be for the good.

Isaura's lips drew into a thin line. *Cryptic as ever, thanks very much.*

The Asena crowded around her, keeping her warm. She lost track of how long she sat with them, staring into space and mulling over everything that had happened.

Asha comes. The Matriarch's head did not move from Isaura's lap, nor did her eyes open.

'Did he send you?' Isaura asked, eyes closed.

'No,' Asha said. 'He said nothing. When he came back on his own, I decided to find you. Lord Karan hides his emotions, but briefly it looked like he could cheerfully cut someone's throat.'

Asha stopped several metres from Isaura and the Asena.

Isaura opened her eyes. 'What's wrong?'

'May I approach?'

'You're worried about this lot? Don't be—they're nice little puppies.' The Asena lifted their heads, growling as one at Isaura. Their blue eyes burned in the darkness. She chuckled deeply, scruffing the head of the youngest Asena.

'You're teasing them! I can't believe you're scared of horses, yet you just did that.'

Isaura sat upright, pointing her finger at Asha. 'That little horse is a fiend of the Underworld! He hates me—all horses hate me.' She covered her eyes with her hand and sobbed melodramatically. 'And tomorrow I've got to get on him again!' Asha's lips twitched in amusement. Isaura leaned back against the trunk resignedly. 'I'm not joking. I really don't want to get back on that damn horse.'

Isaura smiled at Asha and patted the ground beside her. The Asena parted and the two women sat side by side.

'Are you going to stay here all night?' Asha asked.

'Sounds like a plan. The Asena are warm and I threw Karan's cloak at him.'

Asha laughed. 'I wish I'd seen that.'

Isaura's stomach grumbled. 'I don't suppose you brought food with you.'

'Sadly, no … Come back to the fire.'

'I'm comfortable here,' Isaura said. Asha tentatively reached her hand out to touch one of the Asena. 'But you're not, are you? You all seem a little frightened of the Asena, yet you hold them in such reverence. Why?'

Asha's hands remained firmly in her lap. 'Many, many generations ago the Asena were plentiful and roamed all Altaica. They killed our stock; we hunted them. We learnt they are clever, more so than other animals. They hunted us.'

We went to war, Isa-cub, the Matriarch said. *I would not let them destroy us. They'd degenerated into a primitive people ... they still are in many ways.*

'You were at war?' Isaura whispered in astonishment. Her mind raced. *Degenerated?*

'I suppose it was a type of war,' Asha said reluctantly.

'What changed?'

'Nagi. What happened with Nagi changed everything. The Asena had been driven to the forests of the north and beyond to the Plateau long before the Clan Wars. Their numbers greatly reduced, they no longer troubled us and our herds were abundant.

'The Clan Wars forced the Horse and Bear north. The Bear took the forests beyond the Falcontine. The Horse took the Plateau. Our clan thought they would die out, but we could not have been more wrong. Life was particularly hard for the Horse on the Plateau, despite the fact they were allies of the Bear. They had little in the way of crops or livestock in their early days on the high plains. Both the Asena and the Horse struggled to survive. The killing began again—until Nagi. Nagi was the son of the chief of the Horse. He was ...' Asha paused. 'Touched.' She tapped the side of her head and shrugged. 'Simple and very young, only in his fifth year. He and his family had been in the northeast of the plain, finding the stragglers of their goat herd before taking them closer to Targmur for the winter. He had taken his pony and wandered where he should not, away from their encampment.

The pony returned to camp riderless. Autumn still held sway, although winter was beginning show its teeth.

'His parents searched but could not find him before nightfall. The darkness unleashed a storm of such fury that the mountains shook. There would be no finding Nagi that night. Fearing the worst, the chief and his wife prayed to Rana and Jalal for the deliverance of their son.

'Nagi staggered through the rain and sleet. Flashes of lightning lit the landscape and he saw a fallen tree leaning against the mountainside. He crawled through the branches to shelter under its trunk. Shivering as the rain continued to run down his body, he backed further under the tree and fell into a small cave and hit his head. The last thing he heard before he lost consciousness was a deep growl. In the morning he awoke surrounded by the warmth of an Asena mother and her cubs. Nagi became the first Bard Kenati. In the morning after the storm, Nagi followed the Asena and was reunited with his parents. The chief declared that all hunting of the Asena would cease in his clan. When the tale of Nagi was spread, the Bear also followed suit. A proportion of each of their herds since then has been left to repopulate the wild herds for the Asena.'

The killing had to stop. The boy was guileless, innocent and useful, the Matriarch said to Isaura.

'So you've a truce?'

'They've a truce, not the Boar. I'm Boar Clan. Umniga and I are the first Kenati of our clan to have visited Targmur. The tale of Nagi was passed to us from the other Kenati, but many in our clan view it with suspicion. You must remember the Asena have not been seen in the lowlands for centuries. The Plateau was the only place they were to be found.'

No longer, the Matriarch said to Isaura. *No longer and never again.*

'All we've had for generations are our tales and once things become enshrined in stories, the legend grows and is never forgotten. The Asena have become a near mythical terror used to frighten children into behaving. Horse and Bear see the Asena as a saviour. Though I believe even they only see glimpses of them from time to time. This ...' her hands encompassed the Asena surrounding them, 'this is unprecedented.'

Silence reigned between them as each became lost in their thoughts. Isaura's stomach grumbled again.

Asha burst into laughter. 'Are you always hungry? You'll have to return to the fireside if you want food.'

Isaura's lip curled. 'You're right.' She looked at the Matriarch. *Will you come?*

Why should we do that? the Matriarch asked.

Clearly you have chosen to involve yourself in their world again.

Not their world—your fate, the Matriarch countered.

My fate lies entwined with theirs. That will bring you into more contact with them. It might be prudent to dispel some of their fear—some, not all. Begin a new set of stories. Keep their reverence, lower their fear. If you're going to be seen more, then you don't want some terrified farmer attacking a member of your clan and starting another war.

Clan? the Matriarch asked.

Isaura swallowed reflexively, her mouth suddenly dry. *It was a slip of tongue, yet ... No ... I think I mean clan.*

The Matriarch trapped Isaura in her gaze. *Better to use the word 'pack' to any other than myself, Isa-cub.*

'Isaura, are you coming?'

'I can't avoid Karan forever. Let's go. It's going to be a cold night without the Asena.' Asha arched her brow in query. 'No cloak, remember?'

'Oh, you can sleep between Umniga and I. We'll combine our cloaks as blankets.'

Isaura and Asha headed back to camp. The Asena rose and flanked them with the Matriarch to the fore. 'Looks like we'll all be warm tonight.'

Isaura's back hurt every time she moved. She was tired and hungry. The mud in the pen oozed its way up her legs.

A solid timber gate was before her in the moonlight. This was the way out. The man came in and out through here.

It used to be easy to get out, but now she couldn't. Why?

No. She hadn't opened it, someone else had.

A wooden rail slid between brackets attached to the gate and through the fence post, locking the gate in place. Simple.

No! A torrent of anger, fear and frustration almost overwhelmed her. She had to get out, she must leave. She felt a pull upon her spirit urging her to leave here—leave the pain. The images and feelings pounding her were fleeting and confused. She had to find something … someone. Protect someone. Never let them get hurt. Never. Memories of a whip, its crack reverberating through the air. Its tail slicing into her back. The pain still lingered. She must leave.

Isaura stared at the rail that locked the gate. *Why won't it slide? I need to see more.* Slowly her view changed and lowered until she was eye level with the rail. Scanning its length she discovered a wooden pin had been inserted through it and the bracket. Further along, a piece had been cut out of the rail near the end, so that it now dropped over a new bracket where once it had slid through the post. Two locks. *Push the pin. Lift the rail and slide.*

A drunken yell pierced the night.

Isaura woke in a sweat and sat bolt upright. Asha and Umniga still slept beside her and the Matriarch lay nearby.

Karan sat up, watching her.

Asha rolled onto her back and looked at her groggily. 'Isa?'

'Just a nightmare, that's all. Must be from having the shit bounced out of me all day.'

Asha snorted. 'Well, get some sleep. It'll happen again tomorrow, the way you ride.'

'Thanks,' Isaura replied drily, giving her a firm nudge with her boot.

'Ow!' Asha kicked back.

'Stop it you two. You're like children,' Uminga groused.

'Isa, stop being such a child,' Asha said as she rolled over and went back to sleep.

Isaura's worried eyes met Karan's briefly before she lay down.

Ratilal and Niaz leaned over a table within Ratilal's pavilion at the training grounds and stared at a map of Altaica. The clash of weapons and the distant whinnies of horses drifted up to them from the field.

'It needs to be somewhere that they won't think of. Somewhere that won't be patrolled heavily because they don't think anyone will cross there,' Ratilal said.

'There aren't that many places. You need them to be able to hide the canoes …'

'They could just sink them.'

'What about their return?' Niaz asked. Ratilal didn't answer. 'How well do you think they'll fight if they think they can't get home? How will you even get them to go if they don't think they can return?'

Ratilal did not reprimand Niaz. Niaz eyed him closely; his skin looked clammy.

The high lord slammed his fist upon the table. 'There has to be a way! There just has to be!' He spun away from the map in disgust and leaned back against the table, his fingers pressed into his brow. Deep in thought, Ratilal absently rubbed his stomach with his other hand. He lifted his head, gesturing back to the maps. 'Back to work. I'll not let Karan think he can hit us here without repercussions. What will my people think?' As his body turned, he clutched the table and moaned through gritted teeth.

'When did you last have some shadebell?'

Ratilal glared at him. 'Not since just before lunch. Thought I'd take your advice. Not that it's doing me much good.'

Niaz stiffened. 'High Lord, I sought only ...'

'Enough, Niaz. I know. I'm not going to punish you, of all people, for being right.' He braced himself against the table, drawing a hissing breath.

'When did you last eat?' Niaz asked.

'Breakfast.'

Niaz shook his head. 'That's not going to help.'

Ratilal laughed bitterly. 'I need a friend, Niaz, not a mother. The last one was little enough help and you're a poor substitute.' He let out a long breath before straightening up. 'There has to be a way.'

'You need to get out of here, up to your rooms in the citadel.'

Ratilal ignored him. 'You said you need a friend. Then listen to me. If you're going to kick this, it will get worse before the night is over.'

'Niaz ...'

'I know what I'm talking about. You don't want the men to see you—trust me.' *If you are capable of it.* 'I'll bring the bloody map. We'll go over it there.'

Ratilal's hand clutched at his belly and he nodded grudgingly.

'Can you make it?'

The chink of armour sounded nearby. Ratilal's eyes darted toward the noise, his sneer returned. 'Of course I can make it. Don't forget your place, Niaz.'

Chapter Thirteen

WE'VE STILL GOT days to go to reach Bear Tooth Lake and she's the worst rider I've ever seen. Gods, she's aching from head to toe. Yet she'll never tell me. Karan wanted Isaura to talk to him, yet all they had done was train. *It's my own damn fault. At least she's getting better with sword practice. By the time she actually holds a real sword, she might not chop off her own leg.* 'Isaura.'

Isaura stiffened on Toshi, pushed her heels down and adjusted her seat.

'Relax, you're doing fine,' he lied. He ground his teeth in frustration. He didn't blame her for tensing—he'd barely spoken to her other than to correct her. *You've got some work to do to fix this.*

Karan knew that Isaura wasn't sleeping well. Since the night she had woken frightened between Umniga and Asha, she had slept apart from the others. There was always at least one Asena with her when she slept. He felt her agitation in the night as more nightmares plagued her.

Staring directly ahead, Karan said, 'Isa, I want you to tell me what's going on. I need you to talk to me.' No answer. 'Isa?'

Karan sensed a subtle change in their bond. Isaura's hands went slack on the reins. He leaned over and grabbed them, halting his horse and Toshi. 'Isa!'

Isaura slumped in the saddle as Karan snaked his arm around her and held her upright.

'Āsim, get up here!' Their horses jostled each other as Āsim cantered to them.

'Stand!' Karan's voice stilled both animals instantly. 'Āsim hold her.' Karan released Isaura. 'Don't let her fall,' he added with a warning look.

Karan leapt from his horse, reached up and pulled Isaura from the saddle. Half kneeling, he cradled her with one arm. Her head lolled sideways. Gripping her chin with his free hand he turned her head toward him. Her eyes were open. They had changed shape. Isaura's irises had become large so they almost filled her eyes. Their colour was a deep brown, yet a fine rim of green remained around them. Blue lightning danced from the green across her eyes and began to coalesce into the same blue specks that glowed when she was angry. Her pupils were oval and elongated.

Umniga and Asha were beside him. 'What is it?' the old woman asked.

'Look. Is that what I think?'

'Her guardian? It looks like she's bonded to her guardian,' Umniga replied.

'Have you ever seen a first bonding without a guardian present?' Asha asked.

'Never.'

A breeze picked up out of nowhere and curled about them. In the spirit realm the Lady paced. *Isaura!* Nothing. She watched the physical realm in frustration. *By the light of the goddess I will not lose her now. Isaura!*

Nothing, save the scathing voice of the Matriarch. *A little late for you to be praying, don't you think?*

This should not be happening. I have always been able to break into the guardian bond! the Lady said.

Maybe powers greater than yours are at play here, protecting her.

The Lady's eyes narrowed. *You still believe in your goddess? After all this time?*

Yes.

You fool! Look at you. Your goddess has abandoned you.

No. We survived your meddling, thanks to the goddess, the Matriarch said. *We live, we thrive again. We have physical form. You on the other hand are an aberration—a freak. The only mystery to me is why she let you exist even in this form. Perhaps it is the punishment you deserve.*

The Matriarch turned her full attention to the physical world—to Isaura. She lowered her muzzle, tentatively sniffing her. The Matriarch's hackles rose and she emitted a deep growl. She seized Isaura's hand and bit her. Blood welled from the puncture marks as she shook her hand. Two other Asena pushed Umniga and Asha aside. Tense, fixated, their forequarters lowered as if to pounce and they snarled at Isaura.

Karan's arm tightened around Isaura. His free hand lingered near his dagger. If they attacked he could do little other than shelter her with his body and rely on Āsim and his warriors. If he let go of her to fight, then she would be exposed to attack. It would be over in seconds. *The Asena didn't save her for this. Just wait*, he thought.

Āsim stepped forward, his hand hovered over his sword. Karan held up his hand, forestalling him.

Umniga stepped back, waiting; her hand rested on Asha's shoulder. 'Asha, don't interfere. Whatever happens is the will of the gods.'

Asha glared at her and shrugged her off, moving in closer, her hand resting upon her sword. Pio ran up and stopped several metres away, watching anxiously.

The growling rumbled through the air, the bass notes reverberating through those present.

Karan watched as the Matriarch applied more pressure to Isaura's hand. He worried her bones would break. Isaura gasped, her pupils and irises contracted; their blue fire rapidly abated. The Asena relaxed. The Matriarch let go of her hand and proceeded to lick the wounds she had inflicted.

Isaura sat up, staring at those around her. 'What in blazes happened?'

'You tell us,' Karan said.

'You spoke to me. Next thing I know I wasn't looking at anything here. I was back in the forest—injured. I ... I could see almost all the way around me. Colours were different. I was here though, wasn't I? But I wasn't seeing here ... just like those dreams.'

'Calm down, child,' Umniga said shakily. 'We think you bonded with your guardian.'

'An Asena?'

'No,' Karan said. 'Our eyes change shape when we merge with a guardian. Yours did not match theirs.'

'What did they match?'

Karan hesitated. 'I believe your guardian might be a horse.'

'Oh, gods no!' Isaura stared in horror at Toshi, who was eating obliviously nearby.

'It's not Toshi, don't worry,' Karan said with a smirk. He paused, frowning. 'Your guardian isn't here.'

'Not here ... Don't tell me.' Isaura looked between Karan and Umniga in exasperation. 'This has never happened before, has it?'

—∞—

Niaz walked closely beside Ratilal as they made their way to the citadel. Ratilal gave no sign of his distress, and the burgeoning darkness hid his condition. Soldiers bowed as they passed and Ratilal amazed Niaz by stopping to talk to some about their training, commenting on how well they were doing or what he thought they could work on.

They walked into the citadel and the light from candles in sconces revealed Ratilal to be pale and sweating; his jaw was tightly clenched. The doors to the Great Hall were closed as they made their way along the corridor. They climbed the steps to the upper levels; voices filtered up from the hallways below them.

'Has the high lord returned from the field?'

Ratilal bowed his head and his fisted hand rested on the wall; his knuckles shone white as they paused to listen to the chatter.

'Keep moving, Ratilal, before you fall down,' Niaz begged.

Ratilal shook his head, listening intently.

'I know not, Chatelaine.'

'Well, find out girl! He'll want feeding when he returns. Go on, get on with it!' The footsteps faded into the distance.

Ratilal let out a pent up breath; with a grimace his posture sagged. 'She's almost as good a tyrant as I am,' he said with a faint smile. He nodded at Niaz and they continued.

Gods! These damn steps. Just keep going, not much further now, Ratilal told himself as he dragged himself along. Niaz shadowed him. His first reaction was to tell him to leave, though he knew Niaz was merely being loyal. *Just to the end of this corridor. Just a bit more.* They passed another bracket of candles, his eyes watered in the light; he looked away, blinking rapidly. *Damn it!* Niaz's hand grabbed his elbow; he shook him off irritably.

Niaz grabbed his arm. 'Ratilal, here.'

Ratilal stared at him stupidly.

Niaz's eyes flicked past Ratilal and his address became formal. 'High Lord, you were deep in thought. You've passed the door to your chambers.' His tone alerted Ratilal to the fact that they were not alone.

'So I have,' Ratilal replied acerbically. He turned back abruptly, feeling dizzy as he did so. His hand tapped an impatient beat on the wall hiding his need to brace himself, as he barked out, 'Well, open the bloody door!'

A servant hovered timorously nearby. 'High Lord,' she squeaked before bowing. 'Chatelaine Gita sent me to find you. What are your wishes for dinner, High Lord?'

Ratilal pushed his way into the room, saying curtly, 'Tell her to send up food and wine, quickly. Then we are not to be disturbed. We've a lot of work to do.'

'Go, girl. You heard the high lord. Go!' Niaz commanded. She scurried off, the sound of the slamming door chasing her down the hallway.

Ratilal threw off his cloak and struggled with his the buckles on his cuirass. 'Damn it! Help me get this bloody thing off. I'm on fire!'

'Good thing you chose this and not your zirh gomlek,' Niaz said.

Ratilal grunted as Niaz undid the last buckle and took the cuirass from him. Ratilal threw himself into a nearby armchair and began loosening the ties on his tunic. He pulled his tunic over his head and it landed beside the cuirass, revealing a sweat-soaked shirt over the swathe of bandages around his middle and over his shoulder. Ratilal grabbed his boot and began to attempt to pull it off. 'Damn it! Niaz, my feet are on fire. I can't get my boots off. Help me with them, will you?' The boots landed next to the cuirass and shirt. 'Oh, thank the gods!'

'You're saturated.'

'Just leave me be for a bit. I need to cool down.'

Niaz handed him a mug of water before moving to stoke the fire. 'Drink. You've got to drink. It'll flush your system out.'

Ratilal gulped some water, leaned back into the armchair and closed his eyes. The mug clattered to the floor. Niaz spun around as Ratilal vomited up the water and doubled over in pain. Niaz raced forward, grabbing Ratilal's shoulders before he nose-dived into the floor. He shoved him back in the chair. Ratilal drew his legs up onto the chair and hugged his knees.

'Don't move,' Niaz said.

'Bit cold now,' Ratilal said between chattering teeth.

A knock sounded on the door.

'Shit. Hang on.' Niaz dragged the high-backed chair so that it faced the fire fully and its back was to the door. 'Don't move.' He threw the tunic over the pool of vomited liquid before moving to the door. Niaz drew a deep breath, checking that nothing appeared untoward, and opened the door. Several servants stood outside with trays of food and wine. 'Put them on the table there. You'll not be required. We'll serve ourselves later.' He watched the trays pass by laden with a choice selection of food. 'Thank

Chatelaine Gita for a fine repast.' He closed and locked the door behind them.

As soon as Niaz shut the door Ratilal slid from the chair and crawled to the fireside. He held his hands out before the flames. It was not enough. Ratilal moved side on to the hearth and wriggled as close as he could.

Niaz poured himself a glass of wine and ate a piece of meat, watching. *This is just the beginning.* He recalled memories from his childhood of his father shivering, vomiting, ranting, sweating a sweetly foetid smell that comes from long-term use of shadebell. He shuddered. *I never wanted to see this again. Least of all in him.* Sighing, he put the wine glass down.

'C'mon. You're too close to the fire. You'll be alight any second. Move back.'

'Cold!' The voice was infantile, petulant. The eyes were glazed.

Here we go, Niaz thought. 'If you get into bed you'll be warm. C'mon.'

'I'm not a child!' The voice was clear. The eyes were sharp. The brow bubbling perspiration.

'I know that. Ratilal ...'

'Niaz,' his voice hissed as his eyes darted around. 'You must call me High Lord. The servants might hear.'

'We're in your chambers. The servants are gone.' Niaz rolled his eyes.

Ratilal sat up, peering around the room distrustfully. 'I knew that.'

Niaz knelt before him. 'Ratilal, you've taken shadebell for too long. This is the price. It will get worse. You must get into bed.' His hand rested on the bandages on his shoulder. 'We need to put clean dressing on your shoulder. It's soaked and ...' He leaned forward, sniffing, and wrinkled his nose in distaste. 'It smells.'

'It's fine, Zimma has been treating it.' Ratilal's eyes were fixated on the flames.

'It's not fine.'

'Leave me be, Niaz.' Ratilal curled into a ball before the fire and stared at it. His eyes lost focus and he drifted into unconsciousness.

'Shit. Damn it all to Karak! Why in the name of all the gods am I still your friend?' *You know why.* He dragged Ratilal to the chair, hauled him into it and knelt, tipping him forward and over his shoulder. Niaz slowly stood and carried Ratilal to his bedroom. 'Heavy bastard. Don't you dare wake up and chuck down my back or I swear I'll drop you on your head,' he grumbled. Reaching the bed he tossed Ratilal unceremoniously upon it and drew the bed covers around him. Ratilal didn't stir. 'Ratilal?' Nothing. 'Rati!' Nothing.

Niaz slapped him. Ratilal stirred, moaned and doubled up, clenching his stomach and voiding his bowels. 'Ugh!' Niaz stepped back in disgust. Ratilal lay panting clutching at the bedcovers. 'Oh, gods damn it. Seven shades of Karak!'

Niaz paced. He leaned against the mantel over the bedroom fire. *Ratilal could die. If he does ... what then?* Niaz glanced back toward the bed. *What then?* Unable to look any longer at his friend, he stared into the fire. *This is your chance ...* His eyes flicked back to the bed as Ratilal moaned. *Damn it! You owe him still ...* In disgust Niaz strode to the bed. 'Ratilal, stay put!' He shook him. 'Do you hear me? Stay put! I'm getting help.'

'No,' Ratilal murmured, his eyes rolling back in his head.

Niaz fled from the room. Once in the corridor, he slowed his pace to a brisk walk and scanned the upper levels for a servant. *Damn it!* He bounced down the stairs, hopeful that his speed appeared to be from high spirits rather than sheer desperation. Reaching the lower levels, he saw Vikram leaving the Great Hall. 'Captain!'

Vikram turned and approached him. 'My lord?' he asked.

'I would have a word with you. Follow me to the council room.' Vikram inclined his head and followed in Niaz's wake. The door to the council room closed with a soft click, which echoed across the room. Niaz placed both hands upon the table, head bowed, and drew a long deep breath. The sensation of the cold, hard wood beneath his hands calmed him.

'What's amiss?' Vikram asked.

Niaz, torn, studied him for a few minutes. Finally, he let out a long breath. 'Ratilal is ill. He has been taking shadebell tea to control the pain from his whipping.'

Vikram stiffened. 'How much? How long?'

'Since the day it happened. I don't know how much.'

'You should've stopped him.'

'I warned him, but when have you ever known Ratilal to do anything other than what he wants?'

Vikram's lips twisted grimly. 'I apologise, my lord.'

'Never mind.' Niaz waved his hand dismissively. 'I need your help. I need you to find my mother. She'll know what to do.'

Vikram frowned, but nodded. 'Of course. I'll fetch her. I believe she has only just left.'

Niaz nodded tiredly. 'Bring her to Ratilal's chambers. I managed to get him there … Hurry, Vikram. I'm not sure what to do. He is our clan lord now.' As Vikram turned to leave, Niaz snagged his arm. 'She may not want to come. Tell her … tell her the debt must be paid.'

—⚔—

Isaura had insisted on getting back on Toshi. She rode silently between Āsim and Karan. Both kept her within their reach. Despite their fight and the distance he had tried to place between them, the bond had become a gentle warmth that had settled within Karan. *I'm getting used to it.* If he concentrated he could pinpoint where each of her aches and pains lay. Though when he did this she shivered and looked about irritably. *She sensed me.*

When her guardian bonded with her, Karan had not experienced the tug on their heart bond that he'd felt when she entered the spirit realm. *It was like ice had been thrown on it. There's nothing I can do if it happens again.*

Karan looked to the Asena trotting around them. After Isaura's emergence from the Ritual of Samara, the Asena had frequented the camp less often. He sensed them watching and imagined they roamed the forests, revelling in reclaiming them. However, after his fight with Isaura and since her first nightmare, they were always close by. Now they encircled the three of them as they rode. *Like a phalanx. Protecting her from what ... her guardian?*

'Isaura, tell me about your dreams,' Karan quietly commanded.

Isaura rubbed at her face tiredly. 'I've been going over them in my head trying to understand. They're angry, jumbled flashes of memory, pain ... fear ... and hate.'

'What did you see?'

'A pen, bits of forest ... nothing much.'

'Last time?'

'Forest, but ...'

'But what?'

'Karan, what does it feel like when you bond with your guardian? Asha tells me yours is a horse.'

'Feel like? Your guardian is an extension of you. Your senses expand, you can experience the world through their eyes, glimpse their emotions.'

Glimpse? They bombarded me, Isaura thought with dread.

'They aid you in battle. They house the spirits of the Kenati, allowing them to travel great distances, in this world and the spirit world. They are friends, protectors. Nothing to fear,' he added, though for whose benefit he didn't know.

'Nothing to fear,' Isaura murmured. 'Then why does mine hate me?'

Chapter Fourteen

VIKRAM RODE THROUGH the silent streets. The old town was always quiet at this time of night; respectable families were inside dining. *So, Ratilal has been taking shadebell! How much? Will it pass from his system with minimal damage? He could die ... and by his own hand. It would disgrace him ... I could take my time ... say Malak wasn't there. Too easy to refute. I'd be exposed.* Vikram's mind travelled to a world without Ratilal. *Who'll replace him?*

There were those amongst Ratilal's inner circle who were morally little better, but less competent. The war would be over more quickly. *What about the future of the clan? An end to claims to the north, the repairing of relations between the clans? None of his cronies would want that. They're all too hot headed. If we have trials for clan lord? The older generation wouldn't win. Could I? ... Could I be clan lord? How would they react? The lower city will be for me. They see me and my men daily on the streets, keeping the peace. The old blood? They won't accept me. They'll want one of their own. Gods, damn it!* He stopped, staring at the Malak's front door. *No more time.*

Vikram dismounted and looked at the door a moment longer before pounding upon it. He heard footsteps hurrying to the door; hastily a servant opened it.

'I need to see your mistress. We require her expertise with a wounded man at the citadel.'

Malak's voice called out from a room adjoining the hallway. 'I heard. Send the captain through.'

Vikram grinned at the young servant, winking as he passed her. He entered a room lit only by the light of the fire and a single candle. A thick traditional rug covered the floor and he discerned paintings and tapestries at the edges of the flickering light and an ornate shield, sword and bow on a wall opposite the door.

Malak sat before the fire, picking at food on a table beside her chair. She smiled at his obvious distraction. 'Have more wounded come in?' she asked with concern, snapping Vikram back to his task.

'No, Mistress Malak,' Vikram answered hastily.

'Mistress, eh? Where's the 'Lady' as is my due?'

He spluttered. 'My Lady, I understood that you disdained the title.'

She smiled wickedly at his discomfort. 'And you would be correct, Captain. Just wanted to see you squirm. So what's the problem?'

Vikram closed the door. Malak's eyebrows raised, her curiosity piqued. 'High Lord Ratilal is ill.' He announced. Her lip curled. 'Your son is very concerned and, I might add, rather shaken—which I've never seen … He sent me to fetch you.' Malak's face registered faint disgust, yet she said nothing, merely waiting for Vikram to continue. 'It appears High Lord Ratilal has been taking shadebell tea for some days to allay the pain from his whipping.'

Malak's harsh intake of breath interrupted him. 'Boy's an idiot,' she muttered. She lapsed into silence, staring pensively at the fire.

Which boy? Vikram wondered. He roused her from her thoughts. 'Your son seemed to believe that you have the expertise necessary to help … and the discretion.'

Malak snorted. 'He'd be correct.' She did not move, her gaze returned to the flames as she dwelt in memory. 'Ratilal! You know what he's like. He's unstable like his mother—gods keep her in Susurrah. He has only a passing acquaintance with morals! We should let him die.'

'He is clan lord. I am loyal to this clan.'

Malak turned her gaze upon him. Writ therein he saw such sorrow that it took his breath away. 'Vikram, no one who knows you would doubt your loyalty to the clan. Though note that I said clan, not lord. If you were loyal to the clan you wouldn't want him. Tell me, you're well versed in the law. What are our options?'

Vikram cleared his throat nervously. 'Come on, man, speak!'

'Once the title of clan lord was not hereditary. Competition for the title was held. The bravest and most knowledgeable in the lore took the title.'

'Exactly. A competition.'

'The Test of Lore must be given by a Kenati. They have abandoned us.'

'Have they? They have not abandoned the old ways, just the line of Shahjahan—yet more proof of the need for a contest for leadership.'

Vikram paused, thoughtful. 'Who do you think would win, your son?'

Malak sighed. 'No, not against Ratilal. Though he'd make a better leader, particularly with Ratilal gone—dead.'

'Who then?'

She threw her hands in the air. 'I don't know! There must be someone. One of the older generation? Anyone would be better.'

'Mistress Malak.' Vikram resorted to formality. 'What you suggest is within our laws; as you well know it was once standard. I cannot initiate such a thing. The challenge must come from one who wishes to rule.'

'Were such a challenge to come forth, you would support it?'

'It is within the law.'

'So, yes?'

Vikram nodded reluctantly. 'I will uphold the law. But there are no Kenati for the testing.'

'The testing can happen later. There must be a way around it.' Vikram remained silent, waiting. 'Come, you are a man of honour. Do you want Ratilal to lead?'

'He is clan lord and young. He may yet be guided.'

'Pah! You know better than that.' She stood facing him, her finger pointing accusingly and anger blazing from her countenance.

'You will do nothing. No one will do anything. Maybe it's time for an old woman to do something!'

'Mistress Malak, you're a loyal clan member; I respect you greatly. Be careful. I'll not speak of this to anyone but be sure not to be caught instigating this. You may be within the law, but I can only protect you so far.'

'Don't worry about me. I've more tricks up my sleeve than you can imagine. There's plenty of ambitious mamas out there. A word here and there, an innocent suggestion, some well-placed gossip … should stir the pot enough for a challenge.'

Vikram's brow shot up; he barely refrained from grinning at her in admiration. *She should work for me!* 'We should go.'

'Should we? If I let him die, the challenge will happen anyway. Problem solved.' She stared at Vikram. 'What's the matter? What else? You looked like you just swallowed a bitter berry.'

Vikram stared at her for a moment before saying simply, 'Your son said to tell you: the debt must be paid.'

Malak's face became ashen. 'Did he?' Her expression veered from fear, to sorrow, to anger before resting on bitterness. 'Yes, well … damn it … I suppose it does.'

―⚒―

Karan's convoy had left the view of the grasslands behind and skirted a sheer wall of rock that towered above them. Lichen clung tenaciously to the stone face and cascades of tiny white flowers flowed down the wall from dull grey-leafed plants which clung to grooves within the rocks.

Looking up, Isaura saw a young pine growing precariously in the crumbling soil at the top. Turning in the saddle she tried to see the train of horses behind her. Āsim's craggy face filled her view.

He winked at her. 'Lass, you're doing better on that little imp today.' Isaura smiled vaguely. 'Your friends are doing fine,' he continued. 'Young Pio's down there jabbering away to Sarala. Does he ever stop talking?' Āsim joked.

'Not really,' Isaura replied slowly.

'Bet if he does then it's time to watch out, eh? He'd be up to pranks … They're all coming along nicely,' Āsim added cheerfully. 'Except of course for that cranky one. She's got a stick up her ar—'

'Āsim! Shut it,' Karan said.

Āsim waited for Isaura to banter back at him; instead she only half-smiled as she turned away. He shared a worried glance with Karan.

Isaura felt slightly drunk, cut off from the world around her. She flexed her hand. It had begun to heal the moment the Matriarch had licked the wounds. *The Matriarch … she hasn't left my side since.* The Matriarch prowled beside her. All the Asena had moved closer to her. *This feeling, this wall … around me … They're doing it.*

Gradually the rock face to their right merged into a steep hill. The trailing white flowers that had decorated the rock walls vanished and were replaced by spiny dark green tussocks that grew in the dirt between the boulders. The trail steadily climbed, growing narrower as it wove its way around the slope. The path levelled and opened onto a small landing, littered with stone shards.

The cliff face they had been journeying around reared out of the hill again and rose up to meet another such monolith. A defile ran between the two. A few wizened trees struggled to find purchase in the rocky ground. On the left, the largely barren landing gave way to a steep hillside and gradually to forest. Another trail emerged from this forest onto the landing and then disappeared into the defile. All six Asena placed themselves before Isaura's horse and moved cautiously forward, sniffing the air.

'This was once one wall?' Isaura asked.

'Yes, long ago it must have been,' Karan replied.

Isaura craned her neck to examine it. Sharp bulges of rock

protruded from the wall as it rose to a pregnant top that loomed over the defile. Only a small amount of light filtered down through the passage.

'What's this place called?' Isaura asked. Her lethargy began to seep away.

'Hamza's Gate,' Karan answered.

'Hamza, who was he? Umniga hasn't mentioned him in the tales she's been teaching us.'

'Not was—is. Hamza lives down there,' Karan said.

Isaura looked disparagingly about her. 'What is he, a mountain goat?'

'Ach, he's an old goat and make no mistake, but not the kind with four legs,' Āsim said.

'I'm looking forward to meeting him them. Curro and Nic used to call me little goat when I was young.'

'Let me guess, climbing?' Karan asked.

Isaura failed to answer. She shook her head, trying to clear an insistent buzzing in her ears. She caught sight of the Matriarch staring at her.

'Isa?' Concern laced Karan's voice.

'I'm fine. So are we going through here?' Isaura squirmed in her saddle, fighting her rising impatience. The Matriarch brushed her head against her leg, soothing her.

All of the Asena, bar the Matriarch and one other, ran forward through the defile.

They're excited, Isaura thought.

They are young and foolish. They think danger exciting. They don't know what we face. They cannot conceive of it, perhaps none of us can … Isaura waited, anxious for more. Finally the Matriarch continued, *We have been shielding you since your guardian made contact with you. His … efforts increase. I hoped to ease your bonding, but don't know how much longer we will be able to protect you.*

He wants to kill me.

I have no idea, Isa-cub. Child, you are remaking the way of things.

Isaura followed Karan, with the Matriarch preceding her into the darkness. The remaining Asena followed behind. Hoof beats echoed as they passed through the defile. Few slivers of light clawed their way down into the depths of the path. The chill air made Isaura shiver, but she kept her gaze fixed on the brightness at the end of their passage.

She blinked rapidly as they emerged from the defile. The horses stood upon a broad rock shelf. Sunlight glinted off small pools of water that had gathered in shallow depressions in the rock. To her left the mountainside was vertical and on the right a large section of the interior of the mountain had crumbled at one time. Large slabs of rock had cracked and sheered away, sliding down the mountain and coming to rest at odd angles; many nearly horizontal and poised ponderously upon generations of rubble.

The massive caldera in front of Isaura took her breath away. Trees lined the mountain walls from about halfway down before spreading onto a vast, largely forested floor. The lake, which covered a quarter of the crater, was bordered on one side by the mountains and on the other by a cleared area in which Isaura could discern several buildings situated as far back from the lake as the tree line would allow.

'Is this the only way in?' *It's beautiful but I don't want to be trapped in here. Stop it, Isa. Why are you worried?*

'The only way that anyone would willingly take,' Karan answered.

Yet the need to know where the other exit was nagged at her. Unwillingly her mind began cataloguing potential threats. 'Does the lake flood?'

'It does, but has only ever made it halfway to Hamza's buildings. It must drain through the mountain somehow and feed streams on the other side. The ground down there is wonderfully fertile,' Karan said.

'Not that Hamza's much of a farmer. Maris, his wife, is the farmer,' Āsim added.

Isaura was brusque. 'How do we get down?'

Karan raised his brows in surprise at the underlying urgency in her tone. *Is it fear of the descent?* A wicked grin lit his face. 'This way.'

He rode his horse to the edge of the shelf where the horse nimbly jumped down. For a few seconds Karan remained visible, then horse and rider tipped at a precarious angle as they descended again and disappeared from sight.

Eager, Isaura rode to the edge to see a series of rock shelves and Karan waiting several levels below.

'Welcome to the Stairs of the Gods,' he called back.

The stairs stretched down the side of the hill at a varying distances—some only a few inches, some a couple of feet apart, some a leap apart. As the severity of the slope decreased, the shelves were interspersed by sections of steep narrow track created by years of dirt accumulation and other rocky detritus. One misstep, horse and rider would be dead. The final shelf, seemingly miles below, lay partially buried into the steep hillside at the tree line. Beyond that the trail was obscured.

'Stairs of the Gods is right!' Āsim grumbled. 'I hate these bloody things. Every time you descend, you've renewed your faith several times on the way.' He shuddered. 'You might want to close your eyes, lass.'

'I'm not afraid of heights and I don't think Toshi will do anything stupid and risk killing us both.'

'Good for you. I'll just close mine then.'

Malak and Vikram entered Ratilal's suite. A heavy ornate dark timber table dominated one side of the room, ornate carpets covered the floors, richly coloured tapestries hung on the walls, and the chairs were all deeply cushioned and wide. Yet, between the exquisite wall hangings were historic clan weapons and in the pride of place in the room stood a set of armour rumoured to belong to Tarun—their legendary warrior. The room symbolised the decadence Ratilal loved and the aggression inherent in his nature. Malak's lip curled in distaste.

Niaz exited the bedchamber looking harried. 'Thank the gods! Mother …' He rushed to Malak, her unyielding stance halted him before he reached her. His relief turned to dismay and resignation.

'The debt must be paid? Really?' She swept past him into the other room. Her hand immediately covered her nose as a sweet stench, coupled with vomit and faeces assailed her. 'How is he?' she asked bluntly.

'He's lost control of his bowels. There's blood in his vomit. Is he going to die, mother?'

She shrugged as she walked to the bed and placed her hand on Ratilal's brow.

His eyes opened slightly and he said, 'Now I know I'm going die.'

Malak ignored him. Turning to Vikram and her son she said, 'We'll need help. Get Gita up here.'

'No!' Ratilal's voice was strained, yet adamant. 'No one else.'

Malak looked at him, her dislike writ across her face. 'She's your Chatelaine. She's been Chatelaine for decades. If you think she hasn't seen things to rival this, you're wrong.' Ratilal's eyes widened. 'That's right and you'd never hear about it from her. She holds many secrets. That woman keeps a secret better than any I know and holds her duty above everything. Get Gita,' she directed Vikram. He looked to Ratilal who nodded. 'Tell her to get the servants to bring a couple of buckets of warm water.'

'You're going to give him a bath?' Niaz asked in disbelief.

'You're not bathing me,' Ratilal ground out.

Her face stony, she replied, 'No man deserves to die in his own shit.'

Chapter Fifteen

'GET THAT SHIRT off him,' Malak ordered.

Vikram raised Ratilal to a sitting position on the edge of the bed, his nose wrinkling in distaste at the cloying odour.

'It's the shadebell,' Niaz murmured as he pulled Ratilal's shirt over his head. 'It makes the sweat smell like that'

'It's not just that—look,' Vikram replied.

Niaz paled. 'Mother.'

Malak moved decisively forward, nudging her son out of the way. 'Who's been treating this?'

'Zimma,' Niaz said.

'It's infected. Can't you feel it at all?' Malak asked as she stared at the layers of weeping bandages. Ratilal had been struggling to keep his eyes open, yet they widened. He shook his head. 'How much shadebell tea have you been drinking?'

'Not much ... That flask there usually lasted a day.' Ratilal frowned, struggling to remain coherent.

Malak picked it up. 'Just this, each day since ...'

'My whipping,' Ratilal finished drily.

'That's all?' she asked. Ratilal nodded, his eyes closed again.

Malak looked at Vikram. 'He shouldn't be like this so soon.' She shook her head. 'Something's not right. How strong was this?' Malak asked.

'High Lord, where did you get this?' Vikram asked.

'Zimma got it. I asked—he procured, as is his duty. He's good at procuring.' Ratilal chuckled.

'He's delirious,' Niaz offered apologetically.

Malak's lips pursed. 'I'm sure he is.'

'Where's Zimma?' Vikram asked.

'No idea. Should be here though,' Ratilal mumbled.

'Do you know where he got it?' No answer. 'High Lord, where did he get it?' Vikram persisted.

Ratilal shrugged. 'In the outer city.'

'Gods, Ratilal, anything could be in it!' Niaz exclaimed.

'Best way ... he goes disguised, just another poor bastard in Faros. I can't have respectable society thinking I take it.'

Malak shook her head in disbelief.

Vikram said, 'I'll track down Zimma.' As he left, Chatelaine Gita entered bearing an armload of linen. Malak acknowledged her with a grim nod.

'Niaz, lift him.' Malak directed as she tore the dirty sheet from the bed and Gita hastily put a clean one under him. Niaz made move to lower him to the bed. 'Wait! Ratilal needs to be cleaned. He's not going back on the bed like that!' Expressionless, Gita hurried from the room with a pile of dirty linen. Malak watched her departing back with a scowl, before looking at her son. 'You'll have to do it.'

'What?'

'Niaz, there are limits and I'm very close to mine. You will have to clean him up. Prop him against the bed post.'

'He can barely stand!' Niaz was aghast, whether at the treatment of the high lord or that he would have to clean him, Malak wasn't sure and she didn't care.

Malak took Ratilal's chin in her hand and shook his face. 'High Lord?' He murmured an irritated response. 'High Lord, unless you want two elderly women to clean your nether regions,' Ratilal's eyes popped open, 'which will not be pleasant, you will stand up and lean against that bedpost. Do you hear me?' Annoyance flickered across Ratilal's face. She ignored him. 'Bedpost!' she commanded. Niaz turned him toward it and she placed Ratilal's hands on the bedpost. 'Hang on and stand up!'

'I should make you a general,' Ratilal said stiffly, before he gritted his teeth in pain.

Malak placed basin and cloth beside him. 'Be quick, Niaz, before he collapses.' Niaz looked stricken. 'Oh, for the love of the gods! Just do it!' his mother ordered before leaving the room.

Malak leaned against the other side of the closed door, glad to be out of the room. Gita cleared her throat nearby and they grinned mischievously at each other.

It was not long before the door opened. 'It's done,' Niaz said wearily.

'Open the windows, Niaz,' Malak said as she re-entered the room.

'The cold air?'

'Never mind the cold air, it's the stench I want gone!' *I had hoped never to smell it again.*

Malak sighed with relief as the odour began to dissipate. Ratilal doubled up in pain. She sat on the bed beside him. Her hand automatically moved to rest upon his back as if to soothe him; hastily she withdrew it. She held out a basin, catching his bloody vomit before wiping his mouth clean.

Chatelaine Gita returned with Malak's satchel, along with a large wooden box. Malak gave her a tense smile.

'Mistress Malak …' Chatelaine Gita began.

'Malak will do, I think, given the circumstances, Gita.'

'Malak, how can I help?'

'First we clean these wounds,' Malak said.

Gita pulled shears from the box and cut the bandages. Niaz lifted Ratilal up as the women began to remove the dressings. Malak and Gita shared a glance full of distaste, before Gita left to return with a bowl of salt water. Niaz winced as he watched them soak the bandages that had stuck to Ratilal's wounds, before delicately pulling them free.

'I'm sorry, High Lord,' Niaz murmured. 'It must be cleaned.'

Ratilal mumbled, 'Can't feel it.'

Work stopped; they all stared at his back.

'Will it mend?' Niaz whispered in shock.

'In time, but he may never get the sensation back,' Malak replied softly. 'Lie him on his side.'

Gita recovered first. 'We need the wound to dry out.' She passed Malak a stoppered flask. 'It's honeygold mixed with white spirit.'

Momentarily, Ratilal rallied, saying caustically, 'Do your worst, *Lady* Malak.'

Malak began gingerly dabbing the mixture on the open wounds on Ratilal's back. Her frown grew deeper when he did not stir in pain.

Gita softly asked, 'Why can he not feel this?'

'Shadebell. It eases pain, but does so by damaging tissue and thereby delays healing. It can also ruin someone's gut. But this, this is too quick.'

Ratilal stared at her. 'Zimma?'

She nodded grimly. 'Vikram will find him, High Lord.'

'I have not seen this before,' Gita whispered, still staring at the wounds.

'I have,' Malak replied quietly.

Ratilal's eyes shot open at her tone of voice. His gaze held hers in understanding. He opened his mouth to speak, but instead put his hand over hers. Malak pulled it from his grasp, and his look flicked from sympathy to disdain.

'Mother …' Niaz began.

Malak stiffened. 'My satchel.' She held out her hand as Gita placed it in her grasp. 'A mug with water if you please, Gita. A spoon of ground urudahl root for the cramps and a spoon of carid bark powder to coat your gut.' She stirred the mixture thoroughly. 'Gita, thank you. You can return to your other duties.' Gita nodded and left the room. 'Here, drink,' Malak said to Ratilal.

He was too weak to sit up. 'Niaz, help him.' Niaz, as pale as Ratilal, raised him gently then sat behind him, propping him up. 'Drink.' Malak held the mug to Ratilal's lips.' He eyed her suspiciously. She let out an exasperated sigh. 'I'm not going to poison you.'

'You hate me.'

'The debt must be paid,' she said, turning away.

'You hate me.' Ratilal's tone bordered on petulant.

'Yes,' she said vehemently, spinning back to him, '... and no. You saved us ... You took my husband ...'

'He would have killed us ...' Niaz interrupted softly.

Malak desperately sought her son's eyes, to no avail. She drew a shuddering breath, and sat up stiffly before her gaze flicked back to Ratilal. 'You saved us ... but the moment you did, I lost my son.' Lost to memories, she murmured, 'I never wanted to see this again.' Recollecting herself, she stared at him, resigned. 'Drink. You're not going to die if I can help it.'

'How much further?' Isaura stood up in her stirrups, peering for signs of the homestead she had glimpsed.

'Not far.' Karan looked at her riding beside him. Since they'd descended stairs she'd been increasingly alert, and fidgeting in the saddle. He could sense Isaura's urgency and the undercurrent of anxiety that laced through it. She was more assertive with Toshi, who for the first time was anxious and slow.

Isaura kicked him savagely. 'Move.'

They crested the top of a small rise where the forested path opened onto a clear view. The lake sparkled in the distance at the bottom of an expanse of gentle grassland slopes. Opposite the lake, adjacent to the forest lay a collection of farm buildings, including a long timber barn and farmhouse with gabled, shingle roofs.

Karan rode forward, leaving Isaura behind. The other horses began to pass Toshi.

'Are you coming?' Karan called back.

Isaura drove her boots into Toshi. He refused to move.

Āsim slapped his rump. 'Get going, Tosh!'

Toshi refused to budge.

Isaura's eyes narrowed; her lip curled in a sneer. She leaned forward, grabbing the little horse's mane and neck in her hand as if she wanted to rip a piece from it. Hate dripped from her words. 'You will move. You will move now. Or by the end of this day I will feed you to the Asena.' Though barely a whisper, it cut through the air. Toshi leapt forward and trotted down the slope to catch up to Karan.

They halted before a large corral. A deep barn was nearby; its double doors were open.

A burly man in his mid-fifties strode out. 'Karan? What brings you here?' His eyes widened in brief surprise at the two Asena. 'Old Mother.' He inclined his head to the Matriarch.

The Matriarch yelped in pain and all the Asena cringed as their shield around Isaura was shattered. *Isa-cub!*

Isaura gasped in shock as the dull buzzing that had been at the back of her mind burst forth and waves of anger, hate, distrust and longing flooded her mind.

Isaura jumped from Toshi and ran, limping awkwardly, straight for the barn, followed by two Asena.

'Hey.' Hamza grabbed her arm. 'Where do you think you're going?'

Isaura shook him off without sparing him a backward glance.

'Sarala, keep the others here. Umniga, with me,' Karan commanded. He ran to catch up to Isaura. At the back of the barn he saw her open a gate into a large yard with a high fence.

Beside him, Hamza said, 'By the gods, she can't go in there. Stop!' He looked worriedly at Karan. 'He'll kill her.'

'Isa, stop!' Karan yelled.

She ignored them both and stepped into the enclosure. In the centre of the yard stood the largest mule Karan had ever seen. Eyes wide, it snorted at Isaura, tossed its head and reared. *I should run*, Isaura thought. Feet the size of dinner plates pawed the air in front of her and landed with a resounding thud on the packed dirt. *I can't. I just can't.* She stood frozen. *The pull to stay is stronger.* Breathing rapidly and sweating, her eyes grew as wide as the mule's.

Karan reached for Isaura's arm to haul her backwards. A cage slammed around Isaura's mind. She lost control of her limbs and sank to the ground. The mule lunged at Karan, jumping over Isaura and coming between them. He chased Karan from the pen. Hamza slammed the gate shut as soon as Karan was out. The Matriarch peered under the lowest rail. She leapt back as a hoof bashed the timber just above her head.

'We need to get her out of there,' Hamza said.

'He's her guardian, Hamza,' Umniga said. 'It will resolve itself one way or the other. It's up to …'

Karan's harsh words cut Umniga off. 'Do not say this is up to the gods, old woman! This is not the work of the gods. This is the work of men. Look at him.' Karan grabbed her by the back of the head and forced her forward, pressing her up against the fence to gaze through the railings. 'Just look at him.'

The mule ignored Isaura, intent instead on keeping Karan out of the yard. The slamming of the gate registered dimly with her. She could see and hear, but not move. Sweating profusely, Isaura lay panting with one side of her face plastered to the dirt.

Faintly, she heard the Matriarch, *Isa-cub, stay calm. He feels your anger and hate. He is … confused.*

The mule spun and took two steps towards the Matriarch, who backed away from the rail. Satisfied, he turned his attention to Isaura.

His hooves struck the ground loudly as he moved toward her. A large black hoof filled her vision, yet this time it hit the ground quietly. Tentatively, he sniffed her. His warm breath and the hairs on his nose tickled her hand as she lay sprawled on the ground.

Friend, Isaura thought. His snort filled her ears. His massive shadow danced as he tossed his head over her. *Friend*. Nothing. *Friend*, she pushed.

Rage, black and boiling, thrust into her mind; she cowered before it. He ransacked her memories, dredging up visions of her mother, Hugo, Curro, Nicanor and Pio and dragging them before her mind's eye. He singled out images of Elena and Toshi before passing them over. Happiness, grief, misery, guilt … pain, betrayal … anger. Tears ran down Isaura's face as she relived her past. Abruptly it stopped. Isaura, finally able to move, curled into a ball, sobbing.

Two hooves moved back. Isaura felt the mule at the edge of her consciousness. She sat up. They looked at each other warily and Isaura held out her hand. He backed away, then paced between her and the others. Holding his head high he flicked it in agitation while he walked. Isaura stayed still, though she examined him closely.

He carried barely enough weight to cover his ribs. The dried sweat of his coat showed where his harness had lain and rubbed his hair away. In several places, he was missing skin. The way his black mane spiked upright looked as though someone had hacked at it with a blunt knife; pieces of bracken clung to his tail. The lash marks across his rump brought tears to her eyes.

Isaura's anger rose to mirror that of the animal before her. He grew more agitated. *Breathe, Isa. Just breathe, be calm*, she told herself. She focused on her grief at his state, her concern. His distrust ebbed. Wary, he stopped pacing and turned to face her. Cautiously he approached her, gradually lowering his head, blowing harshly through his nose until he touched her outstretched hand.

I'll never hurt you. Gently she patted his head, moved to stand beside him and rubbed his neck. His skin flinched as she examined a wound. *I'll never hurt you. Show me.* A vision of forest floor, the sensation of pulling something heavy entered her mind. Isaura kept patting him and talking softly to him as she walked around him. As she looked at each injury another picture would enter her mind.

Finally back at his head. She placed her hands on either side of his face and put her forehead on his. *Let me in. We're the same. On the inside we're the same.* Nothing prepared her for the avalanche of scenes that she witnessed. She experienced his contentment at Hamza's, his bewilderment at leaving, then being traded again later, leaving one good home to go to another much worse. She saw the ramshackle cabin in the woods, a large man with bloodshot eyes and rancid breath. Bile rose in her throat at his recollections of his life there. *But you got the gate open.* He showed her the man opening the gate; next the man lying in the mud, his head caved in.

Isaura smiled. *Good.*

Chapter Sixteen

UMNIGA, KARAN, HAMZA and the Matriarch remained by the corral.

Hamza looked down at the wooden carryall full of unguents and ground his foot into the dirt next to it impatiently. Desperate to break the silence, he said, 'The boys and Maris should be back from the High Pass and 'ave delivered the shipment to the lake by now. They'll be on their way back.'

'Maris went with them?' Umniga asked.

'Aye, she said she had trading she wanted to do, but that's not it. I would've let them up there on their own. The weather will hold for a bit yet and they'll be fine. But Maris isn't ready to let 'em yet. Not since we lost Jonis.'

For the first time Karan took his eyes from Isaura. 'I pray it was uneventful or Maris will never forgive either of us.'

'Ach, Karan, it will be. I miss the boy as much as she, but we've taken the mule train up that pass a thousand times. It was just an accident. Maris knows it was no one's fault.'

'Her anger and grief will take time, my friend,' Karan said.

'Aye, but I think she's working her way through it. Young Illyria was as desperate to go as the boys were to stop her. Maris let them go- that's something.' Hamza chuckled. 'I think the boys are sweet on a couple of girls in Targmur.'

'Having their mother and their eight-year-old sister along will certainly keep them out of trouble,' Umniga said.

Karan's grin faded; his eyes returned to Isaura. 'You'll need to do another run in two weeks. You'll be taking children from the lowlands to Targmur for their safety. Hopefully there'll be takers on my offer.' Karan began to open the gate.

'Are you sure you want to go in there?' Hamza asked.

'It's been hours,' Karan said. 'It's time to see if Umniga has instructed Isaura properly.'

Umniga sniffed. 'I'll go. It is my duty.'

Karan's look halted her; he closed the gate firmly in her face.

Isaura stood with her head resting against the mule's side. Her hands, which had been gently stroking him, were now still. The mule's head was lowered, eyes closed.

Karan approached her slowly. 'Isa?' Two heads snapped up to gaze at him. 'Isa?' Her eyes' shape and colour mirrored that of the mule. *Still connected. Who has control?*

He reached out to touch her. The mule and Isaura both inhaled sharply; their posture stiffened. Poised for action, their gaze warily followed his hand . Blue lightning streaked through their eyes. Karan placed his hand on Isaura's shoulder.

For several heartbeats, they stared at him. Mule and woman took a deep breath and Isaura's posture relaxed. Her eyes partly returned to their normal shape and colour. 'Karan, we need a medical kit. Our wounds ... his wounds need tending.'

'You'll need help. Will he let us help?'

'Hamza betrayed us,' Isaura said.

'No, Hamza sold him to a good home. He had no way to know that he would be passed on again. Hamza knew nothing of his fate until he returned here.'

'We ...'

'Isa, no one wants to break the merge the first time, but you must let go now. You can't stay connected all the time,' Karan said gently. 'This is the final test of the bonding—learning to relinquish the merge.' She whimpered. 'Separate out your thoughts from his. You need to remember that there are two of you, not one.'

Isaura drew a deep breath, concentrating hard. 'I try, but he won't let me go completely.'

'His job is to keep you safe ...'

She was blunt. 'No, we keep each other safe.'

'Not at the risk of each of you forgetting who you are. Some people fail in this. They remain merged permanently, one entity controls the other who becomes a puppet. That body fails and dies.' The mule shook his head vigorously. *Gods! I think he actually understands me.* 'Either way he'll have failed to keep you safe. Once the merge is ceased, the bond is still there and grows stronger over time. You'll feel a connection and be able to touch each other's thoughts. You'll not lose each other now and you'll have to practise merging regularly—eventually you'll fight merged. You must both trust me.' Nothing. 'Will he trust us to help you both?'

There was a lengthy pause.

'Yes.' Isaura's pupils and irises contracted and their green returned. She smiled. At the edge of her mind still loomed her wary protector.

—⚭—

'Now, Mistress Isa,' Hamza said when they'd finished treating the mule's wounds, 'I'm right sorry Brownie got in this state. If I could find the mongrel who did this, I'd give him what for, I tell you.'

Isaura smiled. 'We know, Hamza, and please just call me Isa. You make me feel old with the mistress bit.'

He clapped her on the shoulder. 'Done, Isa!' The mule's head shot forward, knocking him away from her. 'Hey, Brownie! I mean no harm,' Hamza said, taken aback. 'Isaura, I want him in the barn. It's warmer in there and I'll give him a special feed mix. There's a stall near the front all readied, but I couldn't get near the poor bugger.' Hamza looked at the mule knowingly. 'I'm not sure he'll want to be locked up. You think you can get in there?'

Isaura nodded. 'I'll be close by?'

'Course you will.'

He passed her a halter; Isaura stepped back shaking her head, horrified. 'No, no … he doesn't want it.'

'No ... I don't suppose he does. Follow me.'

The others had long since departed to set up camp for the night. Even the Asena had vanished into the woods.

The mule warily entered the stall, hung his head over the half door and peered out the front of the barn at the campsite.

Hamza chuckled. 'You know, I put him here so he could peek at that lot out there and get to know them a bit.' Hamza reached out and gave him an affectionate pat. 'Poor bastard. He's not ever gonna trust people so easily again and he was such a gentle soul before too.'

Isaura watched while he mixed up a large bucket of feed. 'Hamza, why weren't you surprised to see the Asena? Everyone was shocked and the other lowlanders were afraid.'

Hamza didn't answer directly. 'The Stairs of the Gods weren't always there. There's a back way in here, from the mountains, but it's more treacherous. The Asena were here when we settled. I reckon they never left this spot, just moved from the high plateau to here as they wanted. I thought I'd got a glimpse sometimes, but was never sure. Then my youngest, Illyria, said she'd seen them.' He paused. 'I like this spot and I want to stay here. It's an oasis from the rest of the bloody rot that goes on outside. The Asena didn't bother us, so we didn't bother them.'

'You called her Old Mother.'

'When you travel as much as I do to the High Citadel in Targmur, you hear their legends. You pick things up.' He finished mixing the feed. 'Here, Isa, give him this. He could do with some spoiling.' Hamza gave Isaura a queer look. 'You've got the same look about you sometimes. I think you could do with some spoiling too. Come with me.'

Isaura followed Hamza into his house. At the door she paused, staring back at the barn. 'He'll be all right, lass. Don't you fret. He knows where you are. You can touch each other's mind's now and then for reassurance.' Raucous laughter erupted from the campsite. 'I reckon a bit of quiet will do you both good.'

Hamza grabbed Isaura's arm, gently tugged her through the door and directed her to a seat at the table. He moved to the chimney where a camp oven hung from a hook at the side of the fire.

'Smells good,' Isaura said. 'What is it?'

'Soup. Nice and easy. I set it going in the morning and just have to keep the fire chugging away and it's cooked in the evening.' Hamza ladled out soup for each of them, while Isaura cut thick slices of wholemeal bread. 'You'll have to excuse the bread—it's few days old. Without the young ones here, I don't get through it before it goes stale and I can't cook bread to save myself.'

'How many children do you have?'

'Three of them. Two boys, one seventeen, one fifteen, and a girl—eight.' Avoiding her gaze, Hamza stared at the bowl of soup, then at the fire.

'Jonis made four.'

He looked up, startled.

'I … we heard. I'm sorry,' Isaura said, taking his hand.

'We're not made to watch our children die—any children really.'

Isaura stiffened. 'No,' she replied softly. 'We are not.'

Hamza patted her hand. 'We recover. There are three others that need love and keeping out of trouble. Now for you, Isa,' he continued forcibly brighter. 'You know it's a great honour for me to have Brownie become a guardian. I don't know if there's ever been a mule guardian. I always thought Umniga's mule would be one,' he mused. 'They're brothers you know, but it never happened.' He shook his head. 'Anyway, it's a great honour, but I'm not having you, who now has a mule of impeccable breeding I might add, although I'm buggered if I know how in the name of all that's holy he got so damn big, wearing some bloody fisherman's worn out cast offs.'

Isaura chuckled. 'That was very roundabout way of telling me my clothes are falling apart.'

'Well, they are! They're torn. Gods, what a bruise! That's a horse bite.'

'Toshi. It seems his day is not complete unless he has bitten me or bounced me to bits. I hate that horse.'

'Good thing you've got Brownie then,' Hamza said. Isaura frowned. 'What's wrong? You make a bit of face every time I say his name.'

'I don't think it fits him anymore.'

'What does he think?' Hamza asked.

'He's … waiting,' Isaura said, surprised.

'What for? A name?' Hamza asked. Isaura shrugged. 'Well, it's your turn now,' he said, disappearing into another room and returning with a bundle wrapped in an embroidered blanket. He drew a deep breath. 'They might be a little loose in some places.' He appraised her. 'And maybe not in others, but I think these will fit you well enough.'

Isaura looked stricken. 'Did these belong to your boy? I can't.'

'I know Maris was thinking about giving them away, but she just hadn't found the right person. This feels right. I think she'd agree with me if she saw you.'

'But Hamza …'

'No buts, Isa. These were for Jonis's coming of age. He was killed two days before it. Maris worked hard making them. See she embroidered a mule on each corner? The boar for our clan is there too.'

'I'm not a member of any clan yet. I've to pass the training and prove myself.'

'You can unpick the boar then.' He looked at her shrewdly. 'I've got an idea.'

—⁓—

Isaura stood next to Hamza in his kitchen. 'I'd no idea you'd be so good with a needle and thread, Hamza.'

'Why, because I'm a man? Girl, around here everyone pitches in. We all work our tails off. Why should this be just the woman's work?' he said vehemently.

Taken aback, Isaura said, 'Sorry.'

'Ach, don't be, Isa. Things are different here to the rest of my clan and we like it that way.'

Isaura looked down at her clothes and turned about trying to see them from all angles.

'You look wonderful, girl. You did a fine job on the fiddly small stitches that my calloused old hands can't manage.'

'I feel like I'm pretending.'

Hamza placed his hands on Isaura's shoulders and looked her in the eye. 'Now you listen to me. You wear no clan symbols; you don't need to. No one can be offended. You are the Asena Blessed, that's all you need.'

Karan walked into the room, stopped and stared at her. Remembering Hamza's words, Isaura stood straighter as Karan walked around her, scrutinising her appearance. She was dressed in fur lined, knee length black boots, with loose dark grey woollen pants, the seat and inner leg of which were lined with soft black leather. Isaura wore a thigh-length, light grey, wraparound woollen tunic top, bordered with wide black bands at the hems. Running Asena were embroidered in light grey and blue thread into these dark bands. A black belt about two inches wide with a plain silver buckle was cinched around her waist.

Karan said nothing as he took the caped cloak she held and examined it. It was in two pieces: a shorter outer cape which would end a few inches below her shoulders, and a longer hooded cloak with a gusset at the rear to allow it to hang neatly behind the saddle and over the leg without being too voluminous. Where they fastened, two snarling blue and grey Asena had been embroidered.

'Excellent. Much better. They suit you.' Karan looked at the bedroll at her feet. 'You've been well equipped.' Bemused, he said to Hamza, 'I'll make sure when you're in Targmur that you can take any supplies you need. I'll settle with the traders.'

'The clothes were a gift.' Hamza folded his arms across his

chest and scowled. 'I want no recompense.'

'Hamza, I didn't mean to offend you.' Karan held his hands out placatingly. 'But I'm about to ask more of you and there are things I want you to get from Targmur for me—you should be recompensed for those.'

Hamza grumbled his assent.

Karan flicked his head at the mule in the stall. 'She'll have to ride him. Do you have a saddle Isa can use temporarily? We'll be going soon.'

'Only my breaking saddle. I'll need that. Even that won't fit properly and you wouldn't get away with it for long—he's got too many sores still healing.'

'He's a mountain of a beast—a hand taller than Mirza. He's got legs like tree trunks and a chest like a barrel. What on earth did you breed to get him?'

Hamza looked affronted. 'He's the same breeding as Umniga's mule, Nasir. He's just … bigger.'

'What about Toshi's saddle?' Isaura asked. The mule thundered a kick into the timber of the stall.

'Won't fit him. You'll have to get one made for him later. I can use a surcingle to strap a blanket and sheepskin on him. Isa can ride bareback.'

'He's huge. I barely stay on Tosh with a saddle. Without one I'll slide off.' *Damn, I'll have to ride Tosh.*

'You can try it. But you may as well take your bedroll to Toshi and tie it to the back of the saddle while we finish up here,' Karan ordered.

Not again. Isaura spied Toshi at the end of the line of horses tethered to the hitching posts and headed toward him.

Chapter seventeen

RATILAL TOSSED VIOLENTLY and his arms flailed, smacking those trying to help him.

'Hold him down!' Malak directed Niaz and Vikram.

Once he lay still, sweat pouring off him, his breath coming in short, broken pants, his eyes grew wide and darted between his captors.

'High Lord? High Lord? You must drink this!' Malak said.

'No! You are making me worse!' He began to thrash again. Malak backed away as Vikram and Niaz struggled with him.

'Ratilal! Be still,' Niaz pleaded.

'Niaz? You too? Why? Are we not friends?'

'Yes, yes we are! But you must drink the tonic. It's working. Your cramps have almost gone. Remember, remember earlier?'

Ratilal stopped abruptly, struggling to think. 'Cramps?'

Niaz nodded. 'They're much less now. Let us help you.' He took the mug from his mother. 'Look,' he sipped some of the liquid. 'See, it's not poison. Drink. It will help, trust me.' Niaz nodded at Ratilal, holding the drink to his lips. 'Good. Now rest.'

'He'll sleep soon,' Malak said. 'There's sleepsease in that dose.' She continued tiredly, 'Then we need to retreat those wounds. He's opened them up again, thrashing about.'

Hours later, Malak sat by Ratilal's bed. Niaz and Vikram lay sprawled, asleep in chairs. Gita had left much earlier in the night. *She didn't need to stay for this. No one should have to stay for this.* Malak grimaced at the lingering smell and the memories she could not banish.

Ratilal opened his eyes to see Niaz's mother sitting beside his bed. It was the first time he had seen her looking her age. Dark circles hung under her eyes and her hair was dishevelled.

'Lady …' he paused thoughtfully. 'Mistress Malak.'

'High Lord?'

'It appears I owe you my thanks.' Ratilal's voice was hoarse. He was exhausted and his bones ached to their very marrow. Malak passed him a mug of water. His hands shook so much when he tried to take it that she gently batted them away and held it up to his lips.

'Drink,' she commanded.

'You really should've been a man. You'd make a fine general.'

'There have been women commanders aplenty in our history.'

'Not now, not under my rule. I've no doubt of your courage and strength of will, Mistress Malak, but women in general don't have the endurance or physical strength for war. Their presence is a distraction.' Malak narrowed her eyes defiantly. Ratilal grinned, but fatigue outweighed his enjoyment in battling this formidable woman. 'I'll not debate this further.' Silently, they watched each other. Quietly he asked, 'How often did you have to endure this?'

Malak remained unmoving, looking through him, revisiting the past. 'Too often. Though, I might add not always because of shadebell. No, shadebell was just the … end.' Her eyes met his. Her regret and loss was evident in the tightness of her posture and the hardening of her eyes.

Ratilal nodded. He knew that anyone with any decency would not question her further, yet he could not leave her be. 'He drank a great deal—he and my father both.'

'Your father had more cause than most,' she said without rancour.

Ratilal stared at her, desperate to be offended.

'The loss of your mother.' Ratilal snorted in derision. 'The loss of your sister … He grieved deeply for both.'

'Indeed.' Ratilal's expression grew pensive as he became lost in his own memories.

Good, Malak thought. *You'll drag me through the mire of my past, then so too will you think on your own.*

His visage transformed as he recalled his life thus far. Ratilal's mouth twisted in displeasure; a hardness returned to his features as he regained his focus.

Worry tugged at Malak. *You've poked the bear.* 'Your father had strength enough though. He recovered … was recovering.'

'Your husband did not.'

'No,' she said flatly.

A flicker of hesitation crossed Ratilal's face. 'He'd have killed you both.'

Malak drew a deep breath, her hand gripped her knees and her arms were rigidly straight as if propping her up. 'Probably.'

'Yes.'

'Yes,' she reluctantly acknowledged.

'I saved you both.'

'Yes.'

'Do you want to know why?' Ratilal asked. Malak looked puzzled. 'I always envied Niaz his mother. You were … you are strong. Mine was weak. You were always stable, consistent, protective. Mine was not. Niaz would never tell me where he got the bruises … I thought it was just the training—we trained hard. Or that the others were picking on him, so I stayed by him. I couldn't understand it. Your home … I never suspected. He never said. He kept his shame hidden.'

Malak's head snapped up and she glared at him. 'Shame! He wasn't ashamed of his weakness! How could he be? He was a child! A child cannot defend against a full-grown man—a warrior. He loved his father … he was torn … we both were.'

'A child cannot defend against a full-grown man? What I saw that night … You are alive because *this* child did defend you against a full-grown man. I defended you because you were what I wanted my mother to be. You hid us. But we saw. I saw you try, but you were not enough. You cajoled him, tried to pacify him, it did not work. You fought … it did not work. The look on Niaz's face … I realised this had been going on for years. I was furious.

You could have told my father, your clan lord. You could have done anything …'

'He was not always thus. Only sometimes. He was …'

'You … you were weak! You made me so angry. My *mother* …' he spat the word, 'was bad enough—utterly consumed with herself … But you … I expected so much more. I … your son deserved more,' Ratilal said venomously. 'I was so angry. In that moment I knew … there was no safety … nothing perfect except what you made for yourself.'

Surprise, anger, sadness cascaded across Malak's face. 'That's why you killed him.'

'Before he killed either of you … And you treated me …' Ratilal paused.

Malak swallowed—she waited. She knew what was coming.

He scrutinised her. 'How did you treat me old woman?'

'Like you were a murderer.'

He nodded, falling back onto his pillows. 'You spurned me and I saved you.'

'I loved my husband.'

'You were weak. Women are weak. That was my best lesson,' Ratilal said softly, his anger all but spent for the time being.

The sound of movement drew his attention. His eyes shifted between Niaz and Vikram. Malak stiffened, suddenly reminded of their audience. She made to stand, but Ratilal's hand shot out, drawing her back to sit on the bedside as his eyes flashed a warning at her. She looked at her son, praying for understanding, for him to defend her. Niaz's eyes, unreadable, flicked briefly to hers before he moved to the window. With his back to her, he stared out into the coming dawn.

Predatory, calculating and smug, Ratilal observed the gulf between mother and son.

Vikram cleared his throat.

Malak tried to tug her hand free but Ratilal still bound her to him. 'Captain?' he said.

'I found Zimma earlier in the night. I have him contained,' Vikram said.

'He's in the cells?' Ratilal asked.

'No, High Lord. I believed you would not want his treachery known. My second and I caught him and discretely locked him up.'

Ratilal let out a pent up breath. 'Well done. You were correct. I don't want the clan to know my own valet tried to kill me. What of the herbalist?'

'Legitimate and, I believe, innocent. He'd instructed Zimma that the potion was to be diluted and used for a short time only. He was horrified at the thought that Zimma had not followed his instructions. He begged to tell your healer that he had put ground pedene seeds and carid bark powder in the mixture.'

'Well, healer, what does that mean?' Ratilal asked as he shook her arm. Malak's face twisted in pain.

'It may have ameliorated the damage to your insides.'

'Why would he put this in, if he trusted Zimma?'

Vikram answered, 'A standard precaution. Though he is in the lower city, he has a good reputation and wants it to remain that way. He knew Zimma was your man and has been so for years. He never thought that he would harm you.'

'You believe him?'

'Aye, High Lord, I do.'

'What has Zimma to say?'

Vikram was blunt. 'That, I believe, High Lord, you'll want to discuss in private.'

Ratilal raised his eyebrow imperiously. Vikram cleared his throat. 'I believe, High Lord, that his sister is one of Pramod's girls. Niara is her name.'

Ratilal paled, immediately releasing Malak. 'Leave me, all of you.' Before they had reached the door, he added, 'Mistress Malak, one more word if you please. Close the door,' Ratilal directed Niaz.

Never once looking at his mother, Niaz exited the room, slowly drawing the door closed. Outside his hand lay clenched around the latch and his head rested against the cool timber. He cursed softly, reluctantly releasing the door knob; his hand fisting as if to pound on it, before he spun and left.

With the closing of the door, dread settled inside Malak. Ratilal stared at her, waiting for her to wilt under his gaze. Spine stiff, jaw clenched, she boldly faced him with only the barest trace of contempt in her gaze. He despised the fact that he felt some form admiration for her at that moment.

'Niaz and I both learnt a lesson that night. You were right. You lost a son, I gained my most loyal man … and now you'll never have him back.' He smiled. 'Get out, Mistress Malak, but don't go far. I'll summon you when my wounds need tending.'

'My debt is paid.'

'Not yet it isn't. I'm high lord, you will serve. Now get out.'

Malak bowed and exited with all the appearance of calm grace. As she closed the door softly behind her, her fists balled by her sides and her nails bit into her palms. Tears welled in her eyes and she wiped her hand hastily across them.

Looking up she saw Vikram quietly watching her. She said softly, bitterly, 'May the gods forgive us … we had a chance … yet we saved him. What have we done?'

—ᴍ—

Hamza saw Isaura leave and said to Karan, 'He's a good little horse. I can see why you put her on him. There's no real dirt in him, but he's a right little shit sometimes. She's got whacking great purple bruises from him.'

'It's his only quirk. He doesn't buck, bolt or kick. I thought he'd teach her.'

'Has he?'

'Slowly. He hasn't bitten her in days.'

The closer Isaura got to Toshi, the more the mule fidgeted in the stall.

'I'll get the gear.' Hamza returned with the saddle blanket and surcingle. The mule pushed against the door of the stall, snorting and pounding the floor with his front hoof.

Karan held out his hand. 'Whoa, there now, ssh,' he soothed. The mule subsided.

Hamza looked at the mule dubiously. 'I'm not sure this about this.'

'He's calm now. Once he sees Isa again he'll be fine.' Karan opened the stall door for Hamza. The mule charged forward, knocking the two men into the dirt.

He raced straight for Isaura and Toshi. Toshi shot backwards on his tether, broke it and took off at a gallop, desperate to flee the enraged mule. Isaura stood with her hand to her forehead in disbelief as her guardian chased the little horse. She tried to merge with him, yet hit a wall of rage and hate that blocked her.

Karan and Hamza ran to the nearest horses, mounted and pursued the rogue mule. They didn't have to go far. Jaws open, the mule snapped at Toshi's rump and a streak of red flowed down his rear. Toshi stumbled. The mule lunged, seizing him by the crest of his neck and tossing him like a rag doll, tearing a massive hole through the top of his neck.

Karan and Hamza reached the two and managed to lasso the mule. He spun away from Toshi, kicking out at him and connecting with his cannon bone. Toshi screamed.

Bile rose in Isaura's throat at the carnage the mule wrecked. Toshi, a bleeding mess, stumbled and limped away. She ran toward them, her leg straining with each step. Isaura fought to merge with the mule using her own anger at Toshi's fate and her fear that her guardian would be hurt to break through the barrier between them. *Stop! Why are you doing this? Stop now!* Isaura plunged into his world. He flashed visions, interwoven with her own anxieties, of all her trials with the little horse. The fear that she would not be riding him enraged the mule. Dominating everything was his desire to protect her. His focus was now on the men with the ropes. The men were now the enemy.

Isaura reached them. 'Stop!' She stood between the riders and her guardian. Her hands reached out, halting them both.

You didn't need to attack Toshi. I don't like him, but he didn't deserve this. He's not an enemy. She walked toward the mule, her hand rubbed his face. He lowered his head until their foreheads met. *All will be well. They won't harm either of us. They just want you to stop hurting the little horse.*

'Loosen the ropes,' Isaura ordered Hamza and Karan. They did not. 'Karan, please. I have him, but he won't tolerate the ropes much longer.' All the while her hand still stroked the mule's forehead.

Brusquely, Karan nodded to Hamza; they both released their ropes and Isaura gently removed them from the mule's neck.

'There now, see? It's gone.' Isaura channelled the Undavi; her words sent calming waves undulating through the air.

Hamza and Karan dismounted and went to Toshi.

Isaura rested her head against her guardian's, unable to look toward the little horse.

Umniga touched her shoulder, giving it a squeeze. 'Well done, child. Well done.'

Isaura lifted her head, giving her a faint smile and noticed a small crowd had gathered, staring from a safe distance.

'Take him back to the barn for the moment, put him in a stall,' Umniga said quietly.

With her hand on his neck they proceeded back to the barn. His tension hummed through Isaura; the sight of the small crowd inflamed his distrust and she gritted her teeth as she struggled to pacify him.

The crowd parted widely. On the edge of the crowd to her left stood Elena, with Pio beside her. Distraught, Pio kept looking between the mule and the figures of Karan and Hamza bent over Toshi in the distance.

I'm sorry, Pio.

As they passed, Elena sneered and whispered to Curro, shaking her head. The mule pivoted and lunged at Elena. Isaura fought to control him. She gasped as a heady rush of power flooded her body and her mind filled with his rage. *We could squash her.* Elena pulled Pio in front of herself. *No!* Isaura seized total control as the mule reached over Pio to grab Elena. He stopped, snorted, stepped back and lowered his head in front of the boy.

Beads of sweat trickled down Isaura's brow. *This is not the way, but …*

Curro moved in front of Elena. Nicanor leapt forward and pried Elena's terrified fingers from Pio's shoulders, scooping him up and taking him to safety.

Isaura raked her gaze across her friends. Their harsh intake of breath at seeing her changed eyes brought a cold smile of satisfaction to her face. She glared at Curro. 'Move aside.' He paled. She canted her head at him, sizing him up. 'Move, now!'

Curro stepped involuntarily, haltingly, away from his wife—his disgust and fear plain. The rest of the group had moved back.

Elena darted away. The mule flanked her. Ears back, teeth bared, he snaked his head at her. She backed away and tripped over Isaura's outstretched foot. Elena lay sprawled in the dirt, with Isaura's boot planted firmly on her torso. Isaura stepped back, smiling as a hoof came to rest upon Elena's chest. *Don't kill her.* The command was ironclad.

'Elena.' Isaura's voice was saccharine steel. 'Elena, meet my guardian. Remember this moment, you malevolent, jealous shrew. The only thing standing between you and death is me. He wants to pound your head into the dirt and it's very tempting to let him. It's not the first time I've saved you …' she looked at the rest of her friends, '… or any of you. I think it's about time you remember that.'

Karan and Hamza approached Isaura. Her eyes darted to the prone body of Toshi. She took a deep breath to still the shaking that threatened to overcome her.

'Brownie?' Hamza shook his head in disbelief.

'Brownie is dead. This is Alejo.' Isaura's voice rang sharp and clear. 'His name means "the protector". Remember it.' She smiled at Elena still pinned under Alejo's hoof. 'And if ever you try to use Pio as a shield again, we will rip you apart.'

Chapter Eighteen

KARAN AND HAMZA walked on one side of Isaura and Alejo walked on the other.

'How long can you maintain control?' Karan asked.

'Not much further,' Isaura ground out.

'We'll get him in the stall again,' Hamza said hurriedly.

Isaura, tight lipped, nodded. Alejo was angry and confused; she was trying to reason with him. 'Toshi is dead?'

'Yes,' came Karan's curt reply.

Isaura swallowed and her jaw tightened as she felt Alejo's jubilation. *That was a bad thing. You could have just given him a scare or a warning bite. Karan might not want us now.*

'He would not have survived the injuries,' Hamza said quietly. 'The neck wound was bad enough, but Alejo broke his leg. Karan put him out of his misery.'

'I'm sorry.' Isaura kept her eyes on the barn, grateful that they were nearly there.

Alejo walked reluctantly into the stall and Hamza shut him in. Sighing, Isaura relinquished control of his mind and sagged against the stall door. Alejo shook his head defiantly and belted the wall behind him, cracking the timbers. The Matriarch emerged cautiously from the shadows.

'I could've done with your help earlier, Old Mother,' Isaura said aloud for Hamza and Karan's benefit—she was tired of secrets.

I've done all I can to help you with him, and it was little enough. The rest is up to you two to work out.

'You think he'd target you for interfering?'

I have no doubt. He is potentially as powerful as we are. Together you will be more powerful.

Isaura stood slack jawed. 'How do I fix this?' *He is so angry.*

Indeed, but how did you feel after my gift, when you returned from The Wild?

Strong, angry. I wanted to fight with little excuse.

Exactly. All living things have a connection to The Wild, guardians more so; my clan even more. You were correct when you said that part of it now resides within you. Thanks to the Horse Lord you've begun to control its rage. Your guardian is like no other. He's damaged and he is as strongly connected to The Wild as you and I. He has embraced it, like you, and it helps fuel his anger. Alejo sees everyone as a threat. Even your bond confused and terrified him. Now, he sees you as needing his protection. Isa-cub, Alejo will continue to kill without the slightest hesitation if he thinks you are threatened, unless you teach him control. If not, you must control him.

'I don't want to constantly control him, it's wrong.'

Then you must teach him.

'By the gods!' Hamza whispered as he listened to this one-sided conversation.

Karan pinched the bridge of his nose. 'Hamza, not a word of this to anyone yet.'

Hamza nodded and closed his gaping mouth.

Isa-cub, you will not see us again until Alejo is more stable. I won't risk my kin.

Isaura sucked in a harsh breath. 'But I will see you again?' she begged.

Foolish child, of course. Relieved, Isaura knelt and threw her arms around the Matriarch's neck. The Matriarch licked her face as she pulled away from her.

Karan placed his hand upon Isaura's shoulder. She remained kneeling, watching the Matriarch leave. He held out his hand, helping her to her feet. 'Don't worry, Isa, they didn't help save you only to abandon you.' Softly, he added, 'Nor did I.' Isaura spun, wrapping her arms around him and burying her head against his chest. Hesitantly, Karan embraced her.

Hamza looked away, cleared his throat and murmured, 'I think I'll just go and ... um ... find something to do ... somewhere ... else.'

'Tell the others to leave for the lake. Isa and I will follow later and meet them there,' Karan said.

'I'm sorry,' Isaura mumbled into his chest. *Gods! I've latched onto him like some lovestruck idiot.* She stiffened, released her grip and tried to step out of his embrace. Karan interlocked his fingers behind her back, refusing to release her. 'I'm not usually so damn emotional.'

'Some of it is due to the bonding process. It will settle.'

'Some of it?'

'You've had a harder time than anyone ... ever!' He chuckled.

Isaura thumped her fist on his chest lightly, but relaxed into his arms again. 'Easy for you to laugh, I doubt you've a guardian whose grand plan in life is murder.' Finally she looked up at him. 'I'm sorry about Toshi. I'd no idea Alejo would do that. I didn't know what to do.'

'In the end what you did was amazing. I cannot seize control of my guardian like you did. I don't know of anyone ever doing such a thing. Thank the gods you did though. None of us like Elena, but if he'd attacked and killed her, you'd find it impossible to get a training partner. As it stands they know you can control him. That will add to your reputation, not lessen it.'

'That's something I suppose.'

'And you sat that sour woman back in her box.'

Startled, Isaura laughed then put her hand over her mouth to silence herself. She blurted out, 'It felt so good. I've been wanting to do that for so long.'

Karan's eyes never left hers. *Let her go, man. It's merely the damn bond.*

Isaura bit her lip anxiously and needed to shatter the growing silence. 'We're not going with the others?'

His arms dropped from around her. 'We'll go alone. I'll work with you both. Help you both.' Slowly, as if fearing to be burnt, Karan put his hand upon her cheek.

Isaura waited, breathless—impatient. *He can come to me.*

Karan's finger traced her jawline, then the edge of her lips. *It's not real –it's the bond.* His hand fell and he stepped away from her.

Alejo snorted and sprayed him with slobber. Isaura burst into laughter.

Karan wiped his face and glared at the recalcitrant mule. 'Now, I've some ideas, but tell me what the old mother said, and we'll work out what in Karak we're going to do with this overprotective monster.'

—⚒—

Ratilal sat in his robe before his private dining table poring over maps with Niaz by his side. 'I don't want word getting out that we've crossed the river too early. This area has few inhabitants so a team landing here stands a better chance of moving undetected and finding the strangers.'

'How many teams are you thinking of sending?' Niaz asked.

'Four, I think. Spread out here and here. And,' he said with glee, 'another team landing ...' His finger swirled above the map theatrically before he stabbed it down. 'Here!'

Niaz gasped. 'Really?'

Grinning, Ratilal clapped him on the back. 'You'll lead.' Niaz paled. 'This entire operation relies on stealth, perfect timing and Karan's own spies. All their attention will be directed at our training camps.'

'What's to stop them crossing the Falcontine and hitting us early?'

'Men, supply and winter. He'll still be getting troops and supply. He'll assume the ground is too swampy and we can call on men more rapidly than him. Even if Karan crossed, his supply routes will be longer than ours. If he hasn't got what he needs from Targmur before the pass ices up, then he's not getting it until the thaw. We do this and the psychological benefits will be a huge boost for us and utterly demoralising for them.'

A light knock sounded upon the door to Ratilal's rooms. Niaz rolled up the maps and Ratilal moved to a chair by the fire. 'Enter.'

Malak held open the door for Chatelaine Gita, who carried in a large tray of food and placed it upon the table. She bowed, but before she could exit Ratilal stopped her.

'Chatelaine, how are the newcomers faring?'

Gita sniffed in disgust. 'High Lord, we are slowly overcoming their ignorance; they are learning to be useful.'

Malak scowled at her statement.

'Very good, Chatelaine, you are dismissed.' With a twisted smile he watched her leave. 'Why the scowl, Lady Malak? Surely it's not the prospect of being near me again?'

Malak did not bow. She stalked to his chair and dumped her medical bag on the floor beside it. 'I need to check your wounds, High Lord,' she said curtly.

Ratilal's hands gripped the arms of his chair tightly. 'Answer the question, Lady Malak. I will not tolerate your insolence.'

Malak ground her teeth. 'The good Chatelaine has no clue as to how the newcomers are doing. She has too much to do to adequately supervise them … and their treatment.'

Ratilal sat up straighter. 'Their treatment?'

'Your servants treat them like dogs. They make them sleep upon the floor. They eat only when the others are done and only what is left over. They don't try to teach them the language, then have no patience when they don't understand and strike them for it. They fear them usurping their positions here.'

'This is not the high lord's concern, Mother,' Niaz said.

'It is. Even if it seems insolent to say it, but it absolutely is his concern.' Ratilal remained silent—stony faced. 'High Lord, you do see the problems this could create, don't you?'

'Mother!'

Irritated, Ratilal flicked his hand dismissively at his friend. 'Lady Malak is correct. Niaz, I said I would fulfil my father's promise to these people, to re-home them and integrate them. I need to be seen to be honouring his wishes and in doing so I'll win the total loyalty of these newcomers. That's the point—the entire point. Clearly that can't be done through working in the citadel.' Ratilal shook his head. 'I expected more of Gita …'

'High Lord, it's not her fault. The wounded are taking so much of her time,' Malak said.

Ratilal's fist thumped the chair. He grabbed a goblet of wine from the small table next to him and hurled it against the fireplace. Leaping up, he took a step toward Malak, his finger pointing accusingly at her. 'I don't need reminding about the wounded, old woman. Not from you who never had the courage to fight.'

Niaz moved forward, grabbing his mother's arm and pulling her away. Ratilal's eyes flashed to him.

'High Lord, I did not mean to upset you. I know … I did not mean to anger you,' Malak said, bowing.

Ratilal's harsh breath was the only sound in the room. It hung over her head like an axe.

'Rise, Lady Malak,' Ratilal ground out. 'I feel certain you have a plan in mind to remedy this situation, yes?'

Malak hesitated and swallowed nervously. 'Leave the newcomers in my charge. I'll ensure they are educated. I'll find homes and employment for them.' Niaz stared at her dumbfounded. 'I'll also make sure that they know you have taken a personal interest in their welfare and that it is to you they owe their thanks.'

'Naturally, you will.' Arms crossed, he stared at her. *What in Karak has gotten into her?* 'Why?'

'I … feel sorry for them.'

Ratilal laughed. Niaz gaped.

'Lady Malak,' Ratilal said, smirking. 'I'm astonished, truly I am.'

'Why would you feel sympathy for these people?' her son demanded. 'Or is it that the red-head has taken your fancy?'

'How dare you!' Malak drew back her hand to strike him. Niaz stiffened for the blow. Ratilal watched in anticipation with gleaming eyes. Instead, she hastily lowered her hand and gripped the fabric of her skirt as if she would tear a hole in it. Her voice was quiet. 'How dare you.' She shook her head in sorrow. 'Yes, I feel sympathy for them, but more than that ... it is nice to be needed ... to be useful again.'

Isaura rode Alejo bareback around the large corral behind Hamza's barn.

Hamza worked on a makeshift saddle for her. 'You say her riding's improved?' he asked Karan.

'Yes.'

'Really?'

'Yes.' Karan sighed.

'When are you heading out?' Hamza asked

'Tomorrow. She needs more time and I'm waiting ...'

Alejo's long ears flicked forward and he trotted to the fence.

Karan smiled and turned toward the barn. 'But the wait is over.' Out of the shadows of the barn trotted a black horse with a long mane and tail, wearing a beautiful saddle. The dirty, sweaty animal walked forward and nudged Karan with his nose, demanding a pat.

Karan and the horse approached the corral. Alejo flattened his ears back at the sight of the horse.

'Behave!' Isaura scolded.

Karan stopped several feet from the fence, staring at Alejo warily. 'Isaura, Alejo, meet my guardian—Mirza.'

Mirza walked up to the railing. The two animals tentatively reached out and sniffed each other.

'Isa,' Karan warned as the muscles on Alejo's neck tensed.

Isaura was concentrating on the pair; a rueful grin split her face and she laughed. The stallion and the mule shook their heads simultaneously.

'Are you going to tell me what is so funny?'

Isaura shook her head. 'It doesn't matter. We've reached an understanding. You've nothing to worry about—Alejo won't hurt him.'

Karan narrowed his eyes at her smug remark.

'Looks like he's had long trek,' Hamza said.

'He's come from the Four Ways and the battle there.'

Stunned, Hamza said, 'But that's so far …'

'Battle?' Isaura asked.

'Lord Baldev, leader of the Bear Clan, was victorious at the Four Ways bridge. He burnt down the enemy's fort and the bridge. There are only a few places Ratilal can strike us now and that will most likely be after the winter,' Karan said as he began to unsaddle Mirza.

Isaura went back to practising her riding. She bounced and slid sideways a little.

Hamza shook his head. 'She's trying so damn hard … If she just relaxed she'd do a whole lot better.'

Karan's lips pursed. 'I've been trying to get her to relax her seat for days,' he hissed.

'It's not just her bloody seat that needs to relax,' Hamza whispered fiercely. 'The poor girl's been through the wars herself. She's had a hard time growing up. They've run from one army, she's nearly died at sea, nearly died on land, woken up in a foreign place with new powers, had her head messed with by the Asena, been given a guardian who distrusts everyone and would kill without hesitation, and has a heart bond to you,' he snorted, 'and you've virtually rejected her.' Karan opened his mouth to object, but Hamza cut him off. 'Now she's having to train to fight in another war. For the love of all that's holy, let the girl have some fun.'

'I see you've had a long talk,' Karan said stiffly.

'Don't get jealous, man. I'm old enough to be her father. I wish to the gods she was my daughter.'

'I'm not jealous.' Hamza laughed as Karan's gaze flicked to Isaura again. 'Fun?'

Hamza sighed. 'Mirza needs a good wash. Take them to the lake and go for swim. The water won't be too cold yet and the sun's out. Go on, go. I'll figure out how in Karak I'm going to rig this up for Isa to ride on.'

Chapter Nineteen

VIKRAM ENTERED RATILAL'S chambers and bowed deeply. 'High Lord, you summoned me?'

'Ah, Vikram. Good.' Ratilal sat on the edge of the table, obscuring Vikram's view of the maps rolled out there. 'Report.'

I need to see those maps. What are they planning? 'Māhir's men are making rapid progress on the repairs. Paksis is on the training field. Zimma awaits your judgement.'

'His sister, Niara?'

'There's no sign of his sister. She disappeared from Pramrod's brothel the day of the ... attack. We've not been able to find her.'

Ratilal's face soured. 'Damn it, but what's one whore more or less? Captain Vikram, you've proved yourself an able administrator for Faros under the rule of my father, and in the last few weeks have proved loyal to me. Now I am well I will be out in the field much of my time. I need you to continue your good work here and I hope you continue to impress me.'

'High Lord, I would follow you ...'

Ratilal held up his hand. 'You're needed here, Captain. There is much more to be done to see to the defence and running of Faros. Don't look so disappointed ... I am making you Pasha of Faros. You will govern it while I am away.'

Vikram gaped and stared in wonder at Ratilal.

'Well, Captain, have you nothing to say?'

'I'm stunned. Thank you, High Lord.'

'You may go. Take this.' Ratilal handed Vikram a scroll. 'It's my order making you Pasha in my absence.' Vikram turned to leave. 'Captain, end the problem of Zimma.'

Of course, kill the man who had the guts to stand up to you for hurting his sister. Vikram schooled his features. *At least you won't get the girl.*

Downstairs in the Great Hall, Vikram spied Nada and Deo working amongst the wounded. He made his way to them. 'I have work for you two. Come with me.'

Once in his office in the watch house, he closed the door. 'The others from Parlan are still here?'

Deo shook his head. 'They left straight away. I didn't dare go after being told I had to fight. I mean, I'm clearly elite troop material,' Deo spat.

'And I'm not leaving him.'

'Well you're both going now. Get your wagon ready. I'll re-supply you with what I can to replace what was used in the celebration feast in Parlan as Shahjahan promised. On the way to Parlan, stop by Widow Marwa's. There's a girl there, Niara. She's in bad shape thanks to Ratilal …'

Nada snarled. 'What did he do?'

'She tried to defend one of Pramod's girls against him. The other girl, Sora, fled. No one's seen her since. Just go to Marwa's, get the girl, take her to Parlan, and keep her hidden and safe.'

'What about Ratilal?'

'He's just made me Pasha of Faros while he's away.' Their eyes widened. 'With luck he's forgotten about you. If he hasn't I'll tell him I'm using you here at the citadel, because you'd be a liability in the field.'

Deo puffed himself up to argue. Vikram narrowed his eyes at him. 'Keep your head down and your mouth shut. You just might get home and get to stay there.'

Vikram hurried to find Māhir, who was waiting for him at the southern gate of Faros, so he could approve the repairs undertaken there.

'You've done well here. How are the rest of the guild reacting to your being made Head?'

'A few are disgruntled, but the reality is I've the next biggest workshop and would have got it anyway if something happened to Paksis.'

'Thank the gods he's an arrogant fool then and you're in the position. Has your other work increased?'

'Yes, it seems I'm in favour in higher quarters now, circulating amongst the quality of Faros. My wife wants new dresses. New dresses for the love of the gods! At a time like this!'

'Let her have her fun, Māhir. You've got to mingle, make friends … You'll probably hear some rumours about the high lord in your travels. It'd be a terrible shame if you were to spread them in the right places.'

Māhir laughed loudly. 'Oh, I know where gossip's welcome.'

'Just don't get caught.'

Isaura looked from Karan to the water and back again. 'Swimming?'

'Yes.'

'On Alejo … in the water?'

'Of course.'

Alejo tossed his head and proceeded to walk into the lake. 'Wait! Stop! I'm not getting my new clothes soaked.' Isaura slid from him onto the pebbled shore. She pulled off her boots and their fur liners.

'I haven't been swimming in an age!' she said excitedly. Head bowed, Isaura untied her outer top and hastily shucked it off. She had a quilted vest on underneath it. Isaura's fingers fumbled with the laces, before she tossed it onto the pile. 'This should be fun.'

How many layers of clothes does she have on? Karan wondered. His eyes remained riveted on her hands as she undid the sash at her waist. Still astride Mirza, he watched as she disrobed without any consideration to modesty. Karan's breath caught as her hands deftly undid the drawstring on her pants.

'Do you think it'll be too cold?' Isaura slowly teased the loose pants lower. As the fabric slid down, the blue silk shirt she wore flowed like water, caressing and hiding the glimpse of her hips and thighs. With a delicate kick she tossed aside her pants.

Isaura's gaze rose to meet his with a wry grin. 'Finished looking?'

'Tease,' Karan muttered as she turned her back to him and walked into the water.

'Come on.' The stones were smooth under Isaura's feet as she waded deeper into the lake and the chill of the water brought her out in goose bumps. Waist deep, she sank beneath the water then stood. The silk shirt clung to her form.

Karan's hands clenched on Mirza's reins.

Looking back over her shoulder, Isaura said, 'You know it's only teasing if you're interested. And you're not, are you?'

With strong sure strokes she dived under the water and surfaced further out. Isaura called back, 'Alejo, come on! You could use a bath!'

—∞—

Jaw clenched, Karan watched Isaura swim away. He slid from Mirza's back and stripped. Boots, quilted jerkin and silk shirt landed in a pile on the stony shore. Bare chested, Karan stood with his hands on the waist of his pants. A grin stole its way across his face. *Two can play at that game.* He glanced back to where Isaura was swimming and paused.

She didn't take her top off. Maybe she's not as confident as she makes out. He wanted to give her a taste of her own medicine. He wavered. *Damn it.*

Isaura laughed at Alejo, who stood knee deep in the lake, pounding the surface, splashing water over his belly, head and back. 'Swim, you big baby!'

She merged with Alejo to get a closer look at Karan. Several long, pale scars stood out on the dark olive skin of his chest.

Karan's muscles rippled when he moved, mesmerising her. *Nothing to complain about there ... Soap! He's got soap! Blast, I'd love to wash my hair.*

Karan's gaze slide to Alejo, who had stopped splashing and was staring intently at him. Laughing, Karan discarded his pants and waded into the water.

Disgruntled, Isaura swam away, flipped on her back and floated. She kept her connection with Alejo and continued to observe Karan. *This was meant to tease him and all I'm doing is tormenting myself.*

Karan could still sense Alejo's eyes upon him. The mule was splashing water everywhere, but had turned to face him. He finished bathing, dunked himself under the water and stood, rinsing himself off. Looking at Alejo, he said, 'Seen enough, Isa?'

Isaura spluttered in shock and briefly sank below the water, before swimming quickly further out.

Karan resisted the urge to join her. Mirza entered the lake and tried to shepherd him in her direction. 'No!' Karan waded back to shore. 'I'm not going to be dictated to by a bond I never wanted and an interfering guardian.' Karan stomped to his clothes. Seeing them, he groaned. 'They're soaked!' Mirza emerged from the lake, stood by his side and shook himself like a dog, showering him with more water, before wandering off to graze.

The muscles in Isaura's injured leg coiled. *I've got to head back,* she thought. *I didn't realise I'd come so far. Easy.* She paused, treading water gently. The tension lessened. *Right, keep going. No!* Pain seared through her leg. Isaura flipped herself on her back and slowly backstroked her way to shore, aware that Alejo was ploughing his way through the water to get to her.

Karan concentrated on his bond with Isaura, trying to feel it, to sense if all was well with her. Their connection was drastically muted, he panicked when he struggled to find it. *When did that happen? Is it just distance?* Before Karan realised it, he'd returned to the water. *By all that's holy, why can't I feel her?*

Alejo had reached Isaura and she was clinging to his mane as he towed her back. She limped to the shore.

Karan was terse. 'How bad is it?'

Ruefully she said, 'I'm fine, don't worry. Swimming made it work a little, that's all. It'll be better for it in the long run.'

'I can't sense the bond anymore,' he confessed.

Surprised, she hesitated before saying, 'Well, that should please you. You never wanted it in the first place. I've never been able to feel it anyway. I think you worry about it too much. Yes, I'm attracted to you. I trusted you easily, but I haven't been able to sense how you are feeling physically.' *I'd have to be blind to not see that.* She gulped, remembering he had removed his pants. It took all her will power not to lower her gaze. *Don't look down, Isa! Don't give him the satisfaction!* 'But I'm no more drawn to you than I'd be to any other man I found attractive. Nothing more, nothing less,' she lied. *Don't look down!* Karan's jaw clenched; a vein pulsed in his forehead. Isaura continued on blithely, 'Perhaps the bond thing has nothing to do with us. Perhaps it's simply there so Alejo will trust you and you can train us.'

'Firstly, I am not worried,' he barked. 'Secondly, yes you've got training ahead of you. The sooner you become an asset instead of a liability the better.'

Isaura gaped, staring at him for a few seconds before she marched the remaining distance to him and poked him in the chest. 'My training will go superbly.' Her eyes narrowed. 'I will be the perfect weapon for you.'

They stood toe to toe. Karan's breath fanned her face. His hands were fisted at his sides. He ground his teeth, spun on his heel, grabbed his clothes and stalked back to the house.

'Leave the soap!'

He threw it over his shoulder. It landed on the pebbles at her feet.

She picked up the soap, brushed the sand off and watched his departing back. 'This really should have gone so much better.'

A lake, a naked, gorgeous man … soap … It should have been totally different.'

—⚋—

Hamza sat on a stool outside the barn, stitching layers of thick fabric together in the afternoon sunlight. He glanced up briefly as Karan approached. 'Good swim?'

Karan grunted. 'How's it coming along?'

'Cobbling together well enough. Really it'll just be a glorified saddle pad, but it should do,' Hamza replied.

Karan stalked into the tack room returning with his bridle, saddle and a rag and a clay jar. He hung his gear over a hitching rail opposite Hamza and began furiously rubbing a mixture of fat and beeswax into the saddle.

'You'll wear a hole in that leather if you keep going like that. What's rattled your gourd?' Hamza said.

'*Our girl*,' Karan ground out.

'Ah,' Hamza replied knowingly.

'What does that mean?'

'Nothing, nothing … Some of us fall harder than others, that's all,' Hamza said.

'I have not fallen for her,' Karan snapped.

'No?'

'No.'

'So what's the problem?' Hamza asked.

'She's re-injured her leg while swimming.'

Hamza dropped his work to the ground and glared at Karan. 'Where is she? Why didn't you stop her overdoing it?'

'I've a feeling you don't stop her doing anything. If I'd realised I would have tried to persuade her to return …'

Hamza's eyebrows shot up.

Karan stopped working and paced. 'I wasn't swimming with her. I couldn't tell through our bond … it's not working … or it's gone.'

Hamza resisted the urge to laugh. He'd known Karan since he was a boy and he'd never seen him so unsettled. 'And that bothers you?'

Karan stopped walking, leaned against the barn wall and ran a hand through his hair. 'Yes,' he said in defeat.

'You never wanted it though.'

'No. I thought Umniga had caused it.'

'Daft, man. There's no earthly power that can cause that …'

'I won't be manipulated into falling in love … even by the gods.'

'That's even dafter. I don't believe any power can make two people love each other.' *And if you believe me then you're mad*, Hamza thought. 'What does Isa think?'

Karan pushed himself off the wall and began pacing again. He shook his head, before confessing, 'She thinks I'm worth a quick tumble, but that's it.'

Merriment danced in Hamza's eyes and laughter erupted from his lips.

'Damn it! I'm going for a walk,' Karan said, storming off into the woods.

Still grinning, Hamza watched him walk away. 'Oh, my friend,' he murmured. 'You're doomed.'

chapter twenty

MALAK STOOD BEFORE Vikram's desk in his office in the watch house. 'So you see,' she finished, 'I've come asking for your help.'

Vikram's brows rose and for several moments he could think of nothing to say to her. Malak put her hands behind her back and gazed around the austere room, waiting. A single chair behind a plain wooden desk, a bench seat against one wall, and a cupboard with a collection of scrolls were all that occupied the room. The room revealed nothing of the man. Malak tapped her foot and cleared her throat, prompting Vikram to speak.

'I'd heard that you wanted to help these people, but frankly Mistress Malak, I'm surprised,' Vikram said.

Malak's expression soured. 'I was concerned for the red-head, Daniel. He's alone and his looks make him a target. The rest were just part of a package deal, but now that I've got them I have to find places for them.'

'You need my help?'

Malak nodded. 'Now that you're Pasha, I don't have to ask Ratilal. I've an idea for what to do with Daniel, but the others …' She shrugged her shoulders.

'Have you talked to Chatelaine Gita?'

'Yes, the baker and one or two others have proved worthwhile and Gita says she'll keep them. They appear to want to stay.'

'What are the others?'

'One seems to have been a shopkeeper, the others merely farmers.'

'Do they speak Altaican yet?'

'They're learning rapidly,' Malak said. 'They have to, if they don't want to get a clip around the ear from all and sundry every time they're slow or misunderstand.' Vikram laughed, but Malak was furious. 'What's so funny, Captain?'

He held up his hands placatingly, though failed to wipe the amused grin from his face. 'I've lost count of the number of times I've seen you clip a servant around the ear. Your temper,' he looked pointedly at her, 'is legendary.'

Malak folded her arms across her chest. 'I think I'm getting soft in my old age!' she complained.

'This does you credit, Mistress Malak,' Vikram said. 'Particularly when those around you would do nothing. I'll see if I can find places needing labourers or servants. I know of two farms run by elderly couples with no children who could probably do with help. I'll look into it.' He paused. 'What are you planning for the red-head? I ask only so I can set the gossips straight.'

'I'm going into business with him,' Malak said proudly.

—⚞—

Pio's eyes lit up as he looked upon the campsite. It lay nestled below them in a large clearing near a lake, at the base of a forested mountain range.

'This is Bear Tooth Lake,' Sarala told him. 'Those are the Bear Tooth Mountains.'

Rapt, grinning at the sight before him, Pio could only nod. Smoke from small campfires wafted up into the air. Tents and yurts of varying sizes dotted the field. Two large round yurts sat near the trees. A black and a brown pennant flew from each. Warriors were training; the clash of weapons drifted to them. Archers practised shooting into butts resting against earthen mounds. Mounted warriors galloped and slashed at suspended swinging targets. Other riders appeared to be playing some sort of game. They galloped along, competing at spearing tiny timber targets on the ground.

'Ma, Pa, do you see? Do you see what they're doing?' Nicanor and Lucia smiled tiredly at him. 'This is going to be so much fun!' His attention snapped to Sarala. 'When do I get to do all that?'

'You can start training today. But first you must care for your horse. Give him a rest before you try charging about tent pegging.' Pio's smile vanished. 'Don't worry, I can think of plenty to keep you busy.'

They approached the camp and Baldev came to meet them. 'I told you someone was coming!' Kiriz's strident cry carried through the air as she ran to catch up with him. 'Can you slow down? I want to be with you when you say hello.'

'We'll wait here then, Little General.'

Baldev scanned the riders, desperately seeking Asha. *Thank the gods, she's safe.* Yet Karan was not amongst them. *Just wait, all may yet be well.*

'They look funny,' Kiriz said to Baldev. Eyeing the strangers uncertainly, she slipped her hand into Baldev's.

He squeezed her hand. 'Ssh.'

'But they do!' she whispered before subsiding.

Asha saw Baldev's face light up upon seeing her. *He hasn't changed his mind.* Emboldened, she said cheekily, 'Baldev, is there something you need to tell me?'

'No.'

'Then who is this lovely young woman beside you … holding your hand?' Asha added ominously.

Kiriz's eyes rounded. 'Asha, it's me! Kiriz. You know who I am.'

Umniga chuckled. 'Oh, Asha, I wouldn't believe that if I were you. Kiriz is just a baby, not like this one.'

'Baby! I am not a baby. It's me! Lord Baldev, tell them.'

Asha slid from Honey's back and bent down, peering closely at Kiriz. Her hand entwined with Baldev's as she did. 'Uminga, I think it might be Kiriz … Yes, it is.'

'I told you!'

Asha pulled Baldev's head to her and kissed him soundly upon the lips. 'Just a reminder.'

Baldev let go of Kiriz's hand and embraced Asha. 'I don't need reminding. But I'm so glad you're safe.' He released her from his embrace, but kept holding her hand. 'Where's Karan?'

'There's a lot to report,' Asha said. 'Lord Karan is a day or so behind us with Isaura. She has recovered and been sent her guardian. He is …'

'Crazy as a loon,' Āsim added quietly from behind them.

Asha blanched. 'He is … protective—very protective. Lord Karan hopes to help her with controlling him.'

Baldev gestured to his second, who stood nearby. 'Take them to their tents as we discussed. Come, Asha, I'd like a full report.'

Kiriz went to follow Baldev, but Umniga snagged her hand in hers. 'Child, you've grown like a mushroom. Let Asha and Baldev talk. I want you to tell me all about how you wound up here.'

'I'm Lord Baldev's adviser. I help with the wounded and I know everything that goes on,' Kiriz said proudly.

Umniga nodded. 'Well then I think you'll be the perfect person to help Pio.'

Tugging on her hand, Kiriz made Umniga bend down so that she could whisper, 'Is that the boy who doesn't know anything?'

She looked at Kiriz sternly. 'He knows things, plenty of things— just not about us.'

'I'll fix that.'

—⚭—

Daniel followed Malak through the streets of Faros. She had collected him that morning insisting he come with her. Life at the citadel had been easier since she had taken over the welfare of the refugees. The servants were frightened of her and immediately treated them better. Malak took the time to teach him the language and he, in turn, taught the others. Her bright eyes and the bounce in her stride that morning conveyed her excitement.

At the end of a street near the outer walls they stopped before an old shop. 'This store is owned by an old friend. He has no family. I've known him for years. He's one of the few weavers who specialises in our traditional patterns. In the past his workshop wove rugs and beautiful wall hangings. You've seen some of his work on the walls of my home. His business used to thrive.' Malak looked momentarily melancholy.

'Used to?'

She nodded, drew a deep breath and said, 'We're going to change that.' Daniel frowned. 'I own this workshop now. He still lives here and works here, but now you'll be working with him. You can both share your skills and he can teach you our traditional patterns. Neither of us wants his knowledge to vanish with his passing. This clan has already lost so much.'

'I'll be using my trade again.' A sigh escaped him. 'Thank you.'

'Don't thank me yet, young man. There's a great deal of work ahead of you. I said this shop *used* to thrive. The demand for traditional works has all but disappeared. I don't just want you to learn his ways. I want you to put your own unique stamp on the work here. We'll diversify and produce fabric for clothing too. I'm about to purchase the tailor's next door.'

'I don't want to disappoint you, but who'll want to buy it? You've seen the way they look at me.'

'I'll pray to Rana and Jalal that they will. I've much influence here … and I now also own the seamstress's shop two doors down. Fabric you make will be used there.' Malak linked her arm through his. 'I think we could save a piece of our history, yet provide something new and make money for ourselves. Besides, Vikram has given me names of suppliers in the outer city who may be most helpful. They're tired of being fleeced by the merchants here, so played correctly we should do well. Never fear, Daniel, we shall prevail. Like the rest of my clan, there's nothing I enjoy better than trade.'

Elena lay on the bedroll in their tent. After days of riding they'd finally arrived and she wanted nothing more than to ease her aching bones and to sleep. She listened to the noises from across the camp. Pio stood outside with Lucia and Nicanor, asking to explore with the girl, Kiriz. *How he even understands their babble is beyond me.* She closed her eyes tightly, her hand covered her mouth as she let out a soft sob. *There's no privacy. Everything is strange.* She listened to Curro laugh as he approached the tent and hastily composed herself. *At least Isaura isn't here. Hopefully they'll keep her somewhere else.*

Curro shoved his head through the tent flap. 'Come on, Leni. There's more to be done,' he said.

'We just got here.' She grabbed Curro's proffered hand with a wan smile.

They approached Āsim and Umniga, where the rest of the group had gathered. Umniga summoned Lucia forward and gave her a stave. She moved Lucia's hands to the rear third of the stave and adjusted her stance so that she stood, balanced, with the stave facing forward. Umniga made slow simple movements with her own stave—thrusting it forward, changing sides and alternating her hand position and stance.

'Follow, Lucia,' she ordered. Lucia nodded and worked her way through the movements.

Umniga and Āsim summoned each of them in turn, showing them the same movements. Elena was last. Reluctantly, Elena took the stave from Āsim, her hands holding it loosely before her. He moved her hands into a better grip position and raised her arms to hold the staff at the ready. Elena looked along the line at the others and began the drill.

The staff grew heavier for Elena with each passing moment. She stopped to wipe sweat from her brow and rubbed her hands upon her clothes. Leaning on her staff, Elena paused to watch the others. They were all tired. *Enough, I've had enough. We've been riding for hours and now this. It'll be dark soon. I've had it!*

'A brief rest,' Umniga called. Elena sighed with relief. 'Not you,' Umniga said, stopping in front of her. 'You do ten more repetitions before you stop.' Elena sagged.

'Umniga, she's exhausted,' Āsim said.

'I don't care. So are the others and they didn't give up. Again,' Umniga demanded.

Elena raised her chin defiantly.

Umniga laughed, 'Girl, if we can put that defiance to a better use, we might make something of you. Again!'

'Leni,' Curro said. 'Just finish the drill.'

Elena narrowed her eyes and moved the staff at a leisurely pace through the drill. She finished and smiled sweetly as Umniga's jaw clenched.

'Watch!' Umniga instructed them all as she added another movement into their task. She slid her hands along the staff to hold it out before her, then returned to the original strike position. Āsim aimed a mock strike at her, which she blocked and deflected using her staff. Umniga worked through the movement again, combining the new section with what they had already practised.

'Again!' Umniga ordered.

Elena heard Āsim praising the others. She gritted her teeth under Umniga's withering gaze. *You want me to do this. Fine, I'll do it on my terms ... not yours.*

—⚊—

The Bear captains were bellowing orders and settling the newcomers into the lakeside camp as Baldev drew Asha into his tent. His arms encircled her. 'Thank the gods, you're back.'

'Everything went fine. Apart from Vikram. I can't believe he betrayed us.'

'He won't have betrayed you. He's Karan's spy; has been for years.' Asha's jaw dropped. 'Don't tell anyone. Not even Umniga. If Karan wants her to know, he'll tell her.'

'It was all an act?' She paused. 'They beat the stuffing out of him!'

'It'll help his cover.'

Affronted, Asha asked, 'You couldn't trust us with this earlier?'

'Even the slightest hint of what he was would get him killed. A look, a quiet word—any difference in how you treated him could've given him away.'

'But now you trust me?'

'You're unlikely to see him again until this is over. You can't give him away, but even here you can't breathe a word of this. If we've spies you can bet that Ratilal does too. Besides, I don't want secrets between us. I've wasted too much time keeping things from you.'

'Yes, you have,' Asha said, smiling. 'You promised me at Parlan that you had much to say to me.'

Baldev let go of her and ran his hand through his hair. 'I did and now ... Agh!' He threw his hands in the air. 'I can address troops and go into battle without flinching, but I don't know where to start ... I'm worried about getting this wrong.'

'Just talk—speak your heart.'

'Ever since we were children and Umniga would bring you to train with us, you've always been a part of my life. We had fun. But it seemed from one visit to the next the girl disappeared and the woman arrived. Your training ended, your duties increased, you visited less.' Baldev shrugged. 'I became clan lord and everyone treated me differently. You treated me differently. By the time I realised how I felt, I was certain it was too late. I don't want to be clan lord with you. I want ... After we annexed the North, it made it almost impossible for you to cross the Divide. Then Ratilal ...'

'Baldev, I'm fine.'

'You're still covered in bruises!' he said angrily, pacing. 'I'll kill that bastard ...'

'You'll have to get in line for that ...'

'I've kicked myself for not acting earlier.'

'I would still have gone to Faros. I have my duty.' Asha moved in front of him, placing her hands on his chest and stopping his pacing. 'You wanted to tell me something?'

Baldev searched her face. 'I love you.' A rueful smile slowly formed upon his lips. 'See? No flowery speeches—I don't have it in me.'

'I prefer honest sentiment any day,' she said.

'After all this time I was certain that there'd be someone else.'

'There was no one special,' Asha said softly. She laughed at the scowl on his face. 'Don't give me that look. I'm sure you've had your share of "nobody specials" over the years too.' Asha arched her brow, challenging him to deny it.

'Yes, but not since I realised. Asha, I missed you.'

'Good. So what happens now?'

'Whatever you want. Though I've some suggestions and this is a very roomy tent.'

—ɷ—

Head downcast, Isaura left Hamza's house wiping her eyes.

Hamza gave a cursory wave to Karan. 'I've got stock to tend. Safe journey. I'll see you in when I come for the children.'

Before Karan could comment, Hamza had left and not looked back. *Sentimental old fool,* Karan thought fondly. *He doesn't want to watch Isa leave.*

Alejo waited by the corral fence railing as Isaura climbed it.

'You're not always going to have a fence to climb up, you know,' Karan said.

'There's no stirrups. How else could I get up?' Isaura asked.

'Leap.'

Isaura quirked her brow. 'Could you? Alejo's taller than Mirza.'

'Yes, if he'd let me. How does it feel?' Karan asked.

'Comfortable, more so than on Tos … than before.' Isaura hadn't seen Toshi's body when she woke, but she'd heard the Asena howling during the night. There was little doubt where the carcass had gone.

'You'll need a saddle eventually. Hamza knows what to get and will bring one from my saddler in Targmur in a few weeks' time.'

'This seems fine.'

'A saddle will be more stable and you'll need that to fight. You'll get better leverage with sword or spear that way. You won't be knocked off as easily. Don't worry, Hamza will make sure it's perfect.'

'He's a good man. I'd like to meet his family.'

'I'm sure you will. I think if he could he'd adopt you.'

Isaura smiled wistfully. 'I think I'd like that too.'

Karan cleared his throat breaking the ensuing silence. 'Normally I'd concentrate on using this time for you to practise merging with Alejo and working cooperatively to perform other tasks.'

'Other tasks?'

'Fighting, talking, walking, watching. But you've already proven that you can seize control of him and at the lake you worked together. Did you enjoy watching?'

Isaura had the grace to blush, but would not be cowed. 'I wouldn't have kept doing it if I didn't enjoy it.'

'So did I. Your shirt is see-through when wet.' Isaura's mouth hung open. 'I only did what you were doing.' Karan laughed at her shocked silence, before growing solemn. 'My words regarding the bond have wounded you, for which I am sorry,' he said. 'I'm attracted to you, but the depth of it is too strong. It simply cannot be real. We hardly know one another. Even ignoring the heart bond, you are not yet a member of my clan. You are not of our blood.'

'I'm of your spirit though and I'll pass my testing.'

Karan smiled. 'I'm sure you will. When we get to camp, you'll work on your merged fighting with Pravin. In the meantime we've got time to turn you into a rider and for you to convince Alejo to rein in his homicidal tendencies when he's around other people … Should be easy.'

chapter twenty-one

ENTERING THE LAKESIDE camp, the looks of welcome Karan received turn to astonishment when they saw Isaura riding Alejo.

Isaura tried to ignore the grins and sniggers as they passed. Her jaw clenched. *It's no different than when I was a child.*

Tension rippled through Alejo as he seized upon her memory; his anger rose. *But it didn't hurt me. They made me stronger. We'll prove them wrong.*

Just wait, she soothed him.

They continued through the gathering crowd. Baldev strode to meet them. His head cocked to one side as he studied Karan and Mirza being dwarfed as they rode beside Alejo.

With a half smile, he said, 'Karan, by the gods it is good to see you. And you must be Isa. Asha has told me much regarding you. I'd like you in my clan.' Baldev grinned slyly at Karan. 'But I suspect Karan will have words to say about that.' Karan's lips drew into a thin line and he glowered at his friend. Baldev laughed uproariously and moved beside Alejo to look up cheekily at Isaura. 'I'll walk with you. Isa, you can tell me all about your journey with only this surly one as company.' He paused to grab an apple from a nearby barrel.

'Come on, Isa. We'll tend to our mounts. You can be subjected to Lord Baldev's sparkling wit later,' Karan said.

Baldev stopped, letting them continue without him. 'Ah yes, about your mounts.' He raised the apple up to bite. 'Has the Horse Clan changed its name? Or did you run out of horses?'

Alejo's rear leg shot out. His hoof struck the apple and knocked it cleanly from Baldev's hand. Baldev stood gaping.

Isaura blanched, but Karan winked at her, murmuring, 'Well

played.' Karan called back as they rode, 'I wouldn't take this one too cheaply again, my friend.'

—⚬⚬—

It had been several days since their arrival and Karan decided that morning that he would train early with Isaura. She had not slept in a tent with the others since the first night in camp; the sentries told him where he would find her.

Karan saw Alejo first—he lay slumbering in the forest next to Isaura. The guardian raised his head at Karan's approach, huffed and lay back down. Isaura had scraped pine needles together as a mattress and was curled up tight in her swag. The remains of a fire sat blackened and cold before her. Karan paused, looking at her sleeping form. Isaura's face was free of tension—younger looking. Her toughness was merely an illusion—an armour to protect her. *What am I going to do with you?* His hand reached toward her, then fell to his side. She stirred.

'Wake up, Isa.'

Isaura's eyes shot open and she scrambled to her feet. 'What's wrong?'

'Nothing. It's training time.'

Isaura rubbed her eyes. 'It's still half dark,' she said as she rolled up her swag and rested it against the tree trunk.

'It will be dawn soon. Come. Why are you not sleeping in the tent with Umniga and the others?'

'Someone in there snores loud enough to wake the dead. I'm not training with the others?'

'Not for everything,' Karan said as they walked. 'You must learn all weapons. We each have a weapon of choice. Mine is the sword. Baldev prefers the axe, hatchet or anything involving brute force. Umniga wields the staff.'

'Umniga?'

'Yes, Umniga is brilliant with her staff. She was instrumental in saving you—something you'd do well to remember the next time you want to roll your eyes when she gives you religious instruction. Without her, Baldev and I would've left you all to die. Make sure Alejo knows this is training. I don't want him barging through the trees ready to kill me.'

'He won't. Not with you.'

'Not with any of us, Isa,' Karan warned.

'He understands. He's learning to trust my judgement of who the enemy is.'

'He guarded your tent at night,' Karan said flatly.

'I can't tell him who to trust when I'm asleep, so he thinks he needs to guard me. Sleeping out here keeps him more settled.'

'Tell me, when you communicate with him, how do you do it?'

'He's in my head ... I just think.'

'Words or pictures?'

'Words mostly.'

Karan frowned.

Isaura sighed. 'I gather you don't use words?'

'Not really. Tone, images, feelings. Alejo can understand exactly what's said to him, can't he?' Karan asked.

'Usually, but I think it could be because he's always connected to me. It doesn't work in reverse. Alejo doesn't talk to me. From him I only get images, and feelings—lots and lots of feelings. Part of him is always in my mind, watching. Mirza doesn't do that, does he?' she asked hopefully.

'No. What you and Alejo do could only happen if I were deeply merged with Mirza. Mirza doesn't sit in my mind constantly. I can call him, but he's not sitting there waiting and watching. I'm not sure I'd want him to be there all the time either. Alejo hasn't sought to control you again, has he?' Isaura shook her head. 'Good. Whatever is going on at least you've remained aware of your separate identities.'

'I like him with me,' Isaura said softly. 'It's just like a kind of warmth ...' She shrugged. 'It makes me feel safe.'

The trees thinned, revealing a clearing along the lake and around a willow. The morning mist hung low to the ground and blanketed the water. It was peaceful, beautiful.

Karan looked at her pensive face and threw her a practice sword. 'Let's see how safe you feel after this,' he said with wicked grin. 'Adjust your stance. Remember your balance. The dance you learnt incorporates the basic drill every warrior learns from a young age and more, but it has become stylised. We are going to take that dance and alter it. This time imagine an opponent and think about blocking, attacking, slicing.'

'You're turning the dance back into the drill?' she asked.

'Yes, in a way.'

'Why not start with the drill?'

'You were too tense. Ready? ... Start.'

Isaura mimicked his movements. The dance flowed. She put more strength into the swing of the practice sword. Karan stepped back, watching silently. He lunged, swinging his wooden sword at her, slicing across her arm. She leapt back, glaring.

'You don't want to get hit? Then block it.' Karan swung again, striking her thigh. Isaura growled. 'Block it,' he said calmly. He attacked again. Isaura dodged it, directing a strike at him. Karan laughed. Her eyes narrowed. They faced off, circling—she lunged. He blocked her blow, pressing his attack from high. Isaura ducked and slipped sideways. 'You can't dodge forever. On a battlefield you may not have the room to keep running.' Again he attacked her.

Isaura blocked without thinking; inside she was crowing. Karan attacked again. She blocked. The clash of timber resonated through the forest. Confidence abounding, she attacked.

'Good.' Karan let her push forward. 'Excellent.' Isaura's eyes gleamed eagerly and sweat beaded on her brow. With a mere flick of his wrist, he deflected her thrust and tripped her. Isaura lay on the ground with his sword at her throat. 'Time to leave the dance. An attack won't always follow the pattern.' Karan hauled her up. 'Again.'

Pio hesitated outside the sick bay. Sarala put her hand on his shoulder. 'This is part of your training, Pio. Everyone learns how to tend wounds. This is the best place for it. Come, Kiriz will be here already.'

'Kiriz comes here?'

'Every morning and evening. We each take shifts here. You must too.' They moved through the tents. Harsh moans assailed Pio. He stepped back into Sarala and grabbed her hand. Sarala knelt so she was at eye level with him. 'We all learn how to help heal people, Pio. Here you'll learn to save lives.' Pio looked around uncertainly. 'Maybe one day what you learn here will save the life of your friends or family.' Pio nodded solemnly.

Kiriz emerged from a tent with bloody bandages, which she threw into a large cast iron pot by the fire. She looked up, smiled at Pio, ran up to him and grabbed his hand in her bloody one. He wrenched his hand free and stared in horror at the blood.

'Don't worry, it's just blood. It'll wash off. Come on, we've got work to do.' She grabbed Pio's hand and hauled him along. 'You can help. Sometimes they're a bit cranky—'cause of the pain Umniga says. Don't worry too much about what they might say. Understand?' Pio nodded and shook his head.

They walked into one of the larger tents. Several warriors, men and women, were lying on pallets. Umniga was examining the leg of a young man. 'You're lucky.'

He glared at her. 'I know.'

Umniga shook her head. 'Do you? You didn't die from blood loss and it's not infected. If you want I can open it up again, let it get infected, riddled with pus, bloated and then you can die the usual pain-filled death, or we'll chop it off. Would you like that instead?'

'No,' he said.

'Then try not to be such an utter shit, to me or the others when

I'm trying to help you.' The warrior looked up quickly at Kiriz's approach. Umniga followed his gaze, adding, 'Especially the children. Kiriz, pass me that vinegar.' She soaked a cloth in vinegar and sponged the wound with it.

Kiriz grinned. 'It's not so red today.'

The young man grunted dismissively in response.

'You want more juice of the poppy?'

'No. It makes me want to throw up.'

Kiriz moved beside Umniga and began gently bandaging the leg. Pio watched, transfixed and appalled.

'Who's your friend, Kiriz? He looks terrified,' the man said with a bitter laugh.

'Pio. He's one of the newcomers.'

'If his lot hadn't come here this wouldn't have happened!'

'We would've been at war sooner or later. It's not his fault,' Umniga said sternly. She jabbed her bony finger into his chest. 'Remember what I said. Kiriz, you can bandage up the leg. Pio, you watch, see how it's done.'

Pio nodded. His hand reflexively clutched his flute, which now hung in a bag by his side. In his mind he began hearing a tune Isaura had taught him. She'd said it had been one her mother had hummed when she worked.

They moved among the wounded. Pio began to work with Kiriz, fetching and carrying for the men and women working in the tent. Each tried to explain the various herbs and ointments to him; by the end of the morning, he could remember their names.

Pio's nervousness had not abated. He was acutely aware of the pain-filled, despairing faces around him. Each time he looked around the tent he saw the angry warrior staring at him. Pio's hand strayed to his flute and he held onto it tightly. The tune in his head refused to be silenced. He rocked back and forth upon his toes and fragments of tune escaped his lips. He clamped his mouth shut.

'Let it out, boy,' Uminga said softly. 'It's your gift. Let the gods guide you.'

Pio withdrew the flute from the bag and looked uncertainly at Umniga. She nodded reassuringly. He stood in the middle of the sick bay and played. A hush fell over the tent. Gradually the moaning in the tent lessened; the harsh breathing became slower, relaxed. Those working were silent as they finished their tasks and quietly left. Pio's tune drifted softly away, leaving tranquillity to blanket the ill. He opened his eyes. He was alone. The patients slept.

All bar the angry one who murmured before dozing off, 'You might belong after all.'

Karan walked into his yurt after another training session with Isaura, to find Baldev waiting for him.

'You're being tough on the woman, Karan,' Baldev commented. 'Every morning she trains with you, then does her stint with the wounded, then trains again with those others. Afternoons she spends with Asha working on her riding and mounted archery. Be careful you don't break her.'

'She won't break, but Isa needs to learn to fight quickly. This will also help her earn the respect of the clan.'

'She already has their respect,' Baldev said.

'Because of the Asena, not because of her efforts. If Isa does it the hard way and wins and they'll respect her. Long term it's better for her—better for all of us.'

Baldev looked at Karan thoughtfully. 'You obviously care about her …'

'Of course,' Karan said. 'We've risked a lot to rescue them. Everyone needs to see that she was worth it. You and I are not going to be able to remain here for long before we'll have to be out in the field. Pravin should arrive soon with the others from Targmur. When he comes he can teach her. Āsim can continue with the others. I want her to be able to defend herself.'

'They won't be alone here when we go,' Baldev said.

'I know, but she'll be her own best defence. Isa is not yet a member of this clan. I don't think she can count on unswerving loyalty yet. Did your Kenati meet with Vikram?'

'Suniti spirit walked with her guardian to Faros. Vikram was late, but he made the meeting. He says the levies have been called. Ratilal is assembling an army just out of Faros in the north. Apparently someone tried to assassinate him—Ratilal that is. Vikram thinks he should have let him die and I agree.'

'Perhaps, but it's a good sign that it happened. Ratilal's actions and Vikram's network of spies are slowly undermining him. When we're done they'll want him gone and a truly lasting peace. I regret that Shahjahan had to pay for his son's perfidy, but that too will work for us.'

'Oh, one more thing—Vikram has been made Pasha of Faros in Ratilal's absence.'

Astonished, Karan froze, simply staring agape at Baldev.

'I'm going to remember this moment, forever.' Baldev chuckled. 'I don't think I've ever seen you so stunned. But I imagine you'll recover quickly as even I can see how useful this could be,' he finished smugly.

chapter twenty-two

ASHA AND ISAURA sat alone beside the lake, dangling their feet in the water. Isaura's thick braid hung heavy and wet down her back and Asha's short blonde hair stood up in damp spikes.

'There's nothing so nice as a swim to wash the sweat off,' Isaura said as she pulled on her top. 'I thought Āsim was going to work us until we dropped.'

'Wait till Pravin gets here—then you'll know what work is,' Asha replied as she splashed the water with her feet.

Isaura stared across the water thoughtfully. Asha's body still bore fading bruises from Ratilal's attack. 'Asha, why does Ratilal hate you so much? Why would he risk attacking you so openly? Is he that unhinged?'

Pensive, Asha chewed her lip. 'Probably.' She had a distant look in her eyes. 'I never wanted to be a Kenati. Samia, Ratilal's sister, did, but she never got a guardian. I was the youngest Kenati ever to receive a guardian. She resented me for it; thought my reluctance at training was ingratitude. I just didn't want to leave my family and … she never wanted to return to hers, but without a guardian her training with Umniga was over.' Isaura waited patiently. 'Ratilal—my blonde hair drew his attention. Samia noticed. Twice she found him alone with me, always when Fihr was away hunting. He enjoyed teasing me. She warned him off … she deflected his attention. He thought it was some kind of game with her. Samia watched me …' Asha paused, drawing a deep breath. 'She tried to make sure I wasn't alone. She kept Ratilal from me. I didn't realise …' Asha wiped her eyes. 'Then … by chance … It was late.' Asha shook her head. 'I saw him … with her … together,' Asha whispered haltingly. 'He had her against the wall. Samia was facing me ... The look on her face ... Oh gods.' Asha's wrapped her arms around her middle and rocked. 'She didn't want it. Isa, she never wanted him, I swear. She saw me—my shock, my horror,' Asha said. 'Her face ... that one look—defeat, shame, loathing and a desperate fear. I crept away.'

'You didn't tell anyone?'

'Umniga was out tending an ill, old man. I was scared. I went to my room and locked the door. Later, gods knows what time it was, Samia knocked on my door and asked me to let her in. She begged me not to say anything. She was horrified at the idea that I'd tell. Said she'd deny it. Who'd believe me against the clan lord's children?'

Umniga returned in the morning and I left with her. Samia killed herself a few weeks later. I told Umniga then, ashamed of myself for not speaking up earlier. Umniga returned and conducted the rights of passing. Shahjahan was a wreck, barely functioning. Whatever occurred ... whatever she said, the result was that she never returned to Faros. I'm certain Ratilal knows that I saw him and I told Umniga. I think in some perverse way Ratilal blames me for his sister's death. Umniga and I may be the only two left who know. We're a liability ... I should have told somebody earlier.'

Isaura took her hand, saying, 'The end result may have been the same. You were a child. You can't blame yourself for this.'

Tears ran freely down her face. 'Isa, she saved me. She didn't even really like me, but she saved me. She could have let him swap his attention to me, but she made sure that he didn't. She sacrificed herself for me. I owe her.'

Isaura hugged her tightly. 'We'll make him pay, I promise.'

—∞—

There'd been a slow steady arrival of people at the camp over the last two weeks—Boar warriors who had chosen to fight alongside

Karan and Baldev, and children whose parents had chosen to send them to the safety of Targmur.

Yet this was a procession. Leading it was a grizzled old man, who sat proudly upon his horse, wearing an unadorned zirh gomlek and zirh kulah. His face was scarred and the large hands that held the reins were gnarled; his fierce gaze raked the onlookers. Behind him came long columns of mounted warriors. At the end rode a young girl of about sixteen.

'Now your fun begins,' Asha said. She nudged Isaura. 'That's Pravin, Karan's weapons master. He's as old as the hills and as tough. And Baldev tells me Karan wants him training you exclusively.'

'Not the others?'

'Oh, I'm sure he'll oversee Āsim, but you'll get most of his time,' she replied, smirking. 'I don't envy you.'

Isaura feigned nonchalance. 'Who's the girl?'

'No idea.'

'Look who else's here.' Asha drew Isaura's attention to a figure following at a distance. 'He'll be here for the children.' Behind the column came a string of mules led by Hamza and his sons.

'Hamza!' Isaura called, running up to him and walking beside his mule.

'Isa, girl! Ah, lass, it's good to lay eyes on you. And I see they're treating you well. Come give us a hand and you can meet my boys and tell me all about how you and Alejo are faring. I think you'll find your other friends are here too.' He leaned down conspiratorially, saying softly, 'Look to the woods over there. They've been shadowing us since we left home. Made me feel right important, it did, but I dare say they're not really here for me.'

Isaura's gaze snapped to the shadowed tree line and a smile lit her face. She took off at a run as the Matriarch stepped from the trees. 'Go on then, girl. They're waiting for you,' Hamza called to her, making sure every eye drew in her direction. He smiled in the silence that followed. *Doesn't hurt for them to see the truth of what they have in their midst.*

Pravin stood before Karan. 'What's your assessment?' Karan asked.

'Āsim's doing a fine job.' Derision writ clear upon his face, he continued. 'Considering what he has to work with.'

'They must become competent fighters. They're learning the Lore and conforming, but I won't carry dead weight. Oversee Āsim, but concentrate on the girl.'

'The incoming Boar warriors will not all be up to scratch.'

'I know. Drill them as you would our men, but make no reference to a lack of skills on their part. I want them integrated and they deserve a chance to fight for their homes. It's not their fault their clan let them down.'

'Were the strangers worth it?'

'Isa and the boy were. The rest are unfortunately necessary excess baggage.'

'You've an interest in the woman?'

Karan's expression remained neutral. 'You could say that.'

Pravin narrowed his eyes. 'She's not one of us.'

Karan was curt. 'I'm well aware of that, which is why you are here. She must pass our tests and be accepted into the clan.' *I need her to be accepted.*

'Her skills?'

'Archery and any weapon she can throw—daggers, spears, hatches—she's a natural. Needs work on her riding and swordsmanship. Staff work is coming along nicely.' He paused, eyeing Pravin seriously. 'Her guardian is a force to be reckoned with. Treat her fairly or he'll try to kill you. But if you can work on their combined combat, they'll be astonishing,' Karan finished with a smile.

'You admire her?'

'Greatly. But she gets no free passes, Pravin.'

'The Asena …'

'Are here because of her. Though they keep their distance around camp until her guardian is under control. They're scared of him.'

Pravin's eyebrows shot up. 'Well then. I think I might enjoy this.'

Karan glowered at him. 'Try not to break her or you'll have more trouble than even you can handle.'

—⁂—

Isaura and Asha stood, sides heaving and sweat running down their faces; practice swords and bucklers hung limply in their hands. Their morning had begun with archery training, which Pravin had grudgingly stopped after both Asha and Isaura had excelled at every test he gave them. They'd moved on to throwing knives and hatchets at which point he'd grumbled, 'Well Lord Karan wasn't exaggerating.'

'I thought this was supposed to be your training,' Asha wheezed.

'Gone soft have you, Asha?' Pravin asked.

'I doubt that, sir. She's still injured,' Isaura said flatly.

Pravin snorted. 'I once fought a battle with an arrow shaft in each leg. A little light training's not going to hurt her, young lady,' Pravin said. Uncowed, Isaura met him glare for glare. 'Again!' he bellowed. Once Isaura's back was turned he smiled in grudging admiration.

Asha groaned. 'Stop moaning, Asha,' Pravin said. 'Lord Baldev will skin me if I let you get along without a tune up. All that running around and ministering to the sick and telling stories to folk has made you rusty!'

Asha and Isaura squared off and recommenced training. When Isaura landed a blow on Asha, Pravin called a halt. 'Rest break. Eat, then meet me back here with your mounts.'

They trailed after him. The smell of freshly baked flat bread from the ovens of the camp kitchen wafted to them.

'That's one good thing about Pravin coming—all the cooks came with him,' Asha said.

The chief cook glared at them. 'Not feeding time yet, bugger off you two!'

'Oh, for the love of the gods, feed them!' Pravin bellowed back over his shoulder. 'They've earned it.'

Asha grinned broadly. 'He's pleased.' Isaura looked at her blankly. 'That's praise coming from him. If he wasn't happy he wouldn't have insisted we get fed.'

They grabbed some bread and a mug each of a meaty bean soup, before wandering off. Leaning against a wagon, eating their lunch, they quietly watched the others train. Asha's gaze strayed to Baldev as he strode across the campsite.

Isaura cleared her throat. 'Asha, I need to ask you something.'

'Mmm?'

Isaura frowned, not meeting Asha's eyes. 'Something personal.'

'Go on.'

'Aren't you worried about getting pregnant?'

Asha replied quietly, 'No. There's a small risk, but no. We chew tamagan seeds. Once your moon blood stops, you chew two a day for fourteen days. If it doesn't work then there's a tea we drink to induce our moon flow early. I've administered it. It's effective but not pleasant and ... risky.'

'We'd a similar tea. There was a woman from our village ... she refused help from my mother. She took the tea and nearly bled to death. Her husband came to my mother in desperation. Only after she saved her, did she get enough work as healer for us to survive on.'

Asha put her hand on Isaura's arm. 'People can be stupid, but you're here now. Umniga has a supply of seeds—get some from her. You don't want to rely on the self-control of a man in this regard.'

Isaura looked away. 'I doubt it will be necessary.'

Asha chuckled. 'Maybe not now, but once you pass your testing ... when you're one of us.' Her lips quirked in a cheeky grin. Isaura folded her arms across her chest. 'You don't believe me? Isa, they're already looking at you.'

'I think you're an eternal optimist,' Isaura said. *And deluded.* 'I feel a sudden need to watch the training.' Gabriela and Lucia were sparring. 'I'd never have thought to see Gabi enjoying this so much,' Isaura murmured to Asha.

'Not just Gabi,' Asha said.

Lucia swung and lunged with her stave. Each time Gabriela deflected her blow. They circled each other. Lucia struck again. Gabriela countered, blocked then landed a blow upon her side.

Āsim, arms folded, looked on severely; Pravin stood by his side.

'Next,' Āsim ordered.

Elena stepped up to stand before Gabriela. Asha scowled as she watched. Isaura's jaw clenched and she said nothing. It was over in seconds. Elena made a half-hearted attack. Gabriela struck swiftly, knocking her over and stood with her stave angled at her chest.

'You could at least try, Elena,' she said despairingly as she hauled her to her feet.

'How long has that one been acting like that?' Pravin asked Āsim quietly.

'Always,' Āsim spat.

'Isa,' Pravin beckoned her to him. 'I want to make sure she understands—translate. You.' His eyes bored into Elena. 'You are mocking us. You do not try. You do not work. The rest …' his gesture encompassed the others, '… they try. They work. Your rations are halved.'

Elena jutted her chin out defiantly.

Pravin added with a chilling grin, 'You don't change your attitude, then their rations will be halved too.'

Isaura finished translating, her face tense as the eyes of all bar Gabriela bore into her.

'My thanks, Isa,' Pravin said.

Together Pravin and Isaura turned and walked away from the group. Softly he added, 'Now go and finish your food. Eat where she can see you.'

Isaura's back stiffened, but she inclined her head and returned to Asha. Taking her first bite, she looked up and saw Elena glaring at her. Her food tasted like ash.

chapter twenty-three

ISAURA ENTERED KARAN'S yurt as Pravin left it. Pravin stopped her, gave her a thoughtful look and squeezed her shoulder, before shaking his head and departing.

Bewildered, she looked at Karan. 'Elena,' was all he said.

'She's made her own bed,' Isaura said stiffly. 'I loathe the idea of someone as unstable as Elena being trained to use weapons.'

'She has the right to know how to defend herself and her fate is sealed if she doesn't learn. While her life means nothing to me, what concerns me is that the present situation is affecting the others and Pio. I need to win them and maintain our code. I'd hoped that she would cave in earlier. I want your help.'

'I don't know what I can do. She hates me.'

'Exactly.'

―⁂―

Elena sat alone, under guard, with a meagre bowl of food. Curro and the others sat nearby eating heartily, unwilling to look at her. All were under the watchful supervision of several guards; there would be no hiding food for her.

Elena seethed. *I swear their servings have got bigger.*

Though she could see the others, she was kept isolated from them except for when they trained. *Their laws, their rules ... my life!*

Isaura approached her, smiling at the guard and sharing what Elena assumed was a joke. Elena's eyes narrowed in suspicion. *Probably about me.*

'Elena, how are you?' Isaura asked.

'Don't pretend you care, Isaura. We both know you never have.'

Isaura sighed and folded her arms across her chest. 'You've had it wrong from the beginning. Nothing happened. Nothing ever happened. How many times do I have to tell you?'

'I saw you two.'

Stiffening, Isaura drew a sharp intake of breath, glaring across the distance to Curro. He had paused eating, spoon halfway to his mouth, transfixed at the sight of the two women together. A worried frown creased his brow.

'Even now you can't help but look at him, can you? It isn't enough that you're the favourite of everyone here, but you want my husband as well,' Elena spat.

Isaura squatted before her to gaze directly in her eyes. 'Elena, it's never been what you think. You need to talk to Curro and sort this out. It's eating you up inside, can't you see?' Isaura tried to take her hands, but Elena batted them away. 'Elena.' Isaura's voice held such pity that Elena winced. 'You weren't always like this ...'

'Don't. Don't you dare feel sorry for me. Not when you're the problem.' She leapt up, pushing Isaura and sending her sprawling. The guard moved to intervene. Elena stood, tense, wide-eyed, backing away from him.

Isaura held up her hand and shook her head, forestalling the guard; she slowly stood. Curro had moved forward, but the warriors had stopped him. Isaura was running out of options.

'Elena, I know you're scared.'

Elena's mouth drew into a thin line and her eyes narrowed.

'But you must train. If you don't train, then their rations will be cut. They'll suffer because of you. Elena, you must help yourself and them. If you do, you'll earn everyone's respect. Curro's respect ...'

Pravin strode to them, interrupting. 'It's time.' With a flick of his head he summoned Elena. She stood firm, still glaring at Isaura.

Isaura sighed. 'Elena, no matter what you think, I want you to live a long life happy with Curro. I don't want to see you executed, but trust me, your time is running out. Do you see patience on the faces of Pravin and Āsim? Do you see respect or admiration on the faces of anyone here for you? Do you see it on the faces of your friends?'

Elena's slid her gaze sideways to her watching friends; all bar Curro looked away. Elena spat at her. 'I hate you.'

'Clearly,' Isaura said as she dusted off her trousers. 'You know, there's a betting pool running on whether or not you'll train properly or be killed. The odds aren't good.' Elena paled. 'Although if you do train, then you'll go into the other pool for the competition bouts. Did you know that if we pass the testing, then there are competition bouts?' Isaura scrunched up her nose and scratched her head as if deep in thought. 'No.' She surveyed Elena disparagingly. 'I don't think even those odds'll improve. I wonder who you'd get to fight—if you make it that far, that is.'

Elena's face reddened; the thin line of her lips turned down bitterly.

'Who would you like to fight, Elena? Me? Would you like to see me beaten and humiliated by your hand?'

'Yes,' Elena said stiffly.

'Then you'd better start training. See you in the competition,' Isaura said before casually turning her back on her and leaving.

Jaw clenched, Elena watched her leave. At Pravin's gesture the guards moved forward to take her to the training field. With a sweep of her head she met them and walked toward the training area like a queen.

Ratilal and Niaz left the Great Hall side by side; Vikram followed in their wake.

'It is well that you sit in judgement at these sessions, High Lord,' Niaz said. 'Seeing you fulfil your duties so well will help dispel the rumours.'

'It would be more helpful if Captain Vikram could find who's spreading such lies,' Ratilal countered. 'Slogans charcoaled on the walls of the city!'

'High Lord, patrols on the streets have been doubled into the night. We have yet to catch the culprit, but we will,' Vikram replied.

'Someone must see when they scrawl these vile slogans. Vikram, I want a curfew imposed on the outer city.' Vikram bowed before leaving. 'Come, Niaz, let's head back to the training field.'

Once out of the confines of the citadel, Ratilal heaved a sigh of relief. 'By the gods, that is all that is tedious in the world. Sitting in judgement of petty squabbles amongst merchants and civilians. No wonder my father was such an irascible old bastard.'

'They need to see you continuing the old ways.'

'I know that!' Ratilal snapped. 'You and Vikram never let me forget. You're like old women with your damn nagging. I understand its importance, it just drives me wild and being driven wild by the monthly judgement sessions is not the kind of wild I'd prefer.'

Niaz laughed. 'It's been a while since we went to Pramod's. Are you feeling up to it?'

'Am I feeling up to it?' Ratilal said in disbelief. 'I'm feeling so up to it I could jump that old goat Gita.'

'Then when we've finished at the end of today, we'll go. I'm sure Pramod's got a replacement for you by now.'

'There's still no sign of her?'

Niaz shook his head. 'Not yet, but she can't have vanished.'

'At least Sora got away. That wasn't ruined,' Ratilal said. 'Damn Zimma. He obviously started the slogans.'

'Niara was his sister, and you were a little too drunk and a little too heavy handed,' Niaz ventured.

'You know I haven't lost control like that in long time. Anyway, even you like it rough. Small mercy is that it made it appear Sora had a good reason to run.'

Not that rough, Niaz thought. He shrugged. 'It's done.'

'After we go over the plans, take the men assigned to this mission to Pramod's. Let them have fun, give them a taste of the better goods. If he's got anyone you think worthwhile, bring her discretely back here. I should probably avoid the brothel for a bit,' Ratilal finished bitterly. He paused. 'The more I think about it, there might be a more permanent solution if I can train her up.'

'Who?'

'That mason, Paksis—the one we conscripted for his crimes. His daughter's a pretty thing. She's not used to being a servant and doesn't like it. Handled correctly, delicately …' He grinned at Niaz. 'Oh, don't look so doubtful. I can be delicate when I want. It might take a little longer, but that's part of the challenge. Then I can expand upon her repertoire.'

'Do you still want the other one?'

'Of course. I'm not going without in the meantime.' Ratilal clapped his hands together excitedly. 'To the real business. I believe the squads are ready. The scout reports that the rains have swollen the river enough and the moon is waning, which will help hide them. Time to set everything in motion.'

Pio carried his full bowl of food over and sat on the ground near his father and mother. 'The food's getting better. Wow! They gave me a lot.' He spoke between mouthfuls. 'Auntie Leni, you did good in practice today. I saw you when I came back with Kiriz. You really worked hard.'

Everyone paused eating, eyes downcast, waiting for Elena's usual taciturn reply.

'Thank you, Pio. Today was the first day I felt like training,' Elena said.

'You looked like you enjoyed it, Auntie Leni.'

'I don't know that I enjoyed it, Pio, but it was better than I expected.'

Pio continued blithely, 'We, Kiriz and me, we're training with the horses. Sarala had us shooting our bows off them.' He shoved another spoonful of food into his already full mouth. 'But ... the ...' Food spilled from his mouth.

'Pio! Not with your mouth full!' Lucia said.

Pio swallowed hurriedly, before racing to tell them the rest. 'The horses were standing still. Tomorrow we get to go it again. I can't wait to do it at a gallop.' His eyes grew wider. 'Oh! Do you think Sarala will let me do it at a gallop tomorrow? I've got to find Kiriz.' He scraped the rest of the food hastily into his mouth and took off at a run.

Gabriela asked, 'What was your sudden inspiration, Leni?'

'I didn't think they'd make you suffer for my actions. I thought it was all talk. Once I realised it wasn't, I knew I had to change.'

Gabriela looked at her shrewdly. 'I must remember to thank Isa.'

Vikram's conscience plagued him, though he kept his features calm as he was escorted into Malak's home. *I can see no other means to do this.* A genuine smile lit his face as he was presented to Malak.

'Captain, please sit. I wanted to offer you the hospitality of my table in thanks for your help.' The table was laden with a variety of vegetable dishes and a steaming leg of lamb. Sit, eat and enjoy.' Malak shooed a waiting servant away.

'This is a huge quantity of food, Mistress Malak.'

She shrugged. 'Now you've plenty of choice and the servants have enough for their own celebration too.'

'Your business venture is going well I take it,' Vikram said as he served himself.

Malak chuckled heartily. 'Excellently. I've made business arrangements most advantageous to Daniel and I, and less so for the competition. Thank you, I'm enjoying myself more than I have in years.'

'After all your help with the strangers and with the wounded, I could do nothing less.' Vikram's face grew pensive as he poured them both wine.

She looked at him shrewdly, before rising and shutting the door of her dining room. 'What is it, Captain?'

'You've heard about the slogans painted on the walls of the city?'

'Everyone has. That sort of thing has never happened.'

'And difficult to hide. My men remove the slogans as soon as they can. Yet the rumours still spread … and they're worsening.'

'Perhaps they're true?'

Vikram grimaced. 'At least one is. Ratilal … mistreated two girls from a brothel.'

'Pramod's.' Malak sniffed and curled her lip in derision.

'He'd been seeing one for nearly a year without incident.' Vikram raised his brows and shrugged. 'All I know is he got drunk and snapped. The second one came to her defence.'

Malak's eyes darkened in anger. 'My son goes there with him.' Her old fist slammed the table. 'He would've known. I wish they'd never met. I wish …'

'Take heart, Mistress Malak. The girl is safe.'

'You're protecting him, Vikram.'

Vikram put down his fork with deliberate slowness. 'I was protecting her. When Ratilal inherited the title, I made it clear that I thought he'd the potential to be a good clan lord, but he should modify his behaviour if he wanted to win the people. I thought he had, but now there is Paksis's daughter.'

'What of her?'

'Ratilal's wooing her with promises of an easier life. I fear he is manipulating her for far more than she realises and then …'

'Then.' Malak's voice was grim.

'There are the other rumours … Rumours that it was Ratilal who killed his father.'

Her harsh intake of breath reverberated throughout the silent room. 'Are they true?'

Vikram would not look at her. 'I don't know ... but it's possible.' His hands curled into fists in his lap. *Take the bait. Just take the bait, old woman.*

'You were in Parlan, Vikram.'

'I saw nothing,' he sighed. 'We all knew of the animosity between Ratilal and his father. Shahjahan was about to clamp down on Ratilal and his cronies.' Vexed, he began to tap a tight beat on the floor. 'I witnessed no animosity from Horse or Bear—in fact I saw the opposite. I'd say they came in good faith. I've no proof and few men I can trust even if I did. Ratilal, despite his other faults, is an able warrior and knows how to gain and keep his men's loyalty.'

'Your hands are tied?'

'Effectively, yes. At least for the time being, even if I had proof.'

'You are now Pasha. You have some power.'

'A position given to me by Ratilal. It has changed little about my regular duties, just expanded them, and any real power will only be available when he is away fighting. It's also a position that allows me to protect the people of Faros which, gods willing, I'll be able to keep. I will not jeopardise it. If the rumour is correct—then who will they have?'

'We should've let him die.'

Vikram laughed harshly. 'Neither your nor my honour would allow it.'

'There is still the challenge.'

Vikram nodded. *Careful, don't play it too strong—she's nearly there.* 'Indeed. If one should arise, you know my views.'

Malak leaned back in her chair, thoughtful, gently swirling the wine in her glass as Vikram continued.

'But let us talk about other things, please. You've taken my fears into your confidence and relieved my mind in doing so. I think if I'd not been able to speak to someone, then I would've revealed my true feelings and suffered for it. Now I'd love to hear more about your business venture and how Daniel is faring in our world.'

The conversation turned to the greedy merchants of Faros's textile guild as they continued their dinner. Vikram roared with laughter, placing his wine glass on the table before he spilled it.

'Mistress Malak, I never realised you had such a head for business. They'll rue the day they stood in your way.'

'It runs in our clan, you know that. We love to haggle and bargain and wheedle to our advantage in all things.'

Vikram sobered. 'You're right. At our heart we're a greedy bunch. But they are still my people …' He smiled sadly. 'And that, I'm afraid, is the end of an excellent dinner and the end of my respite. Thank you, but I must return to my work.'

Malak escorted him to the door herself. As he walked through the door, she put her hand on his arm, delaying him. 'There is always the chance of change, Captain. Never fear.'

Vikram nodded.

Walking up the street, his smile became bitter. *Hooked. Damn me to Karak for this night's work.*

chapter twenty-four

KIRIZ SLID SILENTLY from her bedroll and froze. Umniga turned over, mumbling. She crouched, eyes wide, barely breathing. Umniga rolled back and resumed snoring softly. The other occupants of the yurt did not stir. It was pitch black, but she knew where everyone slept. Kiriz rose and picked her way carefully to the door. Without a backward glance she slipped into the camp.

Only the sentries were awake. Kiriz slid from shadow to shadow. Outside Pio's yurt, she paused.

Already out of his bedroll, Pio lay awake fearful—excited. Stiff and silent, he stared toward the door of the yurt. The darkness thinned and the vague outline of Kiriz's head poked through the flap. Pio made his way stealthily to her.

He opened his mouth to speak, but she placed her finger upon his lips. Kiriz grabbed his hand and dragged him along. They ducked and darted their way through the yurts to the edge of the camp. The field kitchen stood before them and the woods just beyond that. Pio crouched, poised to dash to the trees. Kiriz grabbed his arm and shook her head. She pointed to the woods.

'Wait,' she mouthed.

A sentry stepped from the tree line and made his way through camp. He disappeared from their sight.

Kiriz nodded, pushing Pio forward. 'Go, quick—while they change shift.'

Pio ran, half crouched, to the trees. He hid behind a large trunk, waiting for Kiriz.

She did not follow him. His hand gripped the bark as he dared a peek back to the camp. Kiriz scrounged through the kitchen, stuffing a bag with food. His breath caught as she zipped across the empty space to him.

'Come on,' she whispered. 'Let's get out of here.'

'We shouldn't do this.'

'Come on, don't be such a baby. Do you want to go with Hamza?'

'I like Hamza. I want to see Targmur.'

'Targmur is a long way. You won't see your parents in an age if you go there.' Pio shuffled his feet. He looked back at the camp. 'Make up your mind. If we're quick, we'll make it and they'll never find us. We'll come back when he's well and truly gone.' Kiriz stamped her foot. 'I'm going.'

Pio watched her disappear into the trees before racing to catch up with her. 'How do you know they won't find us?'

'They won't. I don't think anyone knows about this place.'

'Then how did you find it? Did you go exploring without me?'

'No. Stop talking,' Kiriz snapped softly.

Pio snagged her arm, halting her. 'Tell me.'

'Come on, Pio ... please. We're not far enough away ... please.' Kiriz grabbed his hand and tugged him. Pio crossed his arms and refused to move. Kiriz sighed. 'Fine, then. I'll tell you if you just keep walking. We're too close to camp—they'll catch us.'

Sharp eyes looked down upon the small boy as he ran through the trees.

They climbed higher and the soft dark soil of the forest floor yielded grey jagged rocks. The pair tramped for hours, clambering around boulders and climbing the mountainside. The sound of water grew from a distant hum to a roar. Mist dampened their hair and clothes.

'It's not much further, I don't think. There should be a little bush with yellow flowers and then ... well ...' Kiriz scratched her head trying to remember. 'Then ... we go behind the waterfall.'

Pio was incredulous. 'You've never been here?'

'No ... I have strange dreams sometimes,' Kiriz said, avoiding his gaze. 'Rana showed me.'

Pio's jaw dropped. 'You've seen the goddess, really? Umniga …'

Kiriz cast him a stern look, shaking her finger in his face. 'We're not telling Umniga. They'll take me from my ma for good … Oh, there it is!' She darted toward a spiny grey bush with delicate yellow flowers.

'Kiriz, wait. I need to sit a bit. My head's buzzing.'

She peered around the side of the hill. 'Come on, up here!'

Pio groaned, rolling his eyes as Kiriz scrambled off. He rubbed the back of his neck. A flicker of pale russet caught his eye against the grey needles of fir tree. In a blink it was gone.

'Are you coming or not?' Kiriz called out.

Red faced and breathless, Pio caught up with her. They were adjacent to the sheer rock face and the waterfall, which flowed into the Bear Tooth Lake far below. In the lee of the mountain the dim grey of pre-dawn still held sway. Pio looked back over the lake and forest. The early morning light was a weak glowing line on the distant landscape, inexorably forcing the slow retreat of the darkness.

'I bet it doesn't get really light here until late,' Pio whispered.

Kiriz tugged on his arm. 'Come on, stop gawping.' She scrambled up a large rock and balanced there before stepping to the next one.

Pio took one step forward. The swoosh of wings filled his hearing, his head buzzed and something sharp stabbed his head. Pio held his hand up to his scalp and it came away bloody. 'Ow!'

'Watch out! It's coming back!'

Pio darted toward Kiriz. A flash of grey and amber feathers and flapping wings dominated his vision. He threw up his hands to protect his face. The little falcon veered away, calling angrily. Pio darted forward, scrambling between and clambering over rocks. The bird kept flying in front of him, blocking his path, trying to drive him backward.

'Quick!' Kiriz hurled a rock at the falcon as it swooped again. Another yellow-flowered bush grew just above them. Kiriz zigzagged her way from boulder to boulder, drawing ever closer to the bush and the cliff edge. She squealed. Arms flailing, she disappeared behind a huge boulder.

Pio gasped. He raced up the slope to her. 'Kiriz!' The falcon dived in front of him again squawking angrily.

'Careful, the rocks are wet!' she called out.

Pio slipped and skidded into Kiriz behind the rock.

Her hair, part of her face and half her clothes were covered in mud. She was sitting on the ground, yet her legs had vanished under the bush. Kiriz grinned up at him. 'Found it.' They pushed the branches on the shrub aside to reveal a cavity behind the rock. 'Let's explore.'

Pio peered over the edge of the boulder. A few feet away sat the falcon. Upon seeing him, it danced from side to side in agitation. Pio rubbed his head and peered at the bird again. 'Maybe we shouldn't.'

'Do you want to stay out here and get pecked to death?' Kiriz asked.

'It's too dark in there.'

Kiriz rummaged around in her bag. 'That's what this is for.' She took out a round metal lamp. There was a handle on one side, a spout on the other with a wick in it and a hole in the middle. She pulled out a stoppered flask and poured oil into the lamp.

'What else is in that bag?' Pio asked. Kiriz grinned as she took out a tinder box and fire steel and flint. 'Where did you get all this?'

'Big B's yurt.'

Pio moaned. 'We're in so much trouble!' He sat with his head in his hands as she tried to light the dry tinder. 'Give me a go.'

He took the flint from her, struck a spark, and the tinder caught. He delicately blew on it, encouraging a small flame. Kiriz moved the lamp closer and they lit the small wick. Pio clamped the lid back down on the metal tinder box, snuffing the flame.

'Ready?' Kiriz asked.

Pio nodded reluctantly and shivered as the little falcon let out a plaintive cry. They lay flat and wriggled their torsos into the cavity.

He held the lamp as far in as he could. They looked at each other before hastily backing out.

'Did you see the walls? They moved. Perhaps we should go back,' Pio said.

'I don't think they moved.' Kiriz held his hand. 'We can do this, together.' They took deep breaths, gritted their teeth and squirmed their way through the cavity into the cave beyond. Their feet sank into damp clay. 'Ow, there're some sharp rocks in here.'

Protruding from the clay was a crystal. Pio drew the fire steel from his pocket and used it to dig the crystal from the damp clay. It was half as long again as his hand, with six sides and tapered ends. 'Have you ever seen black crystals?'

'Never.'

Standing close, still holding hands, they cautiously moved forward. The light winked back at them. The clay gave way to stone. Kiriz held the lamp aloft. Crystal pillars towered around them, jutting out at varying angles.

They moved deeper into to the formation, stopping when the ground became jagged with smaller crystals and they could no longer stand upright.

'It's beautiful,' Pio said.

'A bit, I suppose.' Kiriz shivered. 'Let's go back to the entrance.'

'Maybe we can find another crystal?'

The lamp shook in her hands. 'I'm freezing and … I feel a like the roof is going to fall on us.'

Pio squeezed her hand. 'This'll do then. Let's go.'

Outside in the shelter of the boulders, they cleaned the crystal. 'It's not black, is it?'

'It's like a rainbow, bits of blue, purple—sometimes silver. Oh look, turn it again—green!'

After examining the crystal, they sat at the entrance to the cave, eating day-old flat bread.

'Umniga says there is a purpose to everything the gods do. Do you think we were meant to find this?'

Kiriz shrugged. 'I don't know.'

'If Umniga thinks Rana sent you here, we might not get in so much trouble.'

Kiriz's face screwed up savagely; her voice was stricken. 'No. I'm not telling and neither are you. I told you they'll take me to train me—forever!'

He put his arm around her. 'I promise, I won't tell.'

Pio kept turning the crystal over in his hand. 'A rainbow? A dark rainbow with bits of fire in its heart.'

—⚋—

Ratial and Niaz scrutinised the map rolled out before them on the table in the council room.

'We can mobilise the army, once the signal …' A soft knock sounded on the council room door. 'Enter,' Ratilal barked.

The Castellan's grey head was bowed as he entered. 'A delegation is here, High Lord.'

'Get Vikram to deal with them first before you bother to interrupt me.'

The old man straightened. His eyes flicked to his high lord fearfully. 'Vikram cannot deal with them on your behalf.' He swallowed nervously before continuing. 'It is a conclave of clan elders.'

Ratilal's eyes narrowed and he inhaled sharply. 'As in the Conclave of old?'

'Yes, High Lord.' The Castellan lowered his head.

Niaz's jaw dropped. 'A Conclave has not gathered in generations. They want to replace you?'

Ratilal stalked to the fireplace. 'Naturally. Although I'm surprised they thought of it. I wonder who has stirred them up.' He leaned against the mantel, hands fisted, and stared into the fire. Finally, he said, 'Summon Vikram.'

'I took the liberty of doing so. He should be here soon.'

'You've done well, Castellan. Make sure he finds me first—as soon as he arrives. I assume they are in the Great Hall?' The Castellan nodded. 'Take them refreshments while I prepare.' The Castellan left.

'Why Vikram?' Niaz asked.

'As Pasha he should be here. Besides he has the respect of the lower city. He could be useful.'

Ratilal stood outside the Great Hall. He was in full armour. The engraved plates on his zirh gomlek had been polished and the boar's head of his clan shone amongst the twining branches of oak and willow. His metal greaves and dastanas featured a boar goring a victim; his zirh kulah was topped with a blood red feather. Vikram and Niaz flanked him, poised at each of the huge doors.

'Let's remind them what's at stake,' Ratilal said. At his signal Niaz and Vikram swung open the double doors and he strode into the room. At the base of the dais stood a large gathering of well-dressed men and women. *Soft, used to privilege. Who stirred you up?* Most of them were of his father's generation, though he noted a few younger warriors amongst them. *Challengers.* His lip curled in disdain.

Ratilal's brows rose as he spied several women, unarmed but dressed for combat. *Surely, they don't hope to challenge me? They've no place here.* The entire gathering comprised smaller groups, some with heads bowed in conspiratorial chatter, others animatedly waving their hands in disagreement. A few stood silent, watching. *So not all unified. Or unified in wanting me out, but not in who'll best replace me.*

Conversation ceased the moment Ratilal stepped into the room. All eyes turned toward him. The largest group parted to reveal Lady Malak at its core. Ratilal's jaw clenched and his stride slowed for a beat as he continued to the throne upon the dais.

Niaz drew a sharp breath and halted, eyes wide. He tore his gaze from Malak's and looked imploringly at Ratilal.

'Lord Niaz,' Ratilal said, 'you are in an unenviable situation—one I would not have you suffer in. I can see by your face that you had no inkling of this ... yet you must choose.'

Niaz examined each of the four challengers. Slowly, he closed his eyes and shook his head, before moving to stand at the base of the dais nearest to Ratilal.

'Mistress Malak, I assume you're the cause of this gathering?' Ratilal said.

'No. You are the cause. I merely reminded the elders of the rite of the Conclave to challenge. Your actions already caused them to think you unworthy.'

'My actions?'

'Word has been circulating even unto the walls of Faros that you killed your father; that you scarred a girl from Pramod's beyond recognition in a drunken rage.'

'Rumours. On the basis of this you have deemed me unworthy. I've trained for decades to be a fit leader. I importuned my father to restore this clan to its old ways—he agreed. Why would I kill him? I'd like nothing better than to have him by my side while we take back north of the Divide and to return to our traditional values. I know you want this too because it is best for our clan. What true clan member would not want this? And yet because of these lies you seek to replace me.'

'The Conclave ...' Malak said.

'At your bidding,' Ratilal ground out.

Malak smiled serenely. 'I can't bid them to anything.'

'In truth, High Lord,' an elderly man said, 'Lady Malak merely reminded us that the Rite of Challenge from the Conclave is one of our oldest traditions. Your line came to rule our clan via this ritual. You, who value our traditions so highly, understand how worthy it is to honour this one.'

'Yet, there are those here who are not a part of the Conclave, or even of the elder families. Ladies?'

'Some of us are from the elder families. We are all Boar Clan. Lady Malak informed us of the Conclave. We want a return to our old ways. We want those women amongst us who wish to fight and train to be able to do so—as in days old. To this end we will support whomever encourages this.'

'I see.' *Blackmail.* 'When I win this contest we will talk more.' Ratilal's hands rested easily on the throne. One finger drummed an impatient rhythm on the arm of the chair. 'We don't have time for this. We've a war to win. I've plans that will see Horse and Bear driven to their knees. Every day we linger, Karan has time to bring more troops from the Plateau.'

'He'll not have the numbers to match us. The Plateau must be a harsh place, their numbers cannot be great, thus a week or so will not matter,' an elder said.

Ratilal's fist slammed on the arm of the chair and he leapt upright. 'You think so, do you? Why do you think Karan and Baldev annexed the land north of the Divide? The only reason they'd do it is because he needs the land. We know Baldev's numbers and they did not annex the land for him. There will be no waiting a week for this contest! We will do this now.'

'The necessary preparations must be made. The clan must gather. All must witness.'

'Some of our clan will never make it. They're across the Divide. They cannot be here to witness the challenge. Already do you see the futility of this?' Ratilal said.

Malak smiled triumphantly. 'Are you saying that you refuse the challenge?'

'No. But now is the time we must appear unified. This,' he waved his hand dismissively toward the gathering. 'This serves the purpose of the enemy. If you think Karan and Baldev do not have spies here in Faros, you would be wrong. They spread the rumours. They spread the lies! You're playing into their hands.

The Conclave demanding a leadership challenge sows doubt into the minds of the entire clan—doubt, not only about me, but about our strength. Every delay means Karan and Baldev will amass more troops. If we strike early we'll have the advantage. We are ready. I need no delays.' He eyed them with scorn. 'Captain Vikram has been made Pasha due to his years of loyal service to my father and this clan. None of you can surely object to this?' A murmur of assent hummed through the chill of the hall. 'Good. For the duration of the contest Vikram will be in charge.'

'What! He's no member of the elder families!'

'Precisely. Vikram has risen from lower Faros on his own merit. He has the clan's best interests at heart. He has no loyalty to any of you. He is the fairest choice. He'll make sure that lower Faros is not forgotten.'

'Agreed,' Malak said, loudly cutting off any further objection.

Ratilal gestured to the throne. 'Vikram, you're now in charge. I would respectfully suggest that we deal with this quickly.'

Vikram licked his lips nervously. He ascended the dais slowly, but did not sit upon the throne. 'The word will be spread throughout the city. We will hold the challenge at the training field to the north of the city tomorrow. Then we shall see who is fit to rule the Boar Clan.'

chapter twenty-five

NERVOUS EXCITED LAUGHTER and squeals rioted through the air. Isaura held the reins of Hamza's mount as he checked the string of mules and their precious cargo strung out behind her. She heard his gruff voice, alternately quietening the rowdier children and cheering the more sombre ones with hints about the grand adventure to come. Snatches of his speech drifted back to her.

'You wait till you see the view from the mountain pass—you can see the whole of Altaica. You'll know what it's like to be an eagle then. And them spires on the high citadel, why they're so tall they nearly touch the clouds,' Hamza said.

Karan and Baldev marched up to Isaura. Karan gave her a sly smile, but Baldev's face looked like thunder.

'There's no sign of them! Little wretches,' Baldev thundered. 'Do you know where they are, Isa?'

'No. I'm no longer the person Pio would confide in. Ask Sarala or his mother.'

Baldev strode off, bellowing orders to bring Lucia and Nicanor before him.

'Once I'd have been able to answer him. I knew all Pio's haunts,' Isaura said.

Karan took her hand. 'It will get better, Isa. Pio chafes against his parents' order concerning you. I see him watching you, bursting to tell you something. The more control you have, the more you seem like the old Isa, the less he believes their lies.'

'Thank you. You don't think anything has happened to them?'

Karan shook his head. 'We're safe here. He and Kiriz simply had no intention of going with Hamza. They've taken food from the kitchen, so I'd say they'll wait it out and come back when there's no hope of us sending them away.' His lips curled in amusement. 'I'd have done the same thing. If they're not back tomorrow, then maybe you can ask the Asena to find them,' Karan said.

'They won't run to Kiriz's home?'

'No. From what Baldev said Kiriz's mother would skin them alive if they did. Kiriz has Baldev wrapped around her little finger,' Karan said, shaking his head with a grin. 'She'll be back with Pio.'

'You're pleased he's still here?' Isaura asked.

'He needs to stay with his parents until they pass their testing.'

'And when is the testing?'

Karan's smile vanished; he dropped her hand. 'Tomorrow—for all of you.'

Isaura swallowed nervously.

Hamza returned. 'My Lord, I can wait no longer, not if you want me to do several supply runs before winter closes the high pass. The sooner these little 'uns get to the high citadel the better.'

'I know, my friend,' Karan said. He gestured to a group of mounted warriors nearby. They rode to take up positions along the column.

Hamza grabbed Isaura in a bear hug. 'Ah, my girl, you take care now. Keep training hard and working with Alejo. You've come a long way together, you have. He loves you more than life itself, I reckon. I'll be back before you know it and I'll have a proper saddle for you.' He mounted. 'Make sure they treat you right.' Hamza eyeballed Karan. 'You'll be one of us when I get back.' He scruffed her hair and waved as he headed off.

Isaura smiled fondly, shaking her head. 'Sometimes he talks to me like I'm two.'

'I wouldn't worry, it's just his way. He's always been an old mother hen.'

'Oh, I'm not worried. It's nice.' She shrugged. 'I'm just not used to it.'

The mule train climbed up the rise away from the camp and a large group of Asena joined the guard.

Worry creased her brow. 'That's a lot of escort for somewhere that's meant to be safe.'

'They're children. The escort will spend most of its time stopping them causing trouble.'

Baldev and Karan stood on the rise, looking down on the camp in the afternoon sunlight.

'We've done all the planning we can for the moment,' Karan said.

'Ratilal's not going to attack now. The river's only going to get worse and the land around the Falcontine is getting boggy. Only a fool would move an army across the marsh lands,' Karan declared.

'We should be patrolling,' Baldev grumbled.

'I thought you'd be enjoying having time to spend with Asha.'

'And here I was,' Baldev said cheekily, 'believing you were just thinking of yourself.' Karan crossed his arms and stared at him. 'Oh, don't look like that. I've seen you watch her, check on her progress.'

'We both get regular reports from Āsim and Pravin.'

'You're not fooling me.' Baldev waved his hand dismissively. 'Just tup the girl and be done with it.'

Karan ignored him. 'The newcomers are ready to be tested. I suggest we re-join patrolling once that's done.'

'Agreed. If they pass they can be split up into different squads to continue their training in the field.'

'We need to take a Kenati with each of us. Will Asha be joining you on patrol?'

'No. She can stay here.' Baldev was adamant.

'Protecting her? Asha's not going to appreciate it,' Karan said.

'I can still see the bruising from that bastard's attack. I don't want her hurt.'

'Of course not, but you'll insult her if you're not careful. Asha's a perfectly capable warrior.'

Baldev threw his hands in the air. 'I know, I know! I'm not stopping her from fighting—I can't. But if she comes with me, my judgement will be compromised by worrying about her. Better she doesn't fight with me.'

'We can team her with Isa. They are firm friends. They'll have Asha's guard as the rest of the squad.'

Baldev arched his brow and folded his arms across his chest. 'Protecting Isa?'

'No. She needs more training and now, while the river prevents Ratilal crossing the north, is the time for her to train. When Isa passes the testing, the pair of them will be rostered onto patrolling and she'll learn out in the field like the others. At present she'd be little use in the front line—later though she'll equal the best. Pravin can remain here to continue Isa's training.'

Baldev laughed. 'Good luck giving the crusty old bugger that order.'

'He wants to stay with her.'

'Really? Is she that good?'

'He believes she will be, but Pravin feels that she's always holding back. I think he's having fun,' Karan said. 'Have you given thought about how you want to split the strangers up if they pass?'

'The couples should be split into separate patrols.'

'Agreed. What about Lucia?' Karan asked.

'We shouldn't take both the boy's parents,' Baldev replied. 'Lucia can stay here with Pio. She should pass the test—although she's the weakest of the lot, she is making progress.'

'What of Elena?' Karan asked.

'That one's the surprise, isn't she? She'll pass the testing.' Baldev shook his head in disbelief. 'She's been training like a fiend from Karak's at her door.'

'That fiend would be Isa.'

The site for the challenge lay at the base of a slope, where a rectangular area had been roped off. Large white pennants bearing a black boar's head fluttered at its four corners. A pavilion stood at one end with a raised dais. Upon the dais was the throne from the Great Hall. A black sinan rested upon it. Three wide ornately engraved silver metal bands were spaced evenly along the ebon wood bracing it. The sun glinted off its bright points.

Vikram stood in full armour upon the dais. At its base stood Ratilal and two challengers.

'Where are the other challengers?'

'They withdrew last night,' Niaz replied. 'They've chosen to support the high lord.'

Vikram's mouth drew into a thin line. 'Then they have made this simple. You two will fight, then the winner will fight Ratilal another day.'

Ratilal's eyes narrowed. '*High Lord* Ratilal.'

'No. For the purposes of today you are merely Ratilal.'

'Pasha Vikram,' Ratilal said. 'I'll fight them both today.'

Vikram addressed the Conclave. 'Surely there can be no objection? There is precedent.'

'There is no objection,' Malak said, smiling.

'Are you sure?' Vikram asked Ratilal.

Ratilal tilted his chin defiantly. 'I'd have fought all four of them.'

'That would have been a spectacle worthy of watching,' Malak said. 'Sadly that will no longer be possible, will it? I wonder what prompted the withdrawal of the others.'

Vikram held out his hands, silencing them both. 'Challengers, you will draw straws to determine who fights first.'

'Pasha Vikram, I meant I will fight them together. Although given the odds I would ask the boon of choosing the weapons.'

Vikram hesitated. 'There will be no objection. Choose.'

Ratilal called out to the crowd. 'I choose kilij, buckler, daggers. What we have on us. No sinan, no bills, no bardiche, nothing that keeps me at a distance from my enemies.'

A murmur rippled through the crowd before it rolled into roar of approval.

Ratilal drew his dagger. Niaz passed him a metal buckler, which he held in the same hand as the dagger. The dagger's tip protruded from under the buckler—weapon and shield.

Niaz whispered, 'This is foolish. Two at once? You risk everything for pride.'

Ratilal laughed and clapped his friend on the back. 'Stop worrying, you old mother hen.'

'Your back …'

'Is better. I can't even feel it. Relax. This won't take long.'

Ratilal drew his kilij and moved fully into the combat field.

One of the challengers said to the other, 'Him first, then between us?'

'Done.'

'Begin!' yelled Vikram.

The challengers strode toward Ratilal. One rolled his shoulders, flexed his wrist, and swung his kilij menacingly as he walked. They grinned as they stalked their prey. Bucklers raised, they lunged toward Ratilal.

His sword flashed in front of him—a constantly moving arc slashing a protective wall before his attackers. He danced around them, never still. The two men worked in tandem well; their flurry of attacks kept Ratilal on the defensive. A sword flashed at him; he thrust out his buckler, deflecting the blow, slashing with his dagger and pushing his enemy's arm to the side. Ratial's kilij snaked out, slicing at his opponent's thigh. A sliver of red ran along his blade as he sliced the skin. The man snarled and stepped back.

Cocky, Ratilal grinned, goading him—his attention slipped. In his periphery the second warrior's blade sliced through the air with ruthless precision at Ratilal's neck.

Ratilal, eyes wide, arched back and the blade scraped along his mail. He staggered, tilting sideways. The two men pounced.

Ratilal pivoted and he drove his sword down, knocking the oncoming blade askew. It scraped down his greaves. Desperate, Ratilal kicked his enemy in the side, thrusting him into the other man, but further unbalancing himself. Sweat beaded his brow and the unfamiliar sensation of panic assailed Ratilal. He tamped it down, praying instead for the caress of the velvet rancour that simmered in his soul.

The crowd in the arena grew silent. His mind raced—each attack he thought of would leave him open from another side. The brutal ballet continued as the sun tracked the sky; the arcing dance of swords grew slower. *They'll humiliate you for all to see! They'll mock you for the rest of your days. You will lose everything.* The dark fire stirred within him. *Never! There is none I will bow to.* His rage burst into flame. His eyes alight, Ratilal heaved a deep breath and attacked. His sword blurred and he manoeuvred his enemy.

Ratlilal stood in between them. His opponents grinned, victory was theirs. The man on the left slashed his kilij at Ratilal. The one on the right aimed a blow to Ratilal's head. Ratilal pushed out with both arms. *And now I burn.* Fierce joy filled his face. He punched out with his buckler and dagger, deflecting the blow from the right. His dagger's tip pierced the mail of his opponent. With a turned hand, his sword deflected the slash from the left, thrusting the blade away. He pivoted to the attack on the right. Slashing his blade high he sliced the man's throat. The man dropped his weapons and staggered back, clutching his neck. *Red fire, black fire, beautiful fire. Burn.*

Spinning back, Ratilal punched out with his shield, deflecting another blow and forcing his enemy's arm wide. Into the gap he slashed his kilij down into the man's shoulder. It did not penetrate the mail, yet he staggered sideways, barely able to hold his sword. Ratilal aimed a slash behind his knee. He toppled to the ground. His lower leg hung by thin amount of gristle.

Ratilal left them, calmly walking to the dais. He grabbed the ornate black spear and strode back to his victims. He stood over the man whose leg he'd all but severed and drove the spear between the join of his zihr gomlek and through the centre of his chest. Ratilal pulled it out and walked to the other felled man. He was dead. *But they don't know that.* His body thrumming with adrenalin, he rammed the spear into the corpse. *So too will end all who stand in my way.*

His eyes sought out those of Malak's ashen face. Ratilal held the spear aloft theatrically and turned about so all of Faros could see.

'Before the Conclave and before the clan, by right of conquest,' Vikram shouted. 'I proclaim Ratilal High Lord of the Boar Clan. Long may he rule!'

―❦―

The warriors had formed a large circle. Karan and Baldev stood together. Pravin, Āsim and Umniga flanked them. Within the circle stood Curro, Nicanor, Elena, Lucia, Jaime, Gabriela and Isaura.

Āsim called out, "The time of testing is upon us. Your name will be called. Warriors from the circle will choose to step forward to test each of you. This is not mortal combat. You will be using practice weapons. Weapons are the choice of the warrior testing you. The bout will end when one of you is disarmed, or Lords Karan and Baldev deem a mortal wound would've been delivered, or in the unlikely event that the lords declare the match a draw. It is to gauge your proficiency, your tenacity—your heart. Based on your fight, the gathered warriors will judge whether you are fit to fight alongside with them. Your training has only been short, so that will be taken into account. If you pass, then the real training begins.' Nicanor step forth. 'Who will challenge Nicanor?'

A burly Bear warrior stepped forward. 'I claim that right.'

'Weapons?' Āsim said.

'Sword and shield.'

'Begin,' Āsim bellowed.

Nicanor armed himself, then faced off against the warrior. The kalkan shield protected his hand and forearm. It had a plain metal boss and metal rim. Metal shafts radiated out from its boss, over rolled cane, connecting with the metal rim like spokes on a wheel. He held the shield forward, his hand positioned as if for a fistfight. His other hand held the practice sword. They circled each other. Nicanor darted forward, slashing his sword toward his opponent. The warrior pushed his shield forward, deflecting the blow easily. The clash of sword and shield resounded. The battle drew on.

'Your man's going easy on him,' Karan murmured.

'He's just putting him through his paces,' Baldev replied quietly. 'He'll give him and opening soon—see if he takes it.'

Sweat began to bead on Nicanor's forehead. His pulse raced. His opponent was quick. It took all his skill to defend himself. His focus narrowed as he searched for a sign of the warrior's next move. There! He saw an opening and attacked. His momentum carried him forward.

The warrior stepped to the side. His sword struck Nicanor behind the knee. Nicanor buckled, but did not go down. The warrior struck again. His sword whacked Nicanor in the stomach.

'Hold!' Baldev shouted. 'Nicanor, you've shown heart and stamina. But you'd now have a severed leg and a gaping belly wound. In short you are dead. I call for judgement from those assembled! Will he be worthy?'

A cry of 'Aye' rang out from every warrior and they pounded upon their shields in approval.

Baldev grinned. 'Leave the circle, Nicanor. You are welcome in the Bear Clan.'

Next Jaime was tested, with sinan and shield. Battered and bruised, he passed.

'Jaime, you have our leave to choose between Horse and Bear. You have until day's end to do so.'

Lucia stood, clenching and unclenching her hands in anticipation. Isaura and Gabriela looked at each other and moved closer to her. Isaura whispered, 'Lucia, you'll be fine. You've been working hard, just do your best.' *They want Pio, they have accepted Nic; they'll not let you fail.* Lucia stiffened at Isaura's voice, glanced at her with a half-smile before turning away and staring straight ahead.

Gabriela leaned close to Lucia, saying softly, 'Isaura is right.'

Āsim called Lucia forth. Sarala stepped forward to test her. 'Staves,' Sarala called.

Lucia gripped the staff tightly. She uttered softly, 'Majula and Ariceli, help me.'

Sarala spoke quietly to her, 'Remember, today I am your enemy. Today I would take your son from you if you let me. Just hold that to your heart.'

Lucia nodded with a tremulous smile, took a deep breath and adjusted her grip. Sarala jabbed forward with her staff. Lucia blocked and side stepped. Readjusting her hold, she slammed her staff toward Sarala. Lucia forgot the eyes watching her, she forgot her lack of skill. 'Enemy. Save Pio. Enemy. Save Pio.' The mantra escaped her lips. The rest of the world faded.

Sarala attacked her fiercely. Lucia battled valiantly in return.

'She's doing better than I thought, even though it's just the drill,' Karan said.

'What she lacks in skill, she wins with heart,' Baldev replied.

Lucia lunged forward, swinging her staff. Sarala blocked her easily. Sarala's staff slid along Lucia's and rammed her hand. Lucia dropped the staff.

Dishevelled, weary Lucia slumped. 'I've failed,' she whispered.

'Halt,' Baldev cried. 'Lucia, your skills need much honing, but you have shown us the courage of a mother bear in this and in all your training so far. I call for judgement!'

The clash of weapons on shields nearly deafened her as the call of 'Aye!' rang out. Lucia's jaw dropped.

Pio and Kiriz broke through the circle. 'Ma! Wow, Ma! You did it! You were amazing!' Pio ran up to her and threw his arms around her waist. Kiriz clapped her hands and jumped about until she saw Baldev glaring at her.

'Lucia, you are welcome in my clan! You may leave the circle. Kiriz, I'll see you after the testing.'

'Pio! Where have you been?' Lucia grabbed his shoulders and shook him. She grabbed Pio and Kiriz by their ears and marched them from the circle. 'Now, where were you? I want answers! And look at the state of you!' Her tirade faded into the distance as she hauled the children off.

'Isaura, step forth. Isaura, in this trial you can receive no help from your guardian, is that clear?' Āsim called. 'Who will challenge Isaura?'

Asha stepped forward, but before she could speak, Umniga's voice rang out. 'I will challenge, Isaura. Staves!'

Asha's gaze darted to Isaura's; she shrugged apologetically.

Isaura looked at Karan and Baldev in dismay. 'My lords, I owe Umniga much. I … I cannot …'

'You must, Isaura. She has answered the call to test you.'

'Come on, girl. Let's see what that old goat Pravin's been teaching you.'

Alejo touched Isaura's thoughts briefly, amused at her quandary. He flashed her a smug picture of the old woman sprawled upon the ground with Isaura standing over her. *No, Alejo.*

Umniga struck swiftly. Isaura parried blow after blow. Uminga swung her staff high at Isaura's head. Isaura blocked, her hands and arms vibrating with the force of the blow. Umniga slid her hands along the staff, swinging it down at Isaura. Isaura's staff flashed, deflecting her blow. Both stepped back. Shifting stance, Umniga altered her attack. Staves clashed in the air. In a blink Umniga drew back and jabbed her staff at Isaura's abdomen. Shocked at her speed, Isaura sucked her stomach in and bent back. Eyes wide, she twisted and side stepped. Her staff thrust

Umniga's away. Umniga pressed forward, her staff spinning as she pushed Isaura back. She smiled as Isaura's eyes blazed.

'Come on girl, show me what you can do.'

Karan's jaw clenched at Umniga's taunt. 'What's the matter, worried about your girl?' Baldev chuckled. 'She's quick, I'll give her that, but Umniga won't break her.'

'I'm not worried about that,' Karan ground out.

Isaura felt The Wild within her rising to the threat. Umniga aimed for Isaura's head. Isaura ducked and managed to jab upward at Umniga's midriff. Fire kindled in Isaura's spirit. Alejo urged her to unleash it. *No.* She pulled her staff back at the last second. Umniga grunted as the staff barely connected with her stomach. Umniga's staff was a blur as it came at Isaura. In three successive moves Isaura was on the ground. Umniga's staff hovered above her head.

Karan, arms folded, stared at them, impassive. 'Judgement?' he called. The ring of warriors remained silent.

Umniga hauled her to her feet. 'All your moves bar one were defensive. Why?' she demanded.

Isaura swallowed nervously. 'You're an old lady.'

Umniga threw her head back and laughed. Laughter broke out around the circle. 'So you didn't want to hurt me?'

Isaura shook her head vigorously.

'Our Asena Blessed did not want to hurt a little old lady,' she cried to the warriors, grinning. 'Does she pass?'

Asha cried, 'Aye!' Slowly the warriors began thumping on their shields. 'Aye!' Asha yelled at them again.

'Aye!' they cried back.

Karan held his arms out, silencing the group. 'Isaura, you may leave the circle. You are welcome ...'

'You are welcome,' interrupted Baldev, 'to choose between either the Horse or Bear.' Karan's lips drew into a thin line; his brow arched as stared at his friend. A few chuckles could be heard. 'Although I think Lord Karan ...'

Isaura cut him off. 'I choose Horse.'

'Come on,' Asha whispered as she pushed her out of the circle. 'You were lucky, they expected more.'

'But she's an old woman!'

'She just kicked your butt.'

chapter twenty-six

VIKRAM STOOD AS the women entered his office. 'You are most welcome,' he said, smiling.

'We are pleased to see that the high lord honours his promises,' one of them said.

Vikram's smile vanished. 'The high lord has made no orders regarding incorporating women back into the ranks of his army. I, however, am Pasha of Faros and as Pasha I heartily welcome you into my troops.'

She folded her arms, glancing in shared annoyance with her companions. 'The city guard?'

Vikram held up his hands placatingly. 'It is not what you wanted, but it is a start. It is not war with the others …' He smiled again conspiratorially. 'Not yet. In truth, you are not ready for the front, because prejudice has prevented you from training as you should. I want an end to that. The high lord has chosen his men. I have kept my trusted guard and been left with those he deems too old or too young or too weak to be useful. Amongst the "too old" are some of our clan's best Silahtars—they'll train you. They will make you ready for anything. And none under my command will dispute your place amongst us. Is this acceptable?'

The women turned and huddled in whispered discussion. Finally their spokeswoman said, 'It is.'

'Good. Round up any others who wish to train, rich or poor, I care not. Tell them to bring whatever kit they have to the barracks. We'll assess them and begin training.'

'Yes, Pasha Vikram.'

As they began to leave Vikram said, 'Just Captain Vikram will do. But know this—you will be far more than just the city guard, I promise you.'

'And you should know, it is to you alone we owe our loyalty, Pasha Vikram.'

—⁂—

The Boar soldiers' small canoes were spread out as they silently glided along the river. The only movement from the soldiers was to steer away from obstacles that loomed suddenly before them on the near moonless night.

Hunters' Ford lay miles downstream. The soldiers scanned the shore, futilely seeking signs of movement along the banks. One man closed his eyes, silently praying their high lord was right and no patrols were here.

Their commander sat in the prow. He turned and tapped the arm of the man behind him, pointing to a bulky shape jutting into the river on an outward bend. Each man pulled frantically on the paddles. The closer they drew to the shore, the more hunched and furtive they became.

Willow fronds brushed over the canoes. The lead warrior in the first canoe tossed a grappling hook into the stand of willows. 'Rana and Jalal, don't fail me now,' he whispered. He braced himself as it caught and he began hauling the canoe closer against the current. The bank and willow roots rose above them. As the boat hit the thick, tangled mat of woody and burgundy hair-like roots, the other soldiers sunk bale hooks into them to hold the boat still.

Using the rope, the first soldier climbed up the bank. He clung precariously near the top of the bank, listening intently, trying to glean any sign of the enemy. Slowly he pulled himself over the top. The next man followed. They both prodded the ground amidst the stand of trees.

'Main roots are too close together here. Might be some place further in.'

'I think I know,' the other said, drawing his friend back to the bank. He hung over the bank. 'Hang onto my feet,' he ordered. He pressed and punched the matted red roots. 'Thought so. It felt a bit too springy when we was climbing up.' With a grunt of satisfaction he sliced through the matting of fine roots of the willow. Time and flood waters had created a cavity between the outer roots and the bank. 'We might be able to fit it in here.' Righting himself, he then clambered into the water, using a bale hook to hang from the bank. With a little help from his friend he guided the canoe into its hiding place before re-joining the others.

'If the water rises while it's stuck there it could sink it.'

'Still the best place.'

A second canoe pulled into the bank, aiming for a different spot near the grove. Its crew hastily went to work in hiding the canoe. Stealthily they joined the first group as two other canoes touched the banks.

'We've got a lot of ground to cover and we've got to stick to the schedule for this to work,' the commander said. 'Let's hope the high lord is right and they're at the lake.'

Elena was livid as Curro fought with the heavy wooden bardiche. 'Isaura gets easily beaten by an old woman and passes and we get treated like this. He has not trained in this,' she hissed at Gabriela.

'We've trained with other pole weapons,' Gabriela replied flatly.

'It looks as dangerous as the real thing. If one of them misjudges …'

'The weapon's padded and so is he. They're pulling their blows. He won't be killed. Just watch.'

Finally, Curro stood, sides heaving, leaning heavily on his bardiche as the warriors around him cheered.

'Curro, you are welcome in the Bear Clan,' Baldev called.

The opponent grinned at him. 'You did well.'

'I didn't even land a blow on you.'

The warrior clasped Curro's shoulder. 'No, but I didn't expect you to. I wanted to see how adaptable you could be. I've observed you training and thought that this weapon would be one you may favour. You were undaunted.'

'I do like the feel of it,' Curro said, wiping sweat from his brow.

'Good. I'll train you further. Go and get your leg seen to—you'll have a cracking bruise at the very least.'

Curro hobbled toward Elena. 'All will be well. I've passed. You will too. Just put your heart into it and you'll triumph.' He limped off.

'Gabriela, step forth. Who will test her?'

A young warrior hastily stepped forward. 'I will!' Āsim's contemptuous gaze raked him. He looked at Karan, who gave a small nod. 'Weapon?' Āsim said curtly.

He gave Gabriela a lazy smile. 'Bill.'

Gabriela lowered her eyes demurely, before looking askance at Āsim, who gave her a barely perceptible nod. She took the bill and hefted its long shaft in her hands, appraising the dummy spike on the end with its hook on the side. She hid her smile. Though it was a practice weapon the hook would still work effectively.

'Don't worry. I'll make sure you pass,' he said with a smug wink.

Gabriela held the weapon at the ready. Her opponent feinted. She remained steady, watchful. He lunged. She retreated. He grinned at her worried expression. Cocky, he attacked. Gabriela thrust the bill forward and down, displacing his blow. The end of the bill rammed into the earth against the back of his leg. She kicked him in the groin. He staggered. Hands still on the pole of the bill, she used her weight to haul on it. The hook caught around his leg. He fell. As his legs flew up in the air, Gabriela flicked the bill away. He landed flat on his back. She rammed the tip of the bill at his head. He stared at her wide-eyed as the wooden spike pressed into his forehead. The warriors erupted in cheers. Āsim beamed.

'Gabi,' Karan said. 'I need not ask for judgement for it has clearly been given. Well done.'

'You may choose your clan,' Baldev said.

Gabriela looked from Elena's stunned expression to Isaura's jubilant one. 'Horse, I choose Horse.'

—⚜—

'Who will test Elena?' Āsim's voice rang across the circle. None answered.

Elena clenched her fists to stop them shaking. Curro and the others stood outside the circle, worried and whispering amongst themselves. Curro pushed forward. Two warriors blocked his way. 'My lords, she deserves to be tested. She's made mistakes earlier.' Elena's stared at him indignant. 'But she's tried since.'

'Be still!' Karan barked at him, before nodding at Āsim.

'Who will test Elena?'

The silence was broken by one voice.

'I will,' said Isaura.

Murmurs rippled amongst the warriors.

'A ruling, my lords?' Āsim asked.

Karan and Baldev conferred. 'Isaura has passed and been accepted into the Horse,' Karan declared.

'Given that no other has stepped forward we will allow it,' Baldev finished.

'Well, Elena?' Isaura said. 'It looks like you get your wish. It's time to prove your worth.'

Alejo cantered around the circle. He stopped and pounded his hooves against the ground.

'Isaura, he must not interfere,' Karan warned.

'He will not. My lords, I ask that Elena be allowed to choose her weapon.'

Karan frowned, jaw clenched, then nodded. Elena strode to the weapons rack. Her hand fluttered over the weapons in anticipation.

She chose a spear, eyeing the dummy tip with open disdain. Isaura chose a staff.

Āsim opened his mouth to object. "Leave her be," Pravin said.

'Why don't you take a spear?' Elena asked.

'Because I've no intention of using the pointy end on you, Elena.'

'I will not have them say this was an unfair fight, pick up the spear.'

'My having a spear will not make this fight any more fair.'

Elena's nostrils flared; her lip curled. 'You insult me. I saw you fight. The old woman easily beat you.'

Isaura sighed. 'I want you to pass, don't mess it up,' she said as they walked to the centre of the ring.

Elena's spear flashed toward Isaura's belly. Isaura blocked her blow easily and rammed her arm with the staff, driving her sideways. Elena danced around Isaura, her hands slid deftly along the spear shaft as she rained blows at her.

Isaura began her attack. She kept it simple—mimicking their drill.

Elena parried each blow, growing more bold. 'I knew they kept your training hidden because you were nothing special.' Her spear darted in as she tried to repeatedly stab Isaura's limbs.

Isaura smiled. 'You're doing well, Elena. Keep it up.'

'Don't mock me,' Elena spat. She thrust her spear thrust at Isaura's face, barely missing her.

'Very good.'

A trickle of joy flowed through Isaura as Elena's jaw clenched and lip curled. Elena jabbed the spear forward. Isaura deflected the blow and closed the distance between them, forcing Elena to use the spear like a staff.

Isaura's moves were precise, ruthless. A fire began to build within her. Alejo urged her on. She grinned as she cracked the staff into Elena's side and aimed a sweeping kick into the rear of her leg. Elena toppled backward. Isaura rapped the staff onto Elena's hand and she dropped the spear. Elena hit the dirt.

Isaura pounced on her. She pressed the staff against her throat, pinning her to the ground. A slow grin tweaked Isaura's lips. *Burn.* She pressed a bit harder, watching with detached fascination as Elena's eyes widened. *Just a bit more …*

'Halt,' called Baldev.

Isaura turned her head toward Baldev, her gaze predatory. Her hands still held Elena pinned. Alejo's anticipation filled her mind.

'Isa, no!' Curro yelled.

No? Isaura sought the source of the word. *No?* Her eyes met Curro's. Recognition—Curro. Slowly she saw the others—Nicanor, Lucia … Pio. She swallowed and looked at Elena. *No, she's ill … she doesn't understand.* Abruptly, Isaura stood, her hands gripping both weapons so tightly her knuckles shone white. Her face was impassive, but her eyes were vivid blue as she returned the staff and spear to the weapons rack. She rested her hands upon the rack to steady them. She leaned forward, concentrated on her breathing, slowly inching back her control.

Elena followed her, rubbing her throat and glowering. She picked up a practice sword and shield. She smiled with satisfaction as she ran her finger along the metal edge of the shield. She hefted the sword and took a step toward Isaura. All was quiet.

'Don't, Elena. Not now,' Isaura bit out.

Elena grinned madly. She attacked, sword slicing through the air. Isaura snatched up a shield, thrusting it out and fending off the blow. She pushed Elena away from the weapons rack and grabbed a practice sword. Isaura jabbed the tip of her sword down over the top of Elena's shield. Elena pushed her shield up and bent back. The tip barely missed her head. They circled. Elena sprang forward. Isaura dodged to the side, her blade swiping the fabric of Elena's pants as she passed. The Wild within her rose like a tidal wave.

'Stop them!' Curro cried.

Karan and Baldev stood with their arms folded. Not a warrior moved from the shield wall.

Elena changed tactics. With swifter strikes and shorter

movements, the tip of the curved blade darted snake-like at Isaura. Confident, she aimed for Isaura's head. Isaura punched her shield forward, pushing aside the blow. Her blade sliced through the air at Elena's throat. Elena's shield slammed sideways. She tried to hook her leg around Isaura's to trip her. Isaura danced out of her reach, grinning.

Āsim murmured to Pravin, "It's like watching a cat play with a mouse."

Isaura's body sang with blue fire—joyous, wild. She laughed. Alejo no longer raced around the circle. He stood perfectly still, content to watch. A small part of Isaura struggled to contain The Wild humming through her. *Breathe, control it. Breathe. Gods, calm ... breathe.*

Elena's face twisted in rage. She darted in, slicing at Isaura's side.

Isaura lost control—she became a spectator as instinct took over. Everything was about the fight. She pivoted, chopping her sword into Elena's wrist. Elena screamed as the bone snapped. She dropped her sword and lowered her shield, doubling over in agony.

Isaura swung her shield sideways and hammered it into Elena's jaw.

'No!' Curro yelled as he struggled against two guards.

The bone gave way. Elena's head snapped sideways. Isaura drove the practice sword deep into her belly. Elena slumped to the ground.

Isaura stared at the body, annoyed that she couldn't withdraw her weapon. Alejo gently probed her mind. She frowned, looking about her, puzzled. *Elena. I killed Elena.*

A desperate roaring became a wail that bombarded her. Four men were holding Curro back. Karan was beside her. He put his arm around her shoulders and drew her away. Isaura's eyes darted between Curro and Elena's body. Her friends looked upon her with horror. She began to shake. Karan supported her on one side, Baldev on the other.

'Let him go,' Karan ordered the warriors.

Curro raced forward to kneel beside Elena. Isaura grimaced as he yanked the wooden sword from her belly and cradled her head in his lap. Elena's jaw flopped at an odd angle. Isaura doubled over retching and began to sweat. Her vision grew dark, then was filled with blotches of red.

Karan's arm supported her. 'You'll be all right. It's the battle fever.'

Rage filled Curro's face as he charged toward her. Alejo tore in between them, rearing and striking at Curro. *Alejo, don't kill him.* Asha and Umniga closed ranks around her.

Āsim and Pravin led a group to restrain Curro. Alejo paced between them. It grew quiet.

'Come, we'll take her to my yurt. Baldev will sort this out.'

'If she'd hit her any harder she'd have taken her head clean off,' Umniga whispered.

'Now we know why she's been holding back,' Karan said.

chapter twenty-seven

'ASHA, UMNIGA, GET Isaura to my yurt. She'll probably sleep the rest of this day and the next to recover.'

Isaura straightened, clumsily shaking Karan's arm from her shoulders. 'No. I want to go somewhere quiet.'

'My yurt is quiet.'

'Not there. I can rest elsewhere.' Isaura cocked her head, listening. 'I'm going to the forest—the Matriarch is waiting.' She shook free of his grasp. Alejo lay down and she slid onto his back. Half slumped, she clutched his spiky mane.

'Not on your own. You can barely hang on.' Karan stepped toward her then stopped. He shook his head. 'Asha, Umniga, go with her. Baldev and I will calm things here.'

Asha mounted behind Isaura, wrapping her arms around her friend to keep her upright and on Alejo as he took them to the forest. Umniga walked behind them. Alejo carefully picked his way around trees, fallen branches and through soggy gullies, before stopping at an oak on a small knoll. The Matriarch sat waiting.

Umniga leaned on her staff, catching her breath. 'Greetings, Old Mother.'

Asha and Umniga tried to support Isaura as she walked to the tree, but she pushed them away.

'I can make it. I feel stronger.' Isaura sat on the ground next to the Matriarch and leaned against the tree.

Isa-cub, you need to enter the spirit realm. The Lady watches and is waiting there, the Matriarch warned.

I thought she might be. It was too good a show for her to be able to resist.

'Umniga, Asha, I'm entering the spirit realm—don't panic.'

'Isa, that's not a good idea in your current state,' Umniga said.

Isaura relaxed, controlled her breathing and left the physical world with Alejo.

The Lady was waiting, jubilant. *Isaura, you were most impressive! The power that flowed through you ...*

It did not flow through her! It flowed from her. This is not what you were hoping for, said the Matriarch angrily.

The Lady glowered at the Matriarch. *Can I never have a conversation with the girl without your interference?*

No. Asha and Umniga are calling their guardians to them. They will follow Isa here.

It matters not, the Lady said. *I will not allow them to see me—the time is not right.*

Umniga will probably have a heart attack if she sees you both together, Isaura said.

There was never a woman less likely of having a heart attack, the Lady snapped.

I'm having a hard enough time with the whole Asena Blessed thing without explaining how I failed to mention my casual acquaintance and conversations with someone I suspect they'll think a goddess, Isaura grumbled.

Umniga and Asha appeared with Fihr and Devi. *Isa, you should not ...* Umniga began.

The Wild raced to Isaura, she could feel it pooling around her. Alejo's spirit form glowed blue and red; she marvelled at the strength of his aura—hers was a dull blue-grey. Alejo's aura flared briefly. The outer edges of Isaura's form became more defined. The image of the spider-work of branches and leaves that Asha and Umniga had drawn on her for the ritual of Samara glowed and shone through the illusion of her clothes. A wave of vibrant blue rippled them so the branches appeared to sway. A bloom of blue exploded at her heart, casting a glare. Asha and Umniga looked away, shielding their gazes.

Seeing the change, the Lady glared at the Matriarch. *You knew.*

It's happened before. The question is, why didn't you know?
There is more to occupy my attention than this, the Lady snapped.
By the gods! How? Umniga asked.

Isaura refused to meet her gaze; instead she looked at the Matriarch who said nothing.

The ritual. I was in the spirit realm too long. The Wild is part of me, Isaura confessed.

Fihr and Devi moved in agitation away from Alejo. Asha stared at Isaura and Alejo.

Has anyone noticed that their auras are identical? And ... Asha stepped forward. *He's ... he looks ... nearly solid.*

—⁂—

Elena's body lay atop a pyre. Curro and Nicanor had gathered the wood. Lucia had carried water from a mountain stream and bathed her. A basin of clean water sat on Elena's abdomen and her hands had been placed around the bowl. In her mouth lay a small stone from the mountain.

'This is wrong,' Lucia whispered. 'She should not be burned, but buried.'

Nicanor put his arm about her shoulders. 'They'll not allow it. But she has had our other rites.'

'The water and the stone should be offered up properly.'

'They are still being offered, that's the main thing. I think Umniga is correct. When the fire burns, the water will steam and disperse, rising straight to our gods.'

'The rock? How will it go to the gods?'

'Let Curro decide. Ssh, here he comes.'

Curro carried a torch, and was followed by members of the camp. They formed a solemn circle around the pyre.

Curro's face was haggard; dark circles hung under his eyes. His hand trembled as he touched the torch to the wood. He stood head bowed, shoulders shaking, and fell to his knees sobbing.

The pyre smoke rose black and foul into the chill air.

Isaura watched from the edge of the camp. The taint of the smoke assailed her, yet she stayed until the body had been consumed. *May you find peace.*

Only ashes and bone grit remained, still too hot to touch. The others had gone, leaving Curro to his grief. He rose ponderously, lost and guilty. His gaze rested upon Isaura. Karan stood beside her and they were talking quietly, but Isaura's eyes never left Curro's. There was no regret upon her face, no shame, no apology. Curro's emptiness was replaced by anger and bitterness—his guilt remained.

Isaura left the campsite and headed toward the forest. The weight of the daggers sheathed in the sides of her boots and the one at her waist was of little comfort. Rapidly she assessed her surrounds. Isaura stopped at a stand of maples, bereft of their bright red leaves. *Far enough from camp, open. There's good footing.* Conifers loomed beyond the maples; the winter sun did not illuminate the shadows they cast.

Arms folded, she leaned against a tree trunk and waited.

Curro stepped before her.

Isaura arched her brow. 'Well?'

His face twisted in hate and grief. 'You killed her.'

'Yes.' Isaura looked away.

'Why?'

I didn't mean to. Isaura stared blankly at him. 'She would've killed me.'

'No. No, Elena just wanted to prove herself,' Curro said, shaking his head. 'She … she would've merely taught you a lesson.'

'A lesson? Is that what I need? Are you here to teach me a lesson, Curro, or are you here to end me?'

'I …' Curro's hands fisted at his sides. 'I … just …' He took a step toward her. His hand shook as he pointed at her. 'You … How could you?'

Angry, she stepped toward him. Hands on her hips, she said,

'How could you not tell her the truth? In all these years?'

Curro drew back, shocked. 'I did.'

'You did? Really?' Isaura's tone was venomous. 'What precisely did you tell her?'

'Don't change the topic, Isaura.'

'I haven't. You say I killed her, but surely this path began the moment you didn't confess your crime.'

'I …'

'Yes, you.' Isaura was implacable. 'You were both hurt and angry. The travelling players were in the village. I guessed what you'd do. Gods, probably half the village guessed. But I was the one dumb enough to try to help. I looked for you that night after their performance to stop you doing something stupid. I was too late, so I left. What I've worked out is that Elena must have followed me and waited. I was hoping to stop her finding you … as you were. But Elena saw me leave, followed a short time later by you. The travelling player, whom you dallied with, undoubtedly well-practiced, left by another way. As far as Elena was concerned, we'd slept together.'

'I told her.'

'What exactly?'

'That it wasn't true. That I'd never slept with you.'

Isaura sneered. 'And did you tell her who you *did* sleep with?'

'No.'

Seething, Isaura continued, 'No. Because you were man enough to get it up, but not man enough to own up to the woman who loved you.'

Curro hung his head in shame.

'That's when Elena began to hate me. She had no one else to blame, so why not me? And you let her! So who is really responsible here? I killed her in self-defence, but if not for your actions years ago and your continued cowardice to confess, it would never have come to this.'

Curro held his head in his hands and sobbed.

'Go, see to your wife's remains. Treat her with the honour in death that you didn't in life.'

He remained there head bowed, shoulders shaking.

'Go! LEAVE ME!'

He flinched at the power of her command, turned and left.

Karan and Alejo stepped from between the shadowed conifers. 'I thought he'd react differently. Tell me what you said, Isa,' Karan asked.

She told him the tale in all its sordid glory.

'I'm still surprised he didn't attack you. He may still.'

Isaura shrugged. 'Perhaps he will.'

'Why didn't you tell him that you didn't mean to kill her?'

'It's what I'd like to believe, but it wouldn't have been the truth. I didn't start that way, but by the end it was all I wanted.' Isaura kicked the ground angrily. 'If Elena had more of the truth, things would have been different.'

'The truth is not a universal panacea, Isa,' Karan said softly.

'Oh, I know that. But she would have had one less demon and maybe that would have been enough to change this. To a certain extent she was what he made her. And I helped—we all helped in some way.'

'Would she have left him, if she'd known?'

'Perhaps—I don't know. I know I would have. What's the use now?' Isaura shook her head and wiped away tears.

Karan embraced her. 'Isa …'

She stiffened and pushed him away. 'Don't. Don't hold me like that. Not unless you've made your mind up about us—about the possibility of us. It's too much … too hard, and it's not fair.' Isaura jumped upon Alejo and cantered off without a backward glance.

—∞—

Two days since Elena's death, now we celebrate, Isaura thought. The smell of spit roasting meat drifted from the kitchens.

The head cook yelled out, 'You two, little demons, out! Out now!' Warriors stopped their work, looking up as Pio and Kiriz bolted through the camp near the field kitchen. 'Don't show your faces here again today!'

Gabriela laughed. 'Run, Pio!' He flashed her a cheeky grin and waved as he passed, but his expression fell when he saw Isaura next to her. Isaura's expression was blank as she bent her head, returning to the task of fletching arrows.

'This is far more fiddly than I thought,' Gabriela said lightly.

'You're getting the hang of it,' Isaura said quietly. 'Thank you for your friendship, Gabi. You didn't have to choose the Horse, but I'm glad you did … I'm glad you both did.'

Gabriela took her hand. 'My pleasure. Besides, I want to see this Targmur place where they live. It's meant to be amazing … I can see Umniga coming. Do you think the tattoos will hurt?'

'Yes, and I've got to have two. A horse for the clan and one for Alejo.'

'How will you tell the difference?'

'Probably just longer ears.' Isaura chuckled. 'And maybe a curled lip.'

'And gnashing teeth and a stare that could freeze water,' Gabriela said. An abrasive whinny that became a bray screamed at them. 'Gods help me! Did he hear that?'

Isaura laughed. 'Yep. My demon spawned guardian will get you now. You'd better start showering him with praise and change his mind.' Gabriela paled. 'Oh stop, don't worry, you'll be fine. I think he took it as a compliment.'

Umniga approached them. 'Isa, Gabi. It's time. Your tattooing ceremony is first, then we will do the men,' Umniga said. 'Normally Karan's Kenati would do this, but Hadi is in Targmur and Munira was left at Hunters' Ford. Suniti and Anil, Baldev's Kenati, will work on Lucia and Gabi. Since Asha and I painted your henna tattoos, we will put on your permanent clan tattoos, Isa. You should both know it is considered shameful to cry out while you are being tattooed. Come.'

Umniga led them to a secluded clearing well away from the main camp. A group of female warriors waited, sitting cross-legged in a circle. They sat, sleeves rolled up, clan tattoos proudly displayed.

Lucia sat in the middle of the circle with Suniti and Asha, along with three warriors. 'Gabi, I'm so glad you're here,' she said anxiously.

Gabriela sat in front of her and took her hands. 'All will be well.'

Isaura sat to the side facing them both.

Suniti's sleeves were rolled up, exposing her bear tattoo on one arm and her horned forest owl guardian on the other upper arm. Anil similarly bore a Bear Clan tattoo on one arm, but his guardian, a rufous owl, was on the other. Umniga rolled her sleeves up revealing a boar tattoo and an image of Devi. Asha discarded her shirt, revealing only the Boar Clan tattoo on one arm. She grinned at the three women, turned and revealed her back to them. Spread across her back was a massive tattoo of Fihr, wings spread in flight. The wing tips curled over the tops of her shoulders. Isaura reached out, hesitating.

'Go on you can touch it.'

'How long did this take?'

'Too long time and many sittings. A Kenati's tattooing is a different ceremony to this. It usually involves all of us and smoking ereweed. Sometimes Rana and Jalal provide interesting inspiration as to where the tattoo goes,' she said wryly, eyeing Umniga. Suniti chuckled and Umniga appeared embarrassed and cleared her throat noisily. 'Because of my fight with Ratilal they'll draw Fihr's claws on the backs of my hands at some stage.'

'Remove your shirts,' Umniga instructed. Lucia hesitated as she undid her shirt ties and held her shirt against her breasts to cover them.

Isaura shed her shirt and placed it unceremoniously beside her. She sat straight proudly, revealing her lean, well muscled form. The red-brown of the henna tattoos drawn for the Ritual of Samara had faded, but in its place her skin was starkly white. The sunlight reflected off the ghostly form of the willow and oak.

'Well, now …' Umniga began as she examined the ghostly lines. 'That's … different.'

Lucia gaped at Isaura and looked quickly away.

Gabriela smiled ruefully at her as she placed her top on the ground. 'We, none of us,' she added, looking pointedly at Lucia, 'are the same women who got on that boat and left Arunabejar. Lucia, in many ways this is a good thing. We are more capable now than we ever were—be proud.' She took both their hands. 'I'm proud to be here with you.'

'As am I,' Umniga said.

'As are we all,' one of the women warriors said loudly.

'As are we all,' said the rest.

Together the women, Kenati included, bowed their heads to the three strangers, placing their hands upon their hearts and opening their arms, palms up in respect and welcome.

Raising their heads, the circle of warriors began a low rhythmic humming. The three Kenati sat back on their heels, hands on their knees. They closed their eyes. The warriors' hypnotic humming swelled and resonated throughout the circle before their song subsided and the sound melted away into the trees. After a moment of silence, the Kenati opened their eyes and began chanting; the warriors joined in—some chanting and some humming the opening rhythm. Their hands slapped their thighs in a steady beat.

Each Kenati unrolled a leather bundle. Inside lay several wooden handled tools with dainty, fine bone teeth at their ends; some were narrow, holding only a few teeth while others were about an inch wide. They poured a dark liquid into bowls beside their tools.

The warrior next to Lucia held the skin of her upper arm tight. The tool's teeth were dipped in the liquid and placed on her skin.

It was then tapped with a wooden hammer, puncturing Lucia's skin to implant the dye. Lucia winced but said nothing. Her hand tightened around Gabriela's as they both received their clan tattoos.

Asha looked at Umniga uncertainly. 'Where are we to put Isaura's? Do we tattoo over the oak and willow?'

Isaura's gut clenched. Instinctively she shrunk back from them. 'No.'

Umniga held her hands up placatingly; her voice soothed, 'Easy, child. We won't. We'll place the mule and the horse so that it looks like the branches are embracing them. Do not mark over the branches, Asha.'

'The clan tattoo will not be whole,' Asha said.

'Together they will make a new whole,' Umniga said firmly.

'Do you still have the henna mixture?' Isaura asked.

'Yes, child, why?'

The tension flowed from her body. 'I want you to paint an Asena over my heart, entwined in the branches.' A sense of peace enveloped her, a sense of rightness, of approval.

—⚏—

Nimo stood before Karan. Her hands nervously clasped a satchel that hung at her side.

Umniga entered Karan's yurt, followed by Asha and Isaura.

'You're the girl who was riding at the rear of the column when Pravin and Hamza arrived,' Isaura said.

'I am Nimo,' the girl said softly. Nimo bowed low to Isaura with her hands out, palms up.

Isaura stared slack jawed. Asha prodded her in the back and Isaura hastily mimicked Nimo's bow. 'I'm Isa.' They rose together. 'Please don't bow to me!'

'Isa, it's a traditional gesture indicating good will,' Umniga admonished.

'Oh,' Isaura was embarrassed. 'I've only seen it done to the wealthy or those with power. I'm none of those things.'

Nimo looked curiously at Isaura, but said nothing and bowed even lower to Umniga and Asha. Asha returned her gesture, but Umniga sniffed haughtily, her hand tightened on her staff and she drew herself to her full height.

Karan stood abruptly, moving from the small portable table he was sitting at towards a ring of large cushions on the floor of the yurt. 'Come, all of you sit. Isaura, Nimo is one of my scribes. She has bought something for you to read. I want to see if your gift of language works with the written word as well.'

Nimo sat beside Isaura and reverently pulled a leather tube from her satchel. From inside this she withdrew a cloth-wrapped bundle. Nimo began to unroll the stiff cloth.

'Is that coated in beeswax?' Isaura asked.

'Yes, Isa. To keep what's inside dry and safe.'

'It's precious?'

'Old things are always precious to someone,' Nimo said with a shy smile.

Umniga sat stiffly with her arms folded and her lips drawn into a thin line. Asha and Isaura leant closer as Nimo lovingly unrolled the package to reveal a stained bundle of parchments all written upon with a small neat hand.

'Isaura, can you read it?'

Isaura licked her lips and eyed the parchment nervously. She felt pressure build up in the air around her. 'I've got a bad feeling about this,' she murmured. Gingerly Isaura picked up the top piece of parchment. The words grew blurry. A dull ache began behind her eyes. 'Not again,' she moaned as her head began to pound.

Asha put her arms around her. 'Breathe, Isa. Relax, breathe. It might help.'

Isaura's hands began to shake. Nimo paled, watching in horror as the parchment began to crumple in Isaura's grip.

'Karan,' Isaura gasped in pain. Her eyes, half morphed but almost entirely black, snapped to him. 'Alejo's coming. He's angry ... He doesn't understand my pain ... he thinks you're responsible.'

'Get out, all of you!' Karan ordered. 'Now!'

Asha hauled Nimo to her feet and pushed her toward the entrance. 'Run!' Asha said.

Umniga stood firm.

Isaura leapt up, taking a step toward her. Her gaze wild, she yelled, 'Out! Now!'

Shocked, Umniga quailed at the power in her command before fleeing the yurt.

Isaura reached for Karan as she sagged. He caught her.

'Come on, let's get you out in the open. That damn mule won't fit in through the door and I'm not having him wreck my yurt.'

Isaura took deep breaths, but she half-smiled as he dragged her outside.

The sound of yelling grew closer. A wave of commotion rolled through the camp.

'Gods, I swear I can feel the ground shake!' Karan said.

'That's my boy!' Isaura said.

'I'll remember you said that if he tries to squash me like a bug.'

Isaura chuckled, though one hand shaded her eyes. 'You'll be fine.' She straightened with a groan. 'The pain's lessening, so he's calming. I'm trying to get him to understand what happened. Besides, he sort of likes you.'

Karan's arm tightened around her waist as Alejo slid to a stop before them. The mule paced and pawed the ground. Snorting, his eyes wide, he stretched his neck out and nudged Isaura. Alejo methodically sniffed her clothes and hair, then rested his muzzle on her shoulder.

'Merge with him and reassure him.'

'Karan, he's always with me. Alejo knows everything. I know you said it's dangerous but he refuses to relinquish the merge. It's part of what keeps him calm and in control.'

'In control?'

'Well, other than this he's been fine. He hasn't tried to attack anyone. He hasn't even looked like attacking anyone … lately.'

Alejo shifted his head from Isaura's shoulder and lowered his head to nudge Karan.

Sighing, Karan gave him an affectionate scratch. 'Together you two are going to terrify the enemy. Will you look at the scroll again?'

Isaura nodded. 'I think I'll be fine. My guess is looking at it is like when I hear new words and the Asena's magic kicks in. I should be able to read your scroll. The pain may not come … or not as much.'

'Just make sure he knows I'm not the cause of it. I really do enjoy my yurt the way it is.'

Chapter Twenty-Eight

THE LADY PACED. *This is unacceptable.* She glared at Isaura and Karan as they headed back into the yurt.

Why did that damn scribe have to bring that document? She could have picked up anything else and it wouldn't have mattered.

A soft chuckle floated through the air, before the Matriarch materialised beside her.

You, the Lady seethed. *You abomination. Your interference has gone too far. You knew this would happen!*

How could I have known? How? You are sounding as paranoid now as you did when you were alive, the Matriarch said.

I'm not dead!

It's not living though, is it?

I will kill you for this! the Lady screamed.

The Matriarch turned a baleful glare upon her. *How? Even if you could, do you really think you can afford another death to your name?*

Alejo turned to face them. He shook his head and pawed the ground.

Damn beast, the Lady muttered. *I forget guardians can see into this realm at will.*

I'm going to see what the fuss is about, the Matriarch said. *Are you coming?*

He can't stop me, the Lady said defiantly.

No … at least not yet, but Alejo makes you nervous, doesn't he? He should, he's almost as paranoid as you, and of the two of us it's you he doesn't trust. I can't think why.

The Matriarch vanished to reappear inside the tent, followed by the Lady. Scowling furiously, the Lady observed the scene before her with her arms crossed.

The Matriarch ignored her and focused on Isaura and Karan.

—⚭—

Isaura and Karan sat on the rug and cushions in his yurt. 'Can you read it?' Karan asked.

'Yes, it's a diary I think. These look like some kind of strange dates on each page …'

'Isa, this is wonderful. We've a vault full of such scrolls, and Nimo and her father have been slowly trying to decipher them.'

'What? What do you mean a vault of them? Why can't you read them?'

'They're ancient. Umniga has told you of the clan wars, yes? Well at the end, after the battle told in the tale of Tarun and Safa, both Horse and Bear held the north beyond the Falcontine River. We knew there would eventually not be enough space for us all and we were new allies—we had our own ways and wanted our own land. So the Horse sent out riders to explore. They found a pass, beyond a waterfall that we call the Falcon's Eye, and through the mountain range, which took them to a plateau. The plateau was covered with vast grasslands. Isaura, they found a massive, ancient walled city built at the base and into the mountainside in the south of the plateau. It was abandoned. This city is now Targmur, my home. We found these documents in a locked vault and have been trying to decipher them.'

'Karan, just how old do you think they are?'

He shrugged. 'I've no idea. The clan wars were centuries ago. This place was ancient then.'

'Abandoned?' Isaura's brow creased in worry. 'Why?'

'Its state at the time indicated a disaster had befallen it. Now we can find out. Isa, already we've gained so much from studying some of the diagrams and charts and unravelling their building techniques. Now we can discover more to help my people.'

—⚍—

The Lady's wrath had dissipated. She and the Matriarch silently watched Karan's enthusiasm.

We lost so much, the Lady said sadly.

And this is how it began, the Matriarch finished.

—⚍—

'Please keep reading, Isa ...' Karan paused as Umniga's voice carried to them from outside.

'Damn mule, let me pass,' Umniga fumed.

'Umniga, just leave him be,' Asha said. 'If Karan and Isaura want to tell us what the scroll says they will—later.'

Umniga ignored her.

'Don't know why she's interested,' Asha muttered to Nimo with a wry grin. 'She thinks nothing good comes of such things—no offence, Nimo.'

'None taken,' Nimo said.

Karan stepped from the door of the yurt and walked toward Umniga. 'Umniga, you can begin your work with Nimo.'

'How is the girl?' Umniga demanded.

'Isa is fine. Your task now is to begin telling the tales to Nimo.'

Umniga glowered at him. 'How will I have time to teach Isaura and the others?'

'Asha and the Bear Kenati are here.'

'Asha spends her time training with Isa.'

'Then surely Anil and Suniti can take on teaching the others when you are with Nimo. You can take Pio and Kiriz with you. It will do them good to hear the Lore told and to see Nimo write.'

Umniga jutted out her jaw defiantly.

'You will do this, old woman.' Karan stared at her imperiously. 'Go.'

Umniga rammed her staff into the ground, spun and left. She

stalked off full of angry vigour, not casting a backward glance at either Karan, Asha or Nimo. Karan winked at Nimo and Asha before heading back to the yurt.

'Well done,' he said, patting Alejo happily.

Entering the tent he sat on the rug next to Isaura. 'Well, that's a boon I didn't foresee,' he said wickedly. 'You couldn't stop him?'

'No, not at all,' she lied. 'He was determined to keep her away.'

Laughter burst forth from them both. Karan reclined on the cushions with his hands behind his head. 'I cherish moments like these when the world goes away and I can forget who I am. Thank you.' He closed his eyes and paused, before saying softly, 'Umniga would never admit it but she desperately wants to know what's in that scroll. Will you keep reading, Isa?'

'It's just a journal of some sort. This looks like a date. *"The thirtieth day of Sanskon, Year of Lupala. The city is bustling for the festival of M'Aricel—that will keep prying eyes from me. The first hunt of the season is to take place in two days. The castle is filling with preening nobles for the ball tomorrow night."* There's some more about visiting dignitaries. The writer is annoyed that their work is constantly being interrupted. Oh, it's a woman! *"My final dress fitting has been done."'* Isaura chuckled. ' *"It's a monstrosity of regal proportions, yet deemed thoroughly suitable …"'* She read on silently, becoming engrossed.

Karan cracked open one eye. 'And? Get to the ball. Let's hear what she has to say. Does she find her true love?' he mocked.

'Oh, sorry. Ah here it is. *"The first day of Rendalk. The ball has commenced. My duties are done. Much wine has been consumed so none will miss me. May M'Aricel spare me from the gaping cavern that is the sum of their vacuous intellects."'*

'She sounds like Ratilal,' Karan said. 'I'm not sure I want to hear her arrogant whining.'

' *"Now I can work in peace. Jacoli will join me later to assist. Our abilities have grown through our experiments. Jacoli is able to channel some of the energy into his fighting skills. I seem to be able to influence animal behaviour. He has yet to master this, though I'm sure he will. Jacoli hypothesises that we may eventually be able to influence or compel people through our voice."' Karan and Isaura exchanged a worried look, before she continued. '"Jacoli's main interest in this, of course, is to use it on women." Clearly she doesn't approve of this Jacoli.' Isaura laughed uneasily.

'Keep reading, Isa,' Karan said, tense.

'There's a bit more complaining—about Jacoli. Seems he's her brother ...' Isaura's voice shook. '"*Our problem is that we weaken quickly and it takes days to rejuvenate our spirit.*" This page is damaged.' She hastily moved to the next page. 'There is no date here, part of the page is torn off. All that's left is part of a sketch of a staff. "*The answer was right before us. For once Jacoli's paranoid spying bears fruit. If that bitch priestess, Darya, suspects ... but she has no idea how far we have come. Once we can store the energy of the flumenàniat, we will be able to harness it to our will and the crystal is the key.*"' Isaura rapidly scanned the next page, her face twisted in frustration.

'What in Karak is the flumenàniat?' Karan asked. 'Does she say?'

Isaura hastily leafed through a few more sheets as Karan watched expectantly. 'She seems methodical, yet this is mixed up with what reads like a puerile diary.' She shook her head. 'I'm beginning to think it's deliberate.'

'Hiding the work of real importance?' Karan asked.

Isaura nodded, distracted. Alejo was prodding her mind for her attention. She ignored him. 'Here. "*The twenty-eighth day of Rendalk. Tonight is the penultimate night of the festival of M'Aricel. The hunters have returned; the castle is full. Everyone is engaged elsewhere preparing for tomorrow, when the festival ends and the feasting begins. The crystal has been in our possession for days. Darya has no idea Jacoli replaced the one in the temple. Our research has gone apace. It's fitting that this last night of the goddess's festival will see the culmination of our work. I rejoice in these primitive traditions, for they keep the ignorant away. This night we will succeed—I know it."'*

Isaura shook her head, denying Alejo. He waited no longer. Her vision wavered. She saw her and Karan's auras. Alejo thrust her into the spirit realm.

The startled gaze of the Lady, still watching, met her. *Damn mule!* she said, outraged, before vanishing.

Satisfaction radiated from the Matriarch. Her muzzle split into a predatory grin. *Damn mule indeed,* she said, amused. *He is perfect.*

'That was quick,' Karan said tersely as Isaura returned to her body. 'Though I wish you'd warn me.'

'Sorry. Alejo did that, not me,' Isaura said. She tried to sit up, but Karan's hand gently pressed her back.

'Rest a minute. Such a sudden shift must've been a shock.'

'I'm fine.'

'Just lie a while.' He gave her a lopsided smile. 'Unless you're uncomfortable.'

Isaura opened her mouth to argue, but hastily closed it.

Karan lay beside her, one hand resting upon her stomach. The other played with a loose strand of her hair, curling it around his fingers. 'Tell me what happened.'

Isaura frowned and avoided his gaze.

'What's going on, Isa? What don't you want to tell me?'

What do I tell him? What will be the end of this?

Karan took her hand. 'Isa, you can tell me. I'll listen and I'll help if I can.'

Isaura let out a pent up breath. 'Alejo wanted to show me

something. We were being watched from the spirit realm.'

'Umniga?'

'No, why would … ? Never mind.'

'The Matriarch? Does she always observe you? No, don't answer that. I imagine that she keeps a close eye upon you since she had such an interest in saving you. The real question is why did Alejo want you to know at that precise moment?'

Isaura smiled as he fired questions at her and then answered them himself.

'She wasn't alone. There was a lady there.'

'A lady?'

Isaura rubbed her temple and chewed her bottom lip. 'She was at the ritual too.' *Was she involved in it though, or did she just watch?* Isaura explained her dealings with the Lady.

Karan's eyes grew wide. 'Isa, you've just described Rana. Why didn't you tell me earlier?'

'I was hedging my bets.'

'You don't think she's a goddess?' Seeing her pensive gaze, Karan continued. 'Isa, she must be. Otherwise she would not exist there.'

I bet she masquerades as one. 'Karan, that's the only place she exists. She has no real power here,' Isaura said. 'Wouldn't a goddess be everywhere?'

'She has to be Rana.' He sat up, resting on one elbow and staring intently at Isaura. 'She has to be.' Karan fell silent, staring at the discarded parchment. 'Alejo was warning you.'

'Yes. And Karan, she was furious that I was reading this.'

Karan stood, wandered to the door of the yurt and stared out at the camp with his arms folded. 'We need to keep everything about this a secret. You understand the implications of this … if she isn't Rana?'

'Your religion could be founded on a lie.' *Like most other religions.*

Karan frowned and his lips drew into a line. 'It doesn't mean Rana doesn't exist. You can't tell anyone else. There's only so much change people can cope with.' He shook his head. 'You certainly make life interesting.'

'Honestly, I'd rather not.'

He turned to look at her with a crooked smile. 'Honestly? I'm glad you do.' Karan walked back to Isaura. 'We've a problem though, there are more documents like this—a whole archive in fact, but in Targmur. Other than this you'll find nothing more until we go there.'

'I'll ask the Matriarch. She appears to know her and now I really do want answers.'

'Do you trust her?' Karan asked.

'Yes.'

'Isa, she caused you great pain.'

'It was worth it.' Isaura gestured at the parchment. 'Look at what I can do, I can talk your language—I fit in.'

Karan sat beside her. 'You would've fitted in regardless. Be careful. It may be that the Matriarch has ulterior motives. Most people do, perhaps she is no different.'

'What's your ulterior motive?'

Karan lay on the rug and cushions, his hands behind his head. 'My motives are changing—have changed. Initially—power. I reasoned if the gods had sent you then the Boar Clan shouldn't have you.'

'Now?'

'Well, I'm very glad they don't have you,' he said with slight smile. Lips pursed, Isaura nudged him with her foot. 'Tomorrow Baldev and I will be riding out separately,' Karan said. 'You'll stay here and continue training …' At her sudden intake of breath he continued. 'You're not ready for the front. Don't worry, you will be, and when you are I won't stop you. But Isa, for the first time, I'd like to stay and not have to ride off.'

Karan reached for her hand, but he continued to stare at the yurt roof. 'You know why I've driven you so hard, don't you?' Isaura said nothing, merely stared at their joined hands. 'I wanted you to be accepted into the clan on your own merit; respected in your own right.' Karan's thumb traced lazy circles on the back of her hand. 'Not because of my interest in you.'

'Interest?' Isaura quipped.

He rolled to his side, facing her, gazing at her intently. 'You're not going to make this easy, are you?'

Isaura grinned. 'No.'

Karan brought their joined hands to his lips and kissed her hand. 'I find myself caring less about the bond.' His free hand cupped her jaw. Karan brushed his lips against hers. 'Much, much less.' His kiss deepened. His hand slipped around her waist and he pulled her to him. Isaura slipped an arm about him, relishing their embrace. Karan broke their kiss. Expelling a deep breath, he rested his forehead against hers. 'But I need your position within the clan to be unassailable, before we become involved. We need to keep our distance for a bit.'

'Really?' Isaura asked. Karan frowned at her, puzzled. She looked pointedly at his arm draped around her waist. 'You'd better let me go then.' Isaura sat up stiffly, straight faced.

Frustrated, pleading, Karan said softly, 'Isa …'

Isaura rose from the rug, took the parchment and headed for the door of the yurt. Pausing at the door, her back to him, she said, 'I'll see you off tomorrow when you go.'

Outside, Isaura's eyes twinkled and she broke into a grin. *So that's his version of distant restraint, is it? This will be harder on him than me, I think.*

Isaura sat on a rock ledge by the lake, dangling her feet in the water. Alejo stood guard. If she was correct, the Matriarch would seek her out. Her frustration boiled within her.

The Horse Lord dislikes it intensely when you walk the spirit realm. The Matriarch hunkered down onto the warm rock.

Startled, Isaura swivelled to face her. *Alejo, block my thoughts.* Trying to appear calm, she stretched her feet out before her to dry in a small patch of sunlight. Her mind was brimming with questions. She peered at the Matriarch, looking for any clue as to whether Alejo was successful.

Displeasure radiated from the Matriarch. *You can do that in the spirit realm with her. But I do not like you doing it with me, Isa-cub. You should trust me.*

How far?

Far enough. I'll not see you come to harm, nor will my kind, the Matriarch said.

You want trust? Then I need answers. Not more cryptic crap—real answers.

I may not have them all.

Who is she? Isaura asked.

Misguided and foolish. Loathing dripped from the Matriarch's thoughts. Isaura drummed her fingers on the rock. *Primara. The first born child of King Teofilo. The last ruler of the Salud Empire.*

Not a goddess.

Never a goddess, though she poses as one.

Rana?

The same.

How long ago?

Over a thousand years. I care not, only that it is gone.

Isaura's mouth went dry. She licked her lips nervously, needing to know the answer but afraid of the knowledge that might follow. *Who are you?*

The Matriarch rose, stretching the long powerful length of her body. Alejo moved within striking distance. The Matriarch cocked her head; her gaze drifted between him and Isaura with a too lazy caution.

I? I am Darya.

Darya? The priestess? Isaura was incredulous.

You have no trouble believing that the Lady as you so graciously call her is a former princess of this land, yet you are surprised by this?

Actually, I've trouble with all of it. You say you were a priestess, yet you're ... you are ...

An animal?

Isaura grimaced. *You make it sound like an insult, I'm sorry. I was not always thus.*

What happened to you? Isaura asked. *You want trust, so now you must trust me. You wanted me to read those notes. It's somehow relevant to everything else that's going on now. I need an explanation.*

I would not say it is relevant to everything else, just you.

What happened that night? What you called the flumenàniat is The Wild, yes? She was trying to harness it? To channel it? What?

Both. Primara's experiment was both successful and disastrous. What I tell you is conjecture, though I've had centuries to try to unravel exactly what they were doing. She has revealed only bits and pieces—her failure still humiliates her. The crystal Primara stole from us was called the Goddess's Eye or the Eye of flame. These crystals are common in the mountains and it looked like any other flame crystal. But this one was unique in that it was tangible in both realms.

Primara thought the crystal could amplify her own power, but what it was really doing was acting as a conduit to The Wild. Each time she used it and channelled her will, she drew power through it and herself. In small amounts that was fine as long as Primara expended all the energy. I believe small amounts of energy built up in the crystal.

She must have realised, Isaura interrupted. *She wrote of trying to store energy within it.*

In the end I suppose it matters not. You've felt the pull of The Wild for your spirit's energy. Like calls to like—it is ever greedy for more. Eventually the crystal stored enough energy to lure The Wild to it. Her will was not needed. Primara became the conduit and it consumed her.

The crystal exploded. The power unleashed was catastrophic. M'Aricel put a barrier between the realms for a reason. The flumenàniat fuels life, feeds the aura of all living things. In such quantities it was strong enough to pull lifeforce to it. The wave of power broke through the kingdom; it fed on the living. Those in the castle and city perished. The wave weakened as it travelled, becoming like a plague. People sickened and died slowly.

The explosion happened on the cusp of the ultimate day of the festival of M'Aricel. We were at prayer. Our bodies were destroyed immediately, but our spirits ... The goddess saved us—every single one of her priests and priestess. Our spirits were bonded to these creatures you call wolves. We awoke, confused, in this form. The rivalry between animal instincts and human conscience took a long time to unravel and control ... we were drawn by death. The Matriarch was lost to memories. She shook herself, her long blue-tipped fur rippled. *We are the Asena. I am the Matriarch.* Her lip curled before she continued, anguish fresh in her voice. *Had we our original forms we could still not have helped. There was no cure but time.*

Not all died, though? Isaura asked.

No, Isa-cub, not all died and others fled in boats, hoping to be spared and find another home ... The Matriarch looked at Isaura thoughtfully. *Eventually the flumenàniat dissipated and returned into the spirit realm. Balance returned, but it took centuries. The empire was destroyed, forgotten; the few left knew only to fear the mountains and us. They were primitive clans, who struggled to survive and bickered amongst themselves. The auras of the people changed; the guardians began.*

Horse, Bear and Boar, Isaura said softly.

Indeed.

The anger and grief Isaura felt from the Matriarch touched her. Your goddess may have given you the crystal for a reason. Maybe she still has a purpose.

Perhaps.

How has the Lady—Primara—even survived? Why hasn't she been consumed? Isaura asked.

I prefer to think that she is being punished.

In other words, you have no idea.

Chapter twenty-nine

THE BOAR SQUAD captain listened to his scout. 'There's a farmstead a few miles away. Just a woman and a stripling boy there. Neat little place. But there's something else—it's a patrol base.'

'Perfect. They'll have a cache somewhere. If we can get our hands on their gear and horses, we can really cause a stir.'

The leader shook his head. 'We'll have to plan it right. We can't afford for any of 'em to get away.'

'There's still time to plan.'

—⚜—

The campsite was abuzz with activity. Men and women packed their kits for travelling, donned full armour, and carted their gear to their waiting horses. Tense laughter carried through the air; horses stamped their feet and whinnied in response. Nicanor waited by his horse, packed and ready. His hand rested casually on its neck as he talked calmly to it, yet his heart drummed a frantic beat.

Lucia and Pio headed toward him. *Keep it together. Don't let them see your fear.* Pio raced up to him and Nicanor scooped him up into his arms.

'Pa, how long will you be gone?'

'I don't know, Pio. A few weeks, maybe more.' Pio took his hand and stared up at him imploringly. 'You'll be fine here. Ma is staying and the warriors tell me you are miles and miles from where any fighting will be and that won't happen until after winter.'

'So why go then?' Pio asked.

'Practice, more training. Soldiers always work hard and patrol so that they are fit and well prepared. You must work hard too …'

'So I can be a good soldier!'

'Yes!' *Gods help me, yes. I pray to Majula and Ariceli you never need it.* 'Promise me, Pio, no more running off with Kiriz.' Pio opened his mouth to object. 'Pio, promise. Ma must know where you are.' Pio screwed up his face before he reluctantly nodded.

Lucia stepped into Nicanor's embrace. Words failed her as she clung to him. He stroked her hair as she sobbed. Pio looked away, rubbing his eyes.

'All will be well. Lucia, you and Pio are safe here. These are good people. Keep training hard.' Nicanor held her face in his hands and kissed her. 'I'm so proud of you, my little warrior woman.'

Lucia laughed half-heartedly. 'I'm hardly that.'

'You're well on the way and I'm glad of it.' He kissed her again. 'I'll be back before you know it.'

Lucia smiled sadly, wiping her eyes. 'I know.' She placed her hand upon Nicanor's chest. 'This armour is different to the others,' she said, fingering the lamellar plates covering his torso. 'Is it as good?'

'Apparently it's better. My size meant this armour was what best fitted me. See, it even covers my thighs and the split means even on the horse I'm protected.'

'I think Pa looks tough,' Pio said. 'See, Ma, even his helmet has bits on the side to protect his neck. Āsim told me Pa's armour is old, but very tough and … well … maintained.' Pio nodded his head sagely, certain that was the correct word. 'It'll be fine, Ma,' Pio ended with a crooked smile.

Lucia laughed. 'Āsim told you all that, did he? Then I'm sure it will be fine.'

Curro stood by his horse apart from everyone. 'Go and say goodbye to Uncle Curro, Pio. Your father and I'll follow soon.'

Pio frowned. 'Ma, I tried to play him a tune last night to make him happy, but he got mad and walked away.'

Lucia knelt and took Pio's hands in her own. 'Pio, some things hurt so deeply that your ...' She swallowed anxiously. *His magic ... no!* 'Your music may not have helped. Sometimes we need to feel the bad things, learn to cope with them and then the good things seem even better. Do you understand?'

'I think so. You mean he'll stop being sad and remember the nice times with Auntie Leni—with us?'

'That's exactly right, but it will take time and we'll help him remember eventually. Now go say goodbye to him.'

Lucia's eyes filled with tears as she looked at Curro's stony visage. 'Has he said anything?'

'Not much,' Nicanor replied quietly. 'I've no idea what Isa said to him, but I think now he hates himself.'

Lucia shook her head, saying, 'Why? Isa killed Leni, not him.' Nicanor shrugged. 'Will he hurt Isa? After everything that she's ... that's happened, she frightens me, but I still worry for her.'

'I don't know. I don't want to talk about this, Lucia. I don't even know how I feel about it all.'

Lucia nodded, taking his hand. 'At least he is in the Bear with us and on patrol with you. We'll help him get through this.'

'I hope you're right.'

—⚬—

Jaime listened as the distant camp noises filtered into the tent from outside. The others would not return to the tent for a while; he was grateful for the privacy. Gabriela lay alongside him, her head rested upon his shoulder. She lightly caressed his chest; Jaime's arm tightened around her waist as he kissed her. Jaime longed for these quiet moments alone when he could pretend that she still needed him—that she was still the same girl he'd longed for back home. Jaime trailed his hands along Gabriela's side. Gone were the fulsome curves he'd dreamed of. Muscles were beginning to cord her forearms and back. *Nothing's the same.*

'You've been assigned to a squad?'

'Yes, you?'

'We head out tomorrow too,' Jaime replied.

'Sarala is my commander and mentor, the rest of the squad are nice.'

I know. I've seen the men look at you, Jaime thought. *Nice? They are not nice. Killing is an art form for these people.* He rubbed Gabriela's shoulder absentmindedly. 'Do you miss the old days?'

Wary, Gabriela tensed. 'Of course. Why would you even ask such a thing?'

'You just seem to be enjoying yourself so much. You don't seem to miss it at all.'

Gabriela's hands stilled; she lay rigidly beside him. 'I miss it. I could dwell on what's gone, or I could look at what I've gained.'

'Gained?' Jaime's voice rose in query. 'What about your parents? Do you wonder about them?'

Gabriela rose up, removing her hands from him. Leaning on one arm, she stared at Jaime, her lips drawn into a tight line. 'No. What good would it do? But I'll tell you what I've gained—strength, confidence, new friends, new skills; a chance at a new life.'

'Was the old one so bad?'

'It was laid out before me. Here I have choice. Here I have you. Who knows whether that would've happened at home?'

Bitterness rose within Jaime; he struggled to quell it. 'I wish I'd had a choice about which clan I was in.'

'You did.' Gabriela smiled hopefully. 'Is that what this is about?'

'No … You chose Horse,' Jaime accused, 'leaving me no alternative.' Gabriela sat up, shocked. 'Why did you choose Horse?' he asked, shaking his head.

'Because of Isaura.'

'You'd choose her? You've seen what she can do.'

'Isaura is my friend. She is also the most courageous person I know. Everything we have felt here, as strangers, Isaura has had to deal with her whole life. Think on that. Think about what she's done. None of us have given her any credit. I'm proud to be in the same clan as her.' Gabriela pushed herself to her feet, turning her back to him.

Jaime watched her dress. 'Gabi, I'm sorry. Things are so different now. I ... I don't know ...'

She pulled on her boots, stomping her heels into them. Refusing to turn around, she hung her head and sighed.

'Gabi, stay ... Don't leave—not like this,' Jaime pleaded.

'I don't like being made to feel I should apologise for being happy, for learning, adapting ... for changing.'

'I ...' Jamie said.

'Enough. We'll talk when we both get back.'

'Be careful, Gabi. I won't be there to take care of you.'

'I don't need you to take care of me, Jaime,' Gabi said softly. 'I need you to respect me—respect who I've become.'

—⚋—

Lina stood by the fire with a mug in her hand, stirring a pot of soup. Satish wandered in from his room. 'Why are you still awake? You've a long day tomorrow.'

'Can't sleep. I'm worried about Kiriz. I still don't see why you sent her away. We could keep her safe.'

'Satish, enough! I've problems keeping her out of trouble at the best of times. Lord Baldev will keep her safe.'

'Nothing's going to happen here.'

Lina sighed. 'Just go back to bed or I'll send you outside to keep watch with the others. Would you like that, outside in the freezing cold and drizzle?'

Satish hung his head. 'No, Ma. I'm going.'

Lina filled a wooden mug with soup. 'I'm just taking this out to the stranger—Jaime, I think his name is. Imagine all they've been through to get here and now they're in war. He looked like a drowned rat last I checked.' Lina wrapped her shawl over her head and made her way to the woodshed near the house.

A square shaft of soft light struggled against the darkness as the front door opened. The Boar captain ducked behind the woodpile at the rear of the lean-to that was the woodshed. The light squelching of boots in mud drew closer.

'Jaime, I've bought you a mug of soup to warm you up.'

The sentry's reply juddered with his chattering teeth. 'I won't say no. Doesn't seem to matter what I do, I can't warm up.'

'Enjoy it. I'll leave the pot on the side of the fire. You might be able to sneak in and get some more.'

The Boar captain waited until the farmstead house door closed. The one called Jaime moved further into the shed and sat on the woodpile.

'Ahh.' Jaime wrapped his cold hands eagerly around the warm pottery mug. He stared sullenly at his feet. It had been days since he'd left Gabriela. *I should have said I was sorry, I should have done something, not just left. But damn this place—everything's changed! She shouldn't be playing soldier, that's not a woman's job.* He kicked the dirt. *I was a fool, I should have lied, should have said anything to keep her happy and we could've sorted it out later.*

The Boar captain smiled at Jaime's sigh of delight as he sipped his soup. Slowly, he rose and crept around the pile, his footfalls deadened by the litter from years of woodchips and bark. The Boar captain's arm darted forward around Jaime's neck. He struck Jaime savagely across the throat and drove his knee into the back of Jaime's leg. Unable to cry out, Jaime fell backwards. The mug landed noiselessly on the ground.

Jaime gasped for air—an arm was around his neck hauling him back. He frantically tried to grapple with his attacker, his vision blurred.

The captain's face remained impassive. He felt the lad struggling to draw breath. The moment Jaime's arms rose in resistance, the captain jabbed a dagger under his armpit. Jaime's grip faltered; his strength failed. Eyes wide, Jaime's life fled. The Boar captain held him tightly, easing him to the ground as Jaime became limp. He grunted in effort as he dragged Jaime's body further into the dark.

Another squad member joined him. 'That's the last case of the runs that poor sod is going to have.'

'The body?'

'In the pit under the seat. Nearly didn't fit, but someone dug a good hole.'

They left the shelter of the lean-to and met the others. 'Problems?' His men shook their heads. The captain eyed the barn thoughtfully. The cow, calf and warriors' horses had been brought into the barn hours earlier. There was not a living thing, save them, around the barn.

'Most of them will be asleep. Watch change isn't for hours,' one of the Boar soldiers said.

'Don't get cocky.' They split up to attack from each barn door.

They slipped sideways through the barn doors. The nearest horse, head over the stall door, startled and tossed its head, knocking a muck rake over which clattered into a bucket. The Boar squad shot forward. The cow darted back in her stall, banging into the wall and her calf. The calf bellowed. Six Horse warriors woke up, grabbing their kilijs. The Boar soldiers attacked. Their captain's blade flashed; a Horse warrior fell before he'd made it to his knees, throat slashed his head almost severed.

Another Horse warrior rolled away, rising with his sword, but fumbled reaching for his shield. He leapt backward too late. His hand lay next to his shield. The warrior staggered, raising his sword with his good arm as the blood pumped out of his severed limb.

With ruthless efficiency they were mown down. The bodies of his friends lay around the barn. His vision blurred and the noises around him echoed in his ears. He backed into a stall door. Trapped he slashed his kilij but connected with nothing. The enemy surrounded him, yet they did not attack.

One shrugged. 'He's bleeding out. Just wait.'

'Get to the house—now!' the captain ordered. The remaining Horse warrior slid down the wall, his breath coming in shallow pants. He still clung to his sword. The Boar captain pulled it from his hand. 'You poor sod,' was the last thing the warrior heard.

—ᴡ—

Līna leaned on the mantel, staring into the fire. Her fingers drummed restlessly against the wood. She glanced around her kitchen. Everything was washed, dried, neat and tidy. *You're a fool woman. You should sleep. The patrol is here. They make it more safe, not less.* Walking forward she paused, put both hands flat on her table and drew a deep breath. *Just go to bed you fool.*

Taking the candle with her, she entered her bedroom and walked to the small window. Shifting the hide that covered it to keep out the chill, she checked that the timber shutters were secured. A clatter came from the barn, the calf let out a bellow. Līna froze, listening intently. A distant thump sounded. Her hand began to shake. She dropped the hide covering the window and backed away from it. *It could be nothing.* Her eyes darted to Satish's bedroom.

Līna crept into Satish's room. 'Wake up, son.'

'I'm not asleep. Did you hear something too?'

'It might be nothing, but get up, throw on a coat and boots—quickly.'

Together they moved into the kitchen. Līna blew out the candle. The firelight cast dancing shadows upon the walls. She picked up a carving knife. 'Wait over there.'

Līna held the knife before her and stood in front of the door. She clenched her jaw, drew a deep breath, put her hand on the door latch and opened it a crack. *Nothing.* Līna breathed a sigh of relief.

The door thrust open, driving her back. 'Nice of you to let us in, love.' Līna screamed and charged forward to stab the Boar soldier. He knocked the dagger from her hand and punched her in the face. She collapsed to the floor. Satish ran to his room.

'Go, haul his arse out here,' the soldier said to the man with him. The Boar soldier dragged Lina up and tied her to a chair. He walked to the fire and helped himself to soup to the sound of Satish's door being kicked in.

'He's pissed himself,' the other soldier said as he shoved the boy into the room. 'Some hero he turned out to be.'

'Tie him up too.'

The soldier sat opposite the shaking boy, casually drinking soup and tearing into a hunk of bread. 'Your ma's a good cook, boy. Lucky to have her, you are.' He licked his fingers, then drew his dagger. Reverently, he began cleaning it, never taking his eyes from Satish.

Lina moaned as she regained consciousness. Her eyes snapped open and she struggled against her bonds. The captain casually stoked the fire; he left the fire poker in the hot coals and moved to stand before her.

Lina stared at the heating iron. 'What do you want? We're just simple farmers,' she said.

'Boar farmers who've given aid to the enemy,' the captain said.

Lina scowled. 'You think we had a choice? I never wanted them here. Lord Baldev insisted, said it would make us safer.'

The soldiers laughed. 'Well he stuffed that up. The whole reason we're here is because we knew they were,' said the one nearest Satish.

'I told them they'd just make us a target,' Lina fumed.

'Smart woman.'

The captain stiffened. 'Lord Baldev was here?'

Lina nodded. 'On his way back from the Four Ways with a convoy of wounded.'

'Where were they headed?' the captain asked.

Satish, pale, stared at his mother. Lina moistened her lips and looked away. *Kiriz.* 'I don't know.'

The soldier nearest Satish began carving patterns in the

wooden tabletop. Lina and Satish's eyes followed the graceful swathe of the blade it peeled away the flesh of wood.

'Answer my questions and you'll be free,' the captain said.

'Really? Your kind killed my husband in one of your little raids across the border.'

The soldier carving drove his dagger into the tabletop. 'Our kind? Aren't you a member of our clan?'

'Shut it,' ordered the captain. He stared at Lina. 'I wasn't on that raid; I don't approve of burning homes and killing women and children. Answer my questions and you'll be free. Where was Baldev heading?'

Lina remained silent.

The captain pulled the fire poker from the glowing coals and walked toward Satish. Satish struggled in the chair, trying to jostle it away from him, but two warriors held it still. The poker drew near his face. Red iron filled his vision.

'Stop! They were going to Bear Tooth Lake. I'd bet it's their base.' *Kiriz! Little one, please be gone ... please!* Tears ran down Lina's face.

The soldier nearest Satish was jubilant. 'Ah! So the other team is on target.'

'I told you to shut up!' The captain's hand gripped the poker tightly and he hung his head drawing deep breaths. He wanted to put his trooper's eyes out. He put the poker down, reluctantly relinquishing it. 'How often do the patrols come through?'

'Roughly ten to fourteen days apart,' Lina said.

The captain looked at his men. 'All of you get out.'

'Time for a bit of fun, eh Captain? Save some for us.'

'Get out!'

When the door closed, he went into a bedroom and bought out two strips of cloth. He blindfolded Satish.

Standing behind Lina he said, 'You know what they want?' She nodded sobbing as he blindfolded her. He bent down and whispered into her ear. 'I wouldn't have let them, but I truly wish that fool had not opened his mouth about the other team.' Her head drooped forward as red soaked her tunic. He moved on to Satish.

'I'm sorry. You're free.'

chapter thirty

UMNIGA AND DEVI soared above the camp in the early morning light. *Find the girl, Devi. I want to know if Karan is with her.* Isaura slept in the woods to the side of the camp. The ground that morning was covered in thick frost. She slept under the low-slung branches of a pine, protected from the worst of the chill air. Alejo stood watch nearby, his gaze tracked Devi's progress until he perched in a pine tree. *Yes, I know, my friend. Alejo unnerves me too.* An Asena was curled up with Isaura, but Umniga could see no others. Disappointment filled her thoughts. *She is alone.* Devi perched in the tree. Umniga mused over Isaura. *Ah my old friend, time will tell.* Devi's taciturn mind was utterly disinterested in Isaura and consumed by the thought of food.

Primara, the Lady, appeared before Umniga. She gasped, nearly losing her connection with Devi. Devi barked harshly and Umniga felt a foreign, gentle tug strengthening their connection. Umniga's eyes widened in surprise and awe; she concentrated on her form, strengthening her image and bowed deeply.

'My Lady Rana, I'm deeply honoured.'

'Greetings, Umniga. Oldest and foremost of my Kenati; teacher of my lore.' Umniga remained bowing. 'Rise, old one.'

'Most holy Rana, it's been generations since any of us have seen you or heard you.'

'And yet I have watched my people and in particular my Kenati and guided you in subtle ways. You are never far from my gaze.' Primara smiled gently. 'You and Asha have both felt my hand more than most.'

'It was you who aided Asha to return to her body after spirit walking.'

'Indeed. She needed but a small amount of guidance.'

'You pulled Devi to the boats.'

'Yes. I have watched you for a long time, Umniga. I knew you—oldest, wisest and most loyal—would understand that I had guided Devi there. I knew, too, that you above all the others would realise the importance of the girl when you saw her.'

'Yes, my Lady Rana, but …'

'She disappoints you, Umniga?'

Umniga hesitated, then in a rush she said, 'She is such a heathen. I fear she does not take my teachings seriously. She has no respect for any gods.'

'She is young,' Primara soothed. 'Like all young things she seeks to go her own way and needs persistent, patient guiding to the true path. You have had many such young minds come to you for teaching over the years. Remember, even our Asha—the youngest ever to be gifted with a guardian—was little different as a child. Look what you made of her. I can see Isaura's heart and I do not doubt you will succeed with her.

'I have seen into your heart too, old one. You would have her and Karan together?' Umniga nodded. 'Do not push them, Umniga—you will drive them apart. Neither of us wants that.'

'They have no idea how important this is!' Umniga stormed.

Primara's brow rose; her mouth twisted in small smile.

'My lady, forgive me! It is not for me to rail at you.'

Primara laughed. 'These are momentous times, Umniga. Do not despair. Isaura has a destiny far greater than you realise and to ensure it I need you to do something very important for me, but you must tell no one.'

Asha pulled on her boots.

'Have you got fur liners for them?' Baldev asked her.

'Across the river. So, no, not really. Pio and Kiriz have been trapping rabbits. They've got the skins drying, although I'd rather the children used them for themselves.' Asha shrugged. 'There'll be more game to kill and skin for a while anyway. So I'm sure to be able to make some liners,' she said as she strapped on the last of her weapons. 'Are you ready?'

'Sadly, yes,' Baldev grumbled. 'I'll miss you.'

'Isaura and I can always come,' Asha said cheekily. 'We'd be handy at the front.'

'There isn't a front, yet. Trust me, when there is, you'll be there,' Baldev said.

'Just not near you.'

'No.'

'Because you worry so much? Not because you think I can't look after myself?'

Baldev hesitated. 'Yes.' He shook his head with a rueful smile. 'I think I just walked into a trap.'

Asha laughed at him. 'If I was with you, I'd not be able to resist saving you when you needed it.' Frowning, he opened his mouth to speak. 'See? How did that make you feel?' she interrupted.

'Loved ... and belittled.'

Asha's brow rose imperiously as she folded her arms. 'And?'

'And I understand, but it doesn't change how I feel. But I won't stop you being at the front. I do think Karan is right though. You and Isa need to be together while she learns. You and Pravin are effectively her mentors. When she's ready you'll both begin full patrols.'

'Isa's more ready than the others now, and they're going out.'

'She needs more control.'

'Isa will only get that if she's tested properly,' Asha said. 'Or is Karan being overly protective, like you?'

'Karan is, as always, being careful and calculating.'

'With Isa?' Asha said, putting her hands on her hips. 'He'd better not hurt her.'

'I don't think Karan's done anything with her. That's probably what's wrong with him. Enough about Karan. I've only got a few minutes left with you on my own and I'm not talking about bloody Karan,' Baldev groused.

Asha laughed, launching herself into his embrace. 'Be careful or you'll wind up back in bed.'

—⁂—

Ratilal looked up briefly as Niaz entered the council room. 'Lady Malak has left the city,' he said tersely.

'She's no longer a threat to you, High Lord,' Niaz said.

'No, of course, you're right. I'm just still irritated that she was clever enough to think of it and able to arrange the Conclave so quickly. Probably more annoyed that they backed her. If she was a man ... gods help me ... she'd be worth watching.'

'I'm sorry.'

'I know and it's not your fault. We don't choose our parents. Are you ready? Vikram will be going with you.'

'Vikram?'

'He'll do. He's done well thus far. Treat it as Vikram's final test. I want him gone for a few days and it will be good to be seen running things myself. Come, he's waiting at the northern gate.'

They walked silently through the empty streets of upper Faros. Their semi-shuttered lamp emitted a thin streak of light into the chill night air. Ratilal nodded in silent greeting at Vikram, who waited with two horses at the city gate.

'The gods smile upon us. It's so damn cold any sane person is inside and warm. None will see you. In few hours I'll be up on the battlements watching. Give Faros a sight to remember,' Ratilal said as Vikram and Niaz mounted their horses.

Vikram rode beside Niaz through the countryside north of Faros. A fine low layer of fog had crept up from the ocean and was smothering the land. They halted on the shore of a bay where the Mitta River emptied into the ocean. Waiting before them was a fisherman and his small boat along with two warriors.

'My Lord, what is our mission?' Vikram asked.

'You'll find out soon. None of the others know, Captain.' Niaz paused, staring at him. 'Karan's spies may be everywhere.'

'Hence why the high lord has remained highly visible in Faros,' Vikram said.

'That is but one reason.'

The only sound for the next few hours was the steady swing of the oars through the water.

'The fog will help, yes?' Niaz asked the boatman.

'Aye. They won't notice the boat. We've got barely a sliver of moon to see by. Our only worry is hitting the rocks. Oh, and gettin' back.'

'I think I see the rocks guarding the gap,' Niaz said quietly from the prow.

Vikram peered forward. A dark, jagged mass rose from out of the water on their right. *Gods, there's only one place we can be.* Vikram's heart sank.

'Here!' the boatman whispered harshly. He pulled a pole from under the seats and thrust it at Vikram. 'Pull on those oars, boy.' He ordered the rower. 'There's more you can't see just under the water. Wider, Wider,' he muttered to himself as he pulled on the tiller. The boat hit the hidden rocks. Its timbers shuddered. 'Hold up with the rowing. You there,' he addressed Vikram. 'Use that pole, lad. See if you can push us off.'

Vikram probed the water with the pole and pushed with all his might.

'You lot move to the side a bit,' the boatman said. With a shudder the boat moved freely. 'By the gods we've been lucky. On a breezy day we'd be right buggered to have managed that. Either the gods love us or our high lord's got a knack for plan.'

Niaz passed each of them a backpack. 'Careful with those. Don't break any.'

Vikram loosened the top of the backpack. Round pottery

containers were stuffed into it amongst fleece to stop them from breaking or making noise as they were carried. Carefully, he pulled one out. There was a fuse in it.

'Quickfire. This was banned by the high lord's grandfather,' Vikram said softly.

'Not anymore. Our main targets are the granary, the armoury, the barracks, and the citadel if we can get to it. Anything else is just a bonus. Quiet now,' Niaz said.

The boat glided into the shore, scraping against the pebbled beach. They disembarked and stared into the north.

The comforting smell of smoke from household fires hung low in the air. *Families all tucked safe and sound in their beds,* Vikram thought. Bile rose in his throat.

Niaz smiled grimly. 'Gopindar will never know what hit it.'

No smoke rose from the farmhouse chimney, and chickens roamed freely throughout the house garden and ravaged the well-tended vegetable patch. A raven flew out of the barn. The faint waft of putrescence increased with every step Baldev took toward the barn door. Curro and Nicanor emerged from the dark interior, pale and shaken. They leaned against the outside of the barn wall, breathing deeply before vomiting.

Two warriors hastily opened the other double doors in the opposite wall of the barn, allowing a breeze to draw through the building, dragging the stench of death with it.

Baldev slammed to a halt in the doorway. He stood, hands on hips, lip curled as he tried not to inhale. Light from both sets of doors breached the darkness of the barn, revealing the bodies of Karan's warriors.

They lay where they'd fallen. Weapons gone, bodies scavenged. A black-brown skin had formed over the pools of blood on the hardened earthen floor. Slashes of thick red showed through it where the raven's claws had broken through the congealed crust of blood. Red narrow tracks led the way along a body and stopped where the fallen warrior's eyes had been.

'Get them out of here. Take them to the field north of the house.'

Baldev spun on his heel and headed to the farmhouse. Līna's words hounded him: *You will make us a target.* He paused, hand on the aged wooden gate that led into to the house yard. Anil, his Kenati, stood in the doorway of the house, head bowed. Baldev growled, thrust the gate open and stalked toward the door. Anil looked over his shoulder at him, hastily averted his eyes and moved out of Baldev's way. Baldev stared at the interior of the simple kitchen. He braced himself against the doorframe. *You knew what you'd find. Get a hold of yourself.* Before him still tied to the kitchen chairs sat Līna and Satish. He kicked the doorframe. *Gods damn it. Kiriz, little general, I'm sorry.*

Baldev walked through the house, checking the other rooms. 'It looks like they've left everything untouched,' he said.

Anil looked up from severing the ties that bound Līna's hands.

'I'll take her,' Baldev said quietly. Clinically he examined her. 'Blindfolded. No torture and a clean kill.'

Anil shook his head in disgust. 'I suppose at least it was quick.'

'The question is why?'

'What are you going to tell the little general?'

Baldev stiffened, before scooping Līna's body up. 'Bring Satish.' He walked out of the house.

An agonised wail stopped Baldev in his tracks. 'No, no, no! Jaime!' Curro's cry rent the air.

Nicanor stood before the woodshed, pale, shaking, his face twisted in grief. He turned tear-filled eyes on Baldev only to look away in haste when he saw the body in his arms.

Several of Baldev's warriors wandered over. He handed Līna to two of the women saying softly, 'Take her with the others.' Baldev quietly beckoned more of his troops to attend him.

Curro's voice rose and cracked. 'This is madness!' he yelled.

Arms outstretched, Nicanor moved into the woodshed to pacify his brother. 'No, Curro!' Nicanor staggered back out of the shed.

Curro faced two of Baldev's warriors who were at the open rear of the shed. His sword was not drawn, but he wielded a log like a club. 'You people! You're as bad as the Zaragarians! You thrive on war!' Spittle flew from his mouth. Curro swung the log at the warriors. 'Violence flows through your very veins … your hearts …' He swung again futilely. Curro began to shake; the log fell to the ground. A female Bear warrior advanced toward him, hands outstretched. Red faced, sobbing uncontrollably, he grasped clumsily for his sword.

'Curro!' Baldev barked. He strode to him and grabbed his hand in a vice-like grip. 'Do NOT!'

Curro glared defiantly at him, his eyes deranged. Nicanor appeared at Baldev's shoulder. 'Curro, he's right. These people are not to blame. We swore an oath. This is not the way.'

'Get out of here Nic,' Curro ground out. 'I know what I'm doing.' His hand fought against Baldev's grip to no avail.

'You want to end it,' Baldev whispered. 'I know.'

A look of guilt flashed across Curro's visage. Nicanor gasped at the truth.

'End it on the battlefield, against the people who did this—not against people who would die to defend you. There is no honour in this, and certainly no justice.'

Curro sagged, letting go of his sword.

Baldev kept hold of him. 'Take his weapons,' he said to the nearest warrior.

Curro sat beside Jaime's body. His hand rested upon Jaime's brow as he rocked himself back and forth. Finally he clutched Jaime's body to himself and sobbed uncontrollably.

'Leave him,' Baldev said. 'We'll take Jaime later, when everything is in readiness.' He looked at Nicanor and the two warriors. 'You three stay with him. Ensure he comes to no harm.'

Baldev put his hand on Nicanor's shoulder, murmuring, 'There are many perils in a war—this is but one of them. Watch him well.'

—⚜—

Not a sound disturbed the night as Vikram's party moved through the countryside. The grass was dewy underfoot and every star in the sky winked back at them. There was little cover. Once the forests of the north grew right to the shoreline, but the Bear Clan had cleared much of the land up to the Northern Flow for crops.

There'll be a frost tonight, Vikram thought. *How many more before winter is over? How many cold and hungry if this works? How do I stop this and avoid suspicion? I still need to stick to Karan's original plan until Ratilal's fall.*

They continued on, bypassing farmsteads. Post and rail fences disappeared and soon they found a narrow bridle track to follow. The path joined another wider road, bordered by spiky tea-tree bushes, and an inn stood at a larger intersection on their left. Grouped around it lay a smithy, a barn and many smaller animal pens. Sheep stood quietly in one pen, cows in another, mules and donkeys were in the last pen. The mules turned and looked in their direction with interest.

'Gopindar's market. Not far now. We need to avoid those pens. All we need is for one of those mules to let loose and everyone in that inn will be awake,' Vikram said.

'We need to go around anyway to enter the city,' Niaz said.

Twenty minutes later the walls of Gopindar were before them. The lower town was built around the base of a broad natural hill. The upper town and citadel sat upon this hill. A vast swathe of land around Gopindar had been cleared of all vegetation, save grass. A wide deep ditch had been dug in front of a long steeply sloping earthen wall that culminated in a stone wall the height of four men. Built upon this was a timber wall. Hexagonal timber towers bulged out at regular intervals. Atop each tower sat giant crossbows on rotating platforms. These anti-siege crossbows were armed by two men turning a winch. A drawbridge and massive double gates sturdily braced with thick steel blocked their way. The torch light from the lookouts reflected dully off the pale timber gates.

'Moonwood. Where did they get enough?' one of Niaz's men asked in hushed awe.

'Probably Karan. We've no idea what the Horse have been hiding up there all these years. They've been busy,' Niaz muttered. 'This is what happens when you ignore the enemy for generations.'

'It's why they've protected their borders so well.'

'There's a small pedestrian gate built into the northern gate. It should be unlocked. Come on.'

'You've someone in the city?' Vikram asked.

'The high lord is no fool. He's had someone ready to go to Gopindar since Shahjahan agreed to meet with Karan and Baldev. The operative is in place. We've had word.'

'Word?' Vikram asked.

'Courier pigeon—simple and reliable.'

'Weren't you worried they'd be caught?'

Niaz shrugged. 'They're expendable.'

'What about the gate to the upper city?' Vikram asked.

'It won't be shut. You'll see.'

'How do we get out?'

'There's a gate to the harbour. And before you ask, it was too obvious to come that way. Now shut up, Vikram.'

Two towers abutted the smaller northern gate. Torchlight revealed one guard at each tower post. Laughter carried to Niaz and his squad in the chill night air. A woman emerged at the top of the right hand tower. The guard turned to greet her as she handed him a tankard.

From the other tower the guard called, 'Where's mine, Sora?'

'Sora!' Vikram whispered. 'The other girl Ratilal beat, the one who fled …'

Niaz smiled. 'All part of his plan—no one would suspect her. Come on, who knows how long they'll be distracted?' They scurried across the open distance to the castle ditch, sliding into it near the narrow bridge to the gate. Sheltering under the bridge they picked their way across barricades and sharpened stakes.

Close to the wall they halted, crouching. Niaz poked his head out from under the bridge and dared a glance upwards. Silently he climbed onto the bridge and, pressed against the gate, waited for the others.

With Vikram and the soldiers beside him, Niaz gingerly pushed on the small pedestrian door built into the larger gate. It swung inwards easily.

'Lock it. We want no evidence that anything is awry,' Niaz ordered.

Sora left the guardhouse on the right with another tankard. 'Niaz, the port gate is to the south near the food market. You'll see the canopies and pavilions and you'll smell the fish. Good luck.' She disappeared into the other tower as Niaz and his men moved into the city, flitting through the shadows.

Chapter Thirty-One

HUNKERED IN THE darkness between two houses, Niaz issued his orders. 'You two, wait until you see the granary go up, then have some fun.' A breeze stirred the cold night air. 'The gods bless us. If this wind picks up, our work this night will be easier for it. Hit the market last as we leave.' They vanished into the night, leaving Vikram with Niaz.

Gopindar was a beautiful city. Timber buildings, with shingled roofs and high gables ornately carved with forest animals and plants—a bear was always carved somewhere into the houses.

A door slammed in the house next to them. They flattened themselves against the side of the building. Vikram looked anxiously at the shuttered window beside him. All remained quiet.

Flower boxes sat in front of all the upper windows and the shutters beside him were carved with blossoms, intertwined with willow and oak.

He glanced across the street to see the same craftsmanship. Every building, even the smaller ones had some form of clan embellishment. *This is what we're missing—no pride in our history.*

Niaz tugged on his sleeve and they moved on through the city. The wide paved street continued winding through the city and turned right. They passed a large orchard and field; a few horses and mule raised their heads as the men went past, but none made any noise. A holding yard and set of stables were opposite and before them lay a wide moat and the walls of the upper city. These were much older than the outer walls, yet like them they stood at the top of a steeply sloping earthen bank formed from the natural hillside. The walls were constructed from tree trunks sharpened to points and timber walkways ringed the interior walls.

A massive gate usually stood at the other side of the bridge across the moat. Scaffolding dominated the entrance; the gate lay open. Spanning the middle of the bridge was a two-storied gate tower. Loopholes were spaced evenly along its walls. Visitors to the upper city must first pass through the bridge tower's two sets of double gates. Each of the gates was open.

'How many in the guard house, you think?' Niaz asked. 'The wall?'

'Probably only a few,' Vikram said. 'As for the wall, I think the construction will have taken care of that. Take my pack.'

'We go in together, Vikram.' They walked across the bridge as if they belonged there.

'This is quite possibly the most foolish thing I've ever done,' Vikram murmured. They both drew their daggers.

A young warrior stood in the doorway of the guardroom with her back to them. 'It's bloody freezing out here.'

'Stop ya whining, girl. Shut the damn door and get out there an' do your duty. Thank ya lucky stars ya one of us and not 'em Boar bastards or you'd be stuck at home sewing.'

'Arse,' she muttered, slamming the door shut and turning around. Her eyes widened in fear as Niaz's hand shot over her mouth. He rammed his dagger up under her ribs.

Vikram grabbed her spear before she dropped it. Niaz lowered her to the ground quietly. They left the packs and their delicate cargo by her body.

Vikram burst through the door of the guardroom. He threw one dagger and flicked the other through the air before the guards stood from their chairs by the fire. The first embedded in the throat of the one guard; the second in the chest of the other. Vikram raced up the stairs, sword drawn. There was a dull thump as something hit the floor upstairs.

Niaz dragged the female warrior's body inside and dumped her on the floor.

Vikram came back downstairs. 'All clear.' Looking at the bodies, he said, 'Let's arrange this so a passerby won't suspect anything at a casual glance.'

'Who's going to pass by? You're wasting time.'

Vikram put the girl's body on a cot on her side and covered her with a blanket. He rolled one body under the cot, letting the blanket drape and hide it. The other he propped into the chair by the fire with his back to the door.

Niaz grabbed their backpacks and emptied a bottle of oil on the floor, spreading more across the bridge outside. 'For later,' he said.

Together they exited the bridge tower and moved into the upper city.

'They're replacing the old wall to match the front.'

'This wall will be as tall as the outer wall when they finish. Gods, what a feat,' Vikram said.

'It's still largely wood—it can all burn. Thank the gods they are doing it or we'd not be in this easily. They can't place men on watch up there yet.'

Once through the main gate the road branched in several directions. 'Which way?'

'Right,' Niaz whispered. 'It's broader. I'm guessing the wagons come down here to the granary.'

Warriors were spread thinly along the wall on watch—all looking outward. *If they see me, I'm dead. I need to get their attention at the right moment. I need to keep my cover. Gods help me,* Vikram thought.

A practice area was next to the barracks; next to it the armoury. Nearby stood the smithy—a largely stone building with a slate roof. Along from the smithy stood stables. The sweet smell of hay drifted to them on a light breeze.

They moved behind the smithy. Vikram and Niaz each carried a hollow cow's horn, which hung from their belts. A metal lid with several holes in it capped the horn. Vikram removed the cap. *If I'm lucky, it's out.*

'If we're lucky they're still burning,' Niaz said.

'What was it packed with?'

'Ash, coal, dunghali mushrooms and rush fibre,' Niaz said. He gingerly blew into the horn and a faint glow emitted from it. 'The granaries are mine. When you see it go up, light up the barracks and armoury; see what damage you can do to the smithy.'

Those damn mushrooms burn for hours, Vikram thought as he stared in disgust at Niaz's departing back.

Vikram ran oil along the rear of the barracks and the base of the front door. He did the same with the armoury and the stables.

Sitting at the rear of the armoury he noticed a flicker of flame flare under the granary. He stared in loathing at the grenades in his bag. *Gods curse Ratilal. Why me?* He leant against the building, shaking his head. *He's testing me. I need to be there at the end. My clan needs it.*

Vikram grabbed a wick, lit it and began lighting up the oil along the barracks and armoury. A thin flame raced along the oil and began to lap up the rear and sides of the building. He could see Niaz's dark form moving toward him. Quickly he grabbed a grenade and lit it.

Niaz scudded to a halt beside him. 'Not long now. Come on.' He disappeared into the smithy. Flashes of orange lit the dark interior of the building.

Vikram tossed grenades onto the armoury and stable rooves and walls. He darted through the doorway, hurling more into the building. The screams of horses filled the air. Guards along the wall cried out, raising the alarm. The first granary was aflame.

Vikram heard warriors rousing in the barracks. He threw a grenade on the roof. The pottery jar shattered. A wave of flame rolled down the shingles. The trickle of oil he had cast before the barracks' door burned weakly.

'What have you done? They'll get out,' Niaz said accusingly. 'I knew it—traitor!'

Vikram ran through the night, heading toward the main gate.

The first granary exploded. A warrior threw open the door of the barracks. Niaz hurled a grenade at the guard, whose clothes immediately burst into flame. Niaz tossed another into the building and yet another on the roof, before chasing Vikram.

Screams filled the air as two more fiery men ran outside, their arms flailing. Others thrust them to the ground and rolled them in the dirt to smother the flames.

The warriors stared in disbelief at the fireball that was the granary. The second and third granaries were aflame. All that was left of the drying room was a glowing timber frame. Sparks blew from it into the crisp night air, dancing their way into the sky.

A sergeant bellowed orders. 'You lot get after them. Find them, end them. The rest of you, stop the fire spreading to the last granary. Save what you can.'

Others darted into the armoury, hauling out weapons while it burned. Bits of flaming shingles fell onto them. One woman patted out her singed hair and clothes and prepared to re-enter the building. The warrior nearest her grabbed her arm, dragging her back as the roof collapsed. 'Come on,' he said. 'We need more help to fight the fires.'

Vikram waited inside the bridge tower. *Did Niaz escape?* He could hear pounding feet drawing closer. *Niaz!* Vikram smashed a grenade onto the oil-soaked timber of the bridge. He hurled another into the guardhouse. A blazing wall sprang to life, barring Niaz's way. *Now they'll have you.*

Niaz thundered on. The Bear warriors pursued him. He put his head down, finding a burst of speed. An arrow whizzed past his ear; another sliced the skin of his thigh.

Vikram watched Niaz's approach. *Damn. He's going to make it.* Niaz launched himself through the flames. Running straight for Vikram, he snarled, 'You traitor!' The fire flared behind him.

'Gods' blessings,' Vikram murmured as the fire became an impassable wall of flame, halting the Bear warriors.

Vikram flicked his wrist. His dagger embedded in Niaz's chest. Niaz's hands gripped the dagger as he fell to his knees. Vikram kicked him in the face and knocked him over. He retrieved his dagger, cut Niaz's throat and ran, smashing more grenades as he left. By the time he reached the edge of the bridge, the entire bridge tower was engulfed in fire. He threw the empty satchel away and continued making his way through Gopindar.

Niaz's men had been busy—fires were springing up throughout the densely populated, poorer quarter of the city. The flame moved like a snake following the arsonists' path. *Surely someone will work it out and head them off.* Most of the houses there were thatched. Burning thatch blew over the city in steadily rising wind. The fire spread like a demented web. Soon the entire quarter was aglow.

Horrified, Vikram's jaw dropped as fire broke out simultaneously in four directions at once in the affluent part of the city. *How? Longer wicks to delay ignition. Gods help them.* The swiftest, safest path was no longer sneaking between buildings.

Distant screams merged with nearer ones. Mothers raced from burning homes carrying babes. Vikram ran headlong into a crowd. Shocked eyes turned towards him.

'Quick. Keep your eyes open. The enemy has infiltrated the city,' he said.

They stared at him suspiciously.

'I don't recognise you. Where're you from?'

'The northern forests. I came to sell goods at the market.'

A scream sounded from a side street. Vikram darted down it, chased by several men. A woman stood outside her blazing house wailing. He grabbed her shoulders. 'What?'

Her husband ran from the building, his shirt on fire. Vikram tackled him, throwing him to the ground, rolling him and beating out the fire.

The woman ran to her husband, who lay moaning on the ground. 'Where is he? In the goddess's name where is he?'

'Who?'

'My baby!'

Vikram leapt up. 'Where?'

'Upstairs.'

Two men grabbed him roughly before he could run into the building. 'Nay, you cannot,' one of them said. 'Look.' The roof collapsed. 'Let him go, lads. The enemy would not linger to help us.'

Vikram sagged. 'Dear gods, what have they done?' Tears streamed down his face. They let him go. The burnt man was moaning. 'He needs help. We need to evacuate.'

'We need to fight the fires.'

'How? Wet down the walls and roofs of unburnt houses? With buckets? In this wind? If you could knock down houses in its path maybe, but I fear there will be no stopping this. Evacuate the women with children for pity's sake. Leave those who want to fight.'

The others carried the burnt man back to the main street where people were already moving in droves to the outer gates. Vikram drifted to the back of the crowd. People jostled one another as the crowd grew. More wounded were being carried out. The gates came in sight; the crowd surged forward.

Vikram slipped unnoticed from the crowd and headed to the market. As he neared it the market pavilion burst into flame. A grenade smashed upon a shingle roof shop next to him and fire rolled across its roof. Niaz's men confronted him.

'It's me, let's go.'

'Where is Lord Niaz?'

'Fallen at the bridge. We need to leave. You've done your work well. The high lord needs us now.'

They pushed open the smaller port gate and ran along the jetty to the waiting boat.

'Get us out of here,' Vikram ordered the boatman.

Behind them the lower city of Gopindar burned white hot.

—⚏—

Anil, Baldev's Kenati, finished painting an oak and willow pattern upon the brow of the last of the slain warriors. Each bore their clan's symbols painted on their hands.

A mass grave had been dug not far from Līna's house and large cuttings had been taken from a basket willow in her garden. In the late afternoon, the bodies of the slain were placed into the pit and covered with earth. One willow cutting was planted directly over the grave and one for each of the slain was planted in a wide circle around it. Before each cutting a small fire burnt the personal items of each individual.

Anil began a solemn chant, and Baldev and the others joined in. Their singing faded with the light and ceased. Each stood with their heads bowed until Anil said, 'May Rana and Jalal guide you and protect you on your journey. May you find peace and happiness in the next life—*alvida*.'

'And so we add yet another grove of willow to our land to honour the dead,' Baldev said bitterly.

'There was not enough wood to burn them as we should. Yet this is the way our ancestors followed in times of war. The gods will understand the necessity. Their flesh will return to the soil and be made one with this realm through the trees of the gods. Rana and Jalal will hear us through the song and with the aid of the gods, the burning of their effects will carry the spirits of the dead onwards.'

Baldev nodded. 'I wish we'd had the wood or the time to find it, though, and do this properly. Anil, have you ever really thought about how many such stands of willow or oak grow across this land? How many of those trees in clusters or alone have been planted where otherwise they would not be?'

'Yes, Lord Baldev, I have—too often.'

Baldev sighed. 'How many more will we plant before this is done?'

As they went back to the farmstead, Baldev thought he caught the scent of a heavier smoke upon the air, yet when he tried to catch it again it was gone.

Ratilal stayed on the battlements of Faros watching Gopindar burn all night. *They thought they were untouchable. Baldev will be reeling from the fallout—homeless, dead and hopefully no grain for winter.*

He smiled and rubbed his hands together, warming them against the cold. The sentry behind him had remained stoically silent all night. Ratilal turned to him. 'Jabr, isn't it?'

'Yes, High Lord.'

'What do you think?'

Jabr's face broke into a smile. 'Amazing, High Lord. You've hit the Bear at their heart.'

'Yes, we have. This night's work will not long be forgotten.'

Unable to speak, Jabr nodded heartily in agreement. 'You're not tearing up, are you boy?'

'It's the smoke, High Lord.'

Ratilal looked about him. 'Oh, I suppose it is a bit smoky. I hadn't really noticed.' Grinning, Ratilal shook his head. 'What a sight! Time for breakfast—I'm ravenous. By the gods' teeth it's cold up here. Jabr, I'll send some food and mulled wine up to warm you—you deserve it. There shall be a day of celebration and a feast tonight in the mess hall. The people need to hear about this triumph.' He clamped his arm about Jabr's shoulder in joy. 'But first, breakfast!'

Jabr sagged once Ratilal left his presence. All night he'd fancied he could hear screams on the air. 'Gods, those poor souls. Captain Vikram, where are you? We need you here.'

—⚔—

In his chambers, Ratilal toyed with his wine goblet. Food was piled high on the dining table, enough for the entire squad he'd sent to Faros. 'Niaz should be back soon. We can celebrate. I think a trip to Pramod's is in order,' he murmured to himself.

A light tap sounded on his door. 'Enter.'

Vikram softly closed the door behind him and turned to face Ratilal.

Ratilal drew himself stiffly upright in his chair. 'Where is Niaz?'

'Niaz fell when we were fleeing the upper city.'

Ratilal rushed to his feet. His face reddened; his lips formed a tight line. The sound of his harsh breathing filled the room. 'How? Tell me?'

'The mission went smoothly. Sora let us in. Niaz and I tackled the upper city, the others the lower city. Niaz lit the granaries, and I lit the barracks and armoury. Once the alarm was raised the Bear poured out of the barracks and pursued us. The darkness helped, but the blaze was enough that an arrow found its mark. I fired the gatehouse and bridge. Niaz made it through then died in my arms.'

Ratilal's fist drummed against his thigh. His eyes were distant. 'Will the granaries be destroyed?'

'Yes. They exploded.'

'That's something then. The lower city?'

'The poorer quarter will be gutted. The fire was spreading rapidly, so I suspect much of the other districts will burn too. By now they probably have a vast wall around a burnt husk.'

Ratilal walked slowly to the fire and gripped the mantle with both hands. 'Eat something, Vikram—there's enough.' He hung his head and his face twisted momentarily in grief. 'Eat!'

Vikram took a leg of chicken and stood awkwardly behind what he knew was Niaz's seat. Ratilal shook himself from his reverie. Tersely, he said, 'Sit, Captain. Eat.' Ratilal prowled back to the table to sit, but did not touch any food. He poured himself a liberal goblet of wine and pushed the carafe toward Vikram without looking at him. 'Were the others with you when Niaz fell?'

'No.'

Ratilal steepled his fingers, deep in thought. Finally he tapped his foot impatiently. 'We have other problems. I've not been able to find Lady Malak. She needs to know her son has passed and Faros needs to know she's alive.'

Vikram stared at him. *Good. Rumour has already spread that he killed her for her part in the Conclave.* 'People believe she's dead?'

'More to the point, they think I've killed her.' Vikram carefully placed his wine glass on the table and glanced away. 'Will you dare to ask if I have … ? No, you're not that stupid, are you?' Ratilal snorted, a wry smile curled his lips. 'I haven't.'

'And if she returns, High Lord?'

Ratilal's hand closed around the knife in front of him on the table. With deliberate slowness he peeled an apple. 'Lady Malak will be safe. As furious as she makes me, I also admire the wily old girl. She alone had the gall and brains to organise a challenge.' Ratilal shook his head. 'It was brilliant, for by doing so she ensured her own safety. If I'd lost she was safe. But even if I won, how could I harm even a hair on her head and not make every damn rumour that is still …' He drove the knife into the table. '… still being spread and scrawled on the walls of this city true!' Ratilal wrenched the knife out of the timber, pushed his chair back, put his feet up and faced Vikram. 'By the way, we've put bit of a damper on that. We caught one of the culprits.'

Vikram's pulse pounded. 'Excellent, who was it?'

'Some scum from the lower quarter named Rogesh. Seems he'd had a soft spot for that whore Niara.'

Not one of mine then, Vikram thought. 'Has he given up any others?'

'No, he didn't. And he won't now. He died under torture.' Ratilal devoured apple slices, juice dribbling down his chin. 'I tell you, Vikram, if you want something done right you have to do it yourself.' He shook his head in disgust. 'All we got was that he had a thing for Niara. Everyone thinks I killed her too. Damn women running off—bane of my bloody existence at the moment!'

'To be fair, High Lord, you did beat her badly and the other patrons of the brothel heard the commotion.'

Ratilal chuckled. 'For a man of war, you have a rather delicate way of phrasing things. It wasn't planned. I gave Sora enough bruises to be convincing, and she squealed a bit. Damn Niara runs to the rescue, but at least it gave Sora's story more credibility in the end ... I miss her. How did she look when you were at Faros?'

'It was dark, but I would say as beautiful as ever if the ease with which she dealt with the guards was anything to go by.'

'Hopefully they won't suspect her.' He shrugged.

Bastard. Vikram smiled. 'She seems too clever for that, High Lord.'

Silence dominated the room. Ratilal brooded. He gripped the knife so tightly that his knuckles shone white. Reluctantly he released it. 'I'll remain at the training field tomorrow. My plans cannot wait. Your task remains the same. Govern and protect Faros as Pasha. Find Lady Malak and bring her home. She needs to know about her son. Keep her on a leash.'

As Vikram closed the door he heard the sound of furniture being thrown around the room.

—⚔—

Baldev had not been able to bring himself to sleep in Lina's cottage; instead he slept on the barn floor with his warriors. The acrid scent of smoke tickled his nose and he awoke as his captain reached to shake him.

Smoke hung low across the plains. 'Wake everyone,' Baldev said.

'They're awake, my lord, and waiting.'

'What in Karak is burning? What can make so much smoke?' A wave of dread washed over Baldev. 'Anil?'

'He's already merged with his guardian and is looking, Lord Baldev.'

'Get the horses ready.' Baldev went to the prone form of his Kenati.

'How long has he been gone?'

'Over an hour.'

Dawn was well along when Anil returned to them. Baldev helped him sit up slowly. Anil brushed his hand over the feathers of his guardian, a rufous owl, who sat subdued beside him. When his eyes met Baldev's he said, 'Gopindar.'

Baldev lurched to his feet, roaring in anger. His men parted before him as he paced. He turned back to Anil. 'How much?'

'Three quarters of the lower city. Parts of it still burn; survivors work to put out fires, but it is slow. In the upper city three of the four granaries are gone. There were signs of fire on the armoury and barracks but they looked intact.'

'Dead?'

'Too many to count,' Anil said.

'Find Karan. Tell him I am heading to Gopindar.'

Baldev's captain spoke. 'It could be a trap of some kind.'

Baldev rubbed his face tiredly. 'Yes, it could—but I doubt it. How will Ratilal get a horde of men across the marshlands in the north? You've seen the height of the water in the Divide; the Falcontine will have spilled its banks. The marsh will be in full flood. He can't get an army across that.' The captain nodded. 'We've got to help the survivors,' Baldev continued. 'The weather will only worsen as winter draws near. Food stocks will be low. We'll have to organise supplies from Targmur—Karan will spare what he can. Damn it all to Karak and back!'

'Ratilal has bought himself time,' the captain said. 'He can't be ready to attack in force yet anyway.'

'We humiliated him by escaping his plot in Parlan, and now he seeks revenge,' another added.

'Yes, all of that,' Baldev said. 'He's proving a point with the burning and with what was done here. He knew exactly what to do to hurt us the most now and into the future. Our army will struggle to fight on an empty belly. Anil, join your guardian, find Karan. Tell him what has happened here and to Gopindar. He'll have to deal with the ones who did this to Lina and Satish and he has more men arriving with Hamza. Captain, send a rider to retrieve anyone of ours left at Bear Tooth Lake.' Baldev pulled a red feather from inside his tunic. He gave it to Anil. 'Have your guardian carry this. If you see any of our patrols, swoop low so they see it. They'll know to rally at the Vale of Safa.' Baldev shook his head again. 'We can't abandon them. Ratilal will pay and the wait will be worth it.'

Far from Līna's farmstead, Karan stood beside Mirza, looking at the charred remains of another farmhouse and its occupants. 'How many?'

'Looking at the tracks, maybe six,' one of his men answered.

'Suniti?'

'Yes, Lord Karan.'

'Take to the skies. Find them …' Karan ordered.

Anil's rufous owl landed amid them.

'Lord Karan,' Suniti said. 'The feather!'

'I see it, Suniti—be calm. Find out what has transpired.'

Suniti breathed deeply, waiting as Anil's image formed before her. His words left her pale and shaking. Karan's arm slipped around her as she began to cry. 'Tell me, Suniti.' She related Baldev's message.

'He has no choice,' Karan murmured. 'There can only be a few squads roaming here, Ratilal couldn't get more across,' he mused. 'This is merely a game to him—petty vengeance for foiling him.'

'Lord Karan, the feather.'

'I know, Suniti. You want to return to Lord Baldev. You cannot. I need your skills and I can't spare a squad to escort you back safely, nor will I risk you. Now, you must to get a message to Munira at Hunters' Ford. I want the squad there to destroy our canoes and move out to discover where the enemy crossed the river and destroy their boats. The Boar may head back there or to the ford. Sooner or later Munira and the squad will find them and finish them. Seek out more enemy as you go, report back and we will hunt them down.'

Chapter Thirty-two

THE BOAR SCOUT returned to his squad. 'Most of the camp at Bear Tooth Lake has mobilised. Karan and Baldev took large forces with them,' he reported.

'It means the other squads are doing a good job creating a ruckus attacking the farms, drawing them out,' their commander said.

'Still too many for us to attack the camp though?' a Boar soldier asked.

The scout nodded.

'They're not our objective anyway,' the commander said tersely. 'Did you see the strangers?'

'Some. I saw the small boy in training with a girl—one of ours.'

'Not the woman?'

'Only the mother of the boy, not the one described to us.'

Damn it. Why couldn't it have been the woman he found? The commander kicked a rock into oblivion.

'The boy is special,' the scout said. 'The way they treat him and he plays the flute with unearthly talent … He left with Umniga and a few others this morning.'

The commander groaned inwardly. *Now there's no way out.* 'The mission still stands.'

—⚉—

Umniga ducked and nimbly passed beneath the trunk of a large tree that had toppled sideways across their path and lay wedged in the branches of another. Pio and Kiriz stopped and stared at the vast number of fallen trees around them.

'Ma says,' Kiriz began, 'a huge windstorm came through years ago and crossed Altaica. It tore up trees and threw them around like skittles. But I've never seen so many in one place.'

They both began to poke and play in the thick, soft green moss on the underside of the trunk above their heads.

'Pio, Kiriz! Pick your feet up,' Umniga said without looking back.

They rolled their eyes.

Nimo gave them a gentle push, leaning down to whisper, 'Come on. She's already in a foul mood about having to do this. Don't make it worse, please.'

'I heard that, girl.' Umniga stopped and spun around with her hands on her hips. 'Look at you all! Like you're heading to the slaughter, not a morning of storytelling.'

'Can't you tell us tonight?' Pio pleaded. 'When it's dark and we can't train.'

'Or ride,' Kiriz said mournfully.

'Or shoot,' Pio added.

'No. This will happen every morning until Nimo has written down all my stories.' Nimo withered under her gaze. 'Accurately. Those are Lord Karan's orders. And you two need to learn.'

'When Isa and Asha return from the hill trails with Pravin, we'll stop and then you can train.'

'Damn it to Karak and back,' Kiriz mumbled.

'Mind your language, girl!'

'We've been walking for ages,' Pio whispered. He slammed to a halt as a flash of amber and grey caught his eye, then was gone.

Nimo bumped into him. 'Just keep going. It's not you she's mad at.'

'It's not your fault either,' Pio said softly.

She grunted, adjusting the weight of her satchels as they kept walking. 'We must nearly be there. The trees are thinning.'

'Nimo, will you teach me to write like you do?' Pio asked.

She smiled, ruffling his hair. 'Of course.'

Kiriz gaped. 'Gods! Why would you want to learn letters? You can't eat 'em, wear 'em or fight with 'em.'

Nimo groaned. 'Kiriz …'

Her jaw dropped as they stepped into a small narrow clearing along a backwater of the lake. The grass here was short and much of the bark had been rubbed off the trees by deer. Umniga laid her cloak on the ground, sat on it and began pulling food out of her pack. Nimo cast her cloak on the ground, trying to avoid Umniga's gaze. Umniga's lip curled and she sniffed in disdain at Nimo as the scribe drew out her scrolls, quill and ink.

'Pio, Kiriz. What has Cook put in your packs?' Umniga asked.

'Rocks,' they said, slumping.

Umniga's lips twitched as they despondently opened their packs. 'Apples, cheese, dried venison.' Pio plunked each one on the cloak. 'Walnuts … where'd he get them?' Pio's mouth formed a small 'o'. He drew a sharp intake of breath. 'Honey oatcakes!'

Nimo chuckled. 'I think Cook likes you.'

'And there's this.' Umniga placed a bundle in front of them.

'Fishing line?'

'Best fishing spot north of the Divide. The whoppers live here.' Pio and Kiriz scrambled to their feet. 'After you listen to the stories, quit grizzling and behave, then you can fish. And I want you to practise your flute too, Pio.'

Kiriz and Pio looked askance at each other. 'How long for?'

Umniga's brows rose into her hairline and her lips turned down. The children sank to the ground. 'Right, let's get started,' she said.

Nimo gripped her quill tightly.

The only sound was the shrill cry of a little falcon.

—ᴍ—

Pio sat listening to Umniga's stories. *Lore*, he corrected himself. *Lore isn't so bad.*

Kiriz lay on her back, full and bored.

'Read it back to me, Nimo,' Umniga barked.

'And the rivers ran red,' Nimo said.

'Good now …' Umniga tilted her head as if listening. The harsh caw of a raven in the distance was the only sound. 'Devi?' A twig snapped. Eyes wide, she suddenly yelled, 'Run!' Then she gasped loudly. An arrow had lodged in her chest. 'Run,' came her hoarse whisper. She looked down as another arrow speared her belly.

Kiriz rolled onto her stomach, staying low. A shriek escaped her lips.

Nimo sprang toward Umniga and collapsed with an arrow in her shoulder. 'Go!' she yelled at the children.

Pio leapt up. Kiriz tried to yank him down. 'Stay low, Pio.'

He stared mutely at Umniga and Nimo.

'Pio!' Kiriz grabbed his hand and tugged. Men were emerging from the tree line.

Nimo raised her head. 'Kiriz, Pio, run, hide, get help,' she ordered. 'Do it.'

Kiriz ran. Pio, eyes hard, jaw set, reached for Umniga's staff. His hand closed around it.

A large foot slammed down upon the staff. 'Forget it, boy.' Rough hands seized him.

'Umniga's alive. Finishing her will please the high lord.' A Boar soldier grabbed her grey hair and hauled her upright. In a deft movement a dagger descended towards her throat.

'Leave her, your shot was true. She won't last long,' the commander said.

Nimo lay face down on the grass. Its sweet smell, mixed with Umniga's blood, clawed at her.

'What about this one?'

'Leave her. Find that little girl,' the Boar commander ordered stiffly. 'Stop her raising the alarm.' When they were gone, he murmured, 'Bloody butchers, that's what we've become.'

Kiriz darted between the trees. She slipped on the moss, skidded down a gully and landed sprawled in a pile of damp leaves. She hauled herself up. Mud and leaves clung to her clothes. Her skid marks stood out like a beacon. *Keep running. Get out of the gully.* Kiriz scrambled ahead before fleeing up a narrow animal track. She crouched behind a stump. *Which way is the camp?*

'Here! She's down in there!'

Gods, help me. Rana, Jalal please? The enemy disappeared into the gully following her trail. Kiriz stood up and raced away.

'No, come back,' a Boar soldier yelled to the others. 'She's here!'

The sound of pounding boots dogged her. Kiriz skidded to a stop behind a large tree. The river lay on one side of her; a dense tangled mat of forest regrowth and fallen timber lay on the other. *I've got to hide in there.* She couldn't see anyone. Her chest heaved. She strained to hear footfalls on the damp leaf litter. *Quiet.* Desperate, Kiriz snatched a rock and hurled it with all her might into the lake. The splash resounded through the air.

'Over there!'

Back pressed against the mossy bark, straining to hear, she thought the two men had moved away from her. A hole in the dense undergrowth beckoned. She launched herself forward.

Thorns! No! Kiriz veered away.

A sob escaped her as she searched for a place to hide. *There!*

A large tree lay steeply askew in the branches of a giant cypress. Kiriz clambered onto the fallen trunk and scrambled up its length. She slipped, landing belly first and slid down. Kiriz clamped her fingers in the cracking trunk. Her fingernails tore as she struggled to stop.

'Cunning little bugger. She's not here. Go back. Keep looking.'

Kiriz's breath caught in her throat. She lay clinging to the fallen trunk. She dragged herself up and into the cypress branches and huddled against the far side of the trunk. Kiriz bit her lip, tears streaked her face. *I didn't fight. I ran and left them. Umniga's dead. Nimo? They have Pio. I'm a coward. I should go back—that's what*

Asha or Isa would do. She peeked around the trunk and peered down through the branches. Three warriors stood not far away. The Boar commander joined them.

'Forget her. We need to move now.' Two of the men left. The third stood defiantly. 'You heard me. Get moving.'

The commander stood alone, his eyes landed unerringly upon the cypress. With a sad smile he touched his head in salute and left.

—⚬—

Isaura and Asha, their training done, rode along a high mountain trail with Pravin bringing up the rear.

Glancing back, Isaura laughed. 'Did I pass, Pravin?'

'You did well enough,' Pravin replied brusquely. When she turned away his lips curled into a reluctant smile.

'Come on, Alejo,' Isaura cried. The mule flicked his tail, leapt forward and jumped the log across their path. Honey chased upon their heels.

Pravin scowled. 'Waste of time, tiring the horses further with useless work. You never know when …'

Isaura and Asha laughed at him, flicking dismissive hands toward him before cantering off through the trees.

'Cheeky young buggers.' Pravin shook his head and cantered after them.

They stopped at a fork in the path. 'Asha, you'd better lead the way,' Isaura said. 'I've no clue where this fishing hole is and I'd rather Pio saw you first.'

The horses ambled along the erratically winding track amid fallen trees and dense forest regrowth. Asha drew Honey to a sharp halt. 'Pravin?' she said, staring at the marks on the ground. 'Horses—a patrol?'

'Maybe,' Pravin grumbled. 'Maybe Umniga let those little imps bring their horses to keep them quiet.'

'She was in no mood to indulge them this morning.' Isaura hesitated. 'The tracks run in both directions.' She shared a worried glance with Asha and a weight settled in her belly. 'How long will it take to get there?'

'Half an hour.'

'Asha, send Fihr to check,' Pravin ordered.

'He's not close, but he's coming,' Asha replied as she moved off. 'Can you contact the Matriarch?'

Isaura snorted. 'Only when she wants to hear me and I haven't seen her in days, but I'll try.' Isaura slipped into the spirit realm. *Old Mother?* she called. Nothing. 'It's no good. Looks like we're on our own.'

The only sound as they continued was the soft swish of the scrub as it brushed against their clothes and the horses' sides. As the trail narrowed, broken branches and twigs hung limply from the bushes.

They hurtled along here, Isaura thought.

Asha gasped, leaned forward and grasped Honey's neck. Isaura drove Alejo forward, forcing a way to her side.

'Asha?'

'No! Gods, no!' Asha's hands clutched Honey's mane. She panted and a shrill cry escaped her lips. Asha lurched and spurred Honey forward.

Soon the overgrowth became too dense to continue on horseback. Asha leapt from Honey and tore through the narrow gaps in the trees. Pravin and Isaura chased after her.

Isaura raced to catch her. *Keep going. Nearly ...* She snagged Asha's tunic with all her might. The fabric tore and Asha disappeared around a bend.

Pravin caught up with Isaura and grabbed her arm, halting her.

'How far?' Isaura whispered.

He gestured for her to follow him. The vegetation thinned and through it they could see a small clearing.

'Wait,' Isaura mouthed to Pravin, halting him with her hand.

Alejo, I need to see, but not enter. Isaura began to let herself slip into the spirit realm. Her vision altered. A tug deep within her prevented her from fully leaving her body.

Pravin touched her arm. 'Isa, your eyes ... You're merged, yet in control of your body.'

'Yes. Sort of half in, half out of the spirit realm.' Her voice sounded strange to her. 'I've been practising. Let me look.' Isaura peered through the trees, scanning the clearing and the tree line. Only four auras were visible to her—no one was hiding nearby. Asha's aura glowed before her along with three others: one faint, one dimming rapidly. The third, the smallest, pulsated wildly. *Devi*. He sat bobbing up and down and shifting from foot to foot in agitation. His aura was bright, beating in matching green and brown with Umniga's, but random pulses fractured the pattern.

Where are Pio and Kiriz?

At Isaura's nod, Pravin strode forward into the clearing. Asha sat on the ground, cradling Umniga. She rocked back and forth, brushing Umniga's greying hair from her forehead as she crooned a soft song. Devi fluttered as if trapped a few feet away.

Pravin glanced at them and made straight for Nimo, who was lying on her side. She had managed to wad her cloak around the arrow protruding from her shoulder, before losing consciousness.

'Asha, let me examine Umniga,' Isaura said.

Asha's grip tightened and she shook her head. 'You can't help. You are not one ...' She shook her head again, forcing herself to silence.

'Umniga's not dead.' Isaura's voice remained gentle, yet the timbre of the Undavi filled her words. 'You will let me look—now.' Isaura saw a flick of green flash through Asha's aura. *Hope*.

Umniga's breath rasped. Her eyes did not open, but her hand slid into Asha's. 'My, little whelp. I've waited. Where's Devi?'

Asha smiled. 'He's beside you,' she lied. 'Isa is going to look at your wound.'

Umniga wheezed. 'She'd defy even death.'

Isaura's dagger slashed through Umniga's blood-soaked tunic. The belly wound was black around the edges. Asha looked away.

'Bastards.' Pravin placed his hand on Isaura's shoulder. 'Come, Nimo needs our help. Leave them be.'

Isaura and Pravin snapped the arrow shaft protruding from Nimo's shoulder. Nimo woke with an agonised scream.

'It needs greater skill than mine, Pravin. The bone's probably broken as well.' Isaura tore strips off Nimo's cloak and began winding them around the remaining shaft, padding it and immobilising it.

Nimo stared at Asha and Umniga. 'They took Pio. Kiriz ran. I don't know if they found her.'

Isaura gritted her teeth, trying to quell her fear for Pio, her anger and the raging Wild within her veins. 'Pravin, Umniga's wound … I've never seen a wound blacken like that.'

'Poison. And only on the arrows in Umniga,' Pravin bit out.

'There must be something we can do?' Isaura asked. Pravin shook his head. 'We need to find them,' she said savagely.

'We need more warriors,' Pravin said.

Isaura abruptly stood. 'By the time we get to the camp, they'll be long gone. I'm not waiting.'

'Isa, there are only two ways before them. Northwest toward the Falcontine or southeast toward Hunters' Ford. Lord Baldev's forces stand between them and escape in the north. Lord Karan has many patrols in the southeast. They both have Kenati with them. Asha can get a message to them—they'll find the bastards.'

'Meanwhile they can do whatever they like to Pio and Kiriz.' A plan formed in her mind and Alejo's brutal glee urged her on.

'We're getting Pio back. We'll take them, Pravin, I swear it. And we'll have help.' With a wicked smile Isaura bellowed her thoughts and her rage through the spirit realm. *Old Mother! Matriarch, Asena—come to me!*

Isa-cub. The Matriarch's spirit form materialised before Isaura. *Ratilal's men have Pio and maybe Kiriz.*

The Matriarch ignored her and sat before Umniga and Asha. *For this I am sorry.*

Can you help her?

No.

What? Isaura asked. *I don't believe you. There must be something…*

Umniga is dying, Isa-cub. The wound itself would be slowly fatal, but the poison seeps through her system. She has little time.

Asha lifted her tear-streaked face to the sky. 'Rana and Jalal, help her … help me … What will I do?'

Umniga smiled at her. 'You'll endure, you'll seek vengeance and justice. You'll be magnificent little whelp—the best of us.'

'I don't want you to go,' Asha said plaintively.

Umniga groaned. 'Where's Devi?'

Isaura looked at the Matriarch with tears in her eyes. *We can only say goodbye, Isa-cub.* Isaura's hands fisted by her side; she burned to be gone. *There is time to catch them, Isa-cub. The pack is many miles away. We are coming. We will hunt with you.*

Devi flew to Umniga. Asha reached for him. He bit her, flapped his wings in fear and landed out of her reach, shuffling in agitation. *Their bond is severing,* the Matriarch said. *He is becoming wild. The goddess's grace is leaving them. Umniga will be with us soon. Her spirit will rise and for a brief moment she will be whole here and then The Wild will take her.*

She'll be able to see you?

Of course.

Then there's one last thing we can give her. Primara! Get here now! Nothing. Isaura snarled. *Old Mother?* Isaura asked.

With pleasure, Isa-cub.

What! The pair of you think to summon me? Primara's gaze fell on Umniga. *No!*

Now's your chance for a little redemption, Isaura said. *When her spirit appears you'll show yourself to her. You'll pretend to be the divine, caring deity she has worshipped her whole life.*

How dare you! Primara shook her head sadly. *Umniga is more dear to me than you know. This is too soon. She has not yet ...* Primara paused, staring intently at Umniga, reading her mind. The corner of her mouth turned up slightly and a sigh escaped her.

The Matriarch stiffened, cocking her head. She and Primara locked eyes, until Primara looked away.

Alejo, shield my mind, Isaura asked.

It's not your mind I want to see into, Isa-cub. Fear me not, the Matriarch said. *Umniga has been a loyal servant, has she not, Primara?* Primara sneered at the Matriarch and folded her arms across her chest defiantly. The Matriarch curled her lip in disgust at her.

Umniga moaned. Primara forgot her pique and gazed sadly on the old woman. Devi fluttered in agitation but would not approach Asha or Umniga.

I've had enough. One of you command Devi to her. Let her touch him, Isaura demanded.

I'll try, Primara said. *Perhaps enough of the bond remains. We cannot always command wild animals, but through the bond we can guide.*

Hesitantly, Devi moved closer to Umniga. The closer Devi drew to her, the more his aura matched Umniga's and both strengthened. Umniga reached out and stroked Devi's head.

Old Mother, bond her to Devi. When her essence enters this realm, bond her to him. Like you were to the Asena, Isaura said.

It cannot be done.

Perhaps ... Primara said.

No! the Matriarch snapped.

Why? The Wild pools around me. It comes to me. You called my spirit back into my body, Isaura said. *How different can it be? All we have to do is make Umniga's 'wild', her spirit, go into Devi. She'd be like you. She'd still be here.*

I could do that for you because a faint link remained to your physical, living, form, the Matriarch replied.

It could be possible, Primara said. *With the …*

The Matriarch's thoughts blasted them. *NO! And there will never be a way for you to return, Primara. This is the provenance of the goddess. Isa is not a god.*

'No, no … not yet!' Asha's cries stabbed at them.

The Matriarch continued gently. *Isa-cub, my choice was taken from me. It took an age for me to emerge from the Asena. Some of my friends never regained themselves. It is only now that I understand there may have been a purpose. Would she choose this?*

She would not, came Umniga's strong thoughts. Her spirit form stood before them. She glowed blue and the spirit of Devi appeared with her. *Hello, old friend.* He canted his head at her in a moment of silent understanding. Devi's aura flecked brown and green and he faded from the spirit realm. She watched him leave with longing.

Fear not, Umniga. He will live out his natural life, the Matriarch said as they watched him fly away from Umniga's body. Asha's sobbing increased. Pravin hung his head briefly, but remained near Isaura and returned to watching the tree line.

Primara and the Matriarch bowed before her. Umniga's form flared blue, as The Wild coruscated through it and it began dissolve from the edges, flickering like fading blue sparks into the air.

You have long been my favourite, Primara said. *You have served me well, Umniga.*

Umniga turned toward Isaura with a knowing smile. *I have always done as you bade me, Rana,* she said before fading completely.

Isaura slipped fully into the physical realm to comfort Asha, leaving the Matriarch and Primara alone.

Just remember, Primara, there is no way for you to return. I will not allow it.

What I really want to know is why Devi didn't know they were coming? Primara asked.

The Matriarch turned her hard gaze upon Primara. *Guardians are not infallible.*

Primara arched her brow. *Nor are they usually blind.* She shook her head. *What was the point?* The Matriarch ignored her. *Do they have the girl?* Primara asked.

I don't know, the Matriarch lied. *Why don't you see if you can find her?*

Primara vanished.

The Matriarch took one last look at Umniga's body. *I'm sorry, old one, I did not foresee this, but she needs this test.*

Chapter Thirty-Three

PIO'S CHEEK WAS bruised and swollen and his eye was half closed. *I wasn't quick enough.* The soldier who had caught him had been going to hit him again, but the commander had stopped him. Since then Pio had been riding with the commander. His hands were bound, his wrists red and chaffed. Pio fidgeted with the ropes.

'Stop it, lad,' the Boar commander said. 'They're not coming off and you'll only make it worse.'

Pio sagged. They stopped to water the horses at a creek crossing. The hair on the back of Pio's neck rose; his skin prickled. He looked around. *There!* On a branch watching him intently sat a falcon. *I know you,* he thought.

Small and sleek with a blue-grey back, shifting to dark brown around black eyes. A strip of amber-russet travelled from its beak up the centre of its head. Its soft chest and belly feathers were the same red. The falcon stretched out its wings, revealing amber and brown stripes underneath.

Pio was captivated. He had needed to hold his flute—it made him feel safe and strong. Now his fingers itched to play a tune for this bird. The notes were popping into his head—sometimes light and trilling, soaring, sweeping like the wind; others sharp, short, violent, victorious—fire and grace. The falcon cocked its head at him and moved a little closer along the branch.

'That little falcon's called a hobby, lad,' the commander said. 'They're all over Altaica, but much more common in the north—up in the Bear Clan lands.'

'It's small.'

'Aye, but quick and fierce. They'll take on other birds bigger than themselves. They hunt when and where they like. They're small all right, but clever. Probably a bit like you.' The man's smile vanished quickly.

'Can I have my satchel back?'

'You'll get it back, but not now. I know what you are, boy, or what you will be. I'll not have you lull us to sleep and try to escape.'

Pio craned his neck as they set off, desperately trying to keep the bird in sight. His heart leapt as the falcon launched itself into the air and swooped low over them before shooting skyward. The sun caught her feathers and they glowed with fire.

Pio's grin faded; tears filled his eyes as they cantered off.

Where are we? Pa and Uncle Curro are gone. Did Kiriz get away? Did she get help? Did they hurt her? A spectre of Umniga and Nimo haunted him. Pio began to sob. The arm around him gave him a gentle squeeze.

A new vision filled his mind. One of cloud streaked skies, vast sweeping grass plains, forests and mountains and the form of a sea eagle in the distance. *Fihr! Asha! Isa!* Pio tilted his head as he felt the warm lift of wind under wings. The vista changed as the falcon drew toward Fihr and began wheeling and swooping to get his attention.

—∞—

Isaura tapped her foot impatiently. Pravin stood beside her.

'Isa? Fihr has found Pio. His captors are sticking to the forest trails,' Asha said. 'Kiriz is not with them.'

A prickling sensation travelled up Isaura's spine and a zephyr twirled around her. She slipped into the spirit realm. *This is getting easier.*

Primara materialised before her, her brows raised in surprise that Isaura was waiting. *You knew I was coming?*

Isaura smiled. *I'm becoming attuned to this realm. It's almost like I've not left it. I just choose to see it and it's there.*

Excellent, Primara said. *You are doing well.*

Isaura grew wary. *Excellent for whom though?* she thought.

I've found Kiriz, Primara said. *She is hiding in a cypress a short distance from here.*

You have my thanks.

I wish only to help, Isaura, Primara said before vanishing.

'Asha …' Isaura said.

Asha interrupted. 'We need to get Umniga and Nimo back to camp. Then we need to get some men and find the others.'

Isaura told Asha where Kiriz was. 'You need to retrieve her and either get help or take Nimo and her to camp.'

'I can't leave Umniga alone. There are rituals that must be performed quickly.'

'You can come back with others to claim her and then do what is necessary.'

'Yes … I suppose. Oh, Isa, I'm not like this. I don't know what's wrong. My mind is scrambled. It clears in fits and starts until I remember Umniga is dead. I know we need to act fast … I …'

'It's natural, Asha. Umniga was like your mother. Nimo and Kiriz need your help and you can alert the camp. Pravin and I are not alone in this. The Asena are with us. It's time to go hunting.'

―᙮―

Dusk was falling. Alejo pounded through the forest. The Matriarch emerged from the forest before him and loped head. Isaura caught glimpses of at least ten Asena flitting through the trees on either side of the trail.

Merged with Alejo, Isaura could see almost all the way around her. Pravin's horse dropped back. Isaura slowed, waiting for him to catch up.

'You two might be able to see the path clearly, but I can't. If we continue at this speed we'll break our necks—then where will the boy be?'

Alejo rebelled, pawing the ground and shaking his head. He reached out and snapped his teeth at Pravin's horse.

'Enough, Alejo. Pravin is right. We're not stopping though, Pravin, I want to find them tonight.'

'Agreed.'

Isaura, the Matriarch said. *My scouts have found them.*

Show me, Isaura commanded.

Do not get used to giving us orders, Isa-cub, the Matriarch snapped.

Please.

An image entered Isaura's mind. The path descended the mountain and broke out into a sheltered, rock strewn yet grassy area, bordered by the forest on one side and by a tall outcropping of rock on the other.

'Pravin, they've stopped to rest.' She described the lay of the land to him. 'What do you propose?'

—⚋—

'Time to go,' the Boar commander said. Two sentries at either end of the clearing moved to join the others. Pio sat, hands and feet tied, with his back pressed against a large boulder.

Alejo galloped into the clearing from one end, flanked by Asena. From his back Isaura let loose an arrow, felling the sentry nearest to her. Pravin and the rest of the Asena charged the along the trail from the other side. He hurled a spear into the other sentry. Pravin's horse skidded precariously on the loose stones into an Asena, who yelped shrilly, nipping at its legs.

Isaura saw a Boar soldier take aim at Pravin. She fumbled with reloading her bow and tossed it aside. She let fly a throwing axe, which lodged in the enemy's back. He collapsed to his knees. An Asena pounced on him, gouging his neck, finishing him.

The Boar horses, tied loosely to shrubs, were harried by the Asena. Pulling back and rearing, the horses snapped their tethers and galloped away.

Pravin's horse regained its feet. A Boar soldier pulled the spear from his dead comrade and thrust it at Pravin's mount—the horse sidled away. The spear narrowly missed it; instead scraping Pravin's grieves. Pravin slashed downward with his sword, breaking the spear shaft. The horse danced backward and two Asena pounced upon the Boar soldier, dragging him to the ground.

Alejo slid to a halt, but his momentum had placed him well within the clearing. Two men moved to attack Isaura from either side. Alejo lashed out with both feet, double barrelling one man in the chest, sending him flying backwards. The enemy hit the ground and skidded—dead. Isaura's makeshift saddle slipped sideways as Alejo pirouetted to face the other attacker. She vaulted from his back to face the Boar commander. The Wild hummed within her, blue fire burned in her eyes.

The commander advanced. His kilij slashed toward her. She slid sideways. Alejo lunged at him, trying to bite him, forcing him to turn side on to her. Isaura lashed out with her sword. It barely connected, but sliced through the buckle at the side of his leather cuirass. A faint well of blood flicked off the tip as it travelled.

The commander grunted, but moved in swiftly. His blade came at her in a flurry of slashes. Alejo urged her on. Isaura panicked. Her control slipped. The Wild burned—and she let it. Rage engulfed her. She attacked in a frenzy. The commander smiled, evading her easily. His blade sliced through her jacket. Alejo charged him, enraged. *Alejo, No!* Fear for him jolted Isaura. *Alejo, move!* She drew her dagger in the other hand and flicked it at her attacker. Alejo danced away from him. The cuirass gaped from her earlier work. The dagger slipped through the gap into his side. The commander staggered, but did not fall.

Breathe, just breathe. Focus. Calm. Isaura quelled her rage, visualising The Wild as her sword; trying to channel it into her movements. A sense of detachment, of stillness, enveloped her. Events seemed to slow. Instead of reacting, she watched and analysed—too late.

Isaura felt the breath of the Boar blade as it sliced toward her head. Instinct took over. The commander's kilij flashed toward her head. She arched backwards, turned her wrist and slashed upwards. In her mind's eye, her kilij burned brightly. It sliced through his forearm. His hand and sword toppled to the dirt. Blood poured from the stump. The commander doubled over in pain. As he bent forward, Isaura brought her sword down with all her might and severed his head.

Pravin kept his distance. 'Isa?'

Isaura's sides heaved and her limbs shook. 'I'm in control. I'm fine. You're safe.'

Now she sought out Pio. Several Asena sheltered him and his face lay buried in the ruff of one. Pio was trembling. Isaura took a step toward him. Pravin grabbed her arm, shaking his head and flicked his gaze pointedly to her clothes. Her tunic was spattered with blood. Isaura took it off and tossed it across Alejo's saddle, revealing her clean blue silk shirt.

'Isa,' Pravin said quietly. 'You're ready. When the boy is returned, we join Karan.'

Isaura nodded and went to Pio. The Asena parted before her. *What'll he think? He's just watched me massacre these men.* She sighed, steeling her heart. Isaura prised his hand from the Asena's fur and held it in her own hand, gently rubbing the back of it with her thumb. Slowly he looked up at her.

'Hello, Pio. Didn't your ma tell you not to wander off with strangers?'

Pio threw himself into her arms, knocking her flat on her back. 'Isa! I knew you'd come.' Isaura held him and rubbed his back until his crying subsided. 'Can we go?'

'Yes.' They walked to Pravin and Alejo.

Pio tucked into her side as they stepped around bodies. 'Who'll I ride with?'

'You'll have your own horse to ride,' Pravin said. 'Usually the loose horses don't go too far. We'll find you one.'

'Er …' Isaura said. 'I believe the young Asena enjoyed their job a little too much. The horses are long gone.'

'Isa, Alejo scares me.'

'Lad,' Pravin said drily. 'That mule scares everyone, including me.'

Alejo lowered his head, eyeballing Pio. Pio stepped back, pressing himself against Isaura. The mule stretched his neck toward the boy. Pio's eyes grew round. He grabbed Isaura's hand; his breath hitched in his throat. Alejo closed in on him. Boy and mule stood eye to eye. Alejo wuffed gently through his nose and nudged Pio's chest. He stepped back, shaking his head and gave a whinnie that ended in a bray.

Isaura rolled her eyes at Pio. 'He thinks he's funny, Pio.'

A little falcon swooped overhead and landed on Alejo's saddle.

Pio smiled at it and it glided to his outstretched arm. 'Isa, Pravin, meet Fiamma. I think she's my guardian.'

Asha had worked tirelessly. Umniga's body was bathed and painted with ritual tattoos of willow and oak. Her hair was braided neatly and she lay with her staff on top of a high bier. At sunset Asha held a torch to the timber and watched the flames lick along the wood and burst to life. She leaned forward, rocking, sobbing. A keening wail erupted from her lips. Tears streamed down her face. The words of the lament stuck in her throat. She could not sing. Slowly, those around her began a chant ending with the cry of 'Umniga!' Drums took up the rhythm and the lament began in a harmonious round—the massed voices carrying their sorrow to the gods.

Lucia took Asha's hand and rubbed her back comfortingly. Asha gripped it firmly and stood tall. Her grief, her love and her anger poured forth to the sky as she joined the chanting. They sang until the body was consumed.

Asha placed a portion of Umniga's ash into a carved wooden box. The rest was scooped up and transported to the lake where Asha boarded a small boat and was rowed from the shore. In silence the camp watched as Umniga's remains were committed to the life-giving water. When Asha alighted, she knelt by the lake and wet her face and the top of her head. She dipped her hands into the wooden box and pressed the ash against her skin and hair, transforming her face into a ghostly visage.

'Now we get your son,' she said to Lucia. 'Then we go to war.'

—⚌—

Scowling, Isaura fidgeted, kicking her legs out and pulling them back. She'd been finding it impossible to keep still ever since she'd sat down. Pio slept nearby, clutching his flute, an Asena curled around him. His satchel lay at her feet, its contents half out. *He'll lose things.* Isaura bent to grab it and a warm buzz travelled through her outstretched hand. *What in the world?* Hastily she pulled her hand back. Isaura took the long leather strap of the bag and, holding it out from her, she warily carried it away from the others before placing it on the ground. The Matriarch stalked to her. Alejo wandered over.

Leave it be, Isa-cub.

Isaura narrowed her eyes at the Matriarch. She used a stick to jiggle the bag's contents to one corner, then took hold of the empty corner and shook the contents onto the ground. Out of the satchel slid a half eaten apple and a black crystal as long as her hand.

Isa-cub, don't.

Isaura moved her hand toward it and a rainbow ripple ran along its surface. A multi-hued glow began that became blue. The tattoos on Isaura's hands glowed in response. Her whole arm tingled, filling her with a heady sensation. Slowly, she moved her hand away. The crystal ceased to glow. Yet her body thrummed—strong, invincible.

It's the same type of crystal as the Goddess's Eye, isn't it? How did Pio get it? Did you know? Isaura asked.

Yes it is, and no. This is her work, Isa-cub. Leave it. The Matriarch moved forward, head lowered.

Isaura ignored her. *Did the other crystal do this for you?*

Never. Leave it now. The Matriarch growled low and deep in her throat. A slow full snarl curled her lips as she stared at Isaura. Alejo thumped his massive front hoof between them. The Matriarch tried to dart around him. Alejo flicked a hind hoof. The Matriarch yelped and sailed through the air. She lay prostrate before him, ears pinned against her head. None of the other Asena woke. Those stationed as sentries did not notice the commotion.

Alejo, don't hurt her, Isaura said. Nothing, his mind was blocked to her.

Isaura's vision blurred. Dual images swam before her as Alejo hauled her partially into the spirit realm. She shook her head, disoriented.

Primara was watching. Surprise and wariness warred with glee upon her features. She regained her composure. *Touch it, Isa. It waits for you. Can you not feel it, humming through you? You are the same. It answers your spirit as it never answered mine or my brother's. You will be able to use it.*

Anticipation filled Isaura. *Can I? It could be easy.* All the bodies of those they'd left behind in Arunabejar, the invasion—she'd not been able to protect them. *I could've stopped all that.* Isaura reached for it. The tongues of rainbow flame licked across the crystal. It burst into a vibrant blue blaze. Isaura hesitated, her hand partway toward it.

The Matriarch writhed on the ground, pinned by an unseen force. *Isa-cub, be strong!* She lay on her side exhausted, panting.

Primara flicked her gaze toward the Matriarch—concerned, curious. Smiling, she shrugged. *It seems your guardian and I are of an accord. Isaura, think of the good you can do. Think what you* can do already. *This is just more of the same. You can protect those you love,* Primara wheedled.

Isaura's hand hovered over the crystal. *What's in this for you?*

Primara's form flickered, then grew brighter. Her expression moved from anger, to grief, to resignation. *I need to know I was right. I need to return ... to restore some of my history. You are the key. I need to know a thousand years were not merely punishment and ...*

Iridescent blue flames flicked from the crystal, drawing both their attention. *No, not flames. The Wild. Pulsing not just from it, but to it,* Isaura mused. A flame arced towards Isaura's hand. She stepped back, but The Wild within her answered. The natural currents of energy around her flowed through the crystal and rushed across the arc into her. Isaura's veins thrummed in response, burning as the two attempted to merge.

Drunken euphoria seeped through her. The intensity of the rush grew, nearly overwhelming her. This was no slow, gentle recharging of her energy. Isaura tried to break free. Her legs were welded in place. Her eyes grew wide. *I can't move! I need to do something! This will kill me. I have to let it out.* Yet the crystal continued to arc power to her. *I can't shut it off.* Her legs and arms were cramping.

Isaura, you can do this, Primara urged. *You have come so far. I can see you starting to control it within you. You must now stop the flow.*

Alejo, help! Isaura tore her gaze to him. The Asena had formed a circle around them. They were prostrate before him. Alejo turned his head toward her and his eyes glowed, not with the familiar blue of The Wild, but with the rainbow fire of the crystal. Isaura could only stare into their depths, held captive by the heart of the fire.

A vision of Primara and her brother, with a crystal many times the size of this, invaded her mind. *Twins.* One in the spirit realm, one in the physical realm. *They formed the perfect conduit.*

They laughed, young, confident, arrogant, heady from small successes—heedless of the cost. Primara craved knowledge, her brother craved power. Isaura saw their auras rapidly change, small streaks of blue became dazzling white. Power roared through them killing them and spilling into the world unchecked, then the crystal exploded. *They destroyed everything they loved and coveted.* 'Stop the flow' was Primara's last desperate call from the spirit realm to her brother.

Flashes of memories assailed Isaura—the Matriarch. 'There is always a choice ... decide which trail to walk.' Karan's words lingered the longest—'Control makes heroes or villains of us all.' Visions of her friends, their journey, the hardships. *I don't want them hurt. I don't want to cause it. I want to keep them safe. I've always wanted that! I choose another path. Give me another path please?*

Isaura glared at Primara. *You were wrong then and you're wrong now! You didn't even think about the risk. Your brother had no chance against this, nor do I!* Isaura closed her eyes and prayed. *May the goddess ...* She struggled for coherency ... *M'Aricel, give me strength to fight just to stop this, even if it kills me.*

Frustrated, desperate, Primara screamed. *You must be able to harness it! Your essence is the same!*

Isaura roared at her. *I want to kill you! You've damned us all. I'll not sacrifice my friends for you.* Primara's image fractured, but reformed. A tree trunk split directly behind her. Isaura's teeth clenched. Her skin grew hot and itchy. She fought to shift her feet. Her head swam. *No. Remember who you are, what you want—save them. Breathe. Just breathe.* Isaura closed her eyes. Sweat poured off her; her glowing tattoos pulsed. *Control. Breathe. Focus. Shut it out.*

Isaura found same stillness in her mind that she'd had in battle. She sensed two storms with slightly different rhythms battling for dominance within her. Briefly, they pounded together. Her aura became blinding—nearly white. The discordant beat resurfaced, her aura flickered its familiar blue. *Music. Pio!* Isaura grabbed that discord and focused on it. Thinking of it like a song, singing to it in her mind. It heeded her. The familiar blue flashed back more strongly. Isaura grasped it, forcing that discordance, her Wild, to her hands. Everything slowed. For a second The Wild within her sought release via the path to the crystal, blocking the flow into her—reversing it. Her energy forced its way briefly into the crystal. Isaura could move; she staggered back shakily just as her control snapped. The arc vanished.

Alejo reared; his front feet landed upon the crystal, smashing it. The Matriarch and the Asena shook themselves as if waking from a dream.

Isaura's aura pulsated madly between white and blue. Pure energy whipped around her system, agonising as her as spirit tried to assimilate it. *I have to get it out.*

Isaura, Primara cried. *Use it! It is yours.*

Stay away from me, Isaura snarled, *or we will end you!* Alejo turned the rainbow fire of his gaze upon Primara. She stepped back terrified and vanished.

Isaura forced her legs to move her further away from the camp and her friends. The huge outcrop of rock where Pio had been tied up loomed in the distance before her. *I hope this works.* She picked up a rock, focused on it and hurled it with all her might. The stone struck the massive outcrop and it cracked and toppled into four pieces. The pressure within Isaura lessened. Legs weak, Isaura sat on the ground and kept throwing rocks until she'd reduced the outcrop to rubble.

Isaura stopped when Alejo placed his chin on her shoulder. 'You were a lot of help. What in Karak happened?' She searched his memory, finding only blankness and confusion. 'Never mind.'

She was still there, deep in thought, when hours later the gravel behind her crunched.

'I thought you were out here dwelling on the battle,' Pravin said. He quirked his brow at the rocky devastation. 'I was going to offer you some sage advice, like that way lies madness. Now I'm not sure what to say.'

'It's still good advice,' Isaura replied with a half smile. 'But I think madness lies all around. How's Pio?'

'Just stirring. Before you ask I slept like a baby.' Pravin shook his head. 'Never heard a damned thing.'

'Just as well. The Asena?'

'Still here. The Old Mother has been just sitting, watching you.'

'Isa, what happened?' Pio asked agog.

'I've been trying to figure that out myself.' Isaura stood, dusting off her clothes and winking at him. 'Maybe an earth tremor. Come on.' They headed back to the camp. 'Pio, I'm sorry, Alejo broke your crystal.'

Pio scowled and crossed his arms over his chest. 'Damn it to Karak and back! I'll have to get another one.'

'Pio! If your mother heard …'

'You say it.'

Isaura sagged and smiled tiredly. 'Just don't say it around your ma. And promise me you won't go looking for another crystal. It was magic and dangerous … Promise?'

Pio rolled his eyes. 'I promise.' He held out his arm and Fiamma landed on it. His face lit with excitement. 'Fiamma showed me—Asha is coming … and Ma!' Pio raced to catch up to Pravin.

The Matriarch fell in beside Isaura. 'You're not limping,' Isaura said, surprised. 'Alejo kicked you.'

Alejo did not touch me.

Isaura's jaw dropped. *What? I don't suppose you'll tell me what happened with him last night.*

No. I will only tell you the events were as much a surprise for me as they were for you. Amusement tinged the Matriarch's thoughts. *Do you know how to end Primara?*

Isaura snorted. *No, but if she persists I'll figure it out. Have you any idea how far away Asha is?*

My scouts say a day and a half. Her guard amongst others are with her—a significant force.

Pravin returned to Isaura, leading his horse.

'Pravin, Asha will be here tomorrow.'

'I'll take a look and see if I can find some of those loose horses for the lad to ride,' Pravin said.

There are only three left, Isa-cub. They are over the next ridge by a rivulet in the forest, near an alder tree.

Isaura told Pravin. His eyes narrowed as he listened and he looked suspiciously at the Matriarch.

Only three? Isaura asked.

Hunting is hungry work.

Isaura's lips drew into a tight line and her gaze settled on the bodies of the enemy. She called out, 'Pravin, take Pio with you. I have something I need to do. There are more of our enemy out there and more coming. I want them gone. I want to send a message to those bastards that if they cross into our land they will not live to tell the tale.'

Chapter Thirty-Four

RATILAL WANDERED IN the dark throughout the camp near the training field. He was not arrayed in finery, but in his favourite simple, dark, dusty training clothes, his identity concealed by a cloak. *Niaz should be here,* he thought. The entire camp had been under lockdown for two days. *The men will be restless, they'll talk more to ease the tension. What will I hear?* A select few knew his plans. The common soldiers knew only that they were to move soon. The quiet conversations of the men stopped as he wandered by, but believing him merely another soldier they continued speaking.

'Stroke of genius.'

'Who'd have thought we'd strike at the Bear in their capital.'

'Think of the devastation. They'll be weak come the end of winter.'

They're weak now. Karan's men cannot have arrived. Their forces will split.

'Think of the dead. Families lived in Gopindar. How many little 'uns died in that great fire?'

'Where was the honour in murdering children?'

'They say it razed most of the city.'

'They?' Scorn dripped from the man's words. 'I will tell you one thing. There is no going back from this. Their blood will be up—we'll never have seen the like. We had best win the next battle or they'll wipe us out.'

'Well, love or hate him, Ratilal is clan lord and the best warrior amongst us. The Conclave proved that.'

'The Conclave? Some wet-behind-the-ears rich boys. The new "lordlings"—they never stood a chance.'

'They fight well enough. All they do is train …'

'Once upon a time, there was only one lord, now we've dozens ... never worked a bloody day in their lives either.'

'Keep your trap shut if you know what's good for you.'

'All I'll say is this: our high lord, I'll bet my last coin he's got a plan that'll shit all over Karan.'

Ratilal frowned and moved on. *I'll have to pull the 'lordlings' into line. Can't have a revolt on my hands from the plebs. Vikram.* A niggle of doubt remained about him. Ratilal shook his head. *No, he burned Gopindar, he's quashed the slogans. He's loyal to his clan. Faros is in good hands and soon I'll be back to claim it.*

Besides, he'd left Vikram with the worst of his troops—the old, the weaklings and the women. Faros was in no danger—he and the Divide stood between it and the enemy.

Men began running through the camp, spreading the news. *Ah, they've issued my orders.* Horses' hooves were to be wrapped and padded and the long, large covered wagons' axles well greased—all to deaden sound. Under the cover of night they would move out.

—⚜—

The Vale of Safa was peaceful; its peace galled Baldev. Warriors from Bear Tooth Lake had reported in late the day before. Their tales of the death of Umniga and the kidnapping of Pio infuriated him. *Kiriz and Pio should have been safe.* Isaura and Pravin had hared off on their own rescue mission. *Madness!* Baldev was mollified by the fact that Asha had stayed for Umniga's farewell ritual. *Now, she's off though.* He kicked the dirt.

His captain cleared his throat. 'Asha is a capable warrior.'

'I know that!'

'Chances are Isaura and Pravin made short work of the enemy for they do not hunt alone.'

'I know that too! But four squads of warriors—mine and Karan's—went with her.'

'You'd rather they hadn't?'

'Shut up, just shut up and stop making sense!' Baldev jumped up and stalked a short distance away before returning and sitting again. 'We leave tomorrow morning. The first of the northern watchtowers is two days' hard ride away. Let's pray it still stands. Maybe then we'll see what Ratilal is up to.'

—ᴡ—

Pio scuffed his boots through the dirt. Alejo had broken his crystal. He knew he shouldn't be mad but it was so pretty. *I can get another one.* Fiamma squawked angrily at him. 'I know, I promised!' he said. *It must be here somewhere.*

Pio threw his hands in the air and sat on the ground. He looked at the rubble around him. *Isa must think I'm an idiot. Her magic did this.* He sighed, looking forlornly toward Fiamma. The little falcon was very still. Fiamma cocked her head and made a soft cry.

'All right,' he said to her before pulling his flute from his satchel. Sulking, he played a sad little tune, bemoaning his lost treasure. It bounced off the rocky rubble around him. A dull glow began under the grey dust of rocks.

Pio stared at it, his playing halted. The glow stuttered then was gone. He dived forward onto the spot and began scraping the fragments of rubble and thick dust away. Fiamma emitted a high-pitched squawk and bit Pio. He ignored her and kept scraping. The falcon danced about in agitation. 'Enough, Fiamma. Let's just see.' Pio sat back on his heels.

The dark flame eye crystal fragments lay before him. Carefully he picked them up, dusted them off and placed them on a scrap of cloth from his bag. He lined the fragments up. Joined together they would make the original crystal, except at one end a chunk was missing. Hesitantly, he resumed playing. Fiamma cocked her head, watching the crystals with wary fascination. They spluttered to life; a delicate rainbow shimmer rippled along the pieces. Pio's tune brightened and became faster; the crystals began to pulse in time to his music. The dainty flames danced and changed colours with the song, perfectly controlled by the music—resonating it. *Where are the rest of you?*

Fiamma jumped sideways and scratched at the dirt, revealing the remaining crystal pieces. Pio ceased playing and scraped the dust and rock from three more fragments, which he placed next to the others. These were no longer the dark flame colouring of the others—they were blue.

Pio stared at them before playing a short tune. The dark flame eye crystals sprang to life. The blue ones did not. Fiamma flew to his shoulder. He sat with his eyes closed, concentrating.

Reverently he wrapped the flame eye fragments up, leaving only the blue pieces separate. *Yes, for Isaura.*

—⚬—

Isaura tilted her head back and forth, from side to side and rolled her shoulders, trying to loosen up. The night had been freezing even though they'd been tucked amongst the Asena. It was nearly midday and still their breath steamed in the air and the breeze bit at their skin. The Matriarch sat next to her.

Pio plonked down beside them. 'Isa, you know my crystal …' Isaura arched her brow at him and began drumming her fingers on her leg. 'Well … oh bother … just look.' He pulled a cloth bundle out of his pocket, unwrapped it and revealed the crystal fragments. 'These pieces here changed colour. I like them better like this—they're blue like your eyes go.'

Isaura closed her gaping mouth. She tentatively reached a shaking hand toward them and withdrew it.

The Matriarch sniffed the pieces warily. *Be careful, Isa-cub.*

'It's not going to hurt, silly—look.' Pio placed the blue ones in her hand. A warm buzz ran up Isaura's arm, through her body and subsided. The crystals glowed, pulsed in time with her heart and dulled. The Matriarch paced.

'Wow! They didn't do that when I held them—none of them did. Isa? You look like you might pass out.'

'I'm fine,' Isaura replied quickly. 'I told you to leave them.'

'No, you told me to not get another one ...'

'But I told you it was dangerous. Last time, the rainbow crystal ... it frightened me ... when I touched it ... it was powerful magic ... like the old tales back home.'

Pio swallowed nervously. 'I'm sorry. I won't get another. But the others just light up when I play, that's all—nothing bad.'

'Only when you play?'

'Yep.'

'Did it do that before?'

Pio shrugged. 'Don't know. Fiamma wanted me to play and they were just there and they lit up.'

'You didn't feel hot or tingly or angry ... unwell at all?'

'No. Isa, Fiamma wouldn't let me touch it if it was bad.' Pio's eyes opened wide as he remembered. 'She tried to stop us going to the cave where we found them.'

Isaura ground her teeth. 'Why didn't you listen to her?'

'Fiamma wasn't my guardian then,' Pio stammered. 'I just thought she was a crazy bird. But she let me touch them now.'

Isa-cub, this is pointless.

'Promise me you won't go there again.'

Pio nodded anxiously. 'Should I throw them away?'

Isaura looked to the Matriarch for advice. *Well?*

I have no ideas, Isa-cub. Nothing has been the same since your arrival. The aura of these crystals attuned to yours when you picked them up. Your aura brightened.

'No, keep the pieces safe. Don't tell or show them to anyone, including Kiriz. And don't play around with them until the Kenati are teaching you again or unless I'm there. Can I keep the blue ones?' Pio nodded.

Fiamma swooped by. 'They're coming!' Pio said excitedly. He wrapped up his crystals, shoved them in his pocket and tore off.

Silently Isaura and the Matriarch followed.

Asha rode at the head of the column. Fihr circled above them. As she drew nearer, Isaura stared at her, asking, 'Pravin? What's Asha done to her face?'

'Umniga. All the Kenati will do this when one of their number has been killed. It's more than mourning. It's so when one of them kills those responsible it will be as if Umniga did it.'

'Oh!' Isaura's jaw dropped at the realisation of what Asha had coated on her face. 'I've already killed them.'

'Their revenge will go further than that.'

Asha dismounted before Isaura and Pravin. 'I saw the blood. Where are the bodies?'

Isaura blanched. 'The Asena ... have ... um ... disposed of them.'

'Ma!' Pio raced past to be swept up in Lucia's arms.

Asha smiled. 'I couldn't have kept her from coming even if I'd wanted to. She is a mother bear when it comes to him.'

Pio jabbered excitedly, dragging Lucia toward Isaura and Asha. 'And I've got a guardian. Look out, here she comes!'

Lucia halted abruptly as Fiamma swooped low and landed on Pio's arm. 'That's ... wonderful ... She's very ... pretty.'

'Ma! Fiamma's not pretty! Pretty is for girls!'

'Pio, you've given her a girl's name,' Lucia said, confused.

'She's tough and fierce and smart ... and clever! She's not a girl, she's a falcon!'

Lucia shook her head in bewilderment. 'Well ... good. Watch Fiamma doesn't hurt your arm with her talons.'

'Never! Isa ripped up a cloak, see, and padded my sleeve.'

Lucia darted an anxious glance at Isaura, before quickly looking away.

Pio rolled his eyes and grabbed her arm. 'Isa, Pravin and the Asena saved me. And Alejo too ... he's not really as scary as everyone thinks.'

Pravin snorted.

Pio hauled Lucia to a stop in front of Isaura. 'Say hello to Isa, Ma.'

Isaura folded her arms. 'Pio, your mother doesn't have to …' she began.

'Yes, she does,' Lucia said. 'I owe you an apology—we all do. I don't understand your transformation, but I know that it's not your fault and I believe that the gods have made you our champion.' Lucia drew a deep breath. 'I should've known a heart such as yours would remain true. I was a coward. I wish I'd been stronger and remained as true to you as you did to us. Forgive me?'

Lucia held out her hand. Overcome, Isaura could only nod before dragging her into a hug.

Pio took Asha's hand. She gently stroked Fiamma's chest with the other. He bit his lip anxiously, before taking a deep breath. 'Umniga?' he asked.

'She's gone, Pio.'

'Nimo and Kiriz?'

'Nimo will live. She says as soon as you get back she'll teach you letters. Kiriz is here.'

'Really? Where?'

'At the back. She feels guilty for running away.'

'That's just daft. She was smart. I'll find her and fix it.' Pio wandered off, mumbling to Fiamma, 'She's bonkers. Help me fix it.'

Asha smiled sadly. 'Umniga was right to bring you all here.' She stood taller. 'We need to get the children and Lucia back to camp.'

Pravin spoke up. 'They're going to Hamza's.'

'But Hamza is not there,' Asha said. 'Baldev …'

'Is not here either,' Pravin said. 'I am and I'm senior. Those are my orders. I say Hamza's and I'll bet the Old Mother agrees with me. Hamza is due back anytime soon.'

The Matriarch and Isaura shared a glance. 'Yes,' Isaura finally said.

'We'll lose time,' Asha insisted.

Isa-cub. We will take them to Hamza's. We'll keep Pio safe, the Matriarch said.

But I'm going to the front, Isaura replied, kneeling before the

Matriarch and burying her hands in her ruff. The conversations of the others became a mere burble in the background.

I know, Isa-cub. We will not help you there, not in a full-scale battle. I will not risk more of my kind. We have lost too many in wars with the clans.

Isaura frowned. *There's more, isn't there?*

There are too few of our original number left. We do not age or die naturally, but we can be killed. We breed like your wolves would. Our offspring are intelligent and something more than mere animals, yet not us. When we are killed, the spirits of my priests and priestesses pass on—gone. I need to preserve them and our knowledge for as long as I can and ... I am not sure what our offspring will do when we are not here to guide and control them. Know that I will watch you from the spirit realm and advise you when I can. When this war is over, I pray to M'Aricel that we will have a long association.

So do I.

Asha touched Isaura's arm. 'Did you hear, Isa?'

Isaura shook her head, wiped her eyes and reluctantly stood up, breaking contact with the Matriarch. 'The Asena will take them to Hamza's. They'll watch over them.'

Lucia ran to fetch the children.

'They'll be safer there, Asha,' Isaura said.

'I know, Isa. I'm just ... angry. Ready to kill.'

'Ready to kill is good right now. Pravin, while Lucia and the children are not here will you help me?' They walked into the forest and hauled out two lumpy bundles covered in dried blood, which they tied to one of the pack horses before rejoining Asha.

Lucia, Kiriz and Pio approached.

'Ride safely. We'll see you soon,' Isaura said.

The Matriarch stood waiting for them with her pack. Pio and Kiriz both turned back for one last wave before they disappeared down the rise and into a forest trail.

Asha and Pravin mounted, leaving Isaura staring after the

Asena. 'Isa, are you ready?' Asha said softly.

'It's stupid—I feel like I just lost my mother again.'

'Only this time you're not without family,' Asha said.

—⚏—

Vikram looked out upon Ratilal's empty training camp. *So now it begins in earnest.* He turned his horse back to Faros.

'The high lord wants Mistress Malak found and returned to Faros,' Vikram said to Jabr, who fell in beside him.

'Will she be safe?' Jabr asked.

'You ask that of me?' Vikram shook his head. 'Of course she'll be safe. Mistress Malak is at Umniga's cottage. I want you to fetch her, and a young woman I sent to stay at Parlan; also Deo's grandson. We're going to have another Conclave and Deo's grandson is to stand as witness to the death of Shahjahan.'

'You knew where Mistress Malak and the girl were all this time?'

Vikram smiled. 'Just go bring her and the others back; tell Malak I sent you. And tell her to keep the others with her and safe.'

Jabr cantered off toward Faros and Vikram continued to plan. When he dismounted in the citadel courtyard, Māhir, the mason, was waiting for him.

'The repairs to the walls are finished, Captain,' Māhir said.

Vikram was brusque. 'Come, I want to inspect them.'

Walking along the battlements, Vikram said, 'The camp is empty. We need to step up activity. Malak will return, along with the girl. Keep your ear to the ground. How well are you doing cultivating connections among the wealthier merchants?'

'Fine, it's easy. The merchants loathed Paksis. The news of Gopindar horrified many of them. They're worried what revenge the Horse and Bear may wreak upon us. Their main worry, mind you, is business. Was it as bad as they say?'

Vikram's hands clenched, then he ground out, 'Worse. They are right to be worried—encourage it. Turn talk to how Shahjahan would never have done it, for there was no honour in it.' Vikram peered over the side of the wall, making a show of inspecting the repairs. 'I'll make sure the slogans return and the rumours grow. Lady Malak will help. She has great influence amongst both the merchants and the upper echelons in old Faros.'

'Maybe, but Malak downright annoyed some of the merchants. They tried to stymie her business, and she outsmarted them.'

'Yes, but they need her,' Vikram said.

'You're right and now she's doing so well, they want to work with her. But Captain, don't forget the lower city love her. Malak and Daniel give the poorest citizens work, good pay and discounts on the goods they need.'

Vikram laughed. 'I haven't forgotten, Māhir, it's the best news of all.'

—⚇—

Malak stood beside Vikram in the dimness of the citadel entrance hall. She shivered in the chill air. 'You've taken a long time to decide where you stand, Captain.'

'I've always known what side I was on, Mistress Malak. But for some things the timing must be precise. All things have led to this and yet everything depends on this moment. Are you ready?'

Malak took a deep breath and drew herself up. 'I am, but I've worried for days that someone will try to kill the boy and girl before they're heard. Will they be safe here?'

Vikram paused with his hand on the doors of the citadel. He shrugged. 'I've done all I can.'

Together they walked through the doors of the citadel and stood on its great, wide, arching steps. The courtyard was full. Vikram's warriors—men and women—lined the parapets and inside the walls. The archers stood casually with their bows held loosely in their hands, but their eyes constantly roved the crowd. Along the widest part of the steps, in high backed, imposing chairs, elevated above the crowd, sat the members of the Conclave.

Malak and Vikram stood at the edge of the upper most step. 'As Pasha of Faros, I have assembled the Conclave for a public hearing to pass judgement upon our clan lord.'

A wave of shocked murmurings rolled through the crowd.

Vikram held up his hands. 'Silence! This is not done lightly! Only once before has such a thing been brought before the Conclave. This was once a great clan—a clan of honour. Shahjahan may have let his grief rule him for too long, but in his last days, I saw the return of the clan lord of old. The assault on our Kenati—Asha—was what galvanised him. Shahjahan wanted to restore honour to this clan. He wanted to curtail his son and his followers. You know what I mean.' Heads in the crowd nodded. 'Ratilal has a history of assaulting women. As a young man, as an adult—the assault on Asha, our Kenati, and the brutal attack on two of Pramod's girls. You all saw Asha.'

'He was punished for that!' a voice cried. 'You can't punish him again.'

'No, but we do well to remember it, for it signals a pattern. A pattern which it appears started when he was a child. First I will call Tomak, the former Commander of Shahjahan's bodyguard. He is long retired, but he remembers discovering Ratilal torturing animals as a boy and the patent joy that he appeared to derive from having done so. He'll also tell you of an earlier assault upon a maid within the citadel when Ratilal was but a teen. Remember this and remember Asha when you see Niara—the latest victim. Finally, you will hear from a boy who will tell you what he witnessed the night Shahjahan died.' Silence. 'Those rumours—those slogans on the walls of Faros, they are true. Ratilal murdered Shahjahan on the beach at Parlan.'

'What!'

'No!'

Malak called out, 'I've heard the boy. I believe him. I've met with the girl. They, and I, have only remained safe due to the actions of Captain Vikram.'

'Don't you mean Pasha Vikram? He wants power just like the rest.'

Malak drew herself up. 'Who is it who has kept the peace in this city for years? Who is it who listens to your grievances? Not Ratilal, but Vikram. He didn't seek to become Pasha. It was thrust upon him by a man too consumed with rage, war and revenge to be bothered with his own citizens. Shame on you!'

Vikram smiled inwardly as Malak scolded them. *What an ally!* 'I do not want power in this clan. No matter what the outcome I'll not seek to be made clan lord. But we're forgetting our purpose. You and the Conclave will hear the evidence and they will pass judgement. I call upon Tomak to give testimony before this gathering.'

An elderly warrior strode out in full armour, tall and proud. His craggy face strong and stern, he marched ramrod straight past the Conclave members to stand on the steps just below them. Tomak swore the oath to tell the truth and addressed the assembled crowd clearly. He finished his tale by adding, 'Shahjahan was a good man, an honourable man despite his faults, and would not have allowed his son to rule.'

'Children do foolish things! How can Ratilal be held accountable for his actions when he was a child?' someone yelled from the crowd.

Several members of the Conclave nodded in agreement. Yet the senior member of the Conclave stood and bowed to Tomak. 'We thank you for your testimony, your honesty and your service.'

'I call upon Niara,' Vikram cried.

Through the double doors walked a young woman. Her long dark hair fell lustrously to her slim waist. Niara slowly descended the stairs until she stood below the conclave members, yet high enough on the steps for all the crowd to see her. Her nose had been broken. It was flattened and bent sideways. A long jagged scar ran from high on Niara's cheekbone, following the curve of her jaw to her lip. She held up her arms, showing defensive scarring.

'Do you swear by all that we hold sacred, by Rana and Jalal and upon the spirits of your ancestors, that you will speak only the truth?'

'Yes,' came the soft reply.

'Niara,' Vikram said. 'I know you are scared, but you are safe. You must answer loudly.'

She stood taller and, though trembling, Niara raised her head. 'Yes!'

'You know that to break this oath will dishonour your entire family and see your spirit condemned to Karak by Rana and Jalal upon your death?' the senior Conclave member asked her.

'I do.'

'Then tell us your tale,' the member said.

'I tell no tale, but the truth. I came to the aid of another girl at Pramod's brothel. Ratilal beat me and cut me with a broken pottery carafe. My screams alerted the others. I was only saved because Lord Niaz restrained him. I hid with my brother, then Captain Vikram found me and smuggled me from the city.'

'What of the other girl?' one of the Conclave asked.

'She's just a whore,' one of the crowd yelled.

'The other girl, Sora, fled,' Vikram said abruptly. 'Take a good look at what your high lord did. No one deserves this.' Niara stood stiffly, her terrified eyes roamed the crowd. Soon she began to tremble.

'Niara, child,' Malak said. 'Come, wait here with me.' Niara darted to her side. Malak pulled her close and put her arm around her.

'Next I call forth Mikka, grandson of Deo—Headman of the village of Parlan.'

The small boy, Mikka, exited the great doors, holding onto Deo's hand. He swallowed nervously and with wide eyes earnestly swore to speak the truth. 'My new friend, Pio and I, well ... we got drunk,' he said sheepishly, 'at the celebration Clan Lord Shahjahan put on in our village.' Chuckles and wry grins broke out among the crowd. 'We fell asleep in the dunes and Lords Karan and Baldev came to find us with Asha. Well ... um ... they did—find us that is. And on the way back we heard Clan Lord Shahjahan and Ratilal arguing. We just hid and watched. Then all of a sudden like, Ratilal stabs his father.' The crowd remained silent, stunned at the boy, waiting for him to continue, though they knew the end of the tale. 'And Clan Lord Shahjahan dropped like a sack of spuds—dead.' Talking and shouts erupted. 'We was all pretty shocked. Lord Baldev and Asha snuck us back to the village.'

Vikram thrust his hands in the air, demanding, 'Quiet! What did Lord Karan do?' he asked.

The boy gulped again and anxiously looked around the crowd. 'Lord Karan ran out to the body to check. He said the words of farewell to him.' Mikka scowled. 'Then Ratilal's men saw Lord Karan. It was like they was waiting. I mean, why else would they be there? They said he'd killed our clan lord, but he never did.'

'Why did you not speak of this earlier?' Lady Malak asked.

'Lord Ratilal killed his pa! What'd you think he'd do to me? And Lord Baldev and Asha told us to keep quiet. Everything went to Karak after that.'

'We know the rest,' Vikram said. 'Ratilal blamed the Horse and Bear and started a war—all to come to power and overthrow his father who was about to pull him into line. Clan Lord Shahjahan was determined to see a return to the old ways and our former greatness. He saw peace between the clans as the means to achieve it—through trade and a resurgence of the annual clan games and other traditions.'

'And how long would that have taken? High Lord Ratilal is an able commander. He'll win this war and he's promised a return to our glory days—to the old ways,' came a shout from the crowd.

'Yes, Ratilal is an able commander, his men respect his military skills, but he's without honour. As for returning to the old ways— he has not done so. Ratilal does not care for your welfare as a clan lord should. He palmed off the regular hearings of disputes, he disregards the need to improve the lower city, he neglects the poor and he ignores the rights of half this city—the women. Our clan never cared about the sex of our warriors—only that they fought well and with honour. These women you see here armed and training do not do so under Ratilal's orders.' Vikram shook his head. 'We've able commanders amongst us to match Ratilal— and with more honour. What warrior of honour would've burned Gopindar? Not Shahjahan. No, but the man who murdered his father in cold blood, for wealth and power … the man who has proved himself to be of the most vile character since childhood— yes, he would do it. Ratilal. You see his deeds laid out before you. Is this how you want your clan to go forward?'

'No!'

'Never!'

Vikram shook his head in despair. 'I've worked for the good of this clan all my life. I was prepared to give Ratilal a chance, but no longer! I call on the Conclave to deliver their judgement.'

The Conclave rose as one and entered the citadel. The crowd waited. Silence turned to murmurs. The murmurs dimmed with one call.

'Remove Ratilal and execute him for the crime of patricide.'

'Remove him!'

'Execute him!'

Vikram's face remained impassive, yet his pulse beat more quickly. *So much work, so much planning, so much time. Please gods, let them decide.*

'What's taking them so long?' Malak said. 'How many of them are in his pocket?'

Vikram's lips twisted. 'They're probably fighting over who gets to become clan lord.'

'We'll see about that!' Malak stormed toward the citadel.

Talking began to cease. Some in the crowd jostled their neighbours to silence. 'Look, Mistress Malak will bring them to heel.'

The doors of the citadel opened and the Conclave appeared. Malak slammed to a halt and watched with narrowed eyes as they moved to stand before their chairs.

The entire crowd fell silent, expectant.

The senior member stood. 'For his crimes Ratilal will be executed. There was never any doubt about this. We have been debating how best to go forward from here. A new clan lord must be found. We have …'

'Enough!' Malak shouted. 'This clan is at war over a falsehood. We have a loyal Pasha who is defender of Faros. It is in Vikram's hands that we must now trust ourselves until this mess is sorted out. Then the clan—the whole clan for the first time in generations,' she cried out, 'can decide who our clan lord will be as per our ancient traditions.' A roar of approval ran through the crowd. 'Vikram, what do we do now?' she whispered.

'I've a few ideas. Come, we've a lot to plan and I feel not much time in which to do it.'

―∞―

The stone cabin of farmstead lay nestled not far from a full flowing creek. It was only a small cabin with a lean-to built against the house for a few animals. *A poor steading, but well tended. They didn't have much, and even that was taken from them. We were too late.* Karan placed the woman's abused body on the bed next to her husband. He pulled a quilt over them. *Thank the gods they'd no children.*

Outside Karan's warriors waited. Four of the enemy were dead and lined up before the remaining two who were tied, arms stretched, to timber railings on the house yard fence.

Karan walked to them and drew his kilij. 'I'm usually a man of control. The other day I was telling someone dear to me that control makes heroes or villains of us all. You, however, have snapped my control. I want information.' The sword flashed through the air, slicing across one man's chest. He screamed. The skin parted, revealing bone. 'Trust me when I say I know exactly where to slice, and not have you bleed to death.'

The other Boar soldier's eyes widened in terror as the blade slashed again. His comrade shrieked as Karan's blade cut him and lost consciousness. Karan cleaned his kilij lovingly before sheathing it and drawing a dagger. 'How many squads did Ratilal send?' Nothing. 'I can keep cutting all day. Oh wait, he's unconscious. Your turn.'

'You'll kill us anyway.'

'True, but it can be quick or slow, and after what you did to that woman it will be very slow. Tell me!' The Undavi flowed in Karan's voice.

The man quailed. 'Four squads. He sent four!'

'What else?'

'We crossed with the waning moon. The floodwaters let us reach the top of the riverbank at the right spot. We were to wait until the new moon, then cause havoc while one team headed to Bear Tooth Lake.' The man hung his head resentfully. 'They were to capture or kill one of the strangers and, depending on the situation, deal with Umniga and Asha. By the first quarter moon we should have been back at our boats.'

Isa! Karan's hand clenched. 'Where did you cross?'

The man described the willow stand in detail.

'You should never have come,' Karan said quietly as the life left their eyes. 'Put them in the cabin. Burn it.' Karan turned to Suniti. 'Find Munira, pass on that location and time.'

While the cabin blazed, Karan said to his captain, 'I hoped never to have to do that. It makes me little better than Ratilal. May the gods forgive me for this day.'

'You're nothing like Ratilal. He would not feel the weight of it, nor would he ask for forgiveness.'

As the smoke poured into the sky, Fihr flew overhead, screeching. 'Mount up, we're moving out.'

Chapter Thirty-Five

ALEJO'S BULKY FORM stood out at the head of the approaching column. *Thank the gods.* Karan broke from his warriors and cantered Mirza toward them. He grew sombre when he saw Asha's ghostly face.

'My lord.' Pravin inclined his head. 'Things have been busy.'

'Asha, I'm sorry,' Karan said.

Stony faced, Asha nodded briefly at him.

Mirza swung beside Alejo. Karan held Isaura's hand and kissed it; he did not let it go. Grinning, he held out his other arm. Alejo deliberately sidled closer to Mirza.

'It's a conspiracy,' Isaura muttered, laughing as she allowed Karan to pull her across to sit sideways in front of him on Mirza. 'What are you doing?'

'Showing you how happy I am that you remained unharmed.' Karan tilted her head toward him and kissed her.

'Oh, she's done more than that,' Pravin said.

'Has she indeed?' Karan said.

'She's got the heads of some of those who killed Umniga hanging from a pack horse back there.'

'Really?' Karan kissed her again. 'Pravin sounds rather proud of you,' he said. 'What were you planning on doing with them?'

'I want to stick them on spikes at the fort at the Four Ways so the enemy can see them,' Isaura replied.

'I've a better idea. At the right moment, Fihr can fly them across and drop them on the enemy camp. I think that will be far more effective. That should satisfy some of Asha's need for revenge.'

'It's a start,' Asha said acerbically.

'First we need to meet Hamza,' Karan said, kissing Isaura again.

'Whatever happened to distant restraint?' Isaura asked, laughing.

Karan chuckled. 'Too distant and too much restraint.'

—ɷ—

Ratilal's army lay behind a long, low treed ridgeline. Gopindar still smouldered and this far north the acrid smoke hung low. The wagons were covered in hessian to which grassy tussocks had been stitched. Men sheltered either under wagons or the trees. Mounted troops further away from the Falcontine had lit lots of small fires to disguise Ratilal's true whereabouts and intent. He prayed to the gods that it would work.

Ratilal's scout bowed low. 'Lord Baldev's forces have moved beyond the second of the Divide's watchtowers. They are setting up camp here,' the scout pointed to a spot on Ratilal's map, 'on what dry ground they can find.'

'Does it look like they'll try to cross upstream of the lake?'

'Hard to say, High Lord. There is only one place where they might, but it will add days to their return. It's only a single file track and the river may well have made it impassable. I'd say they aim to push through the marshy ground tomorrow.'

'Good, well done. Dismissed. Get some rest.' To his captains he said, 'We'll move out tonight. Make sure the horses' hoofs are padded again before we cross. We need to travel light, fast and quietly. We must get across the Upper Divide and take those two towers.'

—ɷ—

The warriors in Ratilal's assault team had blackened their skin with a mixture of coal and fat. The polish on their weapons was dulled. They each clung to inflated goats' stomachs and half drifted and swam across the Upper Divide. The newly completed watchtower stood on a raised stone foundation down river to their right. The Upper Divide widened dramatically after that and its banks became steadily steeper. The noise of faint ripples as they crossed echoed gently back to the Boar soldiers. With each stroke closer to the shore they waited to be spotted. Nothing.

The Boar slid on their bellies into the rushes that lined the banks. They froze at an abrupt hand signal from their leader. Nothing. Staying low, they worked their way to the tower and pressed against it walls, listening. Their leader held up two fingers. The tower door opened.

'I'm goin' for a piss.'

A laugh. 'Be lucky if you can find it in the dark.'

'At least mine works.' The Bear warrior flipped a finger at him and turned around the corner of the building. He was seized and a quick knife brutally slid into his neck. Before the light left his eyes, the enemy were in the tower. Muffled thumps came from within. A Boar soldier stepped outside and dragged the body in. It was all over.

Karan's warriors had reached the beginning of the high pass trail where it entered the Forest of the Asena. The smoke from Gopindar had travelled the breadth of Altaica.

Pravin spat in disgust as Karan told him the news. 'I knew it had to be big, but that ...' He shook his head. 'Baldev won't be thinking clearly.'

'Nor would I,' Karan said.

'That's a lie and you know it. Ratilal's had us running around chasing this rabble as they murder innocents. He's split your forces.'

'Not anymore. Munira and the squad from Hunters' Ford will kill the rest. I've dispatched another squad to help. I've also sent a rider to Bear Tooth Lake. All able-bodied warriors will clear out to hide in the forest east of the Vale of Safa and wait for us. We'll intercept Hamza, then join the others.'

'You think Ratilal is planning something too?'

'He's mad enough to do all this for revenge. But Vikram's reports talk of a man who has devoted himself to warfare and strategy. So far we've seen the madness, I suspect the strategy is coming.'

'Poor bloody Vikram,' Pravin said. 'And Baldev's raged on up there.'

'He'd no choice. And ...' Karan shrugged, 'he may be fine. Isaura spirit-walked last night. She said Baldev has camped near the Falcontine.'

'How on earth do you think Ratilal can get him up there?' Pravin asked. 'One or two might get across, but not an army.'

'I didn't think he'd cross the Divide either and that turned out to be painfully simple. I'm not underestimating him again. Let him think we're in the south hunting for his squads. The warriors hiding in the forest are to wait until I am there, no matter what they see.'

'It'll take time to get there. Baldev is on his own till then?'

'Yes.' Karan left Pravin and walked the camp. Suniti and Asha sat together; both now wore the same ghostly aspect. They faced each other holding hands and singing a lament. Karan's warriors had given them a wide berth—a semblance of privacy. There were no campfires, no signs to tell the enemy where they were. The smoke from Gopindar and the keening lament of the Kenati had made the entire camp sombre.

The horses, even Mirza, were exhausted. Alejo was the only mount who remained unaffected by the day's hard riding. He grazed quietly with Mirza while the rest of the mounts were picketed in a line. Karan stopped and patted each of them. 'Alejo, you mad monster, where is your mistress? Mmm?'

'Here,' Isaura said as she approached with her bedroll slung over her shoulder.

'You don't enjoy sleeping out in the open, do you?'

'I like being amongst the trees. The house I grew up in was in a forest. Riding through the grasslands today made me feel exposed, lonely.' She shivered.

Karan took her hand as they walked. 'You'll won't like the High Plains then. It's hundreds of miles of prairie. The only trees are around the edges near the mountains and there's not many of them, though we're trying to regrow them. It's literally freezing in winter and hot in summer. The spring is over in a flash. The weather makes life a challenge.'

'But not impossible?'

'No. And it's beautiful. The city will take your breath away.'

Isaura stopped. 'This is far enough.' The ground dipped gently between the pale trunks of birch trees. She unrolled her bedding. 'Are you staying?'

'If you'll have me.'

Isaura wrapped her hand behind Karan's head, pulled him into a kiss and tugged him onto the bedroll. She kept kissing him as her fingers roamed his chest and she fumbled with the ties on his coat. 'Help me out here?' Isaura said in frustration. He chuckled, quickly divesting himself of the garment.

Karan undid the ties on her wrap-around jacket. It fell open, revealing her blue silk shirt. 'I've loved this shirt ever since the swim,' he said softly. Isaura swatted him playfully. He smiled, kissed her lips, trailed kisses along her jaw and lingered on her neck, while his deft fingers undid the ties of her shirt. Karan slid his hands under the silk to Isaura's skin. She shivered. Slowly, gently, his caresses roved from Isaura's hips up over her breasts, grazing her nipples and moving to cradle her head. Resting his forehead against hers, Karan closed his eyes.

'You've still too many clothes on, you know?' Isaura said. She leaned back, watching Karan excruciatingly slowly undo the ties on his shirt and slide it from his shoulders. 'Tease.'

He laughed, then kissed her again deeply. Isaura felt the ripple of her silk shirt as it glided from her torso. The cold night air washed over her, raising goosebumps upon her skin. Karan traced lazy delicate circles around her nipples.

Isaura revelled in the feel of the muscled contours of his back before gliding her hands to his chest. She hesitated with the sash as his waist. Her hands rested there as she searched his face. Karan moved her fingers to begin untying the sash, never once taking his eyes from hers. Isaura swallowed nervously and sat up. Her hands lingered at his hips. With trembling fingers she undid the sash and drawstring.

Karan kissed her, gently pushing her down. Their kisses grew more ardent. His tongue delved into her mouth. Isaura moaned as his hand delved lower, teasing, exploring. He pressed against her.

Isaura panicked, stiffening. Her hands pushed against his chest.

Karan stopped. 'What's wrong?'

Isaura looked away. *Gods, what will he think? What have I done?*

'Isa, tell me to stop if that's what you want.'

Eyes wide, she tried to speak. 'I …' Isaura shook her head in distress.

Karan eased himself away from her. 'You've done this before?'

She nodded. *Gods, say something!* 'Once … only once. It was the spring festival evening, the only one I went to. Turned out it was a dare. His friends had dared him to kiss me. In the dark we got carried away. The next day I saw him, he said to his friends that it was lucky it was so dark. In the dark he could almost forget the colour of my skin. One of them said no night would be dark enough for him.'

Karan drew a sharp breath. 'Listen to me, Isa. I'm not him. You are beautiful. You are worthy of love and so much more. If he couldn't tell that, then he was an idiot. I see you. I see your beauty, your courage, your prickliness, your fiery nature, and the compassion you temper it with. I see *you*. And I want you beside me for as long as we live. Will you be my partner? Will you rule with me? Be my adviser, my friend, my lover for the rest of our days?'

Isaura gaped. 'Me?'

'You. Always you. No other,' Karan said hopefully.

'Yes.'

Relieved, he kissed her tears away. 'Don't cry, love.'

Isaura's hands roamed his face, lingering near his damp lashes. 'You can talk.'

'Clan lords don't cry.'

'They don't?'

'No, especially not at a time like this.' Karan's gaze raked over her body and his brows waggled outrageously.

Isaura giggled; her lips twitched into a smile. 'No, definitely not at a time like this. There are other things we could be doing.'

'First, I must give you this.' Karan sat up and gripped the gold torc around his neck. He removed it and held it between them. The torc was comprised of two engraved and intertwined bands, each ended in a horse's head. The two heads met in the centre of the torc. Carefully, he separated the bands and placed one around Isaura's neck. 'There.' Karan kissed her. 'Now everyone will know. This is traditional. When two people marry they each take half their torc and entwine it with their partner's. Each of them wears the symbol of the other. As clan lord mine is gold and a horse.' He secured the other half back around his neck.

'I've nothing for you.'

'Yes, Isa you do—you just don't realise it. Don't fret. Not everyone has a torc, but when they find a partner they get one. This torc has been passed down through my family. When we return to Targmur you can design one and have it made. Then we'll combine them.'

'Asha is not wearing one.'

Karan shrugged. 'Baldev's slow. He took years to even let her know how he felt. Asha will probably ask him before too long.'

'Asha?' Isaura said, surprised.

'Don't your women ask men to marry?'

'Um ...' Isaura paused. 'I can't think of one I know who has. I don't know that it's a rule, but they just don't.'

'I shouldn't be surprised. I've seen the way your friends treat their wives. I don't want to coddle you. I want a partner.'

'Good.' Isaura's hands stroked over his back. 'Where were we?'

Their lips met, gently, lovingly. Each kiss lingered, slowly becoming more urgent as their hands roamed. Where his hands went, his lips followed. Isaura pulled him down and they gave themselves up to sensation.

Chapter Thirty-Six

'THE FIRST TWO towers on the Upper Divide are ours,' the Boar captain said to Ratilal.

Ratilal gave the signal and joined his men in hauling the first of the pontoon bridges into place; each was then lashed tightly together. They worked frantically, silently, and Ratilal worked alongside his men for hours.

Finally Ratilal surveyed the result of their labours. A vicious grin creased his face. 'Move out.'

The horses' hooves were wrapped in hessian bags, then they were blindfolded and led quietly across. A string of supply wagons followed; their axles were well greased and hessian was strapped around the metal rims of their wheels.

The pontoon bridges dipped, swayed and held; with calculated efficiency Ratilal's army crossed the Upper Divide.

On the other side, Ratilal's commanders were busy issuing orders to entrench the camp.

'Don't just tell the men, get out there and help them,' Ratilal said.

Ratilal beckoned a group of warriors to him and he grabbed an entrenching tool. 'Come on. You lot with me. We've got work to do.'

—⁂—

Karan caught glimpses of Hamza's mule train as it wound along the mountain trail through the forest. Hamza had taken every mule he owned to get supplies from Targmur and he'd brought back more warriors. These were the warriors Karan had told Hadi, his Kenati—sent to Targmur after the Ritual of Samara—that he wanted mobilised. It had taken weeks for some to answer the call to arms and travel to Targmur from their remote farms, and then they'd had to make the journey along the high pass to the lowlands.

Now we're ready.

When Hamza finally reached them he had a frown plastered upon his face. 'What's gone wrong?'

'Nice to see you too, Hamza,' Karan said.

'Now I'm really worried, you're smiling,' Hamza replied.

'I smile all the time.'

'Not like that.' A knowing grin spread across Hamza's face. 'Well, Lord Karan, I'm glad of it. Now what's gone wrong that you meet me here?'

'Ratilal.' Karan explained their current situation. 'You've arrived in good time, Hamza.'

Karan summoned one of his commanders. 'Brief the new warriors. Let them rest, but don't let them get too comfortable. We've got many more miles to cover this day. We'll restock our kits from you, Hamza. You take the rest to the lake and then head back home. Young Pio is there with his mother and Kiriz.'

'My boys will want to fight.'

'That's between you and them. You're more important to me in supply. Can you get another run down the mountain if I need it?'

'Maybe, but it'll start getting dicey.'

Karan scowled and rubbed his temple. 'I thought so.'

Hamza changed the topic. 'Where's our girl and that fiend, Alejo? I've got her new saddle.'

'Isa won't be far away now she knows you're here. You had no trouble getting the rest of what I asked?'

'None,' Hamza said, dismounting. 'Finest craftsmanship I've seen in years. The tale of our Asena Blessed has spread all over Targmur. The master craftsman were desperate to do the work.'

Karan's lips quirked in wry smile. 'I wonder how that came to pass. Well done.'

Hamza untied a bulky parcel wrapped in woollen cloth from one of the mules and gave it to Karan.

'My thanks. You may as well come with me. She'll want to see you. And you can bring that saddle to Alejo.'

They turned to see Isaura running up to them. She threw herself at Hamza and hugged him.

'Now, now, my girl. That's enough of that.' Hamza gently pushed her back and scrutinised her. 'Well, you look no worse for wear, even if you're covered in dried blood.'

Alejo trotted up to him with a bray and stood tossing his head up and down in joy at seeing him.

'Well, look at you. Much happier lad, aren't you?' Hamza said. He drew a mule forward, unstrapped some packs from it and uncovered a beautifully yet simply tooled saddle, which they quickly placed upon Alejo. The saddle was black leather, with flaps embossed with running Asena. The breastplate matched the saddle, with Asena running its length to meet a large silver emblem in the centre of his chest featuring a snarling Asena. Hamza fastened the girth and then the crupper. The saddle seat was black suede.

Hamza grinned. 'I thought it might help you stay on him, give you better grip.'

Isaura ran her hands over it. 'Thank you, Hamza.' She embraced him excitedly.

'Don't thank me. I was just doing as I was told,' Hamza replied, gesturing to Karan.

'There's more,' Karan said. 'Here.' He passed her the other bundles.

Isaura unwrapped the first to reveal a kilij with a curved black wooden grip. Etched into the top of the blade amid willow and oak was Alejo and an Asena. Next she unwrapped a short recurve bow. Isaura strung the bow with difficulty, but could draw it with ease. The limbs were painted to match the sword. Her mouth hung open. 'For me. How? You?' Isaura threw her arms around Karan. 'Thank you!'

'There's one last thing, I think, isn't there, Hamza?'

'Aye. Just wait.' Hamza went to a pack mule and returned with a black staff. Isaura uncovered the ends. A brushed silver metal braced it top and bottom and in the centre.

'I sense a theme here,' Isaura said, hefting the staff and quirking her mouth at the Asena engraving on the metal.

'There's matching cuirass, grieves, dastanas and a set of daggers somewhere too.'

Isaura gaped at Karan.

'You are the Asena Blessed,' Karan said with a smile.

'And you want everyone to know.'

'I want your enemies to know. It'll scare the living daylights out of them.' His smile vanished. 'Ready to go to war?'

—⚔—

Baldev sat hunched in his cloak. No fires were lit within the camp and a light drizzle had set in. They'd arrived at the area near the Falcontine on dusk. When they'd reached the site the waterlogged soil below glinted gold in the setting sun.

His warriors and their mounts were exhausted. Crossing the flooded area would be dangerous and slow, so they had camped for the night. Anil had scouted the area before they'd entrenched; there had been no sign of the enemy. They were camped on open ground. To the north the ground sloped away to the Falcontine; facing south they had placed a myriad of stakes and a wide shallow ditch as defence. In the west, the hill sloped to the flooded Upper Divide; to the east of the camp lay a gap in the defensive structures, to allow for cavalry egress.

Damn Ratilal. He had us running all over the land chasing those bastards. Cunning sod. Yet Baldev could not rest. *How many homeless? How many injured? We need to be in Gopindar.*

He rose and walked the perimeter of the camp. The sentry nodded in greeting. Baldev peered over the stakes into the mist. 'All quiet?' he whispered.

'Aye, my lord.'

'Stay alert.' Baldev cast one last look into the darkness and shook his head as he walked off.

He sat next to his second in command. 'How's Anil?'

'Exhausted. He's asleep, my lord. Probably the only one of us who can sleep. Anil will not be able to scout again this night.'

Baldev rested his head on his fist and began drumming his fingers on his thigh while he thought.

'My lord, you're worried about attack?'

'I'm worried about everything—that's my job.' Baldev sighed. 'Mostly I'm worried that all along we've taken Ratilal too cheaply.'

'Shall I send out a scout?'

'No, rouse the warriors—quietly. It'll be dawn soon anyway.'

Baldev waited with them. The dawn came, a dull glow struggling through the clouds. The world was shrouded in mist, silent.

The soft hissing in the air was the first sign of danger.

'Shields!' Baldev roared.

He gritted his teeth, eyes forward, trying to ignore the muted sound of bodies hitting the ground and the cries of pain that followed. Out of the mist came the Boar infantry.

The Boar soldiers moved silently across the ground wrapped in the early morning mist. The first wave of their arrows flew overhead into the Bear encampment. Cries rent the air. Shields raised, they charged the Bear camp, silent save for the sound of their foot beats and the chink of chain mail on some of them. Another arrow volley hissed overhead.

The Boar stumbled and fell in the broad shallow ditch that ran before the Bear defences. They hurled themselves up. Sharpened stakes loomed before them.

'Loose!' cried Baldev. Most arrows bounced off their shields, but a few Boar soldiers fell with arrows lodged in legs and faces.

Too few dead and more coming, thought Baldev.

Rows of archers stood in the rear of Baldev's camp. Each archer worked with a shield bearer. They continued to fire return volleys at Ratilal's troops, while the shield bearer strove to shelter them from the onslaught of arrows that pelted down upon them. Wounded warriors lay about them.

Curro dragged those too wounded to walk to safety on the slope nearest the Falcontine. He kept one eye on his brother and the approaching enemy.

Nicanor waited behind the stakes with the other Bear warriors. When the Boar infantry reached the stakes, they attacked all along the stake line, but several wedges attacked specific spots on the defences. The leading Boar troops sheltered their comrades inside the formation, who grabbed the stakes and began working them loose.

Nicanor stood in a gap between the stakes. He lunged forward, jabbing with a spear aiming for legs or any opening to try to wound the Boar attackers and break their shield wall.

One of the Boar teams had succeeded, and almost pushed through into the encampment.

'Push forward!' the Bear captain ordered. 'Nic, forward!'

They desperately drove the Boar back. Bear warriors filled the gap the Boar had made and were able to attack from the sides between the remaining stakes. Nicanor forced his way forward on the other side, but was driven back and stumbled, taking another Bear with him. Curro leapt into the fray and stood over his brother, swinging an axe, while Nicanor and the other man scrambled to their feet.

His face twisted, red and frenzied, Curro unleashed all his anger and grief. 'Miserable damn bastards! I'm sick of you all! Get off my brother! Go! Go!' he bellowed as he attacked.

The Bear now attacked the Boar infantry from the sides and front. Curro pounded on the shield in front of him, heedless of danger. It splintered. He plunged forward, swinging the axe wildly, hacking into the enemy. Nicanor watched him in grateful horror as he fought beside him.

The Bear captain swung his war hammer like a madman on the other side, belting it into the shield before him. The shield tilted. He hammered another blow onto it. It cracked. His war hammer continued its path, breaking the arm of the Boar soldier before him, driving him back. The soldier fell. The Bear captain's next blow cracked his helmet and smashed his skull.

Along the line, other Bear warriors attempted to stop the wedge formations of the Boar soldiers. They tried to jab between the shields with spears and glaives, slicing legs. Boar troops fell; another of their shield walls broke. United, the Bear drove them back, plugging the holes in the stake line. They pushed out further and a brutal melee ensued.

Baldev, surrounded by his guard, watched the battle unfold. The deciduous trees at the forest's edge had lost all their leaves. A flock of birds scattered from the trees. Baldev narrowed his eyes, straining to see. 'They're trying to flank us to the east of the camp. Redirect the archers. Rain down vengeance upon them before we get there,' he ordered one the men. 'The rest of you, to the horses!'

They ran down the hillside to the where their horses were waiting, safely out of arrow range, and leapt upon them.

'Come on!' Baldev spurred his horse forward.

The volley of Bear arrows plummeted into the Boar soldiers as they emerged from the trees. Horses and men screamed in pain.

Two rows of Bear cavalry galloped around the slope, emerging into a clear area between the trees and the camp. Baldev and his riders in the first wave aimed their long spears and met them head on. Riders were jettisoned from horses by the thrust of spears. Men and horses fell, impaled. Long sinan gone, or splintered, the Bear drew their kilijs and hacked away at the enemy.

A second wave of Baldev's cavalry descended upon the battlefield. They swept around the enemy horses and attacked them from behind. Trapped, the Boar cavalry disengaged and fled pell-mell. Half the Bear warriors chased them.

The Boar infantry, driven back and held at an impasse by Baldev's foot soldiers, saw their cavalry routed and began to panic. Their commanders shouted out desperate orders to hold fast and form up using shields, but they broke and ran.

The Bear cavalry chasing the Boar horsemen drew closer to Ratilal's lines.

Ratilal watched and waited. His vast army was arrayed across the land. Ordered, disciplined, they waited. The best troops had been kept in reserve.

'It's working, High Lord,' Ratilal's commander said. 'They've split, they're coming.'

Baldev glared at his pursuing cavalry. 'Recall them!' he hollered.

The strident note of a horn sounded. The Bear cavalry broke off and wheeled back to their camp, hacking at the fleeing Boar infantry as they passed through their ranks.

'My lord, we had them.'

'Don't be a fool. You can damn well bet that Ratilal didn't cross the Upper Divide with just that lot. Get our warriors behind the lines. We need to reinforce the defences. And we'll have bloody little time to do it.'

From the slope of the hill, Baldev stared at the boggy ground below while his commanders awaited his orders. 'Anil, send your guardian to the nearest towers across the Upper Divide. I want to know how Ratilal has crossed. Then I want to know his troop numbers and layout.' To one commander he said, 'Get a small party into the forest and get what you can to shore up the defences before the next wave—quickly.'

Anil lay down, they covered his prone body with shields. He merged with his guardian and the large rufous owl took flight. Its reddish-brown form disappeared from sight.

'My lord, we could try to cross.'

'We could. We'd be slaughtered,' Baldev said. 'Ratilal would sit on this hill and pick us off. Even if some of us were to stay and fight as rear guard I suspect we'd soon be overwhelmed. And once we're gone, he's free to head to Gopindar. Its walls may still stand, but the people will be in no shape to defend them. And even if they were, they no longer have the food supplies to hold out against a prolonged siege.'

'There's still Lord Karan.'

'He's chasing Ratilal's scum, just as Ratilal wanted us to do.'

—⚅—

Hamza had split off to Bear Tooth Lake. Karan's forces stuck to the forest trails to obscure their convoy. Isaura was grateful for all the training Pravin had insisted she do riding through the hills. She'd never thought horses could move so fast over such rough narrow tracks. Alejo never faltered, he never tired; nor did she. Isaura stayed merged with him, half in the spirit realm, and The Wild seeped into them and restored them as they travelled. She glanced back along the column.

Pravin, dogged protector, rode behind her with Gabriela beside him—grim, pale and grieving. *Yet no longer fragile.* Asha was surrounded by Āsim and her guard. After the murder of Umniga they would not let her out of their sight. Suniti rode beside her, another grey ghost seeking retribution.

The autumn leaves were gone in the flatland areas of the forest, only the dark conifers of the slopes were green. The world below looked stark and dead. *A few days ago I wouldn't have thought that, but then I felt so much younger.* Into that bleakness they would ride and bring death. *We'll bring it because sometimes there is no other recourse. Sometimes the path to a better world lies through blood.* A vision of those brown plains swathed in red confronted her; bile rose in her throat.

Karan called a halt, so they could rest the horses briefly.

Isaura pulled the crystals from her pocket and rolled them about in her hand. As always they would glow briefly and fade.

She'd tried focusing on them, trying to will energy into them. 'Damn it.' She sat on the ground and Alejo rested his chin on her head. 'I need to talk to her.'

Karan walked to Suniti. 'Send your guardian ahead to Baldev's camp. I want to know if he is under threat or if I'm just being paranoid. If he is being attacked, Ratilal will have lookouts in the hills. You need to locate them so we can kill them.'

'I can go,' Asha said.

'No, Asha. Fihr is not exactly discreet. If Ratilal sees him, he'll know we are coming. Another forest owl will not attract attention, particularly if Suniti is careful.'

'Karan, I can do it,' Isaura said. 'I can spirit walk there again. I can report more quickly.'

'They won't see you. If they need help they won't know we are coming.'

'But at least you'll know if you need to send Suniti at all.'

'Fine,' Karan said.

Asha scowled. 'The lookouts are mine to kill then.'

Isaura slipped into the spirit realm, knowing Alejo would shield her thoughts and true intent as always.

I've been waiting, Isaura, Primara said.

I've work to do. You can accompany me if you wish.

I'd rather chat.

Then follow me, Isaura said flatly as she began a series of small jumps toward the Falcontine.

Primara smiled smugly at the crystals in Isaura's hand. *I thought you weren't interested in them.*

Inwardly, Isaura groaned. *These are different. Do you know why they just glow and fade?*

No. Events ... took an unexpected turn. You should have been able to harness the energy of the crystal. Everything about you, your aura ... you are closer to my people than the clans are.

So I can't use these at all? They can't help me?

It seems not. Unless you want to try again with a new flame eye ... *you did come very close. You were able to shatter those boulders.*

It's a miracle I'm alive. I should just throw these away, they're no use ... Wait, can you touch them like you could the other?

Primara reached out, and as her hand drew near the crystal arcs of blue light speared out of them, lancing her image and fracturing it.

Primara?

She reformed, some distance away. Her face screwed in distaste. *Clearly I cannot.*

I want to talk to you about Pio, Isaura said. *You know he can use the crystals.*

He's a bard. The crystals only respond when he plays, and what power has he? Music? Pah!

Isaura breathed a sigh of relief. *Perhaps then we can have a truce.*

Primara's lips curled. *Were we at war?*

Don't you get tired and lonely? Ah, you can't get tired, can you? But you know what I mean.

That was cruel. What do you want?

Isaura stopped. Her spirit form hovered over the area of Baldev's camp. In the distance lay Ratilal's forces. Dead men and horses lay on the brown plain between. Primara's eyes narrowed.

I know you feel something for these people, Isaura said. *I know you've guided them in the guise of Rana and you mourn the loss of Umniga. Don't you want to help them now?*

Primara was quiet for some time. *What do you want me to do?*

Help us in this fight.

How?

Use the Kenati Anil. Tell them aid is coming. For them to know their goddess is going to aid them will give them a boost when they most need it. Isaura stared hard at Ratilal's camp. *You can get into most people's heads, yes?*

If they're sleeping—sometimes.

Find this Ratilal. Give him nightmares. Let him think Rana is against him. Let him know that the Asena Blessed is coming. Let him believe that I am the instrument of your vengeance. That I will kill him. Put the fear of the gods into him—literally.

Primara smiled gleefully. *We have more in common than you realise.* She hesitated. *He'll come for you, Isaura.*

I know. I may not have the power you wanted, but I have enough.

Primara, thoughtful, quirked her brow. *I suppose you do at that. I believe perhaps you have more strength than I ever did.* Abruptly she said, *What will you offer in return?*

I'll stop ignoring you. We can work together with these documents Karan wants me to translate. I'll help rebuild your world.

Done.

Chapter Thirty-Seven

ANIL'S GUARDIAN LANDED on roof of the timber tower, his claws making little noise. He heard the voices of the Boar soldiers within.

'That didn't go well.'

'We outnumber them. It's merely a matter of time.'

The rufous owl launched into the air. Dead men and wounded littered the field. Bear warriors quickly dispatched any enemy still alive and ended the misery of the badly wounded horses. He swooped low over the pontoon bridges, never missing a detail and climbed higher to view the array of Ratilal's army. *By the gods*, Anil thought as he looked through the owl's eyes. *He must have mobilised every man in the south.*

Rows of infantry, archers, cavalry—a seething mess of manpower. They were still fortifying the southern section of their encampment with stakes and trenches. They had wicker mantlets as cover for the archers.

How did he get all this across in one night? Why didn't I see them?

On the ground, Ratilal smiled as the owl circled around the camp. He drew back his bow and took aim, carefully tracking his target.

Anil felt another presence overwhelm his guardian. The owl suddenly veered to the side. An arrow brushed past the owl's wing tip. A woman's voice chastised him.

You linger too long, my Kenati. Be gone! Back to your camp. Be not so careless! Aid is coming.

The owl winged its way rapidly back to the Bear camp.

Baldev bellowed at his men as he helped shore up their defences. They dragged saplings and branches from the nearby forest into the line of stakes, filling the weakened spots. 'Quick now, they'll be back for another go before long.'

He left to check on the wounded lying on the far slope of the hill. He asked the field surgeon, 'Of the wounded, how many can fight effectively?'

'About half.'

'Of the rest, how many can at least fire a bow?'

'Half again.'

'Get them up.'

Anil lay nearby. Baldev tensed as the rufous owl landed next to him and Anil returned to his body.

'Report,' Baldev snapped at him as soon as he sat up. He listened to Anil relate what he had seen. His face grew more sombre with each word.

'My lord,' Anil said, clutching Baldev's arm. 'There's more. Rana spoke to me. Ratilal would have shot down my guardian, but she saved us. She says aid is coming.'

Baldev shook him off. 'Unless she means Karan, I hope she has a battalion or two to send us,' he spat. 'I don't suppose she said how far away they are?'

'Er, no, my lord,' Anil stammered.

A grim-faced runner approached Baldev with a message from his second in command.

Baldev's face twisted in frustration. 'Then we'll just have to try to hold on for as long as we can.'

Ratilal left the field hospital and retired to his tent. Baldev had proved more resilient than he'd expected; he'd resisted several assaults during the day. 'I should've thrown everything at him. I will tomorrow. When the wounded are seen to. The men are exhausted.' He lay on his bedroll knowing his aide would wake him shortly.

Ratilal's breathing grew relaxed as sleep overcame him. His dream took him to his suite at Pramod's brothel where three of his favourites awaited him; he was aroused.

A gentle voice whispered to Ratilal, 'There shall be no more such dreams for you.' Her tone caressed him, he moaned in pleasure. Pain like he'd never known assaulted him. He writhed in agony, clutching his groin. Ratilal heard hoof beats in the distance; a gaze laced with blue fire speared him.

His sister, Samia, stood before him, laughing, smiling, then he saw her pressed against a wall by ... someone ... him, a look of despair upon her face. Finally she stood with her arms outstretched and blood dripping from her wrists. 'You caused this. You will pay.'

The hoof beats grew louder.

Asha, beaten and defiant, spat at him. Pain flared in his cheek from where she'd gouged his flesh months earlier. 'You will pay.'

The figure of a distant rider and horse galloping toward him flashed before Ratilal.

The image morphed into his father, Shahjahan, as he fell upon the sand at Parlan clutching his throat. His eyes met Ratilal's and he whispered hoarsely, 'You did this. You will pay.' Shahjahan's eyes streaked with blue lightning before the life left them.

The scene rearranged to a kitchen in a cottage where a mother and son sat bound, murdered. 'You will pay.'

The hoof beats grew louder.

The kitchen became a forest and Umniga, arrows protruding from her, lay dying in the arms of Asha. All the while more and more voices cried, 'You will pay,' until it reverberated through his mind.

They coalesced into one voice, no longer soft and sweet, but ironclad. 'Ratilal, son of Shahjahan—you will pay.'

A beautiful woman stood before him—young, dressed in a

grey robe, with startling blue eyes and long silver hair that ended in blue tips.

'Rana?'

Her smile was predatory. 'For your crimes you have been judged. And my judgment is coming.'

The hoof beats grew louder.

'The Asena Blessed will hunt you down.'

The horse and rider returned, and while Rana's voice condemned him, their image grew steadily larger—the hoof beats became thunderous.

'There is nowhere you can run that she will not find you.'

Ratilal was sweating, he couldn't move. Charging toward him came the Asena Blessed. She rode a giant horse, her eyes burned blue, and in her hands she held the heads of his men. Those heads screamed their terror at him and the Asena Blessed pointed her sword at him and smiled.

He bolted upright, his chest heaving. That voice. *Rana?* Her voice haunted him. Her judgement for his sins was absolute and that judgement was coming.

The Asena Blessed. He'd seen her in the dream. *Those eyes!*

A commotion began outside his tent. 'Look out!'

'By the gods!'

'Damn it.' Ratilal lurched upright and stepped out of his tent.

Three rotten heads lay on the ground outside his tent. Even in the state they were in he recognised his men. The milky eyes stared in horror at him.

'She is coming.'

—⚊—

The soul-rending moans of men and horses had dwindled as they were either tended or dispatched—no wounded enemy was left alive. The silence brought no relief, for first the fog and then the darkness stole any hope of sighting the enemy should they attack again. The stillness of the night became a suffocating blanket relieved only by the dull glow of dawn.

We won't survive another onslaught. Baldev stood, dark circles under his eyes, and rubbed his face. *Why hasn't he sent all his men in? He pecks at us like a vulture.*

'They're coming again, my lord. This time it's his full force.'

Across the plain came Ratilal's army. Cavalry with long spears led the centre, mounted archers to the side. Rows of infantry came behind, many looking as if they'd just left their farms. They carried an assortment of pole-arms: bills and glaives, some bore heavier bardiche. Their faces reflected fear, resignation and grim determination. In the rear, archers on foot moved into positions; sturdy wicker mantlets were being hauled into place to protect them.

Baldev hung his head.

'My lord, look!'

Fihr glided silently up the slope from the Falcontine on the north side of camp, out of sight of the enemy. Baldev broke into a grin as Fihr swooped past him.

'Mount up,' he said as he watched Fihr leave. 'Those who can shoot but not ride, stay here and shoot from behind the barricade. The rest, come with me.'

Baldev arrayed his cavalry. 'We wait until they are committed. Then we move out. Karan is here.'

Ratilal's horses fidgeted, tossing their heads and dancing forward. Their pace steadily increased and their lines became disorderly; they were just over halfway to Baldev's camp.

'Now!' Baldev ordered.

The Bear warriors surged forward, yet remained in formation. Their centre rows carried long spears matching Ratilal's array, while the flanking riders were archers. All the Bear warriors bore swords, some carried axes or flails.

The two armies drew closer.

Emerging from the darkness of the conifers to the east rode

half Karan's force. Their line galloped through the bare deciduous trees and formed several wedge formations. Baldev's forces collided with Ratilal's. Riders fell from their mounts, spears in their bellies. Others discarded broken spears and drew their swords. Mounted archers circled, firing at the approaching Boar infantry, wheeling and coming back for more. Karan's force hit Ratilal's lines from the flank. The wedges scattered Ratilal's infantry. The Boar troops rallied, stabbing their spears at men and horses' bellies, using glaives to slice at horses' legs, downing both horse and rider. Others jabbed, lunged and swung with their bills, attempting to haul Karan's fighters from their horses.

From the forest behind Ratilal's archers poured the other half of Karan's warriors. They attacked the bowmen at the rear of Ratilal's lines. The archers panicked; many moved to the other side of their mantlets, trying to shoot Karan's oncoming forces from cover, only to be targeted by those of Baldev's horse archers who had seen the opportunity to attack them. Many Boar archers held firm, bravely firing as the Horse warriors galloped toward them. Men and women tumbled from horses, wounded or dead. Riderless horses continued the charge in panic, arrows sticking from them. Karan's warriors returned fire at the gallop. Boar archers began to drop; those left panicked and ran only to be mown down by horses, javelins, and hewn by swords.

The battlefield descended into a vicious brawl.

Isaura and Alejo fought alongside Gabriela and Asha. Alejo reared, kicked and bit any enemy he could. His sides were nicked and scratched, but Isaura was unmarked. Isaura's javelins were gone. She swung her kilij, hacking wildly at any who neared. Her eyes blazed blue.

Asha kicked the face of a Boar soldier who tried to haul her bodily from her horse. Blood spurted from his shattered nose. She sliced her kilij at the base of his neck. He collapsed to his knees, clutching his throat as blood seeped between his fingers.

Pravin fought, trying to keep one eye on Isaura. A Boar fighter lunged at him with a bill. Gabriela hurled a throwing axe, embedding it in his attacker's back. 'Pay attention, old man!' she yelled with a grin.

Karan swung his flail down upon a Boar soldier. Mirza reared back as a glaive sliced across his chest. Karan toppled sideways onto the ground on top of his attacker. Mirza screamed in pain. Karan's captain swung his axe, smashing it into the upper back of the Boar trooper with the glaive, who died where he stood. Karan, hands gauntleted, grappled with the Boar soldier he landed on. He rammed his palm up into his chin, snapping his head back just as he drove his fingers into the soldier's eyes. The man howled in pain. Karan leapt to his feet, grabbed his flail and caved his head in.

He ran to Mirza and looked at the wound. 'You'll live, but get out of here. Now!' He slapped him on the rump and Mirza galloped through the melee.

'You need another mount!' Karan's captain said as he reined in his agitated horse.

'One's coming,' Karan said.

Isaura and Alejo pounded up to them. 'Need a rescue?' She grinned. 'You can see a lot more from up here.'

At least a third of Ratilal's troops had broken and were retreating to the river crossing. Isaura unslung her shield from her back and hung it from the front of her saddle.

Karan swung up behind her. 'We need to find Ratilal and end this.'

—⚏—

Vikram's troops halted in front of the pontoon bridges Ratilal that had lain to cross the Upper Divide. There were no Boar soldiers there. Across the swampy ground and river, the battle raged.

He smiled. *Perfect.* Vikram moved the column forward over

the bridges and they formed into ranks on the other side.

The guards on the two towers waved at them in relief. 'You're a sight for sore eyes, Captain!'

Vikram smiled back as he sent two teams of warriors to kill them.

He stepped casually over their bodies as he made his way to the top of one of the towers. Ratilal's troops were in disarray. Most of the archers were fleeing toward the bridges. Karan and Baldev's forces were turning the tide of the battle.

'What do you want us to do, Captain?' Jabr asked. 'Do we attack?'

'I want archers stationed in each tower,' Vikram said as he unfurled a white banner and hung it from the tower lookout. He gave Jabr another one. 'Hang this from the other tower. Then stay with the archers there. Shoot any of Ratilal's soldiers who flee this way. We'll hold Ratilal's force on this plain. They'll be trapped between us and the Bear and Horse. We just wait.'

Vikram returned to his ground forces and mounted his horse.

The fighting across the field was fierce. Vikram hung his head, knowing men he'd trained with in the Boar Clan were dying out there, and men and women he'd known as a child were dying with the Horse and Bear. A knot of loss and loneliness took hold in his gut. *I'm so damn tired. I don't think I know where I really belong anymore.*

The remnants of the Boar foot archers were retreating to him, along with groups of infantry.

'Be ready!' Vikram called as they rushed toward his waiting troops.

Those fleeing looked with relief at Vikram's warriors.

'We're saved!'

Vikram's archers in the towers fired upon them. They milled around in confusion as their number were picked off.

'Back! Go back!'

They turned to see the warriors of Horse and Bear closing in on them.

Vikram stood in his stirrups and bellowed at them. 'Lay down your arms and you will be spared!'

The Bear and Horse warriors stood at their backs, watchful, listening, ready to slay them should they not heed Vikram.

'Betrayer!'

'NO! It is you who have been betrayed! Ratilal murdered Shahjahan to come to power and start this war. The Conclave and all of Faros have heard the evidence against him. He has been found guilty and sentenced to death. This war is over.'

Ratilal's troops looked at one another. They murmured amongst themselves.

As one, Vikram's force stepped forward with weapons drawn.

'I never bloody wanted to be here anyway. I want to go home to my wife and little 'uns,' one man said, walking forward and tossing down his sword.

Slowly the pile of weapons grew as the troops before Vikram surrendered, but the fighting on the rest of the field went on.

Chapter Thirty-Eight

'THE ARCHERS ARE retreating!' Ratilal's captain yelled.

Ratilal spun, spittle flew from his lips. 'Gods, damn it, Karan—the bastard!' He glared at the fleeing archers, tracking their path. 'But look where they're running to. Vikram has come. We'll have the day yet. Go rally them there. Go!' Ratilal cast his gaze around him. 'Hoist my banner higher!' Standing in the stirrups he bellowed, 'To me! Men, to me!'

Fihr cried out harshly, drawing Asha's attention to Ratilal's banner. 'Bastard!' she screamed. Asha spurred Honey on and the little mare leapt forward.

'No, Asha!' Baldev yelled. Distracted, he watched Asha's galloping form weave through the carnage—straight to Ratilal. Boar infantry felled one of Baldev's guard, opening a gap through which the enemy rushed to attack Baldev.

Baldev roared in anger as a spear pierced his leg. His assailant screamed as one of Baldev's guard hewed him in two. Baldev wrenched the spear from his thigh. Blind with rage and fear for Asha, he wheeled his horse around, cleaving a battle-axe into the shoulder and chest of the nearest Boar.

Karan and Isaura were astride Alejo. Karan's guard had closed around them and his flag bearer waved his banner high. He saw Baldev cutting a swathe through his attackers.

'Karan,' Isaura said. 'Look, Asha's going to get herself killed. I can't let …'

He placed his hand on her shoulder, giving it a gentle squeeze. 'I know.' His gaze encompassed the fleeing archers, the white banners unfurling from the towers, and Ratilal's rallying troops. 'Stick with her, Isa, she's not thinking clearly,' Karan said. 'If Asha gets killed, there'll be no peace. Baldev will wipe out every Boar he finds—the hatred will never end. We need to get there before Ratilal regroups.'

Alejo thundered across the battlefield. Karan and Isaura both swung their swords on either side of Alejo at the enemy as they raced after Asha.

Ratilal looked up to see Asha bearing down upon him in distance. 'Finally!' he muttered.

Asha's little mare, Honey, galloped on and Asha fired as she rode. She was dimly aware of her guard struggling to catch her; the sound of battle became a vague cacophony. Focusing solely on Ratilal, in her need for vengeance, she ignored the fact that he stood within a square of his elite troops. She let loose an arrow at Ratilal. It whizzed past his ear and embedded in the back of one of his men.

'She's mine,' Ratilal said. 'No matter what happens, she's mine.'

Boar soldiers braced long sinan in the ground and thrust their points forward; a wall of spears loomed before Asha. Out of arrows, she tossed her bow aside and drew a throwing axe. *I just need one to drop and then I'm through.* Asha never saw the warrior crouched to the side with a glaive. Honey screamed as the glaive sliced through her belly. The mare nose-dived into the dirt, her entrails spilling onto the ground. Asha was jettisoned from the saddle, somersaulted and landed winded on the dirt.

Rough hands hauled Asha to her feet and dragged her before Ratilal. His guards closed ranks behind her, trapping her. Her guard remained outside, desperately fighting Ratilal's troops.

She lay face down, half conscious and groaning as she struggled to breathe.

Asha, my Kenati, get up. Get up now! You must fight. Hold on!

Rana? Asha shook her head, drew a shuddering breath, and winced at the stabbing pain in her ribs. Dusty boots moved into her field of vision. *Boots?* The sounds of the battle came roaring back to her. *Ratilal!* She looked up as Ratilal's hand belted her across the face. Asha's vision blurred and she could taste blood from her split lip.

'Stinking bitch!'

Fihr screamed in indignation and merged with her. Asha's eyes changed shape as his strength and love filled her. Fihr sent her an image of Ratilal with his eyes pecked out. She scrambled away from Ratilal, got to her feet, and drew her sword and dagger.

Asha's eyes widened at the speed of Ratilal's attack as his sword slashed toward her. She parried, wishing she had a shield. Each move set her ribs afire and his blows jarred her arm. His sword swept toward her middle; she pivoted and lashed out, kicking him in the side of his thigh. Ratilal staggered, his shield dropped a little. Asha's blade swiped down across his mail-covered shoulder.

Ratilal's face twisted with hate and he roared in anger. He flexed his shoulder, spat on the ground and swung his shield at Asha, knocking her sword away as it slashed toward him again. His sword flashed, cutting the outside of Asha's upper arm to the bone. Screaming, she dropped her weapon as blood welled along the cut and her flesh parted. Her breathing laboured, Asha struggled to remain upright, yet she still gripped the dagger in her other hand. Her hand trembled and she swayed. Ratilal laughed as he kicked the dagger from Asha's hand and she passed out.

'Too easy,' he said as he raised his sword, ready to plunge it into her.

Fihr screeched. Ratilal looked up as the eagle dived at him. 'First you die, you damn buzzard.'

―⁂―

'Karan,' Isaura said. 'They've got Asha!'

'I know. I saw.' He looked over his shoulder to see his guard, along with many of his other warriors, were with them and that Baldev was free and charging in their direction.

Ratilal's ranks were rushing to him and his officers were

creating order out of chaos. They were regrouping.

'We've got to hit him before he gets too many around him.'

Karan signalled his commanders and the troops behind him fanned out to attack the Boar from multiple sides to cut off the troops rallying to Ratilal. Only Pravin and his personal guard remained with Karan and Isaura.

'No matter what happens, Isa, if you get a chance to get in there and save her, do it! Do whatever it takes to win!'

Alejo careened through the melee, with Karan and Isaura hacking at any who approached.

'Keep going!' Karan said. As they galloped, he gripped her waist, leaned down and snatched a spear from a corpse.

Isaura watched Ratilal's blade rise in the air, poised to strike. Fihr's cry pierced her heart. *No, gods no!* She and Karan were nearly there.

Fihr dived and Ratilal's blade flashed up. Fihr screeched and fell from the sky, fluttering wildly.

Karan hurled the spear with all his might, embedding it in one of Ratilal's guards. The guard toppled sideways. Kilij in one hand, Isaura snarled and channelled her will into breaking through the gap in Ratilal's guard before it closed. Anger and panic for Asha laced her cry. 'Ratilal!'

Alejo ploughed through the gap. Karan was knocked from Alejo's back. He lashed out with sword and fists, attacking the Boar soldiers.

Ratilal spun upon hearing Isaura scream his name. She and Alejo bore down on him. Isaura swung her foot and booted him in the face. He staggered sideways, blood pouring from his shattered nose. *He should have gone down!*

The sight of Asha, unconscious, her arm slashed, with Fihr sitting defiant on top of her, incensed Isaura. A mass of the sea eagle's flight feathers lay on the ground nearby, rendering him helpless.

Isaura slid from Alejo armed with shield and kilij. *Alejo protect them.* He sent her a vision of them killing Ratilal or him attacking Ratilal's guard from behind, creating chaos and aiding Karan and Baldev. *No, if they get in here, Asha could be trampled to death.* Alejo moved to stand over Asha and Fihr.

'Am I meant to quail before you, Asena Blessed? Are you here to deliver my judgement?' Ratilal spat. 'Once I'm done with you I'll finish that bitch there.'

Alejo reared, striking out toward him.

Merged with Alejo, Isaura's field of vision expanded and she saw the fighting almost all the way around her. Ratilal's guards held their ground and more of his troops flocked to him; sheer carnage surrounded them. Umniga, Asha, Pio, Jaime and Nimo, their faces blended with everyone she'd lost and been powerless to protect—a small girl on a desperate boat voyage who should never have died; Asha's parents and those left butchered in her village back home. Inside, The Wild rose with her rage and she harnessed it.

The sounds of the battle around her dimmed as Isaura focused on Ratilal. She canted her head, examining him with a sneer. His aura burned black, whereas she stood at the centre of a blue supernova. Ratilal took a half step back as marks on Isaura's neck, left by her henna tattoos, glowed blue. Isaura laughed as the sword in his hand shook, whether from rage or fear she didn't care.

'Well!' he yelled. Isaura merely smiled, irritating him further.

Furious, Ratilal lunged at her; with every strike his aura pulsed black and its strength travelled through his blows. Isaura thrust out her shield, deflecting his kilij as her blade swiped toward his neck. Ratilal punched up with his shield, barely stopping her, and pivoted sideways. Isaura pushed forward relentlessly, a ripple of Wild powering her every blow. Her blade snaked over her shield, pointing down and aiming at his face. He deflected it seconds too late and a line of red bloomed on his cheek.

Wary, Ratilal circled Isaura. He licked his lips, his eyes narrowed. Isaura pushed forward, slicing her blade vertically at his head, hoping the sheer force of the blow would push past his defence and cave in his head. Ratilal braced himself, staggering under her blow, but his shield blocked her sword and he carved his kilij through the air and lashed at her knee. Isaura launched herself sideways, the fabric of her pants cut, blood trickling down her leg. *Let him think he's winged me.* She scrambled to her feet, dragging her leg. Her eyes widened slightly in fear and her kilij trembled in her hand.

Ratilal grinned cockily. He renewed his attacks with savage glee. Isaura deflected blow after blow, each time slower, and his blade drew closer to striking. Her leg began to buckle.

Don't overplay it, girl, Isaura told herself.

Alejo stood calmly over Asha's stirring form as she surreptitiously reached for her dagger.

Ratilal marched upon Isaura, ready to deliver the final blow. *Women, useless!* His blade cut a swathe straight down at her. Isaura straightened with a small smile, perfectly balanced on both legs, as her shield rose high and horizontal, blocking his sword. Ratilal's eyes widened as he realised he'd been gulled. She pushed forward, her blade carving up into the mail covering his armpit. Ratilal's body jolted with the blow, though it didn't sever his mail. His face twisted in pain, his arm stiffened and his grip faltered on his sword. Isaura flicked her kilij around and slammed it upon his semi-paralysed arm. His dastanas stopped the sword severing the limb, but he howled in rage and pain, dropping his kilij.

'Bitch, you broke my damn wrist!'

Isaura smiled serenely, waiting. His eyes flicked to the sword on the ground and he dove to reach it with his other hand. Isaura drove her sword through the join where his mail coat fastened. Her smile turned to a snarl as the sword skewered him. She channelled The Wild within her and lashed out with her leg, belting him in the torso. Ratilal flew backward, landing in the dirt alongside Alejo. Asha's good arm lashed out, plunging her dagger into his throat.

Isaura pulled his zirh kulah from his head and kicked the helmet away.

Asha stabbed him again and sawed at his neck, sobbing all the while.

'Enough, move away,' Isaura said softly.

Asha pulled the dagger out, clutching it to her; she and Alejo moved back. 'For Samia, for Shahjahan ... for Umniga,' Asha whispered as Isaura's blade scythed through Ratilal's neck, severing his head.

Asha drew a pouch from inside her tunic, seized the head by the hair and pulled it to her. She opened the mouth and poured the last of Umniga's ashes into it.

'There! Now she can choke you forever in Karak!'

Ratilal's guard who'd held the defensive square saw him fall. They faltered, many dropping their weapons in surrender or being killed before they had a chance.

'Alejo, kneel,' Isaura commanded. She hauled Asha to her feet, gently picked up Fihr and passed him to her. 'He'll live and hopefully regrow those feathers. Get on.' Isaura grabbed Ratilal's head by the hair and jumped up behind her, wrapping one arm around Asha to keep her upright. Once they were mounted, Alejo stood and lashed out with his hind feet at the Boar soldiers nearest him.

Isaura held Ratilal's head aloft and breathing deeply she drew on the Undavi, willing her voice to be heard across the field. 'Boar warriors, Ratilal is dead! The towers are taken. There is no retreat. Lay down your arms. Surrender and live!'

The captured Boar troops sat under guard, Ratilal's head was impaled upon a spear for all to see and the wounded were being tended nearby.

Isaura sat with Gabriela and finished stitching up her arm. 'How do you feel?'

'Numb,' Gabriela said.

'I'm sorry about everything, about Jaime.' Isaura shook her head. 'Sorry is such a useless, inadequate word.'

'I'll recover, and probably more quickly than I deserve,' Gabriela said softly.

'Did you see Curro or Nic when we were fighting?'

'Once—they were together. I lost sight of them ... Everything was so chaotic,' Gabriela said tiredly.

'Will you come with me to look for them?' Isaura asked.

Gabriela nodded. They searched through the wounded, but there was no sign of them. Isaura scanned the battlefield, finally spying Nicanor's figure bent over someone. Isaura's mouth went dry and she squeezed Gabriela's hand as they made their way to Nicanor.

'Nic?' Isaura said tentatively.

Nicanor's nose was broken, he had a black eye, his shirt was torn and he was streaked with blood. Curro, head bowed, sat at his feet.

'Isa? ... Isa!' Nicanor drew her away from Curro, pulled her into a rough hug and sobbed. 'Thank the gods! I thought I'd never see any of my family again ... you are my family—always. I'm so sorry. I thought we'd all die ... and you saved us ... you stopped the battle. Gods, Isa, I'm sorry.'

'Lucia and Pio are safe and sound, Nic,' Isaura said. 'They're at Hamza's.'

'Good ... good.' He reluctantly released her and ran his hand through his hair while he looked at Curro. Curro was covered in blood, his eyes were distant. 'He was crazed in the battle. He threw himself into danger. I couldn't keep up, we got separated. Now ...' Nicanor shrugged helplessly. 'I only just got him to let go of his axe. I can't get him to talk and I can't get him up.' Isaura took a step toward Curro. 'I wouldn't, Isa. He hates you since Elena, and when Jaime was killed ... well, it sent him over the edge. You might set him off.'

Face pinched, Isaura nodded. 'I'll send someone to help you.'

'Isa, look,' Gabriela said.

Isaura looked up to see the Matriarch and six Asena walking to her through the camp. The Bear and Horse stopped their work and stared at the Asena, parting before them.

Isa-cub, the Matriarch said. *You did well.* Isaura embraced her and the Matriarch butted her head gently.

I didn't think you'd be here, Isaura said.

There is no danger to us now and our presence here will reinforce what is to come. You are the Asena Blessed, after all, she said. *Come, we should be seen together at the surrender.*

Isaura looked despondently across the battlefield at the slain.

There is only sorrow there, Isa-cub. In loyalty, courage, sacrifice and the peace and justice they achieved—therein lies the honour. Do not forget it or the price. Come, the Horse Lord awaits, the Matriarch said, nudging Isaura to walk.

Ratilal's tent had been shifted nearer to the pontoon crossing. Karan, Baldev and Pravin stood outside awaiting Vikram, who approached under the escort of Karan and Baldev's guard.

Karan raised his eyebrows at the Asena. 'Old Mother, this is unexpected, but not unwelcome.'

'You and she must think alike,' Isaura said with a twist of her lips.

Baldev folded his arms across his chest and glared at Isaura.

Karan's lips quirked. 'He's mad at you, but I'm not,' he said, kissing her cheek. 'He feels you should've made an opening so he could get to Asha sooner,' he whispered. 'Really, I think you just stole his thunder.' Baldev growled. Karan winked at Isaura and took her hand. 'Come, we'll walk out to meet Vikram so the crowd can see the Asena.'

A hush fell over those gathered as Isaura, Karan and Baldev stood out in the open, surrounded by the Asena.

The Kenati stood at the head of the crowd who had gathered. Vikram paused before them, bowing deeply, his palms raised upward in the traditional greeting. 'I mourn your loss.'

Asha, her arm swathed in bandages and in a sling, smiled at him as Suniti and Anil supported her. 'We know you do and we understand that it was none of your doing, that you remain a man of honour.'

Vikram blanched and proceeded. He bowed to Baldev and Karan. 'My lords.' He turned, seeing the torc upon Isaura's neck, and bowed again. 'My lady.' His gaze strayed to Gabriela, whose hand rested lightly upon her sword.

'Gabi is one of my wife's squad, as is Pravin. She is one of the newcomers to our clan and has a heart as brave as any I've met. Have no fear, Gabi—Pasha Vikram is no threat to Isa. Come, let us go into the tent to discuss business.' Karan held the tent flap open and Vikram and Baldev entered.

Isaura lingered, saying, 'What about Asha?'

'She has no place here,' Karan said quietly. 'Only clan rulers may be here. At the moment, with her need for revenge still burning in her heart, it's good that she's not present.'

Isaura nodded in resignation and entered the tent before him. Gabriela and Pravin stood guard outside with Vikram's escort and the Asena.

In the tent, Karan embraced Vikram. 'I'm glad to see you. You've done well. Now to work out a peace that lasts.'

'We'll be merciful,' Baldev ground out. 'Though they don't deserve mercy after Gopindar.'

'I know. I was there,' Vikram confessed.

Baldev leapt at him. Karan jumped between them, struggling to hold Baldev back.

Isaura grabbed Baldev's shoulders and tried to haul him away.

'Explain, Vikram!' Karan ordered.

'I didn't realise where we were going or what was to transpire—Ratilal made sure of it. Niaz watched me like a hawk. I was being tested. I did what I could to minimise the damage in the upper city and I used the opportunity to kill Niaz, saying your men did it. I helped rescue some as I escaped.'

Baldev pushed against Karan, his face etched in anger and grief. 'Vikram had no choice! We've won a total victory due to him.' Baldev snarled at them.

'Enough, Boar Lord! Be still.' Isaura's voice whipped him. 'Have you not had your fill of violence this day?' she hissed. 'Step away!'

He glowered at her. Unable to fight her command, he reluctantly stepped back.

'Control yourselves!' Karan snapped. 'Baldev, what else could Vikram have done? We needed his cover to remain in place.'

Baldev's fists clenched by his sides; he scowled, nodding tersely, before moving further away.

'How did you get in, Vikram?' Karan asked.

'A woman named Sora was there—she's Ratilal's agent. She occupied the guards and let us in.'

'We will find her,' Baldev ground out. 'She will die. In our mercy for the Boar Clan we'll honour the treaty agreed to by Shahjahan,' he said. 'With you as Pasha ...'

Vikram winced. 'My lords, I do not wish to remain as Pasha.'

'What do you want, Vikram?' Karan asked softly.

'Quiet ... an end to intrigue ... to remember who I am and where my real home lies, with the Horse, in Targmur—that's all,' Vikram replied.

'And you shall, but first we must ensure another Ratilal does not rise within the Boar. Who do you suggest as Pasha?'

'Mistress Malak.'

'Niaz's mother? Go on,' Karan said.

'She's strong and clever and has the support of the lower city. Malak is also long respected amongst those in the upper Faros and she loathed Ratilal and everything he stood for. Her appointment would also be supported by the women.'

'Very, very clever. Will she do it?' Karan asked.

'I believe so.'

Baldev remained gruff. 'Who are potential candidates for clan lord?'

'There are several. All of Ratilal's ilk are here,' Vikram replied.

'We'll make sure any who remain alive die of their wounds or never return to Faros. Who does that leave?' Baldev said, flexing his fists.

'There are one or two who'd suit and who'll be malleable,' Vikram said.

'See to it, Vikram. Trade will resume. Eventually families will be able to visit their loved ones north of the Divide, though the borders will be controlled. We'll visit Faros regularly under the guise of trade and clan harmony to check how Pasha Malak and the new clan lord fare.' Vikram nodded. 'See to the arrangements. I'll have an agreement drawn up. Bring Pasha Malak here for the signing. And then come home.' Karan put his hand on Vikram's shoulder. 'You've paid a high price in service to the Horse.'

Vikram sagged. 'Thank you.' He stepped outside the tent into the pale winter light. His eyes rested once more on Gabriela. *I'm going home.* After many years, his heart felt lighter and the winter sun was as warm as summer.

Baldev strode to Asha, embraced her, and led her away.

Karan grinned. 'Finally,' he said to Isaura.

She laughed and looked at the Matriarch. *We've won. Now for peace, now—for the first time—love. Even Primara has changed her tune.*

Really, Isa-cub?

She knows I can't use the flame eye crystal as she wanted and I won't ever try again. She sees Pio's magic as useless and I can't use these. They just glow blue and fade—never anything else. Isaura pulled the three blue crystals from her pocket.

They burned blue. They did not fade. They pulsed with life.

The Matriarch stared at the crystals and, deep in thought, she scrutinised Isaura carefully.

Oh, I don't think Primara is done with you yet, little mother.

Author Note

I love history and I have cherry-picked from various periods of history in creating *Altaica*. The pile of books in my research comprises everything from castle and fortification construction, Roman cavalry training tactics, weaponry, armour, poisons, mules, archery (but that is also a hobby of mine), herbology, sword fighting techniques, staff fighting etc (Osprey publications probably deserve a special thank you for their military books). I have combined them all in creating this world.

In the course of my research for this book I kept returning to the weapons of the Mughals and, particularly, the Ottomans because I loved their combination of beauty and lethality.

Researching wolves, I also stumbled across the Turkic myth of the Asena, which I immediately felt could work with my story extraordinarily well. It seemed fitting that I use it since I was featuring Turkish weapons, and when I saw the term *Altaic* used to describe the language family including Turkish, Mongolian and Tungus—I thought I'd modify it for a title.

By adapting a much-loved Turkish myth and modifying the term *Altaic*, I have intended no cultural offence.

Instead, please remember this is speculative fiction not historical fiction. I would like you to think these things have been an inspiration for a creative mind and hopefully the result will provide much reader enjoyment.

Thank you.

Book Three
coming in 2017

About the Author

Tracy M Joyce is an Australian author of speculative fiction. Her debut novel, *Altaica: Book I in The Chronicles of Altaica*, is published by Odyssey Books. Tracy has long been a fan of the fantasy genre, but particularly likes novels that deal with deep characterisations and that don't flinch from the gritty realities of life. This and her fascination with the notions of 'moral greyness', that 'good people can do bad things' and that we cannot escape our past provide the inspiration for her writing. Combine that with her love of history, horses and archery and you have Altaica.

She grew up on a farm in rural Victoria, in a picturesque dot on the map known as Glenburn. She spent half of her childhood riding horses and the other half trying to stay out of trouble—the only way she did that was by reading books and writing stories. She now lives in Melbourne with her husband, two cats and two (very) lazy greyhounds.

Tracy holds a BA (Hons) from Monash University, spent many years in a variety of administrative roles and fortunately never gave up on her childhood dream to become a writer. In her spare time she tutors a select and unlucky group of students in English.

Tracy loves to hear from her readers.

www.tracymjoyce.com